"Made the hairs on the back of my neck stand up . . . Gailey continues to show themselves to be a versatile, talented writer."
—Cory Doctorow

"I love a good old-fashioned haunted house story, and this one is chilling."
—NPR

"The blueprint for a domestic thriller with a supernatural twist . . . *Just Like Home* interrogates the bloodlust of the true crime genre alongside a good old-fashioned haunting."
—*Paste*

"A superior novel of psychological suspense."
—*Publishers Weekly* (starred review)

"Delightfully creepy and heartbreakingly tragic . . . A must-read for all gothic horror fans."
—*Booklist* (starred review)

"My god, what a book. *Just Like Home* is an insidious book that crawls under your skin and rattles your bones. It poisons your dreams and clouds your senses, keeping you under its beguiling spell. . . . Masterful."
—*The Nerd Daily*

"An excavation of toxic family dynamics, Sarah Gailey's *Just Like Home* uses atmospheric scenes of supernatural horror to reveal the terrors that haunt us all. . . . An excellently crafted thriller."
—*BookPage*

JUST

LIKE

HOME

SARAH
GAILEY

TOR

TOR PUBLISHING GROUP

NEW YORK

JUST LIKE HOME

A Tor Book
Published by Tom Doherty Associates / Tor Publishing Group
120 Broadway
New York, NY 10271

www.tor-forge.com

Tor® is a registered trademark of Macmillan Publishing Group, LLC.

The Library of Congress has cataloged the hardcover edition as follows:

Names: Gailey, Sarah, author.
Title: Just like home / Sarah Gailey.
Description: First Edition. | New York : Tor, a Tom Doherty Associates
  Book, 2022.
Identifiers: LCCN 2022008333 (print) | LCCN 2022008334 (ebook) |
  ISBN 9781250174727 (hardcover) | ISBN 9781250174703 (ebook)
Classification: LCC PS3607.A35943 J87 2022 (print) | LCC PS3607.A35943
  (ebook) | DDC 813/.6—dc23
LC record available at https://lccn.loc.gov/2022008333
LC ebook record available at https://lccn.loc.gov/2022008334

ISBN 978-1-250-17471-0 (trade paperback)

Our books may be purchased in bulk for promotional, educational, or business use. Please contact your local bookseller or the Macmillan Corporate and Premium Sales Department at 1-800-221-7945, extension 5442, or by email at MacmillanSpecialMarkets@macmillan.com.

First Tor Paperback Edition: 2023

Printed in the United States of America

0 9 8 7 6

This is the story of monsters and what they do
to those who love them, those who fear them,
and those who are simply in the wrong place
at the wrong time. Or, from a different
perspective, those who are in the right
place at the right time. Serendipity is
just as cruel as it is kind.

This book is dedicated to anyone who
has ever loved a monster.

CHAPTER ONE

The Crowder House clung to the soil the way damp air clings to hot skin.

Vera had anticipated that coming back to her childhood home would be difficult. She had almost refused, had almost made up an excuse: *I'm really busy at work. I don't have time to come watch you die.*

She shielded her eyes with one flat hand, trying to dampen the too-bright day enough to make eye contact with the windows of her parents' old bedroom. There was only so long she could wait.

There was only so long her mother would wait.

Vera stood with one foot on the lawn and one foot on the driveway, sweating, straining as if she might be able to make out the sound of Daphne dying inside. But the house was built to keep the wind out and the sound in. It stood there, patiently waiting for Vera to come inside, and it did not reveal a single one of its secrets no matter how long and hard Vera stared at it.

Her father, Francis Crowder, had built the house long before she was born, back when his marriage to Vera's mother was new. Back before everything else happened, before everyone knew his name. He'd built it with his two strong hands, built it right in the middle of his square patch of green land, built two stories above the ground and dug one below. He'd built it for Daphne to live in and to die in. From the looks of things she was committed to doing just that.

Francis himself didn't stand a chance of dying in that house, of course.

Not anymore.

That was the only reason Vera was willing to come back at all—that, and the impossible reality of her mother's voice on the phone, rippling with sickness, asking her home.

Vera stood outside the Crowder House much too long, letting the late-spring humidity slide into her throat and choke her. The house was smothered on all sides by a sea of green. The entire block was an eruption of flowers and foliage, just like it always was in the last days before summer broke open and thundered down on everything spring had made. The air was thick with the smell of jasmine and lilacs and wisteria, overpoweringly sweet, so dense Vera wanted to bite into it. It was like trying to breathe fresh sap, relentlessly *spring* in a way that reached down into Vera's lungs with clawed fingers and nested there. Being outside was almost as impossible as going inside.

Almost.

Daphne had never asked Vera to come home before. Not once in a dozen years. Vera knew better than to let this development give her hope, but she couldn't seem to shake the feeling; it bubbled up like a blister and stuck like a scar.

She had come home in spite of that hope and she couldn't make herself go inside until she had sloughed it off. She couldn't afford to bring it inside with her.

Hope was a liability at the Crowder House.

Vera's ostensible task was to clear out the house and to watch her mother die. And after that—after that, she'd get the chance to sort things out. But she couldn't do either one of those things with one foot on the lawn and one foot on the driveway and her eyes full of sun and her lungs full of syrup.

Vera made herself take one step toward the house. The grass underfoot was thick and springy, dense with clover, drunk on snowmelt. She pressed forward, one foot after another pressing the grass flat. It got easier and easier with each step until, just like that, she was right at the lip of the porch.

Tar-smell came off the wood of the stairs that led up to the house. These steps were made of brand-new redwood, nothing like the splintery white stairs that had been there a dozen years before. Nothing like the stairs her father had built. She knew those stairs with her hands and her feet and the backs of her legs, knew the places where Francis had touched the wood with thick-gloved hands and settled it into a shape that would bring the front lawn and the front door together.

Vera examined this new wood and tried to add it to the things she knew, the things that would rid her of foolish ideas about forgiveness and homecoming. Daphne'd probably gotten whichever parasite was currently living in the renovated garden shed to build the new porch for her. Those new stairs meant that she had known what was coming for a while, had been fixing up the house for Vera to eventually sell. She'd waited until the last minute to call her only daughter home.

Vera wondered if, in the destruction of the old front steps, anything had been found. But of course, the thing Vera hid there must have been destroyed. She would have seen on the news if they'd found what she tucked beneath those old boards so many years before.

It was always on the news when something fresh came to light.

The smell of fresh lumber gave Vera what she needed: a reminder of how things really were. A reminder of how little she had been welcome here until this moment. She breathed in the redwood smell and she spread the last of her hope out on those brand-new steps and she watched it die writhing, watched it without pity, watched it until it was still and cold.

It was the right thing to do, giving up that little bit of hope. It was the only thing to do. Some things, Vera knew, were made to die.

The fresh new stain on the wood of the stairs was tacky under the soles of her shoes, sucking her down. As she took her foot off the top step, Vera snapped the fingers of her right hand four times fast. It was an old habit—a childhood tic that she'd dropped when she left the house. She looked down at her hand with surprise, shocked that it would betray her like this, but her fingers did not apologize. They remembered what they were supposed to do to keep her safe, remembered from when she was young enough to develop a superstition without reasoning herself out of it. Vera's fingers knew that snapping four times had gotten her this far.

The front door of the Crowder House was, mercifully, the same as it had always been. It was the door Vera's father hung when he built the house, the door Vera had closed behind her when she left home for good so many years before. It was painted a deep velvety green, with a brass knob and a diamond-shaped window a foot above Vera's eye level. It'd been just the right height for her father to peer through when he'd wanted to see who was outside.

Her old key still fit sweet and snug in the lock. The paint on the door was warm under the flat of her hand. She wrapped her fingers around the smooth brass of the doorknob, and with just a little pressure and almost no resistance at all, she was inside the house that her father built.

The door shut behind her without a sound.

It had been twelve years since Vera had last stood on the inside of that door. The sweat on her skin dried fast in the air-conditioned dark of the entryway, leaving her goosefleshed and sticky.

Without looking, she held out her hand and dropped her housekey in the bowl on the little table that stood beside the door; the bowl that was for keys and nothing else, the bowl that had been there since before she could remember, that would remain where it was until she sent it away along with all the rest of her mother's things. The key landed with a bright chime.

The house swallowed the sound immediately, because it was a house that knew how to stay quiet.

Vera breathed in the windows-shut smell of the place where she'd been born. The place where she'd grown up. The place she'd abandoned.

The place where her mother was going to die.

CHAPTER TWO

In hindsight, Vera could see that she'd started turning toward home two jobs ago. She'd been doing data entry at a plastics manufacturer, and a coworker had seen Daphne on the news. That was a pre-deathbed Daphne, a Daphne who had no interest in her daughter, and she was on the news announcing her plans to host a new artist-in-residence at the Crowder House. There was going to be a series of paintings, an extended tour, a disgustingly lucrative auction. The coworker had seen the announcement and spotted the uncanny resemblance between Daphne and Vera (who wouldn't), and they'd put that together with Vera's last name and they'd figured out who she was. Who her father had been.

It wasn't a hard riddle to solve.

Then had come the usual fraught few days of office friendships disintegrating, emails going unanswered, the break room emptying as soon as she entered. Vera had presented herself at HR to save them the trouble of summoning her. They'd called it a redundancy instead of a layoff, which she thought was kind.

It felt like fate: her next job falling apart in just the same way, and then the lease renewal on her apartment coming up fast, and then Daphne calling just as Vera was about to start looking for her next new temporary life.

Vera told herself that a good daughter would go home after that phone call without hesitation. Besides, it would be a relief to not have to find another furnished apartment, to not have to try to mold her spine into the shape of a new-old mattress and spring-stiff sofa. It wasn't like she had more than a few things to pack.

She'd gifted her three remaining fish to a nine-year-old boy who lived in the unit below hers. He'd promised to keep them alive.

Vera didn't give the fish great odds, but that wasn't her business anymore.

It had been easy to uproot her life and leave it behind. She'd done it so many times before. And because that part had been easy, and because nothing could be easy all the way through, she knew to expect this next part to be hard.

In Vera's memory, Daphne Crowder was a tall, thin, square-jawed woman with a tennis bracelet she never wore and a habit of biting through thread instead of cutting it. She was a woman who swept up broken shards of china and packed lunches in crinkling brown bags and frowned at the laundry as she folded it. She was a woman who had let Vera grow up for exactly seventeen and a half years before shutting the door behind her and bolting it for good.

Daphne had kissed Vera on the cheek that day without looking her in the eye, and then Vera had been outside of the house her father built with a dark blue duffel bag over her shoulder and a light blue suitcase in her hand. When she heard the bolt slide home she knew that the house her father built would never hold a place for her again. The way back, she knew, was closed to her.

Except now, the way was open again.

Vera stood under the arch that separated the dining room from the entryway, holding that same dark blue duffel and that same light blue suitcase, and her head swam. The house was the same, but everything everything *everything* was different.

The dining chairs had been pushed up against the walls. The dining table had been replaced by an adjustable bed. In the bed was a woman.

The woman was looking at Vera with her mother's eyes. But this woman, who was made of paper and wax and seemed too small for her own skin, could not be Daphne Crowder.

A strange hot flush of mortification climbed Vera's throat. It was as if she'd interrupted her mother in the middle of some terribly private moment. Something like bathing or masturbating or digging a kitchen knife into the palm of her own hand.

Dying, Vera supposed, was even more personal than any of those things. She was gripped by the urge to apologize for intruding.

"You look tired," the woman in the bed said. She spoke with the same voice that had once told Vera the reason for the box of baking soda in the refrigerator, the voice that had told her what ovaries were for, the voice that had always been flat and loveless but had turned hateful the year Vera turned twelve.

It was her mother's voice.

Almost.

Something was different. The cold authority had drained out of Vera's mother like brake fluid from a cut line. She spoke slowly, carefully, as if she were pushing each word out with individual effort. Her dry tongue made soft sticking sounds against her lips, against the roof of her mouth.

Her tongue must be dry. The thought clicked the new thing into place between them. Vera wasn't home to visit. She had a job to do. A purpose. She set down her bags and crossed the threshold of the dining room.

"Do you want some water?"

"I have some, there," Vera's mother said, pointing to the sideboard. It was part of the dining room set Daphne and Francis had bought when they moved into the house, back when Vera was just an idea they were disagreeing about. The dining table and chairs and sideboard and china cabinet were all made of golden oak, carved with a grapevine motif that Vera had traced with her index finger as a kid.

There was a thick layer of hard, clear plexiglass on top of the sideboard now, screwed into place at the corners. A plastic hospital-pink pitcher sweated on top of the plexiglass next to a stack of waxed paper cups. Vera poured a splash of water into one of the little cups, filling it to the brim, and brought it to her mother. She wondered briefly if she should get a bigger glass—those little cups barely held a mouthful each.

But then Vera handed the cup over and noted the way her mother's wrists shivered at the weight of it and she understood: this was the most she could expect Daphne to carry.

Vera helped lift the cup. Some of the water dribbled out of the side of her mother's mouth, darkening the cotton at her throat. Vera looked around for a tissue, but Daphne waved her away.

"I've got it," she said, wiping the water away with the side of one hand. The thin, yellowed skin of her face stretched under the pressure of her touch. Her cheeks had caved in like a mid-November jack-o'-lantern—there had to be teeth missing, Vera thought. There was no way her mother had lost enough weight to hollow out her face like that. But then her fingers brushed her mother's hand when she took the little paper cup back, and she reconsidered.

Daphne's fingers had always been slender. Now they were

skeletal. Brittle. She looked at her mother's wrists and saw knobs of protruding bone. So much had been whittled away.

Vera felt the first pang of regret.

She should have come home sooner. The daughter she'd always wanted to be would have come home sooner.

Vera, though, had taken more time than usual settling her affairs, rehoming fish and packing up the few things she wanted to keep and staring at herself hard in the mirror for long stretches of time. She had spread the drive home out over three days when she definitely could have done it in two. She had lingered on the front lawn, gawking up at the house, dreading what was inside.

Vera hadn't known it would be this bad. She couldn't have known. That whole time, her mother had been wasting away.

Daphne cleared her throat, cracking through the silence like the back of a spoon tapping the top of a crème brûlée. "You should take your things to your bedroom and get settled," she said, her voice more even now that she'd had some water. She still sounded strange, but Vera supposed dying would do that to a person. "You must be exhausted from the drive."

"Yeah, um. It was a long way up here from Cape Coral. And I slept in the car." Vera stood at the side of the bed where her mother was dying, unsure of where to put her hands. Sitting on the mattress felt unspeakably overfamiliar but standing there felt like looming. And she didn't want to go to her bedroom. Not yet. "I probably smell awful, I should take a shower."

"Oh, I can't smell anything anymore," her mother said, her lips cracking as they pulled back from her teeth in a clench-jawed smile. "But I'm sure a shower will make you feel better, at least. You can use the one in the upstairs bedroom. I suppose that's obvious, it's not like there's another shower you could use. Unless you want to go knock on the door to the cottage, and ask James if you can borrow his." She cleared her throat again, a thicker, wetter sound than the first time. "Go on and get settled. I'm fine here."

Vera's stomach clenched at the thought of the cottage, which used to be called a 'shed' back before her mother decided to invite people to live in it. Ignoring it—the twist in her belly and the memories she had of that shed—she poured more water into the waxed paper cup and set it down on the rolling table beside her mother's bed.

The dining room was all dark paneling and butter-yellow paint. The flat-pack look of that too-modern rolling table was completely out of place. The bed was similarly wrong: made of smooth white particleboard, nothing like the dark bedknobs of the bed her mother and father had once shared. That bed—the old bed—was probably still upstairs, too heavy for Daphne to have moved on her own.

The realization washed over Vera like nausea: that bed, the matching nightstands, the matching vanity, the half-empty closet. It would be up to her to decide what to do with all of it, and soon.

Sooner than she'd planned for, if Daphne was as sick as she looked.

Vera stood there, dull-eyed, contemplating the rolling table, until her mother spoke again.

"I know. It's hideous. But it was cheap, and it's not like"—she interrupted herself to clear her throat again, her eyes flashing—"it's not like I'll be using it for long."

"It's nice," Vera said automatically. "It seems nice, I mean." She couldn't tell if this was a real conversation or if her mother was just making noise to drive her out of the room.

"That young man brought it in and put it all together for me. I bought a new mattress for your bed, too. I gave him the old one. It seemed like the right thing to do. No sense wasting it, and I'm sure he'll find it inspiring."

Vera knew she was expected to be thankful for the new mattress. The old one probably had moths in it anyway. But she couldn't make herself form words, not over the horror of knowing that *that young man* had been breathing in the smell of her sleep-sweat and skin.

Then again, who could be certain that he was the first? For all Vera knew, Daphne charged all her tenants a little extra for a chance to sleep in her husband's daughter's old bed.

Inspiring, indeed.

"Do you want me to put the table closer?" Vera asked, sidestepping the question of gratitude entirely. Her mother nodded, so Vera tugged on the little table until the wheeled base disappeared under the bed and the flat top slid across the quilt that covered her mother to the waist. The whole thing fit flush around the contour of the mattress and the bedframe.

"They're a set," Vera's mother said. "Just a rental. After I'm done with them, you can just call the number on the fridge and someone from the company will come get the furniture back. Not your new mattress, of course, but these things."

A rental.

This was how she'd always been. Practical, direct, unwilling to bow to the discomfort of others. Vera's mother did what needed to be done, always, and she had no patience for squeamishness.

"How did you get my phone number?" Vera asked.

Her mother's mouth twitched like she was biting through

thread. "Looked you up," she said. "It wasn't hard. You never changed your name."

"It's *his* name," Vera muttered.

Daphne's eyes flashed again, an old dangerous flash that put heat behind Vera's ears. "What did you say?"

"I'll go put my things away," Vera quickly replied. She hesitated beside the bed, not wanting to walk away yet, searching for another sentence. For something a different daughter and a different mother might have said to each other by now, something that would stitch up the open wound that was the last twelve years.

Daphne regarded her beadily. "If you want to take a nap you should go for it. I probably will. I sleep a lot these days."

"Sure," Vera said. "Do you need, um. Do you need help getting up and down? Like . . . to the bathroom? I can come check on you every hour or so . . . ?"

Daphne's chin jerked back into her neck, her revulsion palpable. She loaded a thousand different meanings into her one-word answer. "No."

Vera felt a flush of uncertain guilt. She should have done more research, she thought, should have asked more questions ahead of time about what her mother might need from her. "Are you sure? I don't mind, and you shouldn't have to—"

"I have a system," Daphne responded evenly. "I'm taken care of during the day. The details are not your business. You just focus on the house."

Vera knew she should ask more questions, but being here in this room with her mother was making her blood vibrate. The urge to escape subsumed any thoughts of responsible caretaking. "Great. I'll check on you before dinner."

"It's at six," Daphne replied. "We all eat together. I'm sure James will have questions for you. You'll be polite," she added sharply.

This was more familiar territory. Vera didn't know how to navigate Daphne's vulnerability, but her anger was another matter entirely. "Fine. Yes. Six." Vera walked back across the room to where her bags were waiting, and that's when she made her first mistake.

"Love you, Mom."

Her throat burned in the wake of those words. She picked up her duffel bag, the rustle of it almost covering a soft sound from behind her.

Vera turned around to see her mother looking at her expectantly with heavy-lidded, glassy eyes. She had said something that Vera hadn't heard, and it was important to hear what her mother had said because that 'love you, Mom' had slipped out of Vera unbidden and instinctive—and maybe, just possibly, it would turn out that in her long absence those words had become welcome.

"What did you say?" Vera said, her free hand lifting to her throat unbidden to feel the chain that sat there, the weight of the old key that hung around her neck. "I didn't hear you. Sorry."

Daphne cleared her throat, took a sip of water with a trembling hand. She set the water down carefully before answering. "I said, you don't have to call me that."

Vera couldn't seem to shape her brain around the conversation. Something about being here in the house again, with the dark dining room floor pressing against the soles of her feet—she couldn't think.

"Mom." The woman in the bed briefly pursed her lips as if

she'd just taken an accidental sip of brine. "You don't need to call me 'Mom' while you're here. Just call me Daphne." She didn't look Vera in the eye. "Things aren't that different just because I'm dying. Let's not pretend."

The burning in Vera's throat hardened, expanded, reached a fist down into her belly and clenched it until the knuckles cracked. It forced the air out of her lungs. She made a sound like "oh," and her field of vision shrank to her mother's hollow eyes and dry lips and thin, thin, thin neck.

She wanted to say that was fine, because it was. She wanted to say that she understood, because she did. She knew better than to try saying that accidental sentence again, even using her mother's name in place of 'Mom.' She knew not to do that, at least.

She let go of the chain around her neck and immediately missed the feel of it between her fingers.

"I'll check on you before dinner. Daphne," she said. Her voice came out hoarse, as though she'd let out all the screams she was swallowing.

Daphne didn't answer. She was already asleep, or maybe pretending to be, bolt-upright, her eyes shut and her jaw slack.

"Okay," Vera whispered to herself. She turned and briefly rested her forehead against the smooth plaster of the arch between the dining room and the entryway, letting the house soak in a little of the heat from her blazing face. "That's okay, then."

Vera went back the way she'd come, from the dining room to the entryway, and all around her, the Crowder House exhaled a long-held breath.

CHAPTER THREE

The stairs that led from the entryway to the second level of the house always seemed to have too many shadows. Before, when child-Vera had lived in the house her father built, she'd tiptoed across the entryway at night to use the powder room, swallowed whole by the dark of the house, counting her steps so as not to bump into the wall.

Francis Crowder had built the lower level of the house without hallways because Daphne hadn't seen a need for them, and she was the person he was building the house for. Because of this choice the rooms simply led one to another, separated by thick walls and connected by high, wide, open archways. The stairs were off to the right side of the entryway, while the powder room was on the left, with its connecting door back to the living room. The little room under the stairs—Francis's office, which became Vera's bedroom—stood directly opposite the powder room, the two doorways mirroring each other.

Just past her old bedroom was the door to the basement, squat and wide with a slanted top to follow the contour of the stairs. The two doors stood beside each other like a half-formed wink—one Vera refused now to see as she walked past, dropping her bags at the foot of the stairs and pulling out her last fresh change of clothes. She'd take the bags into her old bedroom after showering, she thought. Laundry could wait for the morning.

She paused at the foot of the stairs, staring up into the darkness of the second floor.

Her hand lifted to the lightswitch and found it right away, without her having to grope for it. When Vera flipped the switch, the upstairs lights flickered twice, just the way they always had. It was a fault in the wiring her father had put in back when he built the house.

Vera smiled as she climbed the stairs.

That little flicker, and then the soft creak of the fourth step, and now the feel of the wallpaper under her trailing fingertips.

It was as familiar as her own skin.

Vera had lived in a lot of places after leaving the Crowder House. She'd been in shitty apartments and nice apartments and even a townhouse for a year, before that situation went bad the way things always did. But she hadn't lived in any of those places long enough to stop bumping into things. She hadn't lived in any of them long enough to feel tenderly toward them.

This house, though. The outside of Vera was shaped like the inside of this house. This was the house her father had built with his two strong hands. This was the goldfish tank where she'd grown to the size she would always be, even after her mother gave her away to the world. There was a space for her here, an indentation she'd left years ago that still held a little of the warmth of her body. No matter what Daphne thought of her daughter, no matter how hard the next few days or weeks or months were going to be, Vera had once *belonged* here.

Now that she wasn't looking at the woman that was in her mother's bed, now that she wasn't listening to that voice coming from that face and looking at those eyes and feeling the ghost of a slap on the rise of her cheekbone—now that she could feel the weight of the house settling over her shoulders like a friendly arm—she felt almost happy to be where she was.

It was the first time Vera had felt that way in a very long time.

The carpet in the middle of the stairs was darker than the carpet at the edges. It was exactly the same as it had been when she left home, already covered in the same layer of thick clear plexiglass as the sideboard in the dining room. The tread on the plexiglass here was scuffed in places, but the carpet—the carpet Francis Crowder had walked on—was perfectly preserved beneath it.

At the top of the stairs there was a hallway, with three rooms set primly away from each other. Upstairs got a hallway even though downstairs didn't, since Daphne had always understood the importance of keeping personal things apart.

All the way at the end of the hall was the bedroom where her parents used to sleep, the bedroom where Vera had been born. Along one wall was her mother's long-disused sewing room and her father's office, separated by the linen closet. The master bathroom was along the other wall. Vera was glad she didn't need to go through her parents' bedroom to get to it. A connecting door met the hallway, just like the powder room downstairs.

Two doors in each bathroom, and none of them locking. Vera was never sure of the exact reason for the dual entrances. Maybe Francis had just forgotten to take bathrooms into account when he'd been drawing up the plans.

It was a thing best left unconsidered, Vera thought. Some questions don't want answering.

❧

Vera stayed in the bathroom longer than necessary. She stood under the weak spray of the shower, losing herself in a chip in the tile on the wall until the hot water started to run out. She lingered for a long time, letting drops of water slip across her flesh and trickle down into the drain, where they'd slide down along the warm metal of the pipes. Letting the house drink her down.

Her skin was still damp as she dressed. Her clothes darkened in places and stuck too close to her, but she didn't want to use the towels in this bathroom without knowing which ones were clean. She braided her overlong brown hair while it was wet and then twisted the braid up into a loose bun to keep it from dripping onto her shirt.

It was how she always did her hair after washing it—out-of-the-way, easy, automatic. But this time it felt wrong. Too tight, too heavy, too close. Before she could think about why, she took her hair down, combed it out, and picked up her mother's ancient pink hair dryer.

It was clumsy work. Vera had a lot of hair and she almost never did anything with it that wasn't a braid and a bun. Daphne had styled it for her on special occasions and picture days before that awful year. And then after that awful year, it didn't matter so much anymore.

It would have been easier to cut it short, but Francis had always liked it best long.

Coordinating the brush and the blow-dryer at the same time was tricky and it took her ages but she managed to do a not-terrible job. Over the course of thirty minutes or so her hair went from a wet, ropy ink-slick to a too-dry fall of deep brown. Loose strands littered the cool tile at her feet, fluttering in the draft from the floorboard vents, drifting toward the grate.

Vera pinned her now-dry, now-straight hair away from her

face using a few old clips she found beside the sink. She took her time smoothing down the stray frizz at her hairline.

The loose hair on the floor gathered next to the baseboard vent, which had steadily sucked the steam out of the air until even the little haze of fog at the edges of the mirror was gone.

Vera made eye contact with herself and was captivated by how different she looked in this mirror now than she had the last time she'd looked into it. She'd seen herself thousands of times in hundreds of different mirrors, had looked at her face under so many different kinds of light—she was accustomed to nothing so much as herself. But this mirror, and this light.

She hadn't seen herself like this since the day she left home.

Her eyes had sat deeper in her head back then; her jawline had been softer; her skin had been worse by some measures, and better by others. But the changes didn't register. In this mirror, now and always, she just looked like *Vera Crowder*. A combination of Daphne and Francis, a girl and then a young woman and now a woman—just a woman, without 'young' attached. Pale the way a person gets when they're indoors all the time, and tired the way a person gets after they've lived too many lives.

But the soft fall of her hair seemed to shine in this mirror. The line of her neck seemed more elegant than usual. She could not help but give herself a little smile. The Vera in the mirror smiled back.

She didn't want to leave this room, the one room that had escaped her mother's efforts at preservation. The one room where there was nothing for visitors to chew on. But it would take a very bad daughter, she decided, to hide in the bathroom ignoring her dying mother. And Vera was trying to be better.

She headed down the dark stairs toward her waiting bags, not bothering to turn the light on. All her earthly possessions were in those bags, not counting whatever her mother was going to leave behind. As Vera approached them, something snagged at the edge of her vision—something unfamiliar in this too-familiar landscape. Something new.

There were photos on the wall. That hadn't been true before she left home. In a fit of rage and spite Daphne had taken them all down one day; for all her furtive searching, Vera had never been able to find them again. Daphne must have had fresh ones printed and framed and hung. Something to give her house-guests, so they could stare into Francis Crowder's eyes and try to find something to sate their relentless hunger for him.

The new photos were notable, but they weren't what caught Vera's eye.

No—the thing that stopped her short was just below where the photos of Vera and Francis and Daphne were hung.

A long, dark line.

Vera ran her palm across it, squinting in the dim light of the closed-up house. It was rough, deep, a gouge that cut through the wallpaper and dug into the plaster. It stretched most of the length of the staircase. It was deep and cruel and strangely smooth at the edges, more of a scoop than a scratch.

Frowning, Vera pressed a finger into it, feeling the way the plaster cupped her fingertip.

She tried to remember walking up the stairs, tried to remember if she'd felt this gash then. Hadn't the lights been on? And hadn't she trailed her fingers along the wallpaper as she'd gone up?

Or had she simply remembered the sensation from a thousand times feeling it? That must be true, she thought. She couldn't have missed this injury. Not if she'd felt it on her way up.

"What did you do," she whispered, not wanting an answer.

The word *inspiring* sat as bitter as old bile on her tongue. Vera reminded herself that nothing ever happened inside the Crowder House without Daphne's knowledge and permission. This injury to the wall had been inflicted by someone who knew they were allowed. There was no sense asking why.

Whatever had caused this—*whoever* had caused it, whichever one of the monsters and parasites that her mother invited into their home—Vera didn't want to know. She didn't need to know. Daphne was dying, now, and the time for answers was long gone. This was just something to be gotten through.

Vera skidded down the last few steps. She could patch up the wall later, when her more immediate work here was over. When the house was hers to sell, she supposed. She picked her things up and walked past the door to the basement again, staying out of the sightline of the dining room.

Her suitcase was in her left hand. The doorknob was in her right. It resisted her, and then it didn't, and then the door was open and she was inside.

❧

Being back in her childhood room wasn't as bad as she'd feared.

Smooth wood floors, just like in the rest of the lower level of the house. The closet she used to hide in when she felt lonely. Chest of drawers against one wall, the top covered with a dusty plexiglass shield. Desk beside it. Rickety wooden chair for doing homework in, pushed all the way under the desk to make walking space.

This room, more than any other, was always the safest place in the house for Vera. This room had been *hers*.

She'd spent so many years sitting in that chair, listening for her mother's footsteps, waiting for the door to open. Waiting to be forgiven.

And there, in the middle of one wall—there was her old bed. It was a queen-sized brass half-poster, familiar despite the bare new mattress resting on the ancient box spring. Vera put her bags down, nudged the duffel halfway beneath the bedframe. She rested her palm against one of the short bedknobs at the foot of the bed and pushed gently.

The whole frame rattled, metal-on-metal. It was even louder than she remembered.

Vera frowned. As a child, she'd assumed that the rattle was predetermined—that it was just how beds were supposed to be, and there was nothing anyone could do to prevent the noise that rang out every time she turned over in her sleep or snuck in and out of her room. But she'd slept in a lot of beds in the intervening years, and she could now recognize the loose shimmy of the metal. It could easily have been silenced: a simple matter of tightening a couple of screws loose in the frame, where the headboard was joined to the platform.

Why hadn't Francis ever fixed it? She only wondered for a moment before the answer came to her. *He wanted to be able to hear.*

Well, he wasn't here anymore, and Vera could handle this without him. She just had to tighten the screws and then the bed would be quiet. That and some bedsheets, that's all Vera needed to make this bed feel like her own.

Back upstairs, then, past the unfamiliar gash in the wall, to the hall closet where the extra bedlinens and the toolchest had always resided together, united in their utility. Francis had always left his tools there, at the bottom of the linen closet, tucked in next to a big basket of cleaning rags, for as long as Vera could remember.

It was still there—a matte black case with bright orange clasps to hold it shut. It didn't look like something that was *his*, and so it had been left alone, too boring for visitors to the house to inspect. Vera bent and snapped the clasps back, lifting the plastic lid of the case, her hands smearing years' worth of thick dust away from the top of the lid.

The tools inside the chest were mismatched and oddly sized. There was a flathead screwdriver with a smooth wooden handle, a large hammer with a worn gray grip, an ancient tub of spackling putty but no putty knife. Vera could remember watching Francis spackling over a thumbtack-hole she'd made in the wall—he'd used a butter knife to do it, leaving tiny parallel grooves in the patch.

There was a pair of work gloves in the bottom of the case. Vera pulled them out and straightened, letting a few loose penny-nails fall to the floor. The gloves were gray and heavy, striped at the cuffs, discolored and unevenly worn.

Her bare toes curled into the carpet absently, feeling for the sudden cold resistance of the dropped nails, as she lifted the gloves to her face. Vera buried her nose in the palm of one glove and inhaled her father deep into her lungs.

The gloves had been alone in that toolbox for such a long time, but they still hung on to him. Must and mildew dominated the bouquet of the old gloves, but Vera concentrated hard on the whisper of her father underneath the age and decay: wood and sweat and sun. He was still here, in this place that he made, in this place that made her.

He was still here.

The moment of longing she allowed herself was an excess, a once-a-year indulgence. It was all she could permit herself in this house, where remembering Francis was compulsory, but missing him was forbidden.

Vera tucked the feeling back away where it belonged, into the spaces behind her back teeth and between her knuckles and under her kneecaps. There was room for it there. She'd found that she could almost forget it entirely.

She didn't bring the gloves with her when she returned to her bedroom.

She carried two screwdrivers in one hand—a flathead and a Phillips-head, since she couldn't remember what the screws on her bed looked like. Under her other arm she'd tucked a set of sheets and pillowcases, light blue cotton with a fine pattern of white flowers. She used her elbow to turn the light off when she got to the bottom of the stairs. It didn't take so much effort to ignore the gash in the wall this time.

She was already getting used to the small differences in the house where she'd grown up, the little injuries that weren't hers to tend. Not yet, anyway.

Not until Daphne was dead.

All was quiet downstairs when Vera turned into the entry-way. The light in the dining room was off, which meant that Daphne was either sleeping or lying silently in the dark, listening to the sound of Vera's footsteps on the stairs and feigning unconsciousness to avoid conversation.

It wasn't too dark to see, not with the thin wash of light from outside that made it into the entryway. But it was dimmer than Vera would have thought for so early in the evening this close to summer. She wondered if a thunderstorm was gathering outside, and she just hadn't noticed.

Vera padded past the basement door to her old bedroom on

quiet feet, nudged the door open with her shoulder, and then leaned back to close it. She bumped the lightswitch with the fist that held the screwdrivers and the overhead fixture blazed to life. Her eyes had already adjusted to the darkness of the entryway; the switch dazzled her for a moment, made her blink, left a shifting shadow across her vision.

She blinked again.

The shadow stayed.

It was next to her bed, a bunched-up thing, something like a man crouching to pick up a penny or tie his shoe. It was a blur in the center of her field of vision, something floating on the surface of her eye, a fingerprint on her retina. It was not there, couldn't be there—but she couldn't see through it or around it either.

Vera pressed the bedsheets to her chest and blinked again, harder this time. While her eyes were shut tight, the fingers of her right hand twitched around the screwdrivers. Her hand was full, so she couldn't snap once, let alone four times, but her dust-smeared thumb and middle finger tried futilely to move toward each other anyway.

When she opened her eyes, the shadow was gone.

Vera exhaled hard through her nose. "Calm down, Vee," she muttered, mostly to adulterate the stifling silence of the house. She told herself that this was fatigue. Maybe a visual migraine. It made sense. She'd been driving for four days, had come into an extremely stressful environment, had spoken to her mother face-to-face for the first time in . . . a very, very long time. Her stomach was hollow and she knew that she should probably find something to eat, but this—the shadow, the little hallucination or whatever it was—proved that what Vera really needed was sleep.

She leaned against the door, thumped the back of her head

against the wood a few times. She closed her eyes and let fatigue wash over her. She wanted to cry. Surely that would help. A good long cry. She couldn't remember the last time she'd had one, which was probably a bad sign.

Her bones were so heavy. She knew she should go and see her mother again. It was the right thing to do, the reason she was here—a daughter should want to spend time with her mother. Plus, Daphne would be furious at her for missing dinner with their guest, the artist that had heralded Vera's most recent unraveling. Whoever they might be.

Then again, Vera reminded herself, Daphne's fury couldn't do anything beyond kicking her back out.

It had happened before.

If it happened again, so be it.

She would not go to dinner, she decided. She couldn't. Not tonight.

Tonight she would take five steps across the room to her bed, and she would put the sheets on the bed and lie down and go right to sleep. She could fix the bedframe tomorrow. She could put pillowcases on the pillows in the morning. She needed sleep, right away, thick rich dark sleep, and in the morning everything would be the same but she would be able to face it all without breaking.

Vera could have fallen asleep just like that, leaning up against the door of her childhood bedroom with her eyes closed. The wood of the door seemed soft against her weary shoulders, seemed to mold itself perfectly to the curve of her spine. She could have nodded off on her feet right then and there.

Until the bedframe rattled again.

Her eyes snapped open.

The noise was still fading, the bedframe still shaking minutely.

Vera watched it move, her breath held tight, a wash of adrenaline burning the weight out of her bones and replacing it with a high harsh buzz of fear. Her mouth flooded with the taste of pennies.

She told herself she'd imagined the sound. But of course that didn't work at all—her mind immediately rejected this as an obvious lie. The bedframe had rattled. Vera was across the room from it and it had rattled. She hadn't touched it, *nothing* had touched it, but it had rattled anyway.

She took a breath. One of the Wellness Packets she'd completed as a teenager had advised breathing in moments of uncertainty. She'd given herself an A-minus on that packet. She took another breath.

There was nothing in the room with her that she could see. There was nowhere to hide other than the closet, and that door was still shut tight against everything that could possibly exist in a house like this. There was nowhere else to go—except for one place.

Before Vera could talk herself out of it, she stooped to look under the bed.

Nothing was there.

Of course nothing was there.

The space between the bedframe and the floor was thick with dust and shadows, uniform in coverage, unbroken by the solidity of flesh and undisturbed by movement.

"Come on," Vera hissed. "You're tired and this is childish. Don't be childish. Just be tired."

She made good on her plan: walk to bed, spread sheets out on mattress. Toss pants and bra onto floor to be reworn tomorrow. Get horizontal. Eyes closed. *Sleep, goddamn it.*

It wouldn't work. The lights were still on. She'd never once

in her life been able to sleep with the lights on. That wasn't going to change now, just because she was in a room where she'd
prefer not to be in the dark. Just because she didn't like the idea
of turning that light off.

Vera knew she was being ridiculous. She knew it. But her
mother was next door, dying, and a ravenous stranger was living in the backyard and her bedroom door still didn't have a
lock on it, and she couldn't shake the feeling that she should
really, *really* keep the light on.

Vera refused to bend to a feeling like that last one. She got
up out of the bed fast and angry. She stalked across the room,
turned the light off with a too-loud slap at the switch. Back
in bed, even faster, rattling the bedframe, back under the flat
sheet with no blanket, her palm still stinging from where she'd
struck the wall. Furious at herself for reasons she couldn't have
articulated even if she'd tried.

The familiar room was full of an unfamiliar quiet. There
must have been a storm overhead, because almost no light at
all came through her bedroom windows. It may as well have
been midnight at the bottom of the ocean.

Vera didn't like any of it, but the deep fatigue of the drive
and the day won out over her vigilance.

It wasn't long before the adrenaline drained out of her, a re-
treating tide that left deep, heavy exhaustion behind it. Sleep
wrapped itself snug around her wrists and ankles and waist and
pulled her down hard against the mattress.

Vera's last thought before sleeping was of how silly she'd
been to be frightened.

This was the Crowder House. The house her father built.

There was nothing to be afraid of here.

CHAPTER FOUR

Vera is eleven years old and she is afraid.

There are noises again.

They woke her up a few minutes ago. Thumps and scrapes and scrabbles, and once a dull wet slap. The noises are coming from under her bed and she is sure, beyond a shadow of a doubt, that they are the result of Something Bad.

Vera still has one ear pressed to her pillow. Her pillowcase has foxes on it. Her hair is long and blond and it fans across the fox pillow in a meander of tangles. This is the last summer she will sleep with the fox pillowcase. It's for little kids and she wants something more mature soon—not grown-up, she doesn't say that anymore. She says 'mature' or she says 'adult.' She wants something more mature soon, but the fox pillowcase stays cool even on the nights when her open bedroom window lets in nothing but stickiness and katydid sounds, so for now it can stay.

She knows that the sounds outside her window are katydids and not cicadas, because her father told her that cicadas mostly make noise during the day while katydids mostly make noise at night. Her mother calls both noises 'that racket' and closes up her own bedroom windows to keep *that racket* out.

The noises that are coming from under the bed are louder than *that racket*. That's how Vera knows that the sound is closer to her than the bugs are.

The bugs are *outside*. The sounds are *inside*. They're inside for sure.

Vera eyes the vague shapes that are scattered throughout the bedroom. The shapes are black against the ambient gray of the darkness, which is cut only by a vague notion of moonlight from outside and the insubstantial glow of Vera's nightlight. That nightlight is beside the bedroom door, a hundred miles away.

Vera always tells herself that the nightlight is there so she can see the door in the dark, so she doesn't trip over the piles of clothes that now in the darkness look like unknowable hungry gape-mouthed monsters. She tells herself that she isn't scared of the dark. She's too mature for that kind of thing. She's outgrown it.

There is Something Bad under the bed and it's making those sounds. She's certain that if she moves, the Bad thing will know she is awake. If it knows she is awake it will get her.

That's how these things work: they wait until a person is awake enough to be scared, they wait until a person is conscious enough to hope for mercy, and then they don't give any mercy at all.

Did one of the vague shadows on the bedroom floor move? Vera tries to remember if she left a pile of clothes in *that* spot, that *very* spot. Surely she doesn't own so many clothes that they could make such a huge black shape on the floor so close to the foot of her bed. Does she?

She can't get to the door now. If she tried, she would have to do two impossible things: get out from under the covers, and let her feet touch the floor. She can't do that. If her foot touches the floor next to her bed then something will reach out lightning-fast and grasp her ankle, and then it will have her.

There's a long, slow scrape from just beneath her head.

Vera breathes through her nose, only through her nose, short shallow breaths that she hopes will be the right kind of quiet. But then she has second thoughts. She's pretty sure that she usually sleeps with her mouth open. Has the thing under the bed been there for so long that it will recognize the difference between her asleep-breathing and her awake-breathing?

The noises are getting closer to her, she's sure of it.

A sound like scrabbling claws reverberates through the wall above her pillow, and she makes tight fists in the cotton of her summer quilt. The cotton wicks the sweat away from her palms. Her sheets wick sweat away from the rest of her. There's a lot of sweat, all of a sudden. She bites down on her pillowcase, trying not to make a sound, trying not to let it know that she's awake.

She's not trying hard enough. A thin whine escapes her throat.

She can't be alone in the room with the thing under her bed. Whatever it is, whatever it wants, whatever it's planning—she can't face it alone. She's too small. She's too scared. This is the first time she has ever felt ashamed of that. In the past, whenever she felt too small or too scared, it was okay and she asked for help and she usually got it. But now she is eleven, and soon she will be twelve, and after that she'll be a teenager, and she knows from the bigger kids at school that she has to get rid of her fox pillowcases and her nightlight and her small bony fearful body.

She isn't there yet, though.

What she needs is her parents. She really wants her father because he's bigger and stronger than her mother and Vera isn't sure how big the thing under the bed is. Either of them would do, though.

But not both. Both would be too complicated.

Her mother, Daphne, is a tight perm with highlights in it, skinny arms with freckles on them, and a full mouth that's always pressed into a thin line. If she comes into the room, she will look at Vera with tired disappointment. She'll still sit on the edge of the bed and tell Vera everything's okay, but she'll add that this can't keep happening, that Vera's getting too old for this, and she'll bring it up next time Vera wants to watch a television show that starts after nine p.m.

Vera's father is a lot easier about these things. He's a big wall of clean soap smell with curly brown hair that's thinning in the back, a crooked smile with a chipped tooth in the front, big ropy muscles in his arms from cutting lumber all day. He'll scoop Vera up close into a hug after he's checked the bed and the closet and the curtains and the corners. He'll tell her that no monsters are there. He'll check twice if she asks.

But either of them is fine. Really. Just so long as somebody comes.

The wet slapping noise comes again, followed by a thick gurgling gasp. Vera squeezes her eyes shut so tight that they ache and she grips her quilt hard, and she decides that the time has come to be as brave as she can, because if she isn't brave *it will get her.*

She sits up in her bed and screams.

By the time she has run out of air her father's footsteps are outside her door, and then he's in the room and the lights are on and he's standing there, solid and breathless, looking at her with wide fearful eyes.

"What's wrong? What is it? Are you hurt?" He looks around the room fast, his gaze hitting every corner of the room before jumping back to her.

"There's . . ."

Her voice fails her. The noises have stopped and the lights are on, and what if there's nothing? What if she tells her father what she heard and he thinks she's being some overdramatic kid? She wonders if she should lie and say there was someone looking in the window, or that she had a nightmare.

But then she imagines her father turning the light off and leaving her alone in the room with the wet scraping sounds from beneath her bed. Her stomach drops. She can't do that. She needs help, even if asking for it winds up making her look like a baby.

"There's something," she says. "Under the bed."

Her father's shoulders drop, and some of the fear drains from his face. "What is it?" he asks, entirely serious. He always does that—takes Vera seriously even when he could roll his eyes at her like Daphne would. "A monster?"

"A person, I think," she says. She only says that because she thinks that it would sound immature to say *yes, definitely a monster.* "A murderer," she adds, because she's not sure if *a person* seems scary enough to justify a middle-of-the-night scream.

Her father nods gravely. His eyes are bloodshot and his cheeks are flushed. Vera figures he must be tired, must have jumped out of bed and run into the room fast when he heard her screaming. "How do you know there's a murderer?" he asks, his voice soft and somber.

"I heard him," she whispers. "He's under the bed. I heard him."

"Let's take a look," he says.

Vera's gut clenches. She bites the inside of her cheek to keep from saying "don't." What if there *is* a murderer under the bed, and they get her father? But if there's a murderer, *someone* will have to be the first to see them, and Vera believes that her father is the best one to do that job. So she clenches her toes under her blanket and she doesn't say anything as her father crosses the room with deliberate steps, his boots falling heavy on the smooth wood of the floor.

She wonders, distantly, when he put his boots on—shoes aren't allowed in Vera's mother's house—but that thought is quickly swept away by the rapid current of her fear.

Vera's eyes stay fixed on him.

His eyes stay fixed on the bedskirt.

He arrives next to the bed and slowly, cautiously lowers himself into a crouch.

Vera takes a deep breath and holds it, ready to scream again.

Her father locks eyes with her. He lifts a finger to his lips.

Vera releases her grip on her quilt and claps both hands over her mouth to keep herself from making a sound because if her father thinks she should be quiet, then she will be quiet.

He nods at her, then looks back to the bedskirt. He reaches out with one huge, steady, scarred hand, one of the hands that he used to build this bedroom, one of the hands that cupped the back of her skull when she was a baby. He reaches that hand out and with sudden fluid speed he whips up the bedskirt and looks at what's behind it.

He looks for a long time. He looks for so long that Vera lets her hands drop away from her mouth so she can brace herself on her palms and lean toward him. "What is it?" she finally whispers, unable to bear it any longer.

Vera's father sits back on his heels, wipes his forehead with the back of one arm, and leans forward to rest both his elbows on her mattress. His fingernails have something black crusted beneath them, dark crescents that Daphne would make him scrub away with a stiff brush if she saw.

"I have bad news, Vee," her father says. "There's something under there, all right, and it's pretty scary."

Half of Vera recognizes this tone of voice, knows that he's about to make a joke. The other half of her is taking in the faint sheen of panic on her father's face, the bloodless pallor of his cheeks, the thready capillaries in the whites of his eyes, and that half of her knows that something is wrong.

But then his face crinkles up into a wide smile. "It's the biggest dust bunny I've ever seen." He laughs and she laughs with him, her eyes landing on his chipped tooth. Not because what he said is actually funny, but because he wouldn't make a joke like that if there was a *monster*.

Vera's father checks the whole room—the corners and the closet and behind the curtains, and one more time under the bed just in case. His boots are loud. Mud falls off of them as he walks, mud that Vera will have to clean up tomorrow before her mother sees.

"Why are you so dirty?" Vera asks when her father has come to sit on her bed and told her that there is, definitely, no one but the two of them in the room.

"What do you mean?" he asks, his brow tight, his eyes darting between hers. There is sweat at his temples, darkening his already-dark curls. Vera isn't sure why she didn't see it before except that she was too busy being scared to really see that, or the mud that cakes his boots. "Dirty?"

"Yeah, your nails are dirty and you have mud on you," she says, pointing.

"Oh," he says. He frowns at his nails. Vera frowns at them

too; now that she's looking at them closely, she can see that the dark grime is tucked in along the sides of his nails, too, and in the creases of his knuckles. "I cleaned the gutters earlier. I guess I didn't scrub hard enough before dinner." He winks at her, the frown so completely gone that it might never have been there at all. "Don't tell your mother. You know how she gets."

Vera winks back, a trick she's only just got the hang of. "I won't tell. Hey, Dad?"

"You don't need to say 'hey,' I'm already listening to you. You only need to say 'hey' if you're trying to get someone's attention."

"Sorry. Dad? If there's nothing under the bed, what were those noises?" Vera swallows hard, afraid that he'll say the noises were her imagination. Adults say that kind of thing sometimes, and it makes her feel ridiculous, or like they might *think* she's ridiculous. Sometimes she does imagine things, but not those noises. Those were real. She's sure of it.

Francis uses one fingertip to trace the outline of two adjacent squares on Vera's quilt. She winces because his fingers look so filthy, but he doesn't leave any dirt on the bedspread—it's stuck to him, all worked-in. "Our house is shaped like this, right?"

"Okay," she says, hesitant because she isn't sure if the house is a perfect rectangle, plus it has a roof on top that isn't flat, plus there's the garden shed in the backyard.

"Here's the top floor, where your mom and I sleep, and where Mom has her sewing room. And I have my office, which used to be your bedroom," he says, pointing to the top of the two squares he'd traced. They'd swapped his office and her bedroom just a few months before, when Daphne had declared that she couldn't sleep with *all that racket* from outside and Vera had declared that she couldn't sleep with her window closed.

Vera's father continues, pointing to the bottom square: "And here's the first floor, where there's the kitchen and the living room and the dining room and your bedroom."

"And the mudroom," Vera adds.

Her father smiles. "And the mudroom." He smells like clean sweat and rich earth and something sharp, something that reminds Vera of the way the air smells right after lightning strikes during the summer storms that shake her windowpane. "And down *here*," he says, pointing below that bottom-story square, "is the basement."

"I'm not allowed," Vera says quickly. This is a firm rule and she obeys the rule even though her best friend Brandon keeps asking if they can sneak down there and look around.

"That's right," her father says. "It's my workshop, and the tools are very dangerous, and—"

"—and there are really big spiders," Vera finishes for him. She remembers this fact and, as a result, is never tempted to go into the basement in spite of Brandon's eagerness and the allure of *not-allowed*.

"Huge," Vera's father says. He holds his hands out two feet apart, making his eyes wide. "Like cats!"

Vera laughs because she is supposed to, because the idea of a spider the size of a cat is supposed to be silly, because she is not supposed to be afraid that maybe it's real and possible and waiting to fall on her face in the middle of the night.

Vera's father smiles at her, then lowers his hands, resting them over the two quilt squares that represent the house he built. "But—and I've never told you this until now, because I didn't want to scare you—there are other things in the basement, too. Things worse than spiders."

A shiver runs up Vera's spine fast as a watersnake vanishing under the garden shed. "Like what?" she whispers, her imagination blossoming faster than her fear can keep up with.

"Possums," her father says. "And raccoons. They come in looking for trash, looking for a place to have their babies. I know you think they're cute," he says, holding up a finger to stop Vera from deciding that the basement now holds fresh appeal. "But they're not. They're wild animals, and sometimes they have rabies. They'll run up and bite you as soon as you set foot in that basement."

Vera isn't sure if she believes him or not. She's never seen a possum before, but she's seen racoons ambling through the sideyard near the garbage cans. They're fat and clumsy and they look soft. They don't look like they'd bite her.

But she remembers the tools and the spiders, and rabies sounds like bad news. She decides that the basement holds no temptation, even if there might be baby animals in there with big eyes and soft fur.

"So . . . that's what that noise was? Possums?"

"Probably raccoons this time. I thought I saw one down there earlier today." Vera's father smooths out the quilt under his palms, his eyes on the movement of his own hands. "I'll set a trap for it and get rid of it. If you hear those noises again, don't worry, okay? It's just animals that wandered in and want a way out. Sometimes they don't understand where they are and they get scared," he adds. "Sometimes they get hurt. And I have to help them escape."

Something has come into Vera's father's voice, some faraway thing that she knows he will not explain to her. Adults do that all the time, talking around big feelings and ideas as if no one will notice that they're saying two things at the same time. Vera knows that he will not tell her the secret of what this means to him. His shoulders are drooping as though a weight has settled across them and his eyes are starting to glaze over, and his fingers are suddenly tight around fistfuls of her quilt.

Vera thinks that he must be very tired. After all, she did make him run into her bedroom in the middle of the night. She lies back, letting her head rest stiffly on her pillow, the clearest I'm-ready-for-bed signal she knows how to broadcast.

"Thank you for checking under the bed," she says.

"Of course, Vee. Hey, will you promise me something?"

"You don't have to say 'hey,'" she replies softly. "I'm already listening."

He smiles, releasing her blanket. "Promise you won't go into the basement to see the animals," he says. "It's really very dangerous. You could get hurt."

His voice is gentle, serious, and he's looking right at her. This, she understands, is big. This is the way adults talk to each other. Her father isn't just telling her a rule. He's telling her a *why,* and he's asking her for a promise.

She nods solemnly, her hair *shush*-ing against the fox pillowcase. "I promise," she says.

Vera's father kisses her goodnight and pulls the covers all the way up to her chin. It's not how she likes to sleep—she prefers her arms on top of the covers—but she likes it when her father tucks her in, and she knows he won't keep doing it for much longer, so she doesn't move until after he's turned off her light and shut her door. Vera closes her eyes and lets her head sink down deep into the soft cool embrace of her fox pillowcase.

When the noises resume under her bed—the long harsh scrapes, and the wet slaps, and the rich gurgling, and the high tight painful squeals—she doesn't open her eyes. It's just an animal, and her father will take care of it by morning.

Still, she can't help but give a little involuntary shiver at the sounds. She slips one arm out from under the blanket and lets it dangle off the edge of the bed. In school that day, her teacher told the class about superstitions, which are things that people believe will keep them safe. Like magic but different.

Vera is still undecided as to whether or not she believes in magic. It ultimately depends on whether believing in magic turns out to be *kid stuff* or *very adult stuff*—but a superstition seems like something outside that question, something anyone might have. Right now, when she's a little afraid even though there's nothing to be afraid of, feels like the perfect time to try out a superstition of her own.

Her small hand hovers in the darkness of the bedroom, her elbow bending ever-so-slightly backward over the edge of the mattress in a casual hyperextension. She waits for the next thud from the basement, which makes her startle even though she knows now that it isn't anything scary.

When the thud comes, she snaps her fingers four times fast.

The sounds fade quickly. Vera smiles at the quiet and returns her hand to the bed, resting her arm on top of the covers. She decides that she likes this new superstition. She decides that it works.

Three years from now, when there are policemen at the door, she will feel afraid. But right now, even with an occasional faint noise drifting up from the basement, she is not afraid. Between her father and this new superstition she's decided on, there's nothing to fear.

She falls asleep so quickly that she doesn't register the faint sound that comes from beneath her bed.

It is the sound of clumsy fingers, trying to learn how to snap four times fast.

CHAPTER FIVE

Vera awoke in the closet of her childhood bedroom, knees bent high in front of her, toes curling on the dark brown wood of the floor.

The closet door was open. She tried to see out into the room, to the moonlit square of the window. She tried to peer under the bed but the night was dense and the shadows in the room were deep and the darkness beneath the bed was thickest of all. She was tucked into the corner of the closet tight, the walls snug against her arms, her bare spine curving into the angle where the walls joined.

When Vera's father built the Crowder House, he did a good job insulating it. The cool fresh air of the night stayed out while the slow-building heat of the day stayed in. The walls stayed as warm as skin. Still, Vera shivered in the darkness of the closet. The night was warm, the house was warm, the room was warm, but she was cold, cold from the inside, a kind of cold that fought against her with grunting strength and bulging veins.

Her hand drifted to the old key that still hung around her neck, squeezed hard enough to feel the bite of the metal against her palm. Then she let her hand drop to her belly because there, right there—that's where the cold was coming from, just a palm's width to the right of her navel.

Right there.

She looked down and could almost see herself through the

pressing-down darkness—a pale, naked, hunched-over thing, vulnerable and alone. Her hair fell around her face as she curled in on herself. She blew a tendril out of her eyes as though that would help anything.

Vera couldn't see much, but she could see just enough. Shades of black and gray. She could see, by straining, that there was something stuck to her. It was dark against the pale plane of her abdomen.

She pressed against the edge with a fingertip, experimental, gentle—she gasped, it was so cold, it was the thing that was making *her* so cold. She had it now. She let out a shaking, shivering breath and pressed against the thing again, harder this time, and she gasped again because when she pressed down, her finger slipped inside the dark thing.

She knew at once that she'd been wrong. It wasn't something stuck to her.

It was a hole.

Of course. This was the hole in her stomach. She knew what to do about this. She knew how to make herself less cold.

She dug her finger deeper into the hole, arched her knuckle to make room for a second finger to slip in alongside it. The movement made the key swing on its chain, bumping back and forth between her goosefleshed breasts.

Her skin stretched tight around her fingers but it didn't hurt—it was too cold to hurt. Her hand was shaking, but it was just because of the thing inside the hole. Once she got that thing out she could go back to bed and be warm. The thing inside the hole in her belly was slippery and freezing, but she knew she could get it if she could just stop trembling.

Vera's fingers were inside the hole in her belly, all the way to the last knuckle, aching with cold. They would be numb soon.

She had to hurry. She took a deep breath in through her nose, let it out slowly through her mouth. She had to stop shivering. It would only take a moment and then it would be out of her and she could be warm again.

She hooked her fingers around the thing inside of her, and carefully, slowly, so it couldn't slip out of her grip, she pulled.

It unspooled fast and sudden like a fish sliding out of a net. She let out a sob of relief as the long gray rope fell to the floor with a wet-laundry splat—but she was still so cold. Her relief turned to dismay, then crystallized into determination: it wasn't all out of her yet.

She had to get it out. She had to get it out in order to be good. She had to get it out so it couldn't go bad inside her.

Vera wrapped her hands around the section that hung just outside the hole, her fists filled with whatever this awful thing was that had been coiled up in her gut. She clenched her jaw at how painfully cold it was.

She pulled hard.

There was so much of it, so much more than she'd expected. She pulled out lengths of it, hand over hand like climbing a rope in gym class which she'd never been good at but she couldn't stop now, piling loops of frigid meat between her feet, her toes curled tight against the wood floor, her teeth chattering—

Vera woke up without a start, without a gasp, her eyes flying open. She was in her bed and her heart was pounding but the nightmare, at least, was over.

She tried to lift her hands to her belly to reassure herself (*it was just a dream, there is no hole, your intestines are warm and pink and they are inside where they belong, there is no hole to pull them out of, it was just a dream*).

She tried to lift her hands, but she couldn't.

She couldn't move her hands at all.

She couldn't move her arms either, or her legs. She screamed silently at her limbs to obey her, but they wouldn't. Her heart was beating so hard and so loud that she was sure she was dying.

She tried to scream, but the only sound that came from her throat was a thin whine.

She squeezed her eyes shut tight. Sleep paralysis, that was all. She'd had it before once or twice as a teenager and now it was happening again. She'd done a packet on it. B-plus, but the content had stuck with her.

She repeated the facts to herself, trying hard not to be afraid. Her brain had just gotten its wires crossed, woken up her conscious mind before waking up her body. That was all. She'd had a nightmare and she'd woken up in the wrong order. It would pass soon and she would be fine.

"Don't worry."

Her eyes snapped open again at the sound of the voice.

"I'm here. You can go back to sleep."

It was right next to her ear. She couldn't make herself turn her head to see it, but she could feel how close it was. The voice was right there, right by her ear, practically on her pillow. Vera's chest ached, bruised from the inside by the frantic racing of her heart. She strained as hard as she could.

She had to move.

"Don't worry. Just close your eyes."

The voice was speaking in a half-whisper, rasping and tender. It sounded so familiar. She had to move, she had to turn on the lights, she had to scream. She could swear she recognized that whisper.

"It was just a bad dream. You're all in one piece now. Go on back to sleep, Vera-baby."

She could feel the breath of the speaker against her ear. It was cool and close, and it smelled like rot and cut grass and turned earth and sweet lemon. But Vera could not see the lips that brushed the tender skin just below her earlobe.

"Hush now."

That did it. Vera's entire body flashed hot with adrenaline and her limbs got the fucking memo and her voice unlocked itself and finally, finally, she could move.

She ran.

She scrambled across the bed away from the voice, half-fell on her way to the door. She screamed and it was a real scream, one that tore out of her, and the long weedy roots of it were wrapped around her pelvic bone and she *meant* it.

She slapped frantically at the wall and on the third try her palm found the lightswitch, and then the room was bright and the shadows were dead and she turned around to see who was there, who was with her, who was in her ear telling her to go back to sleep.

The room was empty.

Her bedsheets were dark with sweat, crumpled around the place where she had been. Quickly, so she couldn't scare herself out of doing it, she ducked down to look under the bed. There was nothing there.

Of course there was nothing there.

There was nothing behind the gauzy curtains that covered the window, either. There was no one in the closet—she flung the door open fast, as though somehow the element of surprise would give her an advantage over anyone who might be hiding there. The corners of the room were illuminated and bare and the floor was clean and Vera was alone.

She crawled back into the bed and sat right in the center of the mattress, the blankets gathered close around her. She clutched her arms, hoping she'd leave bruises so that the next morning she would know this had been as awful and urgent as it felt.

"It was a dream," she whispered to herself. She closed her eyes and tried to dial her breathing down as slow as she could make it. But then with a shiver she opened her eyes again, because she was doing the same calm breathing she'd done when she couldn't move, when she was frozen, trapped, with those lips breathing soft words against her throat, and what if breathing that way again summoned the thing back—

"A dream," she said again, more firmly this time. She said it out loud, trying to compel herself to hear the words, to believe them. She was being absurd, panicky, ridiculous. Breathing couldn't summon anything. And besides, there was no voice to summon. It had been a remnant of her nightmare, a figment of her subconscious. Nothing more.

She had checked. The room was empty, except for her. The door was locked. The lights were on. The sun would come up in just a few more hours.

She closed her eyes and did not allow herself to think about how badly she'd wanted to lean into the comfort that awful voice had promised. She did not allow herself to think about how familiar the voice was.

She did not let her lips form the words that had shot her out of the bed and across the room, that had filled her with a lightning-flash of adrenaline. She did not whisper them to herself as she drifted back into a restless, sweat-soaked sleep. And she did not dream them on a loop, spoken again and again in that soft, rasping voice.

Hush now, Vera-baby. Hush now.

CHAPTER SIX

The town of Marion had changed in the way that all things change, but it was the same town that Vera had left behind so many years before. Main Street was long and straight and featured a combination of small businesses and doomed franchises. When Vera was young, the franchises had been geared toward paint-your-own porcelain and Tex-Mex cuisine. Now there were cupcake shops and places where groups of middle-aged women could drink too-sweet wine while they all tried to reproduce the same painting. The specifics had shifted, but the feel of the place was the same.

Vera wondered which franchise Mrs. Gregson was attempting to keep up these days. When she was a kid, she and Brandon had spent hours, folding brochures for a penny each in the back of the vitamin store. Surely, Vera thought, the vitamin store had gone under by now. If by some miracle that kind of business had survived the first recession, it would have been smothered by the second.

She passed the place between the thrift store and the teashop where the vitamin store had once been nestled. Sure enough, there was a sun-faded FOR RENT sign in the window. An unintelligible sigil of graffiti marked the boarded-over front door.

It looked like it had been empty for a long time. Maybe, Vera thought with a twitch of optimism, Mrs. Gregson had moved away. It would have been the sensible thing. The healthy thing.

Vera parked in front of Alan & Sons, the only hardware store for fifty miles. The windows were painted with a summer sale garden scene, the prices of mulch and shovels illustrated in bright block letters. The store had been owned by the same family for four generations, a monument to the immutability of the town. It was where Vera's father had worked.

He had always smelled just a little bit like sawdust back then.

There was ample street parking available. No one was walking along the sidewalk in front of the store. No one was sitting in the little park across the street, either. Maybe the store would be empty. Maybe some college-age kid would be working the front counter, and he would be the only person Vera would need to speak to before leaving the store.

Maybe things would be easier than she thought.

Vera sat in her car with her sunglasses on, her little canvas purse in her lap. The air-conditioning breathed on her, barely preventing a sheen of sweat from taking hold on the surface of her skin. She told herself not to worry. She was an adult now. She could handle herself better than she'd been able to when she'd lived here as a child. Back then, her whole experience of the world had been limited to a place where the annual ice wine festival was the hottest ticket of the year.

She was a different person now.

She decided not to be afraid.

Vera opened the car door. Immediately she was swallowed by the wet weight of the summer. The green smell of unrelenting bloom worked its fingers up into her skull and down into her throat. She swallowed hard and swam through the thick air to the glass double-doors of Alan & Sons.

The air-conditioned cold inside made her feel damp and bare, as if she'd just shucked a rain-soaked overcoat and let it fall to the floor around her feet. The fluorescent lights high overhead made the concrete floors shine. Bright, cheerful signs hung from the ceiling advertising sales. They did little to cut through the warehouse-feeling of the place.

In spite of the restless nerves that twitched beneath her skin, Vera felt herself sinking into the familiarity of the hardware store. The layout hadn't changed at all. It still smelled like sawdust and sunflower seeds and fresh paint. She hadn't been to Alan & Sons in years and years, not since the days she'd spent wandering the aisles while her father picked out lengths of rope and sturdy plastic tarps and roofing nails for his projects—but it felt just like home. This had been a place they visited together, something they shared only with each other.

Vera let herself feel how good it was to be back in this place. She didn't smile—that would be too much—but she did run her fingers along a cardboard display of paintbrushes as she passed, feeling the stiff bristles beneath her fingertips, remembering the part of her life when things had been good.

Vera passed the paint counter without looking at who was behind it, seeking shelter in the rows of high industrial shelving. She passed the plastic tubs of screws and nails and bolts organized by size, the doorknobs and the lightbulbs and the gardening supplies. She walked fast enough to keep her eyes from straying to the aisle with the huge spools of netting and rope and chain. In that aisle, you could cut whatever you needed to length and buy it by the foot. However much you wanted, for any kind of project. No one would bat an eye.

Vera would not look at those spools.

She kept her head down and walked quickly down the aisle that cut between the two rows of shelves. Alan & Sons was, of course, not empty. It would have been nice for it to have been empty, and imagining that possibility had been a worthy trick to get herself out of the car and into the store, but that's all it had been: a trick. A trap she'd set for herself.

Necessary.

Plenty of people were in the store, having wandered inside to escape the heat like beetles huddling together under a rotting log. There were two in the garden aisle, three near the paint chips, two by the registers, and a few singles scattered throughout the power tools, and all of them had eyes.

Vera did not look at any of them, did not look at their faces, but she could feel their eyes.

She snapped the fingers of her right hand four times fast.

It didn't work. Behind her came the teakettle hiss of a rising whisper. Someone dropped something with a heavy ceramic thunk.

It has nothing to do with you, she told herself. *You're just here to buy storage bins.*

They were on the back wall of the store, their plastic bulk incongruous beside the shelves of cut lumber. Vera grabbed four big eighteen-gallon ones, stacking them inside each other so they'd be easier to carry to the register. They were thick gray plastic with locking lids. They didn't nest inside each other perfectly, and when she lifted them she only just barely saw over the top of the stack. Vera turned to walk back through the store the way she'd come, peering over the gray plastic in her arms.

The whispers were louder now, and the weight of several stares rested heavier on her back. A few people were standing in the long aisle behind her, and even if she didn't want to look right at their faces, it was impossible not to know that they were watching her. She couldn't look at the floor because the gray plastic tubs were in the way. She couldn't dodge all those eyes.

So she didn't. She made eye contact with them. She smiled. The lip of the top tub pressed the key around her neck into the soft meat of her chest. *I'm allowed to be here,* she thought. *I'm allowed to be here just as much as you are.*

It worked until it didn't. It worked until she made eye contact with the middle-aged woman at the end of the garden section. Vera froze at the heat of the hatred in her eyes.

The woman's face was lean and lined in ways it hadn't been the last time Vera had seen her. Her once-auburn hair was cut into a blunt gray bob. Her lips were pressed into a bloodless line. The remains of a large terra-cotta pot were at her feet where she had dropped it just a few moments earlier—she hadn't moved, hadn't bothered to pick up the shards. She had just stood where she was, hating Vera more every second.

Vera swallowed hard and strained to lift her chin over the stacked gray tubs in her arms.

"Hello, Mrs. Gregson." Her voice came out even, but to her own ears it sounded foreign, like her mouth was painted-on and some hidden ventriloquist was speaking through it. "How are you?"

Mrs. Gregson's nostrils flared white as she drew breath to speak. "What," she whispered, "the fuck?"

Vera gripped the gray tubs tighter. She wished that there was someplace on the smooth plastic surface where she could dig her fingernails in, but she could not find purchase. "I'm—"

"What the fuck are you doing here?" Mrs. Gregson interrupted. A fleck of saliva landed on her bottom lip when she spoke, and it stayed there, glistening in the fluorescent light.

"My mother is dying," Vera said simply. "I've come home to . . . to sort things out. To take care of the house."

Mrs. Gregson laughed mirthlessly, a short sharp bark that

made Vera's skin jump. "Burn it down," she said. It wasn't a suggestion or a joke—she spoke with all the authority she'd brought to more mundane phrases of Vera's youth. 'Put your shoes away' or 'curfew is ten o'clock.' It was an instruction. "Burn it down," she said again. "If you've got any decency anywhere in you, you won't make some unsuspecting family live in that house."

Her eyes darted over Vera's shoulder. There was movement in Vera's periphery. People were gathering around them, not standing close enough to be considered 'closing in' but near enough to hear the conversation, and not trying to hide their interest.

A bead of sweat ran down the small of Vera's back under her shirt. There was nothing she could say to this woman, the mother of her childhood friend. Nothing she could say to these people. There was no apologizing, no explaining.

"I have to go," she said, looking toward the register.

"Who's stopping you?" Mrs. Gregson spat. "No one would ever try to keep you or your mother from getting the hell out of here." She was right, but Vera still couldn't make herself turn her back on those hateful eyes. The longer she stayed put, the more venomous Mrs. Gregson got.

"I hope she dies tonight, so you'll both be gone tomorrow," she hissed. "I hope she dies fast, but I hope she suffers when it happens. It's what she deserves. It's what you both deserve."

"That's enough." Someone touched Vera's shoulder and she jumped, looking away from Mrs. Gregson at last. "You ought to get out of here."

At first, Vera didn't recognize the man whose hand rested on her shoulder, but the crease between his brows said that he recognized her. He was tall, blond, thin-shouldered, and he was staring at Vera with a crooked smile. Vera frantically scanned her memories of the town, of her classmates, but she couldn't dredge up anyone who might have turned into this guy.

And then Mrs. Gregson spoke up. "You get out of here too," she said. "You're not welcome here. Not in this store and not in this town. Take your 'art' someplace else," she added, and she pointed at the door.

The blond man shrugged amiably. "If you insist," he said, his eyes still locked on Vera. He was wearing eyeliner, she realized, but only on his bottom lids. It made him look haunted and vaguely hungover. His voice was deep and slow, almost-but-not-quite a drawl. He gave her a wink and nodded toward the door. "Let's get out of here, Vee."

Vera's face burned. She followed him toward the exit on numb legs. Once they were outside she found herself thankful for the stifling press of the outside air, for the way it closed around her like a fist. It made her escape feel complete—like she was in a completely different world from that woman and all the people who still called her *neighbor*.

The blond man started talking the moment they stepped out of the hardware store, the words flowing steady and uninterruptible. "This your car? Well, I mean, I don't know why I'm asking that, of course it's your car. It was outside the house last night. I saw it when I came in for dinner, and your mom told me it belonged to you. I was coming back from an interview with that woman you were talking to, Mrs. Gregson? Well, actually, it was supposed to be an interview with her son, that Brandon guy, but she wouldn't let me near him. Seems like you two know each other? Can I help you carry that?"

Vera squinted at him, not trusting the speed of his patter. This, she easily recognized as a trap. And he'd said *your mom told me.* Daphne was right—the title sounded wrong attached to her.

"No. But you can get the door."

He opened the back door to Vera's car and she loaded in the plastic bins. Not for an instant did she consider going back inside to pay for them.

There was a slam. When Vera looked up, she saw a head of tousled blond hair sticking up over the headrest of the passenger seat. "What are you doing?" she asked, still bent over into the back of the car.

"I'm getting a ride home," he answered without looking back at her. He was fidgeting with something in his lap, something she couldn't see, something that crinkled. "Unless you wanted me to drive for you? I'm not used to driving a manual, but I'm sure I could figure it out on the fly."

Vera considered telling him no—kicking him out of the car, making him walk back to the Crowder House—then decided against it. No point making yet another enemy, especially not one who lived in Daphne's backyard.

Still, she didn't have to be hospitable. She got into the driver's seat and backed out of her parking space without a word.

"So," he said. "That was awfully unfair of those people."

"It's not a fair town."

The man reached forward and swiped at the dashboard of the car, leaving an uneven dark streak across the gray dust that had collected there. His other hand lifted to his mouth, tucking something dark between his full pink lips. "What was that woman so mad at you about?"

Vera hesitated. "She's Brandon Gregson's mother, is what."

"Well, sure," he said. "But it's not like *you* did anything to him."

"Me and him were best friends when I was a kid. Not a lot of people know that." Vera flinched inwardly—she hadn't meant to give this man anything of herself. "She still . . . she's mad at me. She holds me responsible. For all of it. Not like you can blame her for how she feels."

"Seems she doesn't mind blaming *you* for how *she* feels," he mumbled.

Vera glanced over and immediately regretted it. The man's face was carefully arranged and pointed right at her. His eyebrows were raised significantly, his lips pursed around a gas-station cigarillo. He was making a significant point and she was supposed to respond to it with appreciation.

She squeezed the steering wheel a couple of times, just hard enough to feel the stitching dig into her palms. "Sure," she said, not looking over as his lighter clicked. "Sure. What happened wasn't my fault. But it's not like that matters. Dad's not here anymore for them to be mad at. Daphne is. And now I am, too." She glanced at him again. "We're still here for them to hate, because of people like you."

He pressed a hand to his heart, dramatic. Performing. "Me?" A little plume of smoke escaped from between his teeth as he exhaled the word. It smelled like burnt grape flavoring and shitty tobacco.

"Daphne would have had to move away a long time ago if people like you didn't keep her lights on," Vera said, a little edge of acid creeping into her voice. She wanted to tell him not to smoke in her car but she didn't want to let him know that it bothered her, that anything bothered her. "She couldn't have afforded to keep the place without renters. How much did you shell out to sleep in that 'cottage,' mister . . . ?"

He held the cigarillo perched between his index and middle fingers, leaving a trail of smoke wherever he gestured; the thing was cheap enough to keep burning whether he was smoking it or not. "*I* didn't pay a dime. It's all grant money. And the name's Duvall," he added. "James Duvall." He said it with the cadence of importance, like people who ran in the right crowds would gasp with recognition at the sound of his first and last names side-by-side.

Vera wasn't in the right crowd. Still, her mouth flooded with saliva. "Duvall," she repeated, her voice low with the weight of memory and fury. It wasn't a question.

"That's me." James Duvall ran his free hand through his hair too slowly. Vera refused to look over to see if he was showing off a bicep or a wristwatch. "Your mom charges a fair price for access to real, raw, honest inspiration. And of course, I bring some history along with me. Some legacy. It's only fair."

There it was again. *Your mom.* Had Daphne not disabused him of that language yet? Or was he trying to needle a reaction out of Vera by reminding her of their failed relationship? That had to be it.

"I'm glad you're getting inspired, James," Vera replied evenly. She wouldn't give him the satisfaction. "I'm sure your father is very proud."

She didn't know whether or not he'd been waiting for the acknowledgment of who he was, of who his father was. Of how his father had consumed hers. But she couldn't stand to pretend that she didn't know. She couldn't let him think he was getting away with something.

"He doesn't know I'm here," Duvall said easily. "Doesn't know I'm not twelve years old, these days. Alzheimer's."

"Rough," Vera snapped. "What a loss."

What kind of person snaps at someone about that? she asked herself—but the thought was quickly absorbed into her growing anger at this man, this *legacy,* who was in her car and sleeping outside her childhood home, this man who dared to speak to her after what his father had done.

James Duvall laughed long and low. "He told me you were a pistol. Back in the day, I mean. When my father was writing your chapters, he'd laugh to himself, and one day I asked what he was laughing about, and he said, 'That Vera Crowder, she's a real caution.'" He reached over and brushed her arm, let his touch linger for a moment. He wore a ring on every other finger.

"I've been wanting to get to know you for as long as I can remember."

She shook him off. "No thanks."

"Come on," he said, and the weight in his voice drew her gaze for just long enough to see the frank invitation waiting there. "It's kind of inevitable, isn't it? You and me? It's worth considering."

"I don't date men."

"Men like me, you mean."

"Men as in *men,*" she replied. "But you can tell yourself that it's about you, if that'll make you feel better."

"You should have seen this place when I showed up," he said easily, as if they'd been having a completely different conversation, as if she hadn't rejected his advance at all. "Screen door hanging off the hinges in the back, front steps half-rotted through. I think I showed up just in time. It's been a real honor, getting to commune with the house. Getting to seek real, meaningful contact—"

"How long until you leave?" She tried to remind herself that a good person, a normal person, would be more hospitable than this but she couldn't stand it. She couldn't stand *him*.

"Few weeks," he drawled. "But your mom'll probably let me stay as long as I need. She really understands my project, you know? She gets the love-aspect." He returned the cigarillo to his mouth, puckering his lips around it slow and deliberate.

Vera almost smiled then, both at how blatantly he was trying to get her to ask about his project and at the notion of Daphne getting *the love-aspect*. As far as Vera could tell, Daphne had never felt a *love-aspect* about anything.

She didn't ask about the project. She knew better than to talk to a Duvall. As a result, the rest of the drive was silent and uncomfortable. The car filled up with oily smoke. James kept clearing his throat, and Vera kept ignoring him. She drove home too quick and too reckless. She hated the relief she felt when she turned onto the street that stretched out in front of the Crowder House.

She wanted to wrap her fingers around that relief and squeeze it until it popped.

But what she wanted didn't matter. It hadn't mattered for a long, long time.

"We should head in," James said after too many seconds had passed since Vera'd turned off the car. "Or, well, you should head in. I want to get some work done before dinner."

"Right," Vera said. She didn't move.

James cleared his throat again. "Okay then. See you in a few hours, Vera Crowder," he said, lingering on the three r's in her name. He got out of the car and closed the door carefully, quietly. He paused on the driveway to grind out the stub of the cigarillo under his heel.

Vera stayed in the car, breathing in the stench of cheap, infused tobacco, steeling herself to go into the house the same way she'd steeled herself to go into the store. The Crowder House waited, just as it always had. It waited to breathe in the outside-smell of her, waited to seal up her sounds and her movements, waited to wrap her in plaster and wood and old wiring where she belonged.

Inside the house, inside the old dining room, in the newly-rented hospital bed, Daphne waited, too.

CHAPTER SEVEN

Vera had to do what she came home for. And if that was the case—if she absolutely had to dig into the contents of the house—she might as well start in the kitchen.

She'd hadn't been in there since her arrival the afternoon before, not wanting to walk through the dining room. Not wanting to see Daphne again, not ready to try to figure out how to help. It was, Vera knew, wrong to leave her dying mother alone for so long. But then again, Daphne had said she had *a system*. Vera knew that she should have asked more questions about it—was James Duvall the system? Was the system safe? But there was the tempting possibility that maybe that system meant Daphne could be avoided. Maybe it meant she didn't really need Vera's help at all. *Focus on the house,* she'd said. *The details are not your business.*

And so Vera decided to do the thing she knew, without a doubt, *was* her business: she decided to work in the kitchen until it was time to eat dinner with her mother. Her mother and *that man.* She couldn't quite stand the thought of eating alongside him, but that was a problem for the future. Right now, the kitchen was waiting.

A fat permanent marker, new and dizzyingly pungent, worked to label the gray storage bins: KEEP, TOSS, SELL, DONATE. Vera wrote the words in capital letters, wrote right on the plastic. It felt emphatic, like real forward motion. Some petty, small, childish piece of her wanted Duvall to see the boxes and understand that he was not welcome to stay.

The long loose swing of her hair felt right in this house, but it wouldn't do for the work ahead. Vera held the marker in her teeth while she coiled her hair into a high bun, twisting it up tight as a fist.

When Francis Crowder had built this kitchen, he'd done so according to his own arcane understanding of what would happen in it. The counters were long and narrow, and the cupboards were high and deep. This configuration had worked well for a man whose cooking experience was largely sandwich-oriented, a man who was tall and long-armed enough to reach into the backs of the highest cupboards. Vera's mother, however, had always struggled with the too-small surface area of the counters, and Vera herself had never been able to reach into the backs of the cupboards without the assistance of a stepladder. The fire-engine red paint that Francis had inflicted on the walls lent additional urgency to the wrongness of the room.

Now, the front of the refrigerator was covered by a tight layer of heavy plastic wrapping like the film that comes on new electronics, laminating the magnets in place. One of Vera's old report cards was under that plastic, her C-minus in social studies forever preserved against the ravages of time. She couldn't remember that report card ever being on the refrigerator before. Daphne must have gotten desperate for artifacts once the requests for residencies started rolling in.

Once Hammett Duvall's book had been published, everyone wanted a piece of the Crowder House.

Vera started under the sink, pulling out cleaning supplies and dish towels and an absurd volume of plastic grocery bags. She put all of them into the KEEP bin—she didn't know how long she would be staying in the house, and it seemed smart to hang on to the cleaning supplies. The plastic bags would be useful for bagging up the things that accumulated in the TOSS bin.

There was a thermos, too, all the way in the back of the cupboard, under a pile of debris. It had been lost back there and forgotten. Vera knew that, knew it without question, because she recognized the thermos.

It had been her father's.

The green plastic that coated the metal was as bright as she remembered. Vera smiled, gently rolling the thermos between her palms. She hadn't seen it in ages; she could only assume that no one had. She wondered if this was how some people felt when they unexpectedly bumped into an old friend.

Vera closed the empty cupboard and sat back on her heels, relieved at how easy it had been to clear it out. The rest of the house wouldn't compare to that one half-empty cupboard, but that didn't matter. What mattered was that this whole project felt more surmountable than it had an hour before.

It occurred to her that a lot of the kitchen would probably be like that cupboard below the sink. It would be full of things that she would need to keep for as long as she was staying in the house, things that she might as well leave where they were so she could keep using them. Things she wouldn't be able to deal with until after her mother was dead.

The thought startled her with how awful it was, and with how little it made her feel.

Her mother was in the dark dining room, either asleep or pretending to be. Asleep and dying and alone. That knowledge should have buckled Vera's knees. It should have knocked the wind out of her, or at least a few tears.

But it just made her feel awkward. She was here, in this

home, for the most vulnerable and uncontrollable moment of Daphne's life. And she knew beyond a doubt that her presence was the last thing Daphne wanted. She was a last resort, a backup to the backup to the backup. Daphne had only called Vera home because there was no one else to call. They had nothing to say to each other that hadn't been said when Vera was a child, nothing that hadn't been communicated by the years they'd spent as strangers.

Vera rose from her crouch in front of the cupboard, stirring a few loose plastic bags that remained at her feet. There was no point in dwelling on this, on what was and what might have been, on the relationship she and her mother would never have. It was a distraction. There was work to be done here. Best to shake it off and move on.

She decided to clean out her father's old thermos, to make it useful again. Something he'd carried with him to work for years—something his big calloused hands had wrapped around every day, something that he'd thought of as useful and good— shouldn't just sit around. It would be wasteful.

The silver cap squeaked when she twisted it off. The faintest whiff of coffee lingered inside, even though the thermos must have been under that sink for twenty-some-odd years. Vera brought it closer to her face to breathe in that smell.

Something inside rustled.

Vera frowned. She gave the thermos a tentative rattle, and there it was again: a rustle, like the wings of a beetle settling.

She knew better than to look inside, because if something sounds like a bug, it might turn out to *be* a bug, and while Vera didn't mind looking at bugs, she certainly *did* mind them flying up at her face. Instead of looking, she flipped the thermos upside-down over the sink and gave it a good hard shake.

Nothing came out. She shook it again, and then again, and still: nothing. Finally, she tipped it sideways and craned her neck to peer inside, keeping the opening of the thermos as far away from her face as possible.

Something small and white looked back at her. A cocoon, she thought at first. Then, as she looked a little closer, she realized that no—it wasn't a cocoon at all. It was a piece of paper, rolled up into a tight tube.

She held the thermos over the countertop and shook it hard from side to side until the little cylinder of paper stopped catching on the inside of the lip. It fell out and rolled nearly to the edge of the counter, where Vera caught it in her palm. It was the size and length of a cigarette. Really, Vera thought, she should have mistaken it for a cigarette at first, except that as far as she knew, her father had never smoked.

If he'd smoked, she would have known. She almost definitely would have known.

She unrolled the slip of paper. It was white and thin, low-quality unlined notebook paper, torn along one long edge and one short edge. The script was immediately familiar. Her father's handwriting had always been tiny and round and even, the letters bubbling across the page in steady, straight lines.

It was a page ripped out of his journal. The journal Vera had hidden under the front porch. The journal that she'd assumed—that she'd hoped—had long ago turned to pulp.

It was an entry about her.

VERA IS GROWING UP SO CREATIVE AND SO SMART. SHE IS STILL JUST A KID BUT I'VE NEVER LIKED ANY-ONE SO MUCH AS I LIKE HER. SHE IS GOOD AT MATH AND AT SCIENCE BUT NOT SO HOT ON READING. JUST

LIKE ME. I KNOW THAT SHE WILL STAY GOOD SO
LONG AS I REMEMBER TO KEEP BAD THINGS AWAY
FROM HER. DAPHNE DOESN'T AGREE BUT WE DON'T
HAVE TO ARGUE ABOUT IT. I HOPE VERA KNOWS
HOW MUCH I LOVE HER AND THAT I'LL ALWAYS

That's where the page was torn off. That's where the words
ended. Whatever was supposed to be on the line below *always,*
it wasn't here. Vera flipped the thermos over again, peered
close inside it to see if there was another curled-up half page
waiting for her in there—but of course there wasn't.

There was only this.

Vera leaned against the counter hard, the scrap of paper under her palms, her lips pressed tight between her teeth, breathing hard through her nose.

This was a page from her father's journal, and it was all
about how much he had cared for her.

Her head spun hard, a sudden wave of dizziness, and the
momentum of that dizziness swung her right around to the
back door of the house, the one that led out of the kitchen
and into the yard. She crossed to it in three long strides, burst
through the back door, practically fell down the steps to the
grass. Her feet devoured the lawn and blood rushed in her
ears and she wasn't even aware that she was pounding on the
door to the cottage, not until she heard the banging of her
own fist.

It looked almost nothing like the shed she remembered. It
really was a little cottage now, with a new tin roof and a window on one side, and presumably some plumbing within. But
the pressed-aluminum walls were the same and they rattled
with every blow she struck.

She kept banging on the door until she felt the sting in her knuckles.

"Did you do this?" she shouted at the door. It didn't answer. She pounded on it again, this time with the flat of her empty hand. "Duvall! Get out here!"

The door swung inward, revealing a shirtless, damp-haired James. He didn't look afraid so much as confused. Some deep animal part of Vera felt disappointed at that. She fought it down, barely.

"What's going on?" he asked, one hand resting on the front of the waistband of his low-slung jeans as if he had only just finished doing up the button and needed to make sure it stayed put. One side of his mouth slid up into a sly grin. "I thought you weren't interested in coming over to my place."

Vera held up the thermos. "Did you do this?

James looked back and forth between Vera and the thermos several times. "Did I do what?" His brows were crinkled up with what almost seemed to be genuine confusion.

Vera faltered, her thermos-hand drooping. "You didn't—you didn't put anything in this thermos?"

"Nope." He shook his head, leaning against the doorframe of the garden shed. "Never seen it before. Why, was there something in there you were saving for dinner?"

She hesitated. The question she wanted to ask was unaskable. If James hadn't put that slip of paper into that thermos, then the chances of him having found the journal in the first place were slim at best.

"Nevermind," she snapped. "See you in a couple of hours."

His gaze turned sharp. "Wait. Vera. Did you find something? Or did you . . . feel something?"

Her heart was in her throat, was in her mouth, was going to

fly out at him like a cicada in the early-summer heat. She didn't answer.

"Vera," he said, taking a halting step toward her, all the playful antagonism gone from his face. "Vera, tell me what happened. It's important."

"Like hell," she spat. "I know better than to tell a Duvall *what happened*." She turned to stalk inside, furious at herself for having come out here at all.

His slow drawl stopped her in her tracks. Just like that, the serious, sincere James Duvall was gone, replaced by the man who'd answered the door in the first place. "Just a couple hours left between now and dinner, like you said. Does that mean you'll join us tonight? Not gonna hide out in your bedroom again?"

When she looked over her shoulder, he was staring her down, intent. He'd pulled a lighter from his pocket and was spinning it between two fingers. She couldn't stop herself from looking him over, taking in his bare chest and abdomen: the ridge of his collarbones, the slight bump of his ribcage, the taut stretch of flesh across his belly. He was fresh and lithe and whole. His skin looked brand-new.

A shiver ran up Vera's spine. She wanted to ignore it. She wanted to ignore it more than she'd ever wanted anything. When she met James's eyes again, he was smirking.

Oh, she thought. *Oh, no.* "Yes," she said. "I'll see you at six."

"See you at six," he replied with a wink. And then the door was shut, and Vera was alone in the yard, holding a thermos that had just finished telling her that her father liked her better than anyone, wondering who had left the message there for her to find.

CHAPTER EIGHT

Vera sat at the little round table in the kitchen, digging her thumbs into the edge of the plexiglass that was screwed in over the tablecloth. Whoever drilled it in must have cut screw-holes through the cloth, she thought, to keep it from twisting up around the screws when they went in.

There was a lip print in the center of the plexiglass, neat as anything. Someone had tried to kiss this table, and nobody had ever cleaned that kiss away.

It could have been any of them. The artists and the poets and the mediums who paid her mother for a chance to live in the Crowder House, the tour groups who came through to look at the kitchen where Francis Crowder used to make his coffee, the reporters who sat across from Daphne and asked her what it was like and what *he* was like and *did she know? Did she ever suspect?*

It was nearly time for dinner, but she did not want to go into the dining room. She did not want to sit with her mother and James Duvall to share a meal. She did not want that at all.

The dining room didn't seem to want her, either. The arch that separated the two rooms was high and wide and open, but the low early-evening light that streamed through the kitchen windows didn't penetrate the thick dark within. At the place where the black-and-white tile of the kitchen floor met the warm wood of the dining room floor, the ambient light cut off, the sudden darkness as solid as a curtain drawn between the two rooms.

Goosebumps ran up Vera's arms. That darkness was heavy. It reminded Vera of her dream the night before—the way her bedroom had been so oppressively, cruelly dark. Her hand drifted to her belly, to the memory of a cold that had to be pulled out by the fistful.

The doorknob rattled behind her, making her shoot up out of her chair with a sudden shock of adrenaline.

"Just me, settle down." James closed the door behind himself with exaggerated care. Even if he hadn't announced himself, the smell of him came in with the rush of night air: stale tobacco, burnt wrapper, turpentine. He'd been working, then, and smoking another one of those cheap cigarillos while he did it.

"I don't need to settle down," Vera said.

"You look like you've seen a ghost," he replied with an unwelcome wink. "Care to introduce me? I'd kill for an encounter."

Vera decided not to look at him. That, she thought, would surely help. "Are you ready to eat?"

He grinned at her, lopsided and unwarranted. "Always."

Vera pulled plates down from the cupboards with a needless amount of clattering. She handed them to James, flinching at the warmth of his fingers when they met hers. Then she pulled a tray of lasagna from the oven, where it had gone from frozen to edible over the course of the past hour. "I think she's still sleeping," she said.

"I doubt it," James replied easily. "Daphne loves our dinner-time chats. I think she sees me as a kind of surrogate son, you know?"

Vera grimaced, glancing again at the dining room. The darkness didn't look quite so impenetrable as it had before—maybe the light had changed, Vera thought, or maybe her eyes had adjusted sometime in the past few minutes. She didn't like the idea of her mother being awake. If Daphne had been awake, then she would have been able to see Vera perfectly in the bright kitchen throughout the day. Would have seen her lug the plastic tubs in, label them, put her hair up. Would probably have been watching, silently, the whole time Vera had been working, and the whole time she'd been sitting there, avoiding her dying mother. Picking at the cover on the table.

If Daphne had been awake, then she would have seen Vera find the torn-out excerpt from Francis's journal. Vera very much needed that not to be true.

"Shall we?" James asked lightly. Vera's gaze snapped to him.

"Right," she whispered, and as he watched her, unblinking, she took the first step toward the dark room where her mother waited.

Balancing the tray of lasagna on one oven-mitted hand, Vera snaked an arm around the wall that separated the kitchen from the dining room, shivering at the cold. The temperature difference between the two rooms was as stark as the smothering darkness. "It's freezing in here," she said as her hand found the lightswitch at last. She desperately hoped there wouldn't be a reply. "I'm sorry, Daphne, I didn't know. I would have turned the heat up if I'd—"

"I don't mind," Daphne interrupted. "I barely feel it."

The lights flickered on and Vera felt the subterranean fear drain out of her. With the darkness gone, all she had to worry about was Daphne. Vera opened her mouth to ask if Daphne needed anything—a blanket, a glass of water—but she didn't get the chance to speak.

"Glad you're awake," James said, breezing past Vera, leaving smoke in her mouth. "I can't wait to finish our discussion from last night."

Daphne's face transformed. She turned to James like a sunflower seeking light, and her lips curled up into a sweet, almost feline smile. "Oh, you're a precious one," she purred. "Do you have my dinner?"

"I have it," Vera said, lifting the lasagna with both hands now. "It was in the freezer, so I'm assuming it's the kind you like?" She moved to set it down on the sideboard, so she could slice and serve it.

Daphne tracked her daughter's movement, and though the expression on her face didn't shift a millimeter, her eyes had gone flat, everything but the barest acknowledgment draining out of them in an instant.

Vera faltered. "No?"

"That's mine, actually," James said. He slid past Vera and put the plates down in front of her. He was standing so close that she could smell his breath, the faintest trace of vodka and sweet cream. "I don't mind sharing, though."

Vera turned away from him, meeting her mother's cold eyes. "What are you going to eat, then?"

"A lemonade," Daphne said. "Please. From the refrigerator."

"You don't have to tell me 'from the refrigerator,'" Vera said as she stalked back into the kitchen. "That's the only place it'd be."

Vera knew that she shouldn't be annoyed with her mother. It wasn't Daphne's fault that she had made assumptions, hadn't bothered to ask questions. Vera was the one who didn't even know that her mother wasn't eating solid foods, who didn't know what that meant about the progression of her mother's illness.

She didn't have the right to be annoyed. She knew better than to let herself get annoyed. She'd worked so hard to crush that kind of feeling out of herself for so long, because she needed to be the kind of person who could lure love out of someone. But the strange twitchiness that had come over her that afternoon was making everything inside her clench, and so she opened the refrigerator door harder than necessary, rattling the lemonade bottles inside.

There were at least fifty of them in there, crowding the shelves—tall glass bottles with silver caps, each one labeled with a smiling cartoon lemon.

"Jesus," Vera whispered. She grabbed a bottle and used a fingernail to tear off the plastic seal on the lid. She swallowed her rising guilt: she'd been here for over twenty-four hours, and she didn't actually know if her mother had eaten anything in that time. She'd said she had a *system*, but who knew what that actually meant? "Do you want something more substantial than this?" she called, staring down the rows and rows of glass bottles. "I could get you a . . . a meal replacement shake, or maybe some . . . broth?"

Daphne's voice called back from the other room, clear and piping. "No. Lemonade is all I can really taste anymore," she said. "And it's not like I'm ever hungry, anyway."

It didn't seem right—but then again, Daphne *was* dying. Vera didn't suppose that proper nutrition really played a role in her mother's life anymore. She carried the cold bottle of lemonade back into the dining room, set out a row of little waxed paper cups on the sliding table, and decanted the lemonade into them.

"You're good at that," James observed. He was seated in a dining chair, pulled right up to the side of the bed, leaning all the way forward, his elbows denting the covers where they rested. "I always spill half of it."

"I've had practice," Vera murmured.

It did feel grotesquely close to pouring a row of shots, the way she had for the four months she'd spent tending bar at a hotel in Atlanta several years before. That job hadn't been so bad—no one looks too closely at a bartender's face, and the tips had been good. She'd even started to make a few friends. They were the kinds of friends who like you when you're in front of them and don't think about you if you're out of sight, which was just what Vera had wanted.

The job and the friendships had lasted right up until the fateful, predictable shift when one of those true-crime-enthusiast types had walked into the hotel. She had a podcast, that one had said, and she wanted an interview with Vera Crowder, and could Vera confirm or deny Hammett Duvall's more recent claims about a possible haunting in the Crowder House?

It wasn't that her manager hadn't considered all the reasons she might be worth keeping around; it was that her manager didn't think they added up to outweigh the combined troubles of her too-recognizable face and her famous last name.

Vera capped the half-empty lemonade bottle, gave the cap two twists to seal it back tightly. She kept her eyes on her fingers, but she still caught movement in her periphery. Daphne was picking up one of those little cups in her shaking fingers, sipping it with pursed, cracked lips. "How are things coming along, James?"

"Incredibly well," their guest answered, handing Vera a plate with a wobbly rectangle of lasagna perched at its center. "I'm really getting somewhere. This house . . . it's been waiting for someone to come along who could understand it, I think."

Vera lowered herself into a dining chair opposite James's seat. There was no cushion on it, and the bare wood was unforgiving under her thighs. "What's that supposed to mean?" she snapped.

She didn't know why it made her so angry, the idea of him understanding the house.

The idea of the house needing him.

"It's all part of my work," he said in placating tones that made Vera's blood itch. "I'm here to commune with the house so it can grant me permission to express its trauma through the medium of—"

"Nevermind," Vera said, that anger refusing to ebb. "I don't need to hear this. You're exactly like your father and that's all I need to know."

"James is a painter, not a writer," Daphne interjected. "But you're not entirely wrong, Vera. He's just as insightful as Hammett was. And just as charming."

James smiled at that as if he'd expected her to say it. "And what about you, Vera? How's your . . . project?"

He wasn't responding to Vera's anger at all, and that made it so much worse. She bit the inside of her cheek, forced herself to take a slow breath. She would not be the kind of person who picked a fight with Hammett Duvall's son. She would be better than that.

Daphne cocked her head a little too far to one side. "Yes, how is it coming along, sorting through my life and deciding what to keep?"

"Slow and steady," she said, a phrase she couldn't ever remember having used before in earnest. "A little at a time, I figure. That'll do the job."

"Not too slow, I hope," Daphne said between sips of lemonade. "Only so much time before I'm not here to answer questions anymore."

"And only so much time before I'm supposed to be gone, too," James intoned. There was red sauce smudged at one corner of his mouth. "I'd love to be a help to you, Vera. Truly, it would be my honor. I think I have a lot of insight to offer. I could help you understand this place better. The resonances—"

"You have something, right here," Vera said, pointing at her own mouth. The pink tip of James's tongue quested out between his lips until it found the sauce. She looked down at her plate, her stomach twisting. "And I don't think I'll need any help, but thank you."

Daphne snorted. "Don't be rude. You'll have so much carrying to do, and you never were good at lifting heavy loads on your own. Always counted on your father and me, didn't you?"

Vera's ears burned, and she shoved a too-large bite of lasagna into her mouth to keep herself from answering.

"I think it could be good for all of us, having you home during this time of spiritual transition," James said, his voice soft as an overripe plum. "Your mother said I could ask you some questions while we're both here, together. I hope you don't mind?"

Vera looked up, panicked, then glanced between James and Daphne. She was regretting that mouthful of lasagna—the overcooked pasta gummed between her teeth, the mealy cheese stuck in her throat, she couldn't say no fast enough to stop this from happening. Daphne gave her another catlike smile.

"When's the last time you saw your father?" James asked.

Vera swallowed hard, wishing she'd thought to get herself a glass of water, or even, god forbid, lemonade. The under-chewed bite hurt going down. "I suppose . . ." she started, waiting for Daphne to cut her off, to forbid this conversation. But no interruption came. She decided to continue—there could be no real harm in answering this. "I suppose that was when they took him away."

James's head tilted forward and to one side, like a globe tipping on its axis. "You haven't seen him more recently than that?"

Vera shrugged.

James set his plate down, leaned his elbows on his knees, steepled his fingers. It was unsettling, how easily he shifted from slick and slippery to sincere and thoughtful. Vera didn't know which version of him was the real one. "And has he ever visited you? In the time since he passed?"

Vera stared at him blankly. "That's not funny," she replied, the words coming out thin.

"I'm not trying to be funny. Your father . . . he cared about you very much, Vera. That was clear in the interview he granted my father. You're certain you haven't had any messages from him since you came back? A sighting, maybe? Or even just a feeling, like a chill, or a presence—"

A snort from Daphne. "James, please. She didn't even try to visit him while he was still alive. Why would he reach out to her now?"

Vera didn't have anything to say to that. Daphne was absolutely right: Vera could have visited her father, at least in the time since the door to the house he built had been closed behind her.

But Vera hadn't.

"Why didn't you visit him?" James said. His eyes never left her face. He spoke softly, his voice almost tender.

Tenderness was a foreign, forgotten thing that she hadn't encountered since before everything went wrong. She did not want it. Not now. Not from him.

"He didn't want me to," she said evenly. "He would have written if he did." She thought, but did not say, that she had missed her father too much to risk going to see him, to risk the sting of him sending her away like Daphne had. Vera decided to be finished with this part of the conversation. "So. You're not an author?"

"No," he said, with a smile that told her he was letting her off the hook for now, but saw what she was doing. "I'm a spiritual rendering artist."

She shook her head. "What does that—"

"It means I incorporate aspects of the metaphysical into my paintings," he interrupted, gesturing at the room with a vague swirl of his hand. "I try to represent the true character of my inspiration in the work I create. It's an intimate act of co-creation between myself and my surroundings." He slid his fork between two layers of lasagna, gently parting a section of sauce and noodles and cheese. "I like to think of myself as working not with a subject, but with a partner."

Vera set her fork down. "I see. Your partner in this is my mother?"

Daphne let out a strange, soft gurgle, like an infant with a throat full of milk.

"Not at all," James laughed. "No, my partner is never a person. It's . . . history, and geography, and emotion. So much emotion. I find places where those three things intersect, and I distill the essence of that harmony into the visual."

"And people want to see that? For money?"

"Oh, everyone wants to see that. Like here, for instance. There's so much pain, so much yearning. It's perfect. My father always told me about how connected this house was to the other side."

"The other side of what?" Vera said. Then, too slowly, his description of his work fell together in her mind, and she realized what it was that James Duvall painted. "Wait—history, geography, and emotion. Are you saying that you paint haunted houses?"

"*Haunted* is a loaded word," he said smoothly. "And it's not just houses. My series on abandoned hospitals in rural Canada—"

"James brings a wonderfully intimate lens to these things," Daphne purred, but she wasn't looking at him. She was looking at Vera. "So compassionate. He feels so deeply for those who are most affected."

"Like Francis, for instance," James said. "He was a deeply emotional man. When he died, he must have felt—"

"You know, we always seem to end up talking about *my* father," Vera interrupted, the anger she'd bitten back struggling against her teeth. It was a fight she wasn't winning. "What about yours, James? What kind of places do you think Hammett'll haunt once he assumes room temperature?"

"Vera," Daphne said, the two syllables heavy with warning.

Duvall didn't seem bothered. "Dad will cross over peacefully. All his business here was finished by the time he started to get sick. There's no reason to think he'll be haunting anywhere. Your father, on the other hand—his business was never really finished, was it?" He tapped the ring on his index finger against his plate rhythmically as he spoke. "He probably died wishing he could have wrapped things up a little tidier. He really hasn't appeared to you at all in the time since he passed? You can tell me."

Vera met her mother's eyes then, compelling herself to bathe in the cold disdain there. It was the loveless regard of a landscaper eyeing a weed. It was so familiar, so much more familiar than the rest of this conversation, that it was almost comforting.

Before Vera could find an answer for Duvall, Daphne cleared

her throat hard. She made a sound like a coffeepot percolating, going on for long enough that it felt like an act of aggression. After much too long, she worked her mouth into a little knot, then spat something thick and dark into her cup.

"Oh," Duvall said, the revulsion thick in his voice. "I'll, um. I'll just get you a paper towel, Daph."

"Cute nickname," Vera hissed once he was out of the room. "*Daph*."

Daphne wiped the corners of her mouth with her thumb and forefinger, then looked right at Vera, smiling with black-streaked teeth. "You think you're so smart," she said. "Getting his attention."

"What? I don't *want* his—"

"The roll's empty," Duvall called from the kitchen, rummaging loudly through the cupboards. The replacement rolls were on top of the refrigerator, if he'd just look.

"Check under the sink," Vera called, not looking away from Daphne's glittering eyes.

Daphne's smile curled into a sneer. "The disrespect. In my own home, the disrespect. You think you're clever."

"I thought you wanted me to talk to him. Am I supposed to stay in my room again, like the old days? Are we time traveling?" Vera asked, even though she didn't want to hear more. She just wanted this dinner to be over.

But Daphne didn't let go. "Old days. As if you have a right to talk about the old days. If you want to be a time traveler, maybe you can go back and do what I told you to do," she hissed. "You have no idea how much I kept everyone away from you. They wanted to run you out of town on a rail, do you know that? They could see the grease inside you."

Vera's entire body stilled. "Sorry," she said carefully, her lips numb, her tongue thick. "I think I misheard you. What did you—"

"The grease," her mother hissed. She was on the far side of a tunnel, at the bottom of a well, a voice traveling along a string between tin cans. "The grease that's in you, the filth, they saw it and so did I. I locked you up to protect everyone from your *foulness*."

Daphne stared and Vera stared back and it was in that moment that Vera realized with a start that she'd never asked what exactly it was that Daphne was dying from. Why hadn't she asked? If she was honest with herself—and she did not want to be honest with herself—she hadn't asked because she didn't care. She'd just wanted it to be over.

So she hadn't asked. She'd assumed cancer. Was this what cancer looked like? Daphne's eyes were coated with a patchy gray film that shifted every time she blinked, every time her gaze twitched to Vera's mouth. Her skin seemed to slacken, hanging from her face in loose folds. Dark gray mucous gathered at the corners of her mouth, rimmed her nostrils, and she was tapping her index finger faster and faster on the lip of the last empty cup, one-two-three-four, one-two-three-four, tap tap tap tap, taptaptaptap, *taptaptaptap*.

Vera bit her tongue hard, closed her eyes tight, and snapped the fingers of her right hand, four times fast, not as quick as her mother's tapping but quick enough to break Daphne's rhythm. Then, with all her courage, she whispered, "Please. Please, stop it."

It worked. Daphne didn't make another sound. Still, Vera didn't open her eyes again for the space of a few long breaths. She couldn't have heard what she thought she heard. She couldn't have seen what she thought she saw.

She was exhausted, and—although it was unthinkable to admit it—she was afraid. That was all. The strain was too much. Her mind was playing tricks.

Vera wasn't altogether certain that she could handle eye contact with her mother. But she heard Duvall thumping back toward the dining room, so she opened her eyes.

Daphne was fast asleep again, chin-to-chest, a string of saplike black ooze hanging from one corner of her half-open mouth.

"They were on top of the fridge," Duvall said, and then he froze, his eyes on Daphne.

"It's fine," Vera whispered. She took the paper towels from him. "Dinner's over anyway. You should take yours to go," she added, looking pointedly at his half-eaten pasta.

"Sure," he replied. He looked nervous. "Sure, that's fine—you'll deal with this, then?"

"Oh, is this not inspiring enough for you?" she hissed, then grimaced at herself, wished she could be better than she was. "Sorry. Yes. I'll deal with this," she confirmed.

"Sleep tight," James murmured. "And Vera?"

Vera did not look at him. She didn't want that can-opener feeling of his eyes on hers, his curiosity and his hunger biting into her. "What?"

His voice was horribly gentle. "If you notice anything out of the ordinary tonight, I hope you'll tell me. You could be an integral part of my work here. You could really help me understand this place, if you just open your mind a little."

She didn't move until he was gone.

Once the screen door that led into the backyard banged shut behind him, Vera walked into the kitchen and held a clean dishrag under warm water for a few seconds. She stared out the back window as she ran the water, tracking Duvall across the yard. He left the door to the garden shed ajar.

Vera held her fingers under the tap to feel the warmth flowing over them. She wanted him to shut that garden shed door, but he didn't. She'd just have to hope he stayed inside.

After much too long, she returned to her mother's bedside and gently wiped her lips, her nose, her temples. Daphne didn't stir.

"Maybe you won't have to see it, Daphne," she murmured. "James's collection, I mean. The paintings. When they come out, maybe you won't have to know." She warmed as she said it, as she finally let herself give in to the dark fury that had been twisting between her teeth the whole evening. "Maybe you'll be dead by then."

She might as well have been talking to herself—Daphne was still and silent, and there was no reason to think she'd heard a word Vera had said. Still, a hot flush of wicked satisfaction burned through Vera, as sudden and forbidden as the first time she'd ever slipped her hand between her legs and felt a shock of recognition.

She'd never, ever spoken to her mother the way she'd been speaking to her tonight. It felt terrible. It felt wonderful.

Leaving her mother for the night, Vera went into her bedroom and sat in the center of her bed, her legs crossed under her. The as-yet-unfixed metal bedframe rattled. She could feel the pull of a familiar temptation. She was about to fall into a dangerous internet spiral, one where she'd be reading everything fresh and new that she could find about her father. About the man he had been. The things he had done.

And the things that he had said—to the police, to the court. To the man who'd written that awful book about their family.

Maybe, if she was very lucky, the things that he had said about his daughter. His daughter, who he had liked better than anyone else. His daughter, who he missed.

His daughter, who he just might have forgiven.

Vera pulled the too-long chain that hung around her neck until the key at the end of it slipped from inside her shirt. It was skin-warm and worn smooth from years and years of worry. She did not hold it or rub it for luck or put it in her mouth, the way she did when she was fourteen and alone in this bedroom with no hope of hearing a knock on the door or footsteps in the hall.

Having it out was enough.

She pulled her laptop open and typed in the first two letters of a search term that autofilled with predictive text. She could tell herself that she was getting better about looking her father up, but the algorithm knew the three words she typed in the most. It knew them by heart.

Francis Crowder Murders

CHAPTER NINE

Vera is eleven-and-a-quarter years old, with newly short hair that is just starting to darken from cornsilk to chestnut and an end-of-summer tan and legs that keep growing out from under her, and the police are at the door.

The police car is parked at the curb. The lights are not flashing.

Vera is holding her big math textbook. It's large and heavy. She doesn't like putting it into her backpack while she's walking home from school, because the weight of it will make the straps hurt her shoulders, so she usually hugs it close to her chest. Now, taking in the scene on her front porch, she clutches it tight so that the edges of it dig into the soft skin of her inner arms.

Vera knows from watching television that there's one very obvious reason for the police to be at her house. She peels her fingers away from the edge of her book, bracing it against her wrist to keep it from slipping out of her grasp.

She snaps her fingers four times fast and she hopes that nothing bad can happen to her now.

Vera stands at the edge of the lawn, looking between the police car and the policemen on her front porch. There are two of them. One is short and fat and white; the other one is tall and thin and Black. Their uniforms are dark blue and the weight of the fabric looks too heavy for the early-September heat. Each one is holding his regulation cap in his hands.

Vera's mother is not holding a hat. She's holding a dishtowel, and she's twisting it between her fists, winding it into a tight creaking rope of fabric. From the end of the driveway, Vera can't quite hear their conversation, but she knows that the dishtowel is bad. It means that her mother's very worried or very angry or both.

Usually, when Vera's mother has the dishtowel in her fists like that, Vera finds a reason to go directly to her bedroom and stay there until morning.

The lawn is brown from the too-dry summer that has just ended. It crunches under her shoes as she walks up to the front door. She thinks the noise of the grass underfoot is probably loud enough, but she pauses at the bottom of the porch steps just in case. She doesn't want to get yelled at in front of the policemen. Her mother has told her several times not to sneak, as if it's Vera's fault that nobody pays attention to the sounds of her life.

Thankfully it's only a few seconds before her mother notices her. "Vera! Thank goodness you're home." Then Daphne spreads her arms wide, the twisted-up dish towel swinging loose from one hand.

Vera knows her cue. The police officers part so she can race up the steps to where Daphne's open arms are waiting. She hugs Daphne tight, breathes in that dishsoap and hairspray smell that means rules and disapproval and safety.

Her mother's hands rest lightly on her shoulders.

After a few seconds, Vera allows her mother to push her away. She looks up and sees warm satisfaction in the pressed-thin line of Daphne's mouth. Vera has accomplished the necessary task of showing strangers that she is loved, that she is cared for, that everything at home is just fine.

Her mother's approval settles over her like a jacket that's just a little too thin for the weather.

"What's going on?" Vera asks softly, hoping that her mother will hear the question she isn't asking.

But it isn't her mother who answers. It is the short white fat police officer. He speaks to her in a slow voice, the kind of voice that is the preferred mode of communication for adults who think that kids are innocent and inattentive as a rule. "We were just in the neighborhood," he says. "We're asking everyone if they've seen this man."

As he talks, the tall Black police officer crouches in front of Vera. He's holding a photograph. Vera can feel the cool pressure of her mother's hand between her shoulderblades, urging her steadily forward. Vera takes an obedient step toward the police officer and his photograph.

"Have you seen him anywhere?" The tall Black police officer has a high, nasal voice.

The man in the photo is an adult. He's got brown hair and a brown moustache and he's wearing a striped shirt in the photo. He looks like someone's dad, or maybe someone's math teacher.

Vera stares at the policeman, uncomprehending. She feels that she's probably seen the man in the photo before, but the truth is that he looks like so many of the adult men she's met in her life. He could be almost anyone. "I don't think so?" Vera says, and the policeman's face doesn't tell her whether this was the right answer or the wrong one.

It doesn't matter, because before the policeman can say anything else, Vera's father is running up the front steps, his heavy boots landing hard enough to shake the porch. "Vera? Daphne? What's the matter? What happened?" He's breathless, sweating hard, his eyes wide, his hands running frantically through his brown curls. He touches Vera's face right away, checking to be sure that she's okay.

Daphne does not touch her own hair, because bothering a perm will make it limp, if she's told Vera once she's told her a hundred times.

"Nothing happened, Francis. Calm down." Daphne's eyes rest on Francis's hand, on the place where it's cupping Vera's jaw. Her voice is tight with restrained impatience, the way it usually is before she sends Vera to bed early so that she and Vera's father can have a 'conversation' in the living room. "Leave Vera alone. You'll upset her."

Vera doesn't like this at all. She doesn't like the police on her front porch, and she doesn't like how her mother is looking at her father—like she wishes the police were holding a photo of him, instead of this other man.

Vera makes eye contact with her father to try to let him know that of course she isn't upset at him for caring about her, that she can't see why she would ever be upset about that. He gives her the tiny don't-worry half-smile that he saves just for her, for the times when ice starts forming around the edge of her mother's words.

She collapses into him then, finally dropping her math book, almost knocking her father over. But his arms are strong and he wraps her up tight, and she lets all her fear bleed out through the porch at her feet. "It's okay, Vee," he whispers into her hair. "Everything's all right." He does not push her away; he rests his hand on the top of her head and lets her cling to him like a younger version of herself would.

"There's a man missing." Vera's mother replies to her father's unvoiced question at a normal volume. The ice in her voice is thicker now. "These officers are—"

The short white policeman interrupts. "You're Francis Crowder, is that right?"

Vera, who is still wrapped up tight in her father's arms, feels him go very still. "That's right," he says softly. He gives Vera a squeeze, then straightens up, keeping his hands on her shoulders even after she turns around to face the police.

She leans back against him, the sure weight of him reminding her that nothing can go too wrong. Nothing very bad can happen. Not as long as he's there.

"You work at Alan & Sons, don't you?" The tall Black policeman stoops to pick up Vera's dropped math textbook as he asks the question.

Vera's father's fingers twitch on her shoulders. "That's right," he says. "Cutting lumber."

"Do you work with this man?" The photo emerges from behind the math book.

Vera's father doesn't hesitate. "Of course," he says. "That's Laurence Adamowicz, he works the register at the store. Why?" He pauses, and his fingers twitch on Vera's shoulders again. "He in some kind of trouble?"

"We hope not," the short white policeman says, giving Vera and her father a smile that's as reassuring as any lie. "Why don't we send these two ladies inside, and you can tell us about the last time you saw Laurence?"

Vera's father grips her shoulders far too tightly but she doesn't make a sound. After a few seconds, he lets her go.

"Come on inside, Vee," Daphne says, snapping her fingers. By the time Vera reaches the doorway, her mother's already inside and out of sight.

Vera knows she's supposed to go to the kitchen, where her mother will ask her to help with some fiddly, menial aspect of dinner preparation to keep her busy without actually involving her too much in the cooking process. She'll be tasked with shelling peas or picking thyme leaves from their woody stems, or brushing the dirt from mushrooms with a dry, wadded-up paper towel. Vera knows she's supposed to do this without being asked.

But Daphne's already in the kitchen, banging pots and pans around to fill the house with the noise of her displeasure, and it'll be a few minutes before she notices that she's alone in there. So Vera lingers just inside the shade of the front door, listening to her father's conversation with the police.

The short white police officer is speaking. He's discarded his slow, syrupy talking-to-a-little-kid voice, trading it for gruff directness. "You and Laurence spend a lot of time together outside work?" he asks.

"Not really," Vera's father replies. "He was a little young for me to be socializing with, and I've got the wife and kid at home, and all."

"He ever talk to you about his extracurriculars?" This is the high, nasal voice of the tall Black police officer, and it's the exact same voice he used to speak to Vera before. Because of this, she decides she likes him. "He have a girlfriend, maybe?"

"Oh, I think he had a few," Vera's father says, and the three men laugh in a way that makes Vera's toes curl inside her shoes. One of them mutters the words *hound dog*, and then they all laugh again.

Vera is holding her breath, leaning as close to the doorframe as she can while staying out of sight, which is why she doesn't hear her mother coming up behind her. She about jumps out of her skin at the weight of Daphne's hand at the nape of her neck. Her mother's grip is tight enough to hurt; the throb of it turns Vera on her heels and steers her toward the kitchen, shoes squeaking on the hardwood.

Vera doesn't bother to apologize, and her mother doesn't bother to admonish her. They both already know everything that would need to be said. They go into the kitchen and work in tense silence. Vera sits on a stool that is too tall for her, pulling the tails off shrimp, swinging her feet until her mother tells her to stop kicking the counter because she'll leave scuffs.

"You shouldn't be wearing your shoes in the house anyway," Daphne says. She's chopping an onion with slow, deliberate strokes of her big kitchen knife, the one that Vera is still not allowed to use. Daphne's eyes don't water at the fumes from the onion, but Vera's do.

"You didn't give me a chance to take them off," Vera mutters into her bowl of shrimp tails.

This is a mistake. It's true, and it's sound reasoning, but it's still backtalk. Vera's mother looks up with sharp, angry eyes that promise a bad night ahead for Vera, the kind of night that involves a tense dissection of her behavior over the dinner table. Vera glares back at her with the courage of a girl who knows that she will be punished, and who knows that her punishment will be unjust—but before either of them can say anything, the front door slams.

They both wait for Vera's father's heavy footfalls to fill the house, but the sound doesn't come. Not for a long time. When it finally does, it's as slow and deliberate as a pulse.

Francis leans against the kitchen doorframe for a few moments, the way he must have leaned against the front door after he closed it.

His face is gray, his breath labored. He's got one hand pressed tight to his chest. He looks up at Daphne, and there's something on his face that Vera doesn't recognize, something desperate. His eyes are glazed. He is breathing hard through his nose, and sweat darkens the collar of his shirt. Vera has never seen him like this before—he's like a small, broken, found thing that will need to be fed from an eyedropper and held under a lightbulb for warmth.

Vera is holding a shrimp in the palm of her hand and she reminds herself over and over not to squeeze it in her fist.

"Dad?" It comes out as a whisper, but he hears her. His eyes flash up to meet hers, and there is something animal in them, something raw and ragged.

"Do you want to sit down?" Daphne asks.

He shakes his head hard, like he's trying to dislodge something from his ears. "No," he says, and then again, more softly, "no. I'm fine."

Daphne's mouth twists a little, tucking itself into a sympathetic frown. "I don't think so. Vera, go to your room."

"But—"

"Now. Your father and I need to have a conversation." Daphne sets down the big knife and wipes her hands on a kitchen towel.

Vera drops the shrimp in her hand onto the countertop. She slides off the stool and leaves the kitchen, her steps heavy and reluctant. When she reaches her father, still braced in the doorway, she pauses.

"Are you okay, Dad?" This feels strange to say—she's not

used to thinking of her father as someone who might not be okay.

"I'm okay, Vee. Go on," he adds with a frown. He tricks the frown into being a smile, sort of, and even Vera can see the desperation in it. "Go on and I'll come get you when it's time for dinner."

She goes into her bedroom, and she waits. But he doesn't come get her all night, and she falls asleep without ever hearing his footfalls on the stairs above.

Days later, Vera is sitting at her desk, writing a paragraph about the water cycle for her Earth Sciences class, when she catches a snippet of her mother's voice. It's rising again.

It's been rising a lot lately.

Vera swallows and stands up, succumbing to the draw of a habit she's been trying to break. She opens the closet and pulls out her laundry basket, kicks aside a couple of pairs of shoes, and sits down inside. She pulls the door most of the way shut after her. Leaning back into the corner of the dark closet, she squeezes her eyes shut. She can still hear the fight, though, and it makes her prickle all over with an elemental kind of fear.

For the first time in the closet, Vera snaps her fingers four times fast.

Her mother's voice fades as though someone is turning down the volume.

It's quiet enough now that Vera can hear her own breathing. She frowns at that silence. It's a familiar quiet—the quiet that fills up the bedroom at night when she can't sleep, the quiet that surrounds her when there have been bad dreams or when she's been sent to bed early for some infraction. This kind of quiet is the reason she sleeps with her windows open, so she can hear something other than herself, alone.

It's a quiet that she usually thinks of as belonging to the night. But the warm late-afternoon sun is streaming through Vera's bedroom windows and leaking in through the gap in the closet door, and the absence of sound is thick and close and sudden, and it's just a little too much to bear.

Vera extends her leg and nudges the door open a little more. It's still too quiet. Tentatively, carefully, she leaves the closet and cracks her bedroom door.

Her mother's voice slices into the quiet like the blade of a shovel opening up the earth—*trying to hurt me? You won't be able to save*—and then Vera firmly shuts the door again, and the silence returns.

This could be a coincidence—Daphne's volume rising and falling at just the right moments. But Vera thinks, as she scrambles back into the safe nest of her closet, there is also the possibility that she has magic powers. This is an appealing option. Daphne would say that Vera is too old to believe in things like that, and she's mostly given up on the notion of magic powers, but there's a part of her that still hopes to discover something special and vibrant within herself.

She rolls her eyes, as if someone's watching her and might think she's silly for what she's about to do.

Then she whispers, "I want to hear them," and she holds her hand out toward the open closet door, and she snaps four times fast.

A noise comes right away—her mother's voice. Just a few words, sharp and sudden. *Go tell her.*

Vera hears the familiar tread of her father's footsteps outside her bedroom door.

"Vee?" His voice is just on the other side of the wood.

For a moment, she finds it impossible to answer him. Is the fight over? Or did she actually end it by snapping her fingers, like casting a spell? A damp wave of panic threatens to rise in her, and she presses her palms flat against the floor, not knowing quite why she feels so afraid.

She flexes her fingers, feeling the comforting ridges of the woodgrain. The floor creaks under the pressure of her hands, and two of the floorboards slip apart, making a gap just large enough for her fingers to slip between them.

The wood is warm and snug against her skin. Her breathing slows. Everything is okay, Vera tells herself. She just got caught up in her own imagination.

Francis raps gently on the bedroom door with one knuckle. "Can I come in?"

She climbs to her feet, steps out of the closet, shoves her shoes and laundry back inside so it won't be obvious that she was hiding in there like a little kid. When she opens the bedroom door, Francis is standing there, waiting patiently. He still looks pale but he gives her a weary smile and she knows that the worst of the fight is over.

"How much did you hear?" he asks.

"Almost nothing. Are you getting a divorce?"

He lets out a short laugh. "What? No! Your mother and I— she just needed to set me straight about a couple of things, that's all. There's nothing to worry about," he adds.

"I wasn't worrying," Vera lies.

Francis lifts his eyebrows in a silent acknowledgment of the lie but he lets her have it. "Well, good, because there's nothing to worry about," he repeats. "Anyway, Brandon's at the door. He wants to ride bikes. Your mother says we have about an hour before dinner, if you want to go."

Vera frowns. Some part of her raises a warning bell, tells her to just go, but she hasn't learned yet to listen to that warning. "Aren't I supposed to help with dinner?"

Her father shrugs. "You can go into that kitchen if you want to, but I'll warn you, it's not the friendliest place in the house right now."

Vera turns to grab her shoes from inside the closet. She doesn't want to ride bikes with Brandon right now, but she doesn't want to be within Daphne's sight, either. She looks for the comforting gap between the floorboards as she bends to pick up the shoes, but she doesn't see it.

She'll think to look for it later, soon, and that's when she'll see the light below her bed.

The light that will let her understand the world in a way she never has before.

But that's later.

For now, running down the porch steps, she forgets all about that gap in the floor, because Brandon Gregson is there.

He is her best friend and she accepts this the way she accepts the fact that dinner is at seven o'clock. They hang out together almost every day—they started calling it 'hanging out' instead of 'playing' earlier this year, before she'd caught up to him in age and in height, and before he'd caught up to her in speed and in stubbornness. Now Brandon puts gel in his hair to make it stick up in limp spikes and he got really tan over the summer because his family got an aboveground pool, one that Vera is never allowed to swim in. He is her best friend and she loves him, although most of the time she is not sure that she likes him very much.

"You have something on your hand," he says, pointing. Vera looks and sees that he's right—something thick and dark is smeared across her fingers. She wipes it on her pants; then, when it doesn't come off, she bends to rub her fingers hard against the grass. It smears at first, spreading out gray like old grease, but then the grass breaks and the dampness of it loosens the filth from her skin, lifts it off and leaves her at least a little bit cleaner than before.

"Gross," she says.

"What is it? Is it from the basement?"

Vera rolls her eyes because Brandon doesn't really think it's from the basement, he just wants an excuse to talk about what might be down there, behind the forbidden door.

"It's just gunk," Vera says, and then she takes off.

They ride their bikes fast, their helmets dangling from the handlebars. Vera stands up on the pedals and pumps her legs hard, then coasts for a while to let Brandon catch up. He is leaning forward over his handlebars—he has an idea, she recalls, that this makes him aerodynamic—and sweat soaks his shirt.

"You don't have to go so fast," he snaps.

"You don't have to go so slow," she says back. She says it in a slow, easy voice she's been learning to use with the boys at school. It's a cool voice, she hopes. Sometimes it works to defuse their strange sudden moods, and sometimes it doesn't.

This time, it does.

"Race you to Maple Street," he says, and he's already gone, even though it's not fair of him to give himself a head start like that.

She pedals hard to catch up, wanting to beat Brandon at this sudden race. Vera wants to win.

She doesn't want to be angry, but she is anyway. It isn't fair, what he's done.

Brandon is ahead of her, his legs working hard to keep distance between them, but she's closing in on him. The wind is in Vera's hair and she feels fast as a diving bird. She clenches her fingers hard around her handlebars. She thinks of the photo the police showed her, the photo of her father's missing coworker. Her legs are starting to burn, but not so much, and she's almost on Brandon now. She thinks of how Brandon will look when he's an adult, how a photo of him will probably be indistinguishable from that photo of Laurence. She thinks of how Brandon, one day, will be the same as every other adult man who isn't her father, and how they're all the same as each other, too, with their wet eyes and their bristly hair and their slow, deep voices that laugh at things she doesn't find funny.

Vera wonders if she will still be angry at him, when they are grown up.

This is the last thought Vera has before she realizes, almost too late, that she's directly behind Brandon's back tire, and still going much too fast. She jerks her handlebars to avoid smashing her bike into his. There is a heart-stuttering moment when she knows that she could crash into the curb, but she lifts the handlebars and pops the front tire of her bike up onto the sidewalk and somehow, by what she is sure is magic, she keeps the bike upright.

"Hey!" Brandon yells, and he sounds impressed. Vera lets out a whoop, because she's pretty sure that was a wheelie, and she's never done one before. She won't tell him that it was an instinct, an accident. She'll let him think she knows how to do a wheelie on purpose.

They both coast across Maple Street without stopping to

check for oncoming traffic. Brandon cheated a little at the start of the race, but Vera has definitely won. She brakes hard, letting her back tire skid a little, and turns to look at him. A broad grin splits his face, and seeing it, Vera's anger evaporates.

"That was *awesome*," he says.

Brandon's eyes are bright and his grin is guileless and Vera cannot help but smile back at him. In that moment, she loves him, in part because he is not the type to get mad at losing a race to a girl and in part because she beat him and so she can afford to be magnanimous. In that moment, she feels that it is fate that they are best friends, that she will know him forever, maybe marry him, and their marriage will be one without icy stares and twisted-up towels and fights in the evening.

In that moment, Vera cannot think of a reason why she should ever have been angry at Brandon at all.

They will know each other for fifteen more months.

CHAPTER TEN

Seventeen years had passed since Francis Crowder last slept under his own roof.

Vera dropped her plastic bins on the floor of the bedroom he used to share with Daphne. She swallowed back revulsion at the sight of the worn-down carpet, the lopsided mattress, the plexiglass-topped nightstand on the left side of the bed. The empty spaces, everywhere, that had never been filled.

This bedroom, like the rest of the house, was a set piece. It was a tourist trap. It was all for the eyes of strangers who wanted *inspiration*.

It had not been a bedroom for two bodies to sleep in since everything went wrong.

When he went away, most of his possessions went with him—or, not *with* him, because where he was going, personal possessions weren't an option. But they went away at the same time, Francis and his things, to be inspected and examined, studied and tested, entered into evidence whether they mattered to his case or not.

At the time, Daphne had said that they were trying to prevent any of his things from becoming objects of spectacle. That's how she put it. Vera can remember the way her mother bit out the words: *objects of spectacle*. Ridiculous, in hindsight, Vera thought—her mother had turned the entire house into an object of spectacle just as soon as the money had run out.

But Daphne couldn't have been planning on it from the start, because she let the police take what they wanted. She must have regretted it later, not keeping some things back.

They didn't find everything, though. They didn't find the toolbox in the closet with his gloves in it, and they didn't find the drafts of his confession, the ones he'd ripped up and tossed into the trash can beneath his desk. Vera had hidden the box all the way at the bottom of her laundry basket, and she'd gathered up those precious scraps of paper and put them down the garbage disposal just in time. She'd done what she could. She'd tried to save him.

They also didn't find his journal. Vera knew where he kept it—she'd fished it out from under his side of the mattress and hidden it under the front porch, where she thought it would be safe until he got home. She'd figured that he'd want it back, or at the very least that he wouldn't want strangers reading it.

That was it. His toolbox and his journal and his trash. And, Vera now supposed, his thermos, forgotten beneath the kitchen sink. That was all they had left behind. They took his reading glasses and his clothes and his shoes. They took his one good suit—a blue one with gray stripes that he wore to every day of the two-week trial, letting it rumple and darken with sweat and wear. They took his toothbrush, his hairbrush, the books from his bedside table.

Francis Crowder was never going to come home to claim that journal. A tuberculosis outbreak at the supermax facility took care of that. And now the front porch was rebuilt. For all Vera knew, the journal had been digested by mushrooms, or shredded into bedding for a family of possums, or torn up and turned into papier-mâché for a *sculptural element* long before the porch had been rebuilt.

Daphne'd had seventeen years to fill up his side of the double-wide closet, to put her own books on the nightstand. She'd had seventeen years to fill those empty spaces.

But she hadn't done any of that. His half of the closet was home to empty hangers and a mothball-smell. A shoebox sat on the floor beneath those bare hangers, its lid askew, its previous inhabitants gone.

Those had been his good dress shoes, Vera remembered, the black ones with the stitching around the gore.

Now there was just the empty shoebox. She picked it up and threw it overhand into the bin marked TOSS. The hangers went to DONATE, and with that, Vera's father's half of the closet was finished.

She slid the mirrored door shut and marked it with tape, then moved four feet to the right and opened her mother's half of the closet.

She took two steps back. That was the distance she needed to take this side of the closet in.

It was packed.

Vera took a deep breath. She eyed that shelf, trying to imagine how she would go about taking a sweater down without risking the whole pile collapsing on her. She didn't wonder why her mother hadn't expanded to the other closet—that seemed transparent enough—but she did allow herself a good hard slug of judgment. There had to be twenty years of rayon and poly-blends in there.

The rounded, pastel plastic hangers of Vera's youth were gone, replaced with a tangle of thin wire hangers that could slide close together. The closet rod, assuming there was one under all that wire, bowed with the weight of them. All her

mother's dresses and skirts and blouses pressed so tightly together that Vera could hardly distinguish them from each
other. Two layers of shoes covered the closet floor, and the shelf
above the rod was stacked with shirts and pants and sweaters
right up to the ceiling.

The performance of sentiment, the guilt, the melodramatic
self-indulgent drama of it, was so thoroughly in-character for
Daphne. Vera thought she could see a Christmas sweater in
the sediment on that shelf, and for what? Who was her mother
wearing Christmas sweaters for? It wasn't as though she'd been
invited to any parties in the aftermath.

The truth of her mother's isolation should have pulled Vera
up short. It was a vicious loneliness Daphne must have experienced, a loneliness with rows and rows of teeth on it. It should
have stopped Vera in her tracks, that thought; it should have
brought up some kind of compassion. It should have reminded
her that Daphne had been alone for nearly two decades, trapped
in a notorious house in a town that hated her.

But the problem was the second thought, the one that followed right after the notion of her mother's loneliness.

It was the thought of strangers, standing in this bedroom,
looking at the empty places where Francis Crowder's life
used to be. Strangers who had been invited in where Vera had
been cast out. The thought of all the strangers looking at the
places where a life used to be. And one stranger in particular—
Hammett Duvall, tall and cigarette-musty, standing in this
bedroom and planning his book.

She'd read the book. Of course she'd read the book.

Vera had been sixteen years old when it came out, desperately lonely, and gullible enough to think of Hammett as a

friend just because he smiled at her and asked questions. There
had been a pile of limited-edition paperbacks on the dining
room table, *complete with photo inserts!* according to the cover,
waiting for Daphne's signature. It had been easy enough to
grab one, to hide it under her pillow for late-night reading.

Being in her parents' bedroom now surfaced the memory
of reading that book, of realizing how wrong she'd been about
the first Duvall she'd met. Vera remembered how the flashlight
beam had trembled across the page as she learned about the
scope of that man's violation.

*I laid my head down on the pillow that had once supported Francis
Crowder's rest, and I breathed in the air that had once filled his lungs,
and I wondered how such a quiet house could create such a vile, un-
speakable, repugnant monster.*

Daphne had let that man into their home, let him into this
bedroom, let him lie down on that bed. She had let him write
his book, the book that had cemented Hammett Duvall as a
legendary true-crime author. The book that had secured Francis
Crowder's status as one of the great villains of the twenty-first
century.

Daphne had let him in, and then she'd let the rest of them
in. Vera knew with absolute certainty that at some point every
goddamn poet and painter and journalist and spiritualist who
passed through this house had put their head on her dead father's pillow and tried to breathe him in, too. She knew it like
she knew her way through this house in the dark.

She knew it the way she knew her own skin.

That sharp snap of fury gave Vera the energy she needed to
rip into the closet.

She struck at the center mass of the hangers, tearing down
fistfuls of old work-and-church clothes. She threw them to

the ground, the khaki slacks and the cap-sleeved blouses, the crystal-buttoned cardigans and the linen sundresses, the sensible skirts in sage and lavender and cream and desert rose and denim. The musty smell of unworn fabric rose around her until the room was choked with stagnant fog.

"Fuck," she whispered to herself, not knowing why but knowing that the word was right for the moment. She sat down in the middle of the clothes and looked at them, unable to see them for what they were.

They didn't seem like things a person could wear. They didn't seem like things Daphne had ever purchased. She couldn't imagine the jaw-clenched woman who had locked her out of this house twelve years ago slipping into a skirt set and driving to the store. She couldn't imagine the woman in the bed downstairs walking into a changing room and modeling a dress for herself, bringing it home and pulling off the tags.

Maybe, Vera thought, she was just out of practice.

She'd learned to stop thinking of her mother as a person a long time ago, back when it still hurt to want Daphne to love her. Forgetting that her mother was human had been necessary. It had been the only way to survive the years when she still lived with a mother who looked at her daughter as if she were black mold blooming across the kitchen counter. It had been the only way to get through the years after that, when Vera was all alone in a world where someone always seemed to find out who she really was.

But now, she had to think of her mother as a person. As a person who needed things. As a person who was sick and deserved care and dignity.

"Fuck," she whispered again, and she folded herself up until she was on her feet again, scooping up an armful of fabric for the DONATE bin. As she turned to drop it in, something came loose and drifted to the floor at her feet.

Vera let the clothes fall into the plastic bin, then turned to see what she'd dropped. It took her a moment of digging through the piles of fabric to find it, but after a few seconds, her fingertips met something that wasn't rayon. It crinkled at her touch.

She withdrew her hand from the blouses. It was a slip of paper. She told herself that it was probably a dry-cleaning slip, or maybe even an old cheque that had been crumpled up in a pocket—but she knew.

Of course she knew.

It was folded into eighths. She unfolded it, and there were those even, rounded letters. There was her name.

VERA'S GROWING UP TOO FAST. WE WENT FISH-
ING TODAY AND HAD THE TALK. I WONDER IF SHE
KNOWS I'D DO ANYTHING FOR HER. I WONDER IF
SHE UNDERSTANDS HOW I JUST WANT TO PROTECT
HER AND KEEP HER SAFE. DAPHNE TOO. SHE'S SO
GOOD INSIDE AND I NEVER WANT TO LET ANYTHING
HAPPEN TO HER, NO MATTER WHAT. I THINK SHE'S
STARTING TO GET IT I JUST HOPE SHE DOESN'T EVER
HATE ME FOR WHAT

And that was it. Just like before, the writing cut off midsentence, only this time it wasn't because the page was ripped—it was because the page ended. Vera flipped the paper over as if she didn't already know the back side was blank. Francis Crowder had only ever used one side of a page to write. There was a dark smear at the edge of the page, like an inkblot or a fingerprint. When Vera touched it her hand came away sticky.

She reconsidered the dunes of clothing that surrounded her. This note had to have fallen out of a pocket. She dropped to her knees beside the plastic bin and pulled out each shirt, one at a time, feeling for hidden folds where more pages from the journal might be hidden, but there was just flimsy poly-blend fabric, rough and pilled with age and too many washes in too-hot water.

Vera read the page again.

SHE'S SO GOOD INSIDE.

This was a little piece of her father. A little piece of a family that had loved Vera. A piece that had cared about her so much that he had to write it down, had to put pen to paper and memorialize that his daughter was *good*. She was *good*.

Maybe her mother had found it and torn it up and stuffed it in a pocket to be forgotten. Maybe some visiting artist had shredded it and left it strewn around like so much trash.

Or maybe Francis, knowing he was going to disappear from his daughter's life, had left these for her to find.

Vera sat back on her heels. Then she reached out and grabbed a cardigan. She folded it carefully, feeling along every inch of it. It took hours, but she checked every garment, folded each one neatly and slowly surrounded herself with piles of the clothes that had sheathed her mother for the last few decades of her life.

She checked every pocket. She turned up every collar. She shook out every sleeve.

There was nothing. Not a receipt, not a loose dollar, and certainly not any more of Vera's father's words.

It should have felt like defeat—all that effort to no real end—but Vera felt somehow steadied. This was the second scrap she'd found of her father's journal. There might be more pieces of it littered around the house. If there were, Vera decided, she was going to find them all. Every piece of him that was left, she would gather and keep. It was her job to clear out the house, and she was going to do just that.

Until now, it had been about erasing the evidence that her mother had lived and died here.

Now, it was about more than that. Now, it was about finding evidence that once, half a lifetime ago, love had lived here too.

First, though, the folded-up clothes had to go. She could drive them to the pick-and-pull that afternoon, get rid of them for good. She loaded a few stacks into the plastic bin, then realized that what she really needed was bags, and a lot of them. Those plastic ones from under the kitchen counter, maybe, or some big garbage bags—whatever would be enough to get all of this out of here. She'd need to take the bin downstairs to figure out how many bags she needed, and then back up to load all the clothes into the bags, and then back down again, however many trips it took to empty the room.

Her arms ghosted with fatigue at the thought of heaving all that weight down the stairs and into her car, but there was no way around it. No one would be helping her. Certainly not the son of Hammett Duvall, whom she had no interest in inviting up to the second floor of the house. Vera might as well just let her arms ache until this part of the job was done.

Once it was, she'd be able to move on to another part of the house, to find what secret pieces of her father might be waiting for her.

CHAPTER ELEVEN

On Vera's third trip from the bedroom to the car, she happened to glance into the dining room. It was dark and cold, just as it had been the day before when she had tried to clean out the kitchen. The house was quiet, still, as if all the air in it had been condensed into a single point. She couldn't see a thing, but she could hear her mother's labored breathing. It was a heavy noise with a click at the bottom of it, like ball bearings falling through cottage cheese.

"Daphne?" she said, standing at the threshold of the dining room, the door to the basement shadowing the edge of her vision. It occurred to her that, even with the lights off in the dining room, it shouldn't have been so dark in there. The light from the kitchen window should have shone through, even if only a little.

She set down the overloaded bin of clothes. The half of it that was on the dining room side of the threshold vanished into blackness.

Maybe her mother had gotten up and drawn the curtains in the kitchen. Maybe she'd wanted it dark, and she'd drawn the curtains, and the sun was on the other side of the house so there wasn't much light coming through anyway.

Vera didn't want to walk through that darkness. She scolded herself for her childishness. It was just a dark room with a dying woman in it. Fourteen feet across, give or take a few inches because Francis Crowder had never been too precise in his measurements. There was no reason why those fourteen feet of impenetrable blackness should have made her so aware of her throat and her bladder and the way her high bun exposed the bare skin on the back of her neck.

She made a fist with her right hand, determined not to indulge her sudden, childish fear. It was just a dark room.

"Daphne, I'm coming in," she said, her voice an imposition in the too-quiet house.

She was answered by another sucking, rattling breath.

"Fine," she hissed to herself. She snapped the fingers of her right hand four times fast, and then, before her fear could talk her out of it, she reached around the wall and turned on the light.

Daphne was sitting up in bed, looking right at her, blank-faced.

"I'm just going through to the kitchen," Vera said. Her mother didn't answer—she just watched with glittering black eyes as Vera passed through the dining room.

The kitchen was warm and bright, suffused with afternoon sun like honey in tea. Vera let the warmth unravel a little of the strange panic that had seized her at the prospect of walking by her mother. She wondered if she could bring herself to ask about the pieces of Francis's journal. She got the bags from under the sink, and when she passed back through the still-lit dining room, she forced herself to stop.

"How are you feeling?" Vera thought that Daphne's eyes were back to normal now, brown and tired. Had they really been so dark just a moment before? "Do you need anything?"

"I feel fine," Daphne answered, and her voice was a thing with claws, painful to hear and surely painful to use. Vera got her a cup of water without asking if she wanted it, ignoring the corner of her mind that was preening at the idea of her mother's silence. "What are you doing up there?"

". . . Closets," Vera said after a moment, because it didn't feel right to tell her mother that she was emptying a bedroom the woman would never see the inside of again. She eyed Daphne's cracked lower lip. "That's gotta sting," she ventured. "Do you want some lip balm?"

Daphne looked up at her with exhausted eyes. "That would be nice," she said softly. "It does sting."

Vera retrieved lip balm from a drawer in the kitchen. It was in the same drawer it had always been, and it was the same brand her mother had always used—it came by the jar and had a shepherd on the lid. She opened it and held it out, but Daphne didn't move.

"Will you?" Daphne asked, not making eye contact.

Vera swallowed around the catch in her throat. "Sure." She dipped the pad of her middle finger into the jar, then patted her mother's lower lip as gently as she could. The skin of Daphne's mouth was thin but tough, like crinkled-up wrapping paper. The balm left a thick sheen everywhere Vera touched. Daphne's eyes stayed on her the whole time, flat and evaluating. Vera wondered if this meant anything to her mother, or if it was simply a matter of practicality.

"There," she said, looking away from her mother's mouth as soon as she was finished. "That should be better."

"Thank you," Daphne murmured. She picked up the paper cup of water and drained it, leaving a waxy crescent on the lip of the cup. "So. Closets."

The room felt too, too small. "Yep. I think I'll finish the bedroom today or tomorrow. It's going fast, since there's only the one side to do."

"I'm glad it's convenient," Daphne said, the edge in her voice just a shade duller than it had been a moment before. "Not too much trouble, then."

Something pathetic and small inside Vera leapt at that hint of gentleness, like an alley cat standing on its hind legs to plead for a scrap of trash. She tried to slap the yearning down, but it got away from her. "Not too much trouble, no."

"Do you know," Daphne said softly, staring down at her own trembling hands, "that my life began the moment I laid eyes on you?"

Vera's skin prickled the way it did when she was walking at night and stepped off a curb without realizing it, the feeling of a sudden drop and a near-fall. "What did you say?"

"You were covered in blood and screaming loud as your lungs would let you, choking on your own voice," Daphne continued. Her voice was low and even, like she was reading out loud to herself. Vera had never heard her mother like this before, not once. "Everything you'd ever known had just been torn away from you. Everything was cold and everything was awful and you didn't understand what had just happened to you. I saw you there in that bedroom, raw and miserable, and I loved you more than I'd ever known I could love anything."

There was no air in the room. Vera sank slowly into the chair near the foot of Daphne's bed, the one James usually occupied during dinner. She couldn't remember her mother ever saying *I love you,* even in the time before it all went so wrong. She couldn't remember her mother talking to her this much, either.

The lights flickered overhead. Vera ignored them. Hadn't they just been talking about closets a moment before? What was happening?

"You didn't know it yet," Daphne said, her voice taking on

a rough edge, "but you were mine and I was yours. I knew right then that we'd always have each other. We'd be tangled up together until the day one of us died. I remember thinking that maybe we'd both die at the same time, and wouldn't that be the best way for it to happen? Both of our lights snuffed out at once, so I'd never have to imagine a world where there was *you* without *me* or *me* without *you*. Of course I knew that wasn't how things would go—we'd be pulled apart by time, by circumstance, the way the world works. But that seemed so far away back then. It seemed impossible."

Heat flared in Vera's chest, because it wasn't time or circumstance that had pulled them apart. Old fury warred with a deep and profound hunger to hear these words, to hear her mother telling her that she was wanted, that she'd always been wanted, and Vera pressed her palm to her mouth to keep from gasping at the pain of those two emotions meeting each other.

"The night you were born, the doctor had to come here because it was the middle of the night and the hospital was so far away. He handed you to me and you didn't know what love was yet. You were the most selfish thing that ever was," Daphne added, "claiming every inch of love your new family could scrape together, demanding it all for yourself without giving any back at all. You came into the world on a wave of pain and exhaustion and that was just the beginning. All you knew then was needing and wanting and getting. There's nothing so pure as a yawning pit of need, and that's the kind of animal you were."

"Please," Vera whispered. "Don't." Because this was familiar. Daphne had called her selfish and thoughtless and burdensome more times than she could count.

But Daphne didn't seem to hear her. "I felt the weight of

you—of who you'd be in our little family and in the world—
and that's when I became whole. I existed for a reason then. I
existed for you. Do you know that? I existed for—" And then
Daphne cut herself off with an extended coughing fit, her chest
spasming violently, her fingers clawing at the bedsheets. She
hunched forward in the bed, making an almost mechanical
hacking noise.

It was a spell-breaking kind of sound. Vera rose from her
chair with her hands half-raised, her heart pounding, paralyzed
by the onslaught of tenderness. She couldn't think of a thing
to say or a thing to do, so she just stood there as Daphne con-
vulsed around her own lungs. Maybe, Vera thought, this was
it. Maybe it was happening. Tears sprang to her eyes and she
didn't know why, didn't know what she was afraid of, because
wasn't this perfect? Wasn't this the way she'd imagined Daphne
when she'd agreed to come home?

But then again, the Daphne she'd imagined coming home to
didn't tell loving stories of Vera's birth.

After far too long, Daphne lurched and heaved and made
a thick, underwater noise. She gestured frantically with one
hand, motioning toward the edge of the bed, the doorway, her
own stomach.

"What?" Vera asked, "What do you need?"

But Daphne couldn't answer, for reasons that shortly became clear: her mouth was simply too full. Her back was still
hunched with the strain of her coughing fit as she let her jaw
tip open.

An uneven stream of dark gelatinous tissue fell from between her parted lips. It was threaded with something black
and dense like veins under skin. Daphne sighed with evident
relief as she released it from her mouth, her shoulders sagging

as the clinging wet mass rolled down her chin and dropped into her lap.

Vera made a noise that started as "oh" and ended somewhere far afield from human speech. She ran to the kitchen and dove under the sink, grabbing as many rags as her hands could accommodate.

When she came back into the dining room, her mother was motionless, still curled over her own lap. The stench of the room was close and choking. It was an amphibious smell, like turned earth and rain, dark mold and half-rotted wood. There was an undercurrent, too, of sweet lemon. It filled Vera's mouth until she closed it tight, and even then the taste of soil and citrus stayed with her.

"Here," Vera said uselessly, her voice trembling. "Here, now. Let's get you cleaned up."

She eased Daphne's shoulders back and started wiping at her chin and chest. Daphne didn't move to help, but she didn't resist, either. Her thin skin rucked into wrinkles at Vera's every touch. Her breathing was quiet and even, now. It was like the breath of a person who would live.

To clear up the mess, Vera sacrificed three kitchen rags, two wet and one dry. It took dedicated scrubbing—whatever this was that had come out of her mother stuck stubbornly. Vera decided she wasn't going to try to rinse those rags in the sink, renew them in the wash. They were ruined in a way that would never come clean.

Vera eased Daphne's shirt off and replaced it with another one, trying not to see how the mottled fishbelly skin of her mother's torso stretched drumtight between her ribs. She changed the blanket that covered her mother's legs, too. She left the sheet, both because it was pretty clean and because she didn't want to expose her mother's bare legs. It felt like an intrusion beyond bearing, revealing her mother's skin to the room. Looking at the parts of her that she'd kept tucked away all this time.

Vera bundled everything into a trash bag and held it, feeling like she hadn't done enough, which was, of course, true. There was no such thing as 'enough.' Not anymore.

She couldn't stop her mother's death. She could barely even ease it. All she could do was clean up after it.

"Do you want to wash up more than this?" Vera asked. Daphne didn't answer, not even with a gesture. She was studying her own hands. Her eyes were something worse than vacant. She looked clean enough, but Vera couldn't shake the feeling that there was something more she ought to do. "Daphne? Do you want a shower? Or a bath? Or something?"

"No. I have a system. Please, just go. Just go."

Vera hesitated. "Are you sure? What . . . what's the system?"

"It's not your business," Daphne said immediately. Her voice was almost normal. "I'm fine. I feel much better now, thank you."

Fine didn't seem like the right word at all. "Are you sure?"

Daphne picked up a cup of lemonade and sipped at it placidly, as though nothing had happened. "Of course I'm sure. Get on with your work, I'm going to rest. And Vera?"

You don't need to say my name, I'm already paying attention to you. Vera thought it but did not, could not, say it. "Yes?" she said instead, at a complete loss for how she was supposed to look at this woman who had never ever loved her and who was, in her dying moments, unsheathing a violent wave of tenderness.

"Thank you for the lip balm."

Vera did not go back upstairs. She left the dining room,

stumbling past the bin of her mother's clothes that she'd left on the threshold. She slipped on the shoes she'd left by the front door and walked out onto the porch, then took the porch steps two at a time, nearly falling. The tied-off garbage bag full of her mother's rot went into the trash bin around the side of the house, and then she was in her car and driving, her hands trembling on the steering wheel, her foot too heavy on the gas pedal. She braked too hard at a stop sign, jerking forward against her seat belt, catching herself with a slap of her palms on the steering wheel.

She stared at the road in front of her and tried to have a thought, but none would come. Snatches of songs swam through her head, none of them catching. She was far from herself, far from the idea of a self, far from the thing she had seen and the things she had heard and the thing she had cleaned off the woman who she could not, in this moment, pretend to know at all.

She stayed there at the stop sign, her foot on the brake and her hands on the wheel, her breath coming slow and shallow, until someone pulled up behind her and waited long enough to honk. Then she drove, because it was the only thing to do in a car that was running.

CHAPTER TWELVE

Vera had never been a drinker. She didn't like the slippery feeling of alcohol in her brain, the threat of drunken carelessness.

She had a long-held suspicion that drunkenness would be a threat to her. It was a suspicion which had been confirmed by that short-lived bartending job she hadn't been able to keep. She'd watched people trust each other without thinking, watched them share secrets and space, watched them melt into each other and exchange room keys with strangers. Strangers who could be anyone once a hotel room door was closed. Strangers who could ask anything, say anything, do anything.

It wasn't for her.

But Vera needed a place that wasn't the house her father had built, a place where she could catch her breath and eat something other than a microwaved meal from her mother's lonely freezer and drink something other than metallic tap water or lemonade. Anything to drink but lemonade. Most crucially, beyond anything else, she needed a place where she could sit without being noticed. Without being remarked upon.

She needed a bar.

Nobody in a bar wanted to look at her. In the right bar, she could be alone without having to be alone. In the right bar, she could move among people without having to pretend to be one of them.

That was precisely what she needed: a moment alone. Not the kind of alone she felt when she was pouring lemonade for her mother, and not the kind of alone she felt in her childhood bedroom, with the walls of the house pressing in close around her like a cupped palm.

She needed a moment alone that didn't feel like a punishment.

Vera drove for an hour without bothering to notice where she was headed—the only thing that mattered was that she was going *away*. After that hour had passed, she pulled off the road and looked up local bars on her phone. There was one a block away, and it sounded like the kind of place that promised to be dimly lit and sparsely populated.

Perfect.

She hoped that she looked tired enough to avoid having to show anyone an ID with the name Crowder on it. She could have changed that name—probably should have, certainly should have. But she was a Crowder, just like him. How was she supposed to give that up?

Vera walked into the Cat's Medallion with her head down and her hands in her pockets. She took a stool in the far back corner of the bar, near the wall but not near the entrance to the bathrooms—the spot where no one wants to sit and no one wants to look. The place was a little too well-lit, but otherwise, it was perfect. She kicked her feet back and forth between the stool and the bar, feeling the squeak of her shoes against metal and wood.

The bartender clocked her right away with a salesman's intent. He was a young guy with a cool enough haircut and bright enough eyes that Vera would have put money on him being from somewhere that wasn't Around Here. It was too much to hope that he wouldn't know about her father, but she hoped anyway. Maybe if she paid cash, he wouldn't connect her to her father. He was short, puffed out with marshmallowy muscles as if to make up for it. His smile was the kind of sharp that made Vera think the word *amateur* without knowing what, precisely, she was judging him for.

He made too much eye contact with her. It was as if he hadn't noticed that she didn't want to be looked at. She frowned at him and he just smiled right back at her. The smile was too sharp, and it didn't reach his eyes, which were filled with a blank flavor of anxiety that let Vera know she hadn't chosen the right bar at all.

He was going to be relentless. She could tell. This was a kid who prided himself on remembering customers, who would want to make conversation, who probably thought of himself as a charmer, who probably thought that he got tips because of his personality and not because his customers were scared to be assholes. Sure enough, he put a glass of water in front of her and leaned his elbows against the bar as if they were both people.

Vera did not want this. She did not want to be a person. She did not want his smile or his elbows or the elaborate mixed drink he was going to try to convince her to try.

"A glass of white wine," she said. "Dry. Whatever you like best."

The bartender winked at her, made a clicking noise with the corner of his mouth, and Vera felt a vicious flutter in her belly.

Something old moved in there, something she'd spent years ignoring, something James Fucking Duvall had woken up with the smooth new skin of his belly, stretching outside his truck.

Foulness.

Reckless.

"Nothing wrong with keeping it simple," the bartender said, pouring the wine with an unnecessary flourish of his wrist. He set the bottle on the bar and turned the label toward her with the kind of precision that she could tell he prided himself on. His forearms were heavily veined, his fingernails short and clean and whole, and Vera clenched her jaw at the sight of them.

Being home was pulling something out of her that she didn't want. *Not worth it,* she reminded herself. The bar wasn't air-conditioned. In the unmitigated heat and humidity of the day, condensation was already forming on the side of the wineglass.

A bead of moisture dripped slowly toward the stem. She tracked the path of the droplets as they rolled together to keep herself from looking at the bartender's pale, bare wrists.

Never worth it.

She left the right amount of cash tucked under the bottom of the untouched glass of wine. Hopefully the condensation from the glass would soak the paper, hopefully the money would be cold and clammy in the bartender's hand, hopefully he would shiver when he felt it—

Vera stood up fast and walked out of the bar without looking at anything but the door. The inside of the car was stifling. She sealed herself in with the stale air, tremors flooding her body, something in her shaking free that was never, ever supposed to be released.

It was plenty dark by the time Vera stopped trembling. She turned her headlights on and drove home slow, the twin smells of night air and sweet wine invading her brain. Halfway home, she noticed a smear on her arm, something dark and sticky. She scrubbed it on the inside of her shirt until it felt like her skin was coming loose.

Maybe by the time she got back, Daphne would be asleep. Maybe by the time she got back, Daphne would be dead. Vera drummed her fingers on the steering wheel and let herself chew on that combination of hope and dread, let herself chew on it all the way home, all the way until she was in front of the house her father had built.

She parked and got out of the car and stood there with her back braced against the driver's side door, trying to convince herself to go inside.

"Vera?"

She looked up wearily, ill prepared for any kind of interaction with any person, only to see the person she was least prepared for.

"Brandon," she breathed. "Hi. Are you—do you still live around here?"

He looked around, shoved his hands deep into his pockets. "Yeah. Yeah, I'm still at my mom's. I was just walking home." He looked away from her as if he was considering walking away already.

There was so much to say that there was nothing to say, so much between them that it all fell away flat. "You look good," Vera lied. He didn't look good. He looked a decade older than her. He looked like he hadn't slept in seventeen years.

"I should go," he said.

Vera took a halting step toward him. He flinched at the movement. "Please," she said. "Please talk to me. I'm so sorry about—"

"I can't. I'm sorry, I can't." He shook his head, but he didn't leave.

"Please," she said again, and then she said something she never would have imagined herself saying to Brandon Gregson, something she hadn't let herself so much as *think* since the last time she'd seen him. "Please. You were my only friend."

"No, Vee," he said with a smile that Vera couldn't quite read. "I think we both know you had another friend."

Vera let out a low laugh. "I really didn't. Not a real one."

Brandon shook his head. "I should go," he said again. "Sorry about your mom. I hope . . . I hope she goes easy."

And then he was leaving, and Vera couldn't make herself call after him. She couldn't quite dodge an awful thrill of hope that maybe they'd be able to make things right, to be friends again, to fix what had been so broken all those years before. She couldn't dodge it so she didn't—but she also didn't linger there, leaning against her car and letting that hope linger on her tongue. Instead, she swallowed it whole, like a cherry pit, and she walked up the front steps without pausing, without feeling the weight of the house, without snapping her fingers. She walked right in and she let the house close around her like it always did.

She exhaled and the Crowder House sucked up the air that left her. She took her shoes off and the warmth of her feet went into the cold floorboards. She brushed her teeth and when she spat into the sink, whatever had been in her mouth coated the insides of the drain like plaque lining an artery. The skin that fell from her body and the hair that dropped from her scalp drifted into corners and under furniture, a soft lining for every gap and every edge in the house.

Going out, she saw now, had been a mistake. This house, the house her father built, the house where her mother would die—this place was safe. This place knew her.

This place was where she belonged.

CHAPTER THIRTEEN

Vera is twelve years old and her lip is bleeding. It's bleeding a lot. She has her hands cupped under her chin, but blood is running between her fingers anyway, dripping onto the cement of the curb between her knees.

If Vera were at home, she would imagine having a friend nearby to say *oh no, what happened?* They would have a kind warm voice and they'd wrap Vera up in a hug that would smell like dust and old pennies.

Brandon is what happened. This is all Brandon's fault. It started when he stopped his bike under the big larch tree with the lightning-strike scar down the middle, the tree Vera thinks of as dead but it still grows out tiny new leaves on some of the branches, so it can't be dead really.

"What?" she'd said, almost mad at him for making them stop riding just when she had really been building up a good head of speed. But she didn't stay almost-mad, because his face was so serious that worry flashed through her with a sharp snap.

She feels small and foolish, later, for having been worried about him.

"Come here," he'd said, and his voice was so loud and imperious that even then, Vera knew that he was nervous.

"You're not the boss of me," she'd snapped. But she let her foot drag along the ground anyway as her bike coasted closer to where Brandon was standing, and when she reached him she put her heel down, grinding to a final stop. "What is it? Why are we stopping?"

Brandon cleared his throat and wiped his palms on his jeans. They left dark tracks on the denim. "I have to tell you something," he said. "I don't like you. I mean, I like you, but I don't . . . *like-like* you."

Vera was upset by this in a way she didn't really understand. She wanted to laugh in Brandon's face, but she also wanted to kick him hard in the stomach, and she also, a little bit, wanted to cry. In the end, she didn't do any of those things. "So?"

"So, I had to tell you that first." Brandon stepped toward her with a frown of fierce determination. "Now, I'm going to kiss you."

This time Vera did laugh, a high surprised yelp of laughter that made her wobble on her bike. She put the kickstand down, but did not climb down off the seat.

"Don't laugh!" Brandon's face fell. "I'm going to kiss you because we should just do it, right? Everyone thinks we're a . . . a thing, and anyway I know you want to try it."

Vera did not want to try it. Or at least, she'd never wanted to before. But now Brandon was offering, and she wasn't sure. Did she want to try it? Had she always? Would she ever?

"Okay," she said, and she tightened her grip on the handlebars of her bike, and she closed her eyes, and she leaned forward just a little, not enough to tip over but enough to put her face into the part of the air where a kiss might happen.

After a few seconds, something soft and very wet brushed her mouth. She startled and her eyes flashed open and there was Brandon's face, too close to hers, so close that she could see the pale veins in his closed eyelids, and that soft wet thing was his lips on hers. She moved her mouth a little, pursing her lips out toward his, and Brandon exhaled through his nose and his breath was warm on her cheek.

Vera didn't know when this was supposed to be over. She smacked her lips together to make a kiss-noise and then pulled her head back. Brandon's eyes fluttered open, and they looked at each other knowing that they were somehow different now than they had been before.

"Wow," Brandon whispered. Vera did not know what he was saying 'wow' about. "Can we do it again?"

"No," Vera said, loud and fast, before she even knew she was going to say it. She pushed off and wheeled her bike around and then she was riding away, pumping her legs hard, letting her bike wobble from side to side. Brandon was calling her name and his voice was getting closer, and then he'd caught up to her and they were riding together fast the way they had been before he decided he wanted to kiss her.

"Are you okay?" he called out over the sound of their tires spinning. "What's wrong!"

"Nothing," Vera called back. "I just think I don't like kissing!"

Brandon didn't say anything for a while. They reached Vera's street and slowed down to avoid getting yelled at by adults who couldn't seem to mind their own business. Vera took her feet off the pedals and coasted with her legs stretched out straight, not looking at Brandon, hoping that he would let her forget the whole thing.

Because she wasn't looking at him, she didn't see what his face was doing when he swerved toward her. She couldn't know what he was feeling when he kicked his leg out toward her, knocking her down. All she knew was that one moment she was on her bike and the next she was on Jan Haverbrook's lawn, sprawled headlong in the grass with a ringing in her ears and no air in her lungs.

She turned over and there was Brandon at the curb, straddling his bike and glaring at her with a tender kind of fury she didn't recognize. It was uncanny, seeing this completely new emotion on his face.

It made her feel unaccountably hungry.

"Fuck you," he said. She could tell from the way he said it that he'd been practicing in his head. "I didn't want to kiss you anyway. You're ugly, and anyway I *told* you I don't like you like that."

Vera tried to answer but her lip was burning and when she opened her mouth she felt a gout of warmth run down her chin. She slapped her hand to her face and felt the warm tickle of blood running down the back of her knuckles. "Ugh," she said. The sound came out of her bubbly and thick.

Brandon looked like he was going to spit, or maybe cry. But instead of doing either of those, he added, "You know what, Vera? My mom says that *your* mom's a loser to believe your dad's out sugaring in the summertime. Nobody sugars once it gets above freezing at night. She says"—he gave a wet sniff—"she says he's off having an affair and he probably has a whole other family somewhere because you and your mom suck so bad. I bet that's what he keeps down in that creepy basement you're too scared to go in," he added, his eyes bright with cruel inspiration. "I bet it's pictures of his real family that he loves more than you."

His eyes were shining. He wouldn't look at Vera anymore. And then he rode his bike away, and now Vera is sitting here on the curb in front of Jan Haverbrook's house, letting her blood stain the pavement.

She feels paralyzed. Getting up and walking home with all this blood running down her chin feels wrong, but she's not sure when it's going to stop bleeding, and she has to go home sometime.

It doesn't even hurt yet.

Her bike lies on its side, half on the sidewalk and half in the road, one wheel slowly rotating. Her mouth tastes of brine and metal. Her knees and elbows are starting to sting, the skin an angry red under the smeary green of crushed grass.

She can't believe Brandon said 'fuck.'

Someone calls Vera's mother—probably Jan Haverbrook—and it isn't long before there is a pair of shoes in front of Vera's bike. "Oh, Vera," Vera's mother mutters. She's holding a pale pink plastic pitcher, the one that's usually full of iced tea in the refrigerator. "Get up and come inside. You're bleeding all over Jan's sidewalk. What on earth happened to you?"

Vera thinks, but does not point out, that it isn't Jan Haverbrook's sidewalk. The sidewalk can't belong to a *person*. It's supposed to belong to everybody.

She stands in the street with her hands still cupped under her bleeding mouth, waiting. Her mother upturns the pitcher, dumping water over the sidewalk, washing the blood away and leaving behind a dark wet stain. Then they walk home. Vera's mother pushes the bike by the handlebars. Blood drips from between Vera's fingers, leaving a trail behind them.

By the time they walk through the front door, the bleeding has mostly stopped. Vera's face is swollen and hot. The two of them sit on the edge of the tub in the upstairs bathroom, and Vera winces as her mother sponges blood from her chin with a wet dishcloth.

"What happened?" Daphne's breath smells like old coffee.

Their faces are close enough together that Vera can see the mascara clumps that glue her mother's eyelashes together.

This *what happened* isn't like the *what happened* Vera's imagined friend would say, the friend who would comfort her and listen to her. It isn't a *what happened* that anticipates unfairness, that invites the telling of a slightly-embellished story. It's a *what happened* that's already tired of the answer.

"Brandon pushed me," Vera says. The lip of the tub digs into the backs of her thighs. It feels alien to snitch on Brandon like this, but the betrayal is so fresh that the words slip from her unbidden.

"Brandon did this?" Daphne's surprise is mild, but sounds genuine, and it validates Vera's own bewilderment at her friend's sudden violence.

Tears well mortifyingly in her eyes as she nods. "Yeah," she says, her chin twitching in that strange way it does whenever she's about to cry. "I don't know why," she adds. "He, um." The air grows heavy with the weight of what she's about to say, the significance of it. "He kissed me."

Vera's mother pulls away from her, examines her hard, and Vera feels cold all over. She's certain that she's in trouble—the only question is, how bad is it going to be?

But when Daphne speaks, she doesn't sound mad. "He pushed you down and he . . . kissed you?" Her voice is gentle in a way that's more frightening than her anger would have been. "Did he hurt you anywhere else? Tell me exactly what happened, sweetheart."

Vera cannot remember her mother calling her 'sweetheart' any other time, ever. It shocks her out of crying, and she's so stunned that she almost forgets to answer the question. "No," she says at last, shaking her head and then wincing at the way the movement makes her split lip throb. "That isn't how it happened. He kissed me, and then I rode my bike away from him, and *then* he pushed me. And then"—she decides in an instant that she will not tell her mother about the *fuck you*, it's too much to share the sting of that with any adult—"and then he said that Dad doesn't love us."

Daphne considers Vera for a long time, looks into her eyes with a bright, curious intensity that Vera does not understand.

"Now why would he say a thing like that?" she asks, and she's still using that strange, soft tone, like Vera is an outside cat she wants to coax into the house.

Vera doesn't move, not a single muscle. This is the side of her mother she so rarely gets to see, the side she so deeply longs for. There is the most softness and allowance here that Vera ever gets to see. This kindness, this interest. Vera wants to lean toward it like a flower turning toward sunlight. She wants to eat it.

But she feels that maybe if she stays perfectly still, it won't end. It won't change. "He said Dad's cheating on you," she whispers eventually. "He said . . . he said Dad doesn't really go sugaring in the summer."

Daphne takes the cap off a dark brown bottle of hydrogen peroxide. "This is going to sting," she says, and before Vera can even brace herself, her mother pours the clear liquid over the ragged patch of skin on her knee. It stings a little, and then it stings a lot. The hydrogen peroxide begins to foam and hiss. "That's good, those bubbles," Daphne says. "That means it's working."

Vera bites her swollen lip, fascinated, as the bubbles do whatever it is that they're supposed to do. Her mother pours capfuls of liquid over both of Vera's knees, the heels of her hands,

her elbows. It hurts every time, a raw, immediate kind of pain
that makes her suck air through her teeth. The hurt carves a
deep valley into Vera's heart because it's braided together with
Daphne's attention, Daphne's gentleness, Daphne's care.

Maybe, Vera thinks, this is just what love is like.

"Why did Brandon do that?" Vera asks as her mother dabs
petroleum jelly over the split in her lip. Daphne uses her middle
finger, and Vera tries to memorize the warmth of her touch.
She doesn't really expect an answer, but she gets one anyway.
"Why did he say that stuff about Dad? It's not true, right?"

"He was probably confused," her mother says absently.
"Boys that age are confused all the time. They want things
that they don't understand, and they don't know how to stop
wanting them, so they get mad. I'm sure he'll apologize to
you soon."

Vera wrinkles her nose, which makes her lip hurt more.
Normally, she wouldn't risk asking questions, but maybe her
mother's kindness can bear the weight of interaction today.
"What kinds of things do they want?" she asks.

But she never gets to find out what her mother means—what
the thing is that boys want but don't understand—because a big
hand lands on the half-open bathroom door, pushing it open.

"Hey, ladies, what's going on in here?" Vera's father pads
into the room on sockfeet. His eyes get big when they land
on Vera's swollen face. "Oh, wow, Vee. What happened to the
other guy?" His voice is light but his hands are both clenched
into tight fists, and Vera feels a low thrum of guilt, knowing
that he's upset. Knowing that he's worried, and it's her fault.

"Vera fell off her bike," Daphne says softly. "Going too fast
around a corner, I bet. I keep telling her to slow down, but she
never listens. Just bad inside, I suppose."

Vera draws breath to protest this lie, this blame—she didn't fall off her bike like a baby, she can go fast and it isn't dangerous no matter what her mother thinks, and the accusation of falling down is an injustice that she will not let stand. But then, with a quick hand, her mother grabs her by the elbow, pressing against that raw patch of flesh in a way that stings even worse than the hydrogen peroxide did.

Vera looks to her mother, shocked at the sudden pain of this touch, and their eyes meet for the briefest of instants, and in that instant, Vera sees her mother's eyes flash *don't*. She doesn't quite shake her head, but it's there, between them: a warning, an insistence, a demand for silence. And so Vera turns to her father and dips her chin into a nod.

"Yeah," she says. "Mom's right. I was going too fast and I . . . I ate shit."

"Vera!" Daphne's voice is sharp, but her grip on Vera's elbow vanishes, taking the pain along with it. "Language."

"Sorry," Vera says, knowing that, somehow, she has done the right thing.

Vera's father clicks his tongue. "We all forget ourselves sometimes, but you shouldn't swear around your mother," he says. He winks then, and Vera gives him a very tiny smile, because he's the one who told her that *ate shit* could mean *fell down,* and it's their secret. He smiles back, just as small. "I'm going to go take a look at the bike, make sure it's in good shape. I'll be in for dinner."

When his footfalls disappear down the hall, Vera's mother grabs her again, by the arms this time. Her grip is tight and painful and her face is drawn, urgent, tight-lipped. She gives Vera a tiny shake, not hard but hard enough that Vera feels her lip start bleeding afresh.

"What!" Vera says, an unwelcome whine in her voice.

"Don't tell your father what really happened," Daphne hisses. "Don't tell him what Brandon said about him. Do you understand me?"

Vera does not understand, not at all. She has almost no secrets from her father, and she can't think of a single reason why this should be one of them. "You're hurting me," she says, but her mother doesn't let go of her, doesn't stop punishing her with that hard wild gaze.

"Tell me you understand," Vera's mother says. "You can't tell him what happened. You can't tell him about Brandon, or the kiss, or any of it. Promise me."

Vera tries to wiggle out of her mother's fingers, but there's no breaking that iron grip. "Fine," she says, "I promise, I won't tell. I said I *promise*," she repeats, and only then does her mother release her.

Daphne's lips are pursed together into a bloodless knot. She will not look Vera in the eyes. "Good," she says.

"It's not true, though, right? Dad loves us."

"He loves me," Daphne says crisply. "Your relationship with him is your own business."

Vera knows that she has done everything right, that she has done exactly what her mother wanted from her, but it doesn't matter. The Daphne who might have loved her for a few minutes there is gone, vanished without warning. She stands up, walks to the door, pauses with her hand braced on the doorframe. She looks like a made thing, like someone poured plastic into a mold and then chipped her out of it.

"Put band-aids on your knees," she says, not turning. "So you don't get blood on everything if they ooze."

And then she's gone. Vera grabs a wad of toilet paper and

uses it to mop the fresh trickle of blood from her chin. She bites back tears, pointless baby tears, no reason for them.

She doesn't understand everything that's just happened, and she *knows* she doesn't understand it, and that's a horrible, terrible feeling. Somehow, Brandon hurting her has turned into a secret that she has to keep from her father. She's only ever kept one secret from him before and it's not one her mother knows about.

Maybe this—the secret she's sharing with Daphne—will bind them closer, give them something to wink at each other about behind her father's back. Maybe it will turn into love. But then again, this secret is also something that made her mother hurt her on purpose. It's something that made the room feel thick with fear and heavy with urgency. And once the secret had solidified, Daphne was gone.

Vera imagined the friend she could have, the kind of friend who would find her here in the bathroom fighting back confused tears and ask *what's the matter* in a voice like the tap of fingernails against the side of the tub.

"Nothing," Vera mutters. "Nothing's the matter. I just wish I knew . . ." There's no end to that sentence, none that satisfies, and trying to find it makes her eyes well up with more unwelcome tears.

It was really cool how you didn't even cry when you fell off your bike, her friend would say. *And Brandon was wrong to push you.*

Vera's fingers curl around the lip of the tub, leaving a little smear of blood behind. Her smile is wobbly, but real. Brandon *was* wrong to push her. "Yeah," she whispers. "Yeah. It doesn't matter. Whatever."

Whatever, her friend echoes, and it sounds just a little less cool than when Vera says it. Just a little more hesitant.

Vera stands slowly and washes her hands in the sink. Gummy blood is caked between her fingers from where she tried to keep from dripping on the sidewalk and on the floor. She watches the bloody water swirl down the drain, so fast it's as if the sink is drinking it up.

"Dad wouldn't cheat on Mom," she mutters to the sink.

He wouldn't, her friend answers easily. Vera is trembling with an emotion she can't name, but the thought of a friend so nonchalantly dismissing Brandon's accusation makes her stand up a little straighter. Something that easy to reject can't carry any weight.

"He wouldn't," she says again, and it comes out stronger this time. "It's a lie. He's lying." The part she can't say aloud, even to the walls of the empty bathroom, is how badly she needs it to be a lie—because she knows, in her bones, that her father loves her. He would never betray their family. And if that's not true, then nothing can be true ever again.

Brandon and his mom must not know very much about sugaring, that's all. And they certainly don't seem to be so suspicious of Francis Crowder when they get a bottle of maple syrup from him every February. It probably just takes a really long time to make the dozen or so bottles he gives away every year. He must *need* to collect all spring and all summer.

He's lying, her friend repeats, and she takes it as confirmation: Brandon doesn't know what he's talking about.

She prods the swollen part of her lip with her tongue, tasting the way the raw flesh is different from the rest of her mouth. It tastes like the hole left behind by a fallen-out tooth—not quite bloody, not unpleasant. Just strange.

She is not sure whether she likes that taste. Maybe not. Maybe it's just new.

Maybe you'll get a cool scar, her friend whispers.

She tongues the split in her lip again. "Maybe you'll get a cool scar," she echoes under her breath, liking the sound of it. She laughs softly. The laugh seems to double as it echoes off the tile and glass of the bathroom, and the pain of the day fades a little, because Vera feels the way she always feels when she's at home.

She feels like she isn't alone after all.

CHAPTER FOURTEEN

A week after her return to the Crowder House, Vera stood in the wide arch that divided the entryway from the dining room where her mother slept. She didn't move, and she didn't breathe, because she was listening. Listening for anything. The creak of James shifting his weight in one of those uncomfortable dining chairs, the hiss of fabric shifting against itself. A cough. A breath.

Anything.

The dining room was much too still.

Vera's hand remained on the lightswitch where it had landed after just a few frantic gropes. When she'd turned the light on, her first thought had been that her mother would surely need another blanket to ward off the strange chill that seemed to inhabit the dining room. Now she wasn't so sure, because dead people didn't tend to need blankets, and as far as Vera could tell her mother wasn't breathing.

"Daphne?" Vera didn't say it too loudly, didn't want to risk startling her mother, just in case. Didn't want to kick off another of those awful coughing fits. But the sound of Vera's voice had no effect.

Daphne didn't stir.

Vera set the banker's box that was tucked under her arm down on the floor. She took a few steps closer to the bed, peer-

ing hard at her mother's concave chest, looking for any sign of
a breath.

Daphne's chin was tucked down into her neck, her face hidden in the shadows of her hair, which had come loose somehow
since the last time Vera had checked in on her. She wasn't moving. Not at all.

Vera cleared her throat and tried again. "Daphne? Are you
awake?"

A low rattle came from the shape in the bed. The sound
pecked at something buried deep in the recesses of Vera's
mind—some summertime memory of sweat and oil and grass
stains on a stinging knee—but before she could exhume the
precise shape of that memory, Daphne spoke.

"I am now." Her voice was clotted and slow.

Vera's heart caught at the sound of her mother's voice. Alive.
Awake. Unpleasant relief pooled under Vera's tongue. She
wasn't ready for Daphne to die. Not anymore. Not after that
strange conversation.

I existed for you.

Vera stalked past the bed and into the kitchen, trying to give
herself time to abandon the idea—the fear, if she was honest
with herself—that it had all been over. She opened the refrigerator and took out a glass bottle of lemonade.

She stared at it for a moment, feeling the cold wet weight
of it in her hand. Vera had never been a praying type, but just
then, she begged whoever might be listening for a favor. She
prayed that the acid in the lemon would wash away whatever
was in her mother's throat, whatever was making her voice
sound like that. She prayed that the lemonade would wash it
away so it wouldn't have to come up.

So it wouldn't interrupt them again.

Daphne didn't speak again until after she'd finished three tiny paper cups of lemonade. "It's that time, is it?" She nodded to the banker's box.

"Just some things to sort through," Vera said, fetching the box and working the lid off it. "There's not too much." That was a lie—the box was packed as full as she could get it without tearing the cardboard at the corners. It contained everything she hadn't been able to figure out on her own. All the papers she'd found in her parents' bedroom, her mother's sewing room, and the kitchen.

There had been nothing in her father's office. Nothing but a few dime-sized burn marks and a lot of smudged fingerprint powder and a smell like bitter cocoa. That room had the same gutted feeling as his side of the bedroom, the feeling of a half-rotted baby blanket by the side of the highway. It was something worse than abandoned. Seeing it like that had left Vera furious and hollow.

She began to pull out stacks of paper instead, laying them out in neat piles at the foot of the bed. "Is it okay with you if I sit?" she asked, gesturing to an empty spot near the very end of the mattress. Daphne replied with a strange shiver that seemed to lift her skin from the flesh beneath. "Nevermind," Vera said quickly, and she pulled a dining chair from its place against the wall.

Sitting in that chair took Vera back to the family dinner table of her childhood. Trying to remember to keep her elbows off the table. Getting scolded for fidgeting. Catching her father's wry smile as her mother tried to teach her table manners.

Daphne let an empty paper cup fall from her hand to her lap. "There's no point sorting through whatever you've got in there.

It's all trash," she said. There was no venom to her words—she said it as if it were a plain fact, free of judgment, immutable.

"Let's make sure," Vera said. "How about these?" She held up a stack of sealed envelopes. Each one had her mother's name and address written on the front in pen.

"Trash," Daphne replied.

"You don't want to know what they are?" Vera asked, pulling an envelope at random and starting to slide her thumb under the flap. She was looking at the envelope in her hand when she heard the sound again, that faint noise that had come from her mother's throat before.

She froze, her eyes locked on the envelope, and listened. That sound—a low, muted, metallic clicking—was definitely coming from Daphne. It went on and on, growing in volume, and Vera could place it now.

She could place it, because it sounded just like the plastic-coated links of a bicycle chain sliding through an O-ring, rattling against a cement floor—

She looked up at Daphne, and the noise cut off, leaving the room heavy with silence.

Vera's ribs felt too small for her lungs. The walls felt too close. She struggled to blink, to swallow, to breathe.

"No, thank you," Daphne said evenly. "I don't need to open any of those. I already know what's in them." She lifted the last paper cup of lemonade to her lips, swallowed loudly. "They're letters from the penitentiary."

"From Dad?" Vera asked. "He wrote to you?"

Daphne shook her head, her eyes sliding to a far corner of the room. "He never wrote to me, no." The next words she spoke were so casual, so off-handed, that Vera almost didn't understand them. "No, those aren't for me. They're from back when he still used to write to you."

Vera dropped the envelope as if it had breathed in her hand.

"What," she said. It wasn't a question, wasn't even really a word so much as a sound that her mother had knocked out of her. "He used to—what do you mean, when he used to write to me? He never wrote to me," she added, even though she suddenly knew that her words weren't true, felt ridiculous even bothering to say them.

"Of course he did," Daphne replied. "He loved you more than anyone. He wrote to you every month that first year." She pursed her lips, still not meeting Vera's eyes. "He got . . . upset, when he realized I wasn't passing his letters on. He stopped accepting my calls. And then he died, so."

Vera was standing in the kitchen doorway and she didn't know how she'd gotten there, only that she was gripping the doorframe in both hands. She turned around slowly, saw Daphne picking at the lip of the paper cup in her hand. A violent wind swept through her then, leaving her goosebumped and empty. Everything she could think to say felt hollow, ultimately answerless. *How could you?* What could her mother possibly say to that?

She wanted to be angry. She wanted to rage and storm and she wanted to hurt Daphne, wanted to grab her and squeeze and squeeze until the flesh split open—but then, what would it do? It wouldn't bring Francis back. It wouldn't make it so Vera could go back in time and pluck up the courage to write him, the strength to risk visiting him and being turned away. It wouldn't make anything that was her fault stop being her fault.

It wouldn't get the box of papers sorted out.

So Vera did what she had so much practice doing: she took

the hunger and the anger and she pressed them down into the empty aching void inside her where those letters should have gone.

And then she returned to sit heavily in the dining chair at the foot of her mother's bed. She picked up the stack of envelopes, feeling the weight of them in her hand. "Why would you save these?" she asked, because it was the only thing she could think to say that wouldn't feel like bleeding.

Daphne shook her head. "I thought someone would make use of them, maybe," she said. She'd shredded the paper cup, leaving a snowdrift on the surface of the little rolling table. "I thought they'd come to some kind of good. It's a ridiculous question, Vera. Why did I save those letters? Why did I save you? It doesn't matter anymore, does it? Maybe you'll understand when you're about to die. None of it matters."

The lights in the dining room flickered then. Vera looked up at the light fixture that hung from the middle of the ceiling, the brass-and-ceramic semi-chandelier her father had hung there before she was born, and watched the lightbulbs stutter.

"It's not as if I can undo any of what I've done," Daphne continued. "It's not as if there's any way to turn back time and do things differently. I just have to live with it."

Vera glanced down at her mother, then looked back up to the lightbulbs. They were still flickering, but there was something strange. They were going dark and then brightening in perfect unison. "Does this happen often?" she asked.

Daphne didn't seem to hear her. "I have to live with it, and so do you, not that you care," she muttered, her words flattening into a low monotone. "I'm the only one that hurts for all of it."

"When's the last time you had the wiring in this place looked at?"

"I have to sit here knowing what I know, all on my own, and you get to be out in the world—"

"Let's just finish this, please," Vera said, gesturing to the banker's box of documents. She tried to cordon off the part of her mind that would need to decide what to do with the envelopes. Whether to open them, whether to read them. Whether to let herself think about her father as someone still-living who might miss her as much as she missed him.

All of that could come later, when everything was over, when her mother wasn't looking at her anymore.

Vera bent double to tuck the envelopes under her chair and out of sight. When she straightened, the lights had stopped flickering. She made a mental note to have an electrician come and look at the house once her mother was dead.

CHAPTER FIFTEEN

Vera and Daphne spent most of the afternoon going through the box, the unopened letters burning beneath Vera's chair like banked embers. Together, mother and daughter sorted through old tax returns, bank statements, an unsigned contract for a documentary project. Several of the papers were cut in places, or torn a little too strategically.

Vera was willing to bet that those shreds of her father's history had found their way into collages and scrapbooks and wallets. Souvenirs for all the artists who had nursed themselves on the Crowder House over the years, turning Francis's notoriety into their own. Maybe James Duvall had claimed a few scraps of his own.

Daphne's energy flagged before they were halfway through the box, but Vera pretended not to notice. She needed answers about the documents. She couldn't afford for her mother to fall asleep and never wake up again, not until they'd discussed what needed to be done with the accumulated paperwork of her life. Vera poured Daphne cup after cup of lemonade, hoping that the sugar would keep her awake long enough to finish their business. But by the time the kitchen windows started to darken, Daphne's eyelids were drooping. Vera frowned at the half-full box of documents.

"Hey. Hey." Vera dropped a binder-clipped stack of documents onto her mother's lap, hoping to startle her into alertness. "What about these?"

Daphne's eyes didn't open, but her head rolled on her shoulders. "For so long, you had a soft skull without a single thought in it," she murmured. "You were nothing but hunger. You were an animal."

Vera froze. "I was—I was an animal?"

"You were simple," Daphne sighed. "And it's easy to love a simple thing."

And then she fell silent, her chest rising and falling with slow, silent ease.

Vera wanted to scream. It wasn't fair for Daphne to fall asleep, not now, not in the middle of what could have become an actual conversation that might mean something, connect something between them, reveal some hidden truth between them. It wasn't fair that she'd hidden those letters. It wasn't fair that she was starting to talk to Vera like a mother might talk to a daughter, not when she was dying so fast that parts of her kept erupting with black ooze.

It wasn't fair that this was the first time Daphne had ever spoken to Vera in a way that made Vera long to listen.

She didn't bother to be quiet as she cleaned up the paper cups and documents. She purposefully knocked into the bed, rattled the papers that remained in the banker's box. She wanted Daphne to wake up. She wanted to be able to pretend that she'd been trying to let her mother sleep, that she'd been respecting Daphne's need to rest—but she didn't want the conversation to be over.

That was what stopped her, what made her catch herself. "God, Vee, what's wrong with you," she muttered to herself. She couldn't be the selfish person her mother had always accused her of being.

She couldn't do that.

Vera stooped to get her father's letters from under her chair, half-expecting them to sting her fingertips. But they were just old paper. They weren't heavy, even though she felt sure that they should have been.

By the time she got to her bedroom, all of the myriad emotions of the day had settled into a sense of deep loneliness, like spilled water seeping into soil. The Crowder House had none of the satisfied warmth of a house with two people in it, of a house that was full. It was even worse than it had been when Vera was that quiet, almost-invisible teenager. Even back then, during all the long hours she spent in her bedroom with the door held shut by the weight of her mother's contempt, the house hadn't felt quite this empty.

Vera's breaths had an inescapable echo to them. Every exhalation was oppressively loud in the locked-up quiet of her bedroom, and each one seemed to be doubled, like the stutter at the end of a heartbeat with a murmur. Maybe it was her imagination running rampant in the space left by her solitude—or maybe it was the house breathing behind her, absorbing whatever breath she expelled, sighing along with her exhaustion.

Maybe, she thought, the Crowder House missed Francis too.

She put the letters into the bottom drawer of her dresser, alongside the pair of jeans she wasn't wearing. The envelopes were a perfect white bundle of whatever it was her father had wanted to say to her. Vera pulled the jeans out and tossed them onto the top of the dresser, then shut the drawer too hard, letting the noise fill the room so she wouldn't have to listen to her own breathing.

There. Now they were put away, and that drawer wouldn't need to be opened again until she was ready. If she was ever ready. The sentiments in those letters were aimed at a girl she hadn't been in a long time. Vera didn't know if she could bear to read her father's long-overdue disappointment, his reproach, his resentment. Knowing that his old vision of her, his love for her, had been tarnished by what she'd done.

Of course, the alternative was worse. If he had already forgiven her, if he had still loved her after all, if he had missed her and thought that she had just been ignoring him all the way up until his death—it would be so, so much worse than anything else she could imagine. Vera didn't have to think about it even for a moment to know that she wouldn't be able to survive his kindness. It would break her heart.

She would never know what might have happened if her mother had given her the letters. She would never know what kind of relationship she could have had with Francis before he died. What she could have asked him. What he could have taught her.

Either way, those letters were a gamble, and not a safe one. They'd stay in the drawer, where they might say anything as long as she left them unread.

The smell of cheap tobacco and artificial strawberry drifted through the room. Vera startled hard, as though the smell had stroked the back of her neck. She crossed to the window, trembling, and looked out to see James Duvall leaning against the side of the house, just outside, a cigarillo between his lips.

He was staring at a tall, thin board that was propped against the garden shed. The surface of it had a ragged, aggressive texture, like ripped-up fiberglass insulation rendered in wet clay.

Duvall's white T-shirt was streaked with bright, harsh ochre, and something of the same shade was caked around his fingernails. Paint, Vera thought. The canvas was white, but that had to be paint all over the man.

With one quick twitch, he turned his head to meet her eyes.

Vera jerked back, slamming the window shut. She didn't want to look at him. She didn't want to breathe in the smoke he exhaled, didn't want to feel it clinging to the underside of her tongue. She didn't want any of it. Not tonight. Not ever. Vera decided to skip dinner.

She changed into a clean T-shirt and fresh underwear. She left the clothes she'd worn that day in a pile on the floor in front of the dresser. She checked that the window was closed. She took her hair down and then put it up again, wished she could lock the bedroom door. Folded the clothes from the floor and stacked them on top of the dresser.

As she checked the window again, she recognized what she was doing, chastised herself for being silly. There was no need to circle the bed like a wary dog approaching a stranger. It was just a bed. It was the same bed she'd slept in for the entirety of her childhood. She was shaken up from the revelation of her father's letters, and from being home. That was all. There was nothing to be afraid of.

Except that her eyes kept dropping to the bedskirt.

She flinched away from the memory of her dream. The memory of squatting on the floor and pulling icy coils of intestine from her own abdomen. Pulling all that cold out of her belly had felt just as necessary as removing a splinter from her palm.

"You're being ridiculous," she whispered to herself, needing to say the words out loud to make them louder than the memory of the dream. She was talking to herself more and more often the longer she stayed in the Crowder House.

The lights flickered.

She wrapped her arms around herself, gripping her own elbows. Goosebumps peppered her bare legs. She was, she admitted to herself, afraid. She was afraid to get into the bed. She was afraid to fall asleep, to dream again, to wake up paralyzed with a sweet, tender voice whispering in her ear.

"Okay," she whispered. "Enough. You just have to look." Her words were reasonable, and her brain believed them, but her body did not respond. She tried again. "You have to look. Just check and then you'll know." The muscles of her abdomen felt unearnedly tired, as though she'd been doing crunches all day instead of trembling at her own bed for the past ten minutes. She tried to breathe, to make herself relax, but the breath came out shaky and the sound of her own fear made her somehow more afraid.

She decided to startle herself into action. She clapped her hands purposefully—the sound of the clap was too loud and she regretted it right away—then stalked to the closet and flung the door open.

The light overhead flickered, casting strange shadows in the closet. It was empty except for her suitcase and duffel on the floor. She looked over her shoulder, then crouched and opened them, looking inside, telling herself that she was checking for mice. Of course they were empty.

You never thought there would be mice, she chastised herself, and then she paused, because she'd said it out loud without meaning to, without noticing that she was doing it.

She licked her lips. She'd heard the words, that much was certain. She'd heard them spoken aloud. That could only mean that she'd been the one to say them.

Except that the voice she'd heard wasn't her own.

"You never thought there would be mice," she said softly.

The sentence was familiar and yet unfamiliar in her mouth, like the time she'd eaten an underripe strawberry without noticing what she was doing, not until the texture and the flavor didn't match up to what she'd been expecting. "You never thought there would be mice," she repeated, and then she slammed the closet door shut. The sound of it was as loud as her too-loud clap. Before the noise could fully die, she was on her knees beside her bed, lifting the bedskirt.

"God, Vee," she hissed to herself, saying the words out loud so her own voice would be the only one in the room, surveying the emptiness beneath the bed. "Being in this house is fucking with you."

She was getting herself worked up because of a nightmare and some vermin, that was all. She pulled the sheets back and looked at the bed, not wanting to slide her feet beneath the covers without looking for—what? For mice, she told herself again, and this time she almost believed it.

She looked around the room once more. The door was shut, and the windows were latched. There was nothing behind the curtains, nothing in the closet. Nothing under the bed, nothing in the bed.

She turned off the light and crossed through the darkness to her bed. As she sat on the edge of the bed, in the darkness, with her feet planted solidly on the floor, she told herself that she was safe. As she pulled her feet up after herself, tucking them beneath the covers, she told herself that nothing could hurt her. As she compelled herself to lie back with her head on the pillow and her throat exposed to the open air, she told herself that she was the only living thing in that room, and that there was no reason she shouldn't sleep peacefully through the night.

She was almost right.

CHAPTER SIXTEEN

Vera is twelve and a half years old. She has a mostly-healed scar on her lip and a stick in her hand. The stick is long and sturdy. There is a string wound around it and knotted at both ends. Vera's fingertip is bleeding, and the rock she's sitting on is digging into the backs of her thighs, and she can feel the skin on her nose cooking in the bright afternoon sun, and she has never been happier in her entire life because she is learning how to fish and her father is the one teaching her.

"That's all right," he's saying. "Everyone jabs themself with the hook their first time. Try again."

She sticks the bleeding fingertip into her mouth and smiles around it. It only takes her two more tries after that to thread the fishing line through the eye of the hook. While she ties a knot with clumsy fingers, she asks her father questions about their shared project. She asks, even though she remembers the answer from the drive here, when he told her what they'd be doing. "Why can't I just tie the string at the end of the stick, again?"

She knows that her father enjoys explaining things to her, enjoys teaching her. He likes to be the one who shows her how the world is. So she asks questions she already knows the answer to.

She does it to be kind to him, but she also does it because some part of her always wonders if she'll get the same answer as last time. She wonders when he'll stop telling her the little-kid answers, when he'll stop softening reality for her.

The approach of that day feels a lot like the approach of her first period—she's not sure if she's excited for it or dreading it, but she knows that she should be on the lookout.

He reaches out a big hand to correct the knot she's botching; a quick few flits of his fingers, and it's almost done. He hands it back to her to finish. "Well," he says patiently, "you don't want to tie your line at the end because if you catch a *big* fish, he might snap this little stick right in half. If you wrap the line around the stick, though," he adds, tracing the string with a rough fingertip, "it doesn't matter if the stick breaks, because you've still got the line handy. If you don't do that, the fish might get away. You never want to let a big fish get away." He looks at her somberly. "Fish are big old gossips. They'll tell all the other fish to stay away from where you're standing."

Vera holds up the hook, which is secured to the line by a huge, clumsy tangle of a knot. Her father nods his approval before standing up and wading into the creek.

Vera hesitates—she isn't sure if she should take her shoes off or not—but then her father turns and looks back at her, and his face looks like *what are you waiting for?* So she stands right up and puts the narrow imprint of her own sneakers in the big footprints his boots have stamped into the mud, and she walks into the water.

It's colder than she expected, and murky. The silt of the creekbed swallows her feet right up. Mud fills her shoes in a way that isn't entirely unpleasant, but which she knows will give her mother a fit. She wades in until she's standing next to her father. The water comes up to the middle of his thighs; it rises just over the waistband of Vera's shorts. Her belly sucks in of its own accord, and a strange, ugly shiver goes through her at the thought of that cold water filling her navel.

Vera's father tucks his fishing pole under his arm, reaches into his pocket, and pulls out a little jar. It's a jar Vera knows well: every time her father plans to go fishing, he hands it to her the night before, so she can go out to the yard and fill it up.

He opens that jar now and reaches in with a thumb and forefinger. With the deft ease of long practice, he pulls out one of the stretchy, sinuous nightcrawlers Vera dug up for him last night.

Vera mirrors his posture, tucking her fishing pole under one arm so she can grab the hook with one hand and accept the worm with the other.

She doesn't hesitate. She slides the hook through the worm's soft, pink, mud-speckled skin. Out of the corner of her eye, she sees her father smile, and she feels that same smile on her own face. The nightcrawler is squirming hypnotically, thrashing in a way that is nothing like the usual slow undulation its brothers make when Vera digs them up in the yard for her father.

It looks muscular. It looks furious.

Watching it, something in Vera begins to solidify. Usually, worms are boring, but this one—all it took was a poke to turn this one into something completely different, something fascinating. Something *alive*. A creamy kind of hunger Vera's never felt before puts an ache in her jaw and a twitch low in her belly.

She doesn't want to eat this worm, but she can understand why a big fish might.

When she looks up at her father, there's a tightness around the corners of his eyes. "Are you ready?" he asks, and Vera almost says *no*, but she knows that the right answer is *yes*, so she nods. "Good," he says. "Now, watch. Watching is the only way to learn."

Vera nods again. She watches as her father casts his line. He lifts his arms high over his head, letting the hook dangle far behind him. Then he whips his arms forward, and a second later, the weight on his line drops into the water six feet away.

He nods to Vera. She cautiously raises her own arms.

"Careful the hook doesn't catch you," her father says. "Watch it close."

She's careful. She watches the hook with the worm on it as it arcs through the air in front of her, landing not far from the ripples of her father's cast. She looks to him to see if she got it right, but his eyes are already on the little float that's bobbing in the water in front of him.

"You have to keep the tip of your pole kind of straight out, like this, see?" He demonstrates with his own stick, holding it almost parallel to the surface of the water. "That way, when you get a bite, you can yank it up and set the hook. Watch that float there," he adds, pointing at her float. It's blue and white where his is white and yellow. "If it disappears, you're in luck."

She twitches her fishing pole up and down, smiling at the way the lightweight line rests on the surface of the water for a few seconds before it disappears. She wonders what the fish think when they see the line touch the water like that. But then she smiles to herself, knowing that the fish don't think or feel anything at all. Probably ever.

After all, they're only animals.

❧

After an hour, Vera's toes are the same temperature as the mud that fills her shoes, and her shoulders ache from holding the stick up at the proper angle, but none of that matters. Her father tells her jokes about elephants in trees, and she laughs even though she could roll her eyes, and twice he hands her the jar of nightcrawlers and tells her to change out the one on her hook because "nobody likes a soggy dinner, not even trout."

Each time she presses her hook down into tender flesh—each time a worm turns into a tense thrumming fighting thing in her hand—she feels that same lush thrill. Here is something that she controls. Here is something that responds to her with the kind of frantic immediacy she's always wanted from the world.

"Hey, Vera, why couldn't the two elephants go swimming?" her father asks. Vera has heard this joke before, but she loves this exchange, her father producing jokes for the sole purpose of making her laugh, her laughing for the sole purpose of making him happy. She doesn't love the jokes, but she loves that he tells them, so she always acts like they're fresh.

But then, before she can say *I don't know, why couldn't the elephants go swimming*—the blue plastic circle of her fishing float vanishes beneath the surface.

What comes next is frenetic in a way she couldn't have anticipated. Her father shouts at her to set the hook, and she's not sure what that means but she's so startled that she yanks her fishing pole up hard and feels a sharp *tug* and that turns out to be the right thing after all. She can feel the fish on the line under the water, trying to pull the stick out of her hand, it feels just like the yank she gets behind her bellybutton when her teacher catches her passing a note, like whispering the word *bitch* when that same teacher's back is turned, like pressing her face to the bedroom floor. Her mouth is open and her eyes are wide and she's looking to her father because she's caught something, and she couldn't possibly imagine what to do now that she has it.

"Pull it in!" he says, reaching up and grabbing his own fishing line. Vera mimics the gesture without thinking. She grabs the line in her hands and pulls on it, and it cuts into the flesh of her palm but she keeps pulling and pulling, tucks her stick under her arm so she can reel in the line hand-over-hand—and then the fish finally breaks the surface of the water, and oh.

Oh, it's *so* much better than the worm.

The fish flails in the water, splashing and spasming wildly. Vera finishes pulling it in, holds it up by the hook in its mouth so its head is level with hers. It seems to calm down for a few seconds. She peers into the wet black glass of its pupil, looking for any sign of fear or desire or thought.

"That's a beauty," her father says, wading closer to her. "When they get that big, you know, they'll eat anything. Frogs, salamanders. Baby birds that fall in the water. Little girls, maybe." He nudges her and she laughs even though she's not little anymore. She doesn't look away from the fish's glossy eye. The iris is green and brown and yellow and strange, and she has a deep impulse to touch it.

"Where's the hook?" she asks. The fishing line is in the trout's mouth but the hook isn't jabbed out through its lip. It isn't stuck anywhere she can see.

"He probably swallowed it," her father answers. He grabs the fish by the lip and holds it up, turning it in the sunlight. It thrashes again, struggling against his grip. It's silver-green and covered in dark brown spots. It looks smooth instead of scaly. Vera can't help thinking it looks like a frog that took a wrong turn. "It's okay," her father adds, not looking away from the fish. "We're going to have him for dinner anyway. We'll just pull the hook out when we gut him."

Vera grins so hard she feels like she's going to swallow her own teeth. "I did it!" she says, her voice coming out so childish that she'd be embarrassed if she weren't so excited.

"You did it," her father agrees. He grabs the fish in both hands and points it at Vera, squeezes it by the face so its mouth puckers. "You deserve a congratulations fish-kiss, don't you think?" She fake-barfs, clutching her stomach and putting on a show, hoping to make her father laugh, and he does. But he doesn't put the fish down. "Come on, Vera," he says in the same voice he used to use for every storybook character, back when Vera still wanted bedtime stories. "Gimme a fish-kiss!"

Vera wrinkles her nose at the fish. "Well, since you asked so nice, Mr. Fish," she says. She blows a loud, smacking kiss, her mouth a safe inch away from the trout's gasping lips. "I guess it's better kissing *you* than kissing nasty old Brandon."

This is the worst wrong thing to say.

The air forms a crust, like when the entire top of the skating pond ices over all at once. The sound of the current in the creek seems to grow very loud, and the bottom falls out of Vera's stomach as she shifts her gaze from the fish to her father's face.

"What did you say?" he says.

Vera scrambles to think of a lie, to think of a way to turn the whole thing silly. She wants to save this, but some part of her knows that's not possible. So she doesn't say anything at all. Her father's looking at her like he's never seen her before, like he can suddenly see all of her at once. "Have you been kissing Brandon?" Her father's voice is so soft.

He doesn't sound dangerous—he sounds wounded, small, lost.

If Vera didn't know better, she'd say he sounds afraid.

"N-no," she says. A tear slips down her cheek, and then another, and then she can't stop crying and she's not sure why but her arms are tight around her father's middle and her face is pressed into the soft flannel of his shirt.

The whole story comes out of her, just like that. The kiss, the shove, the *fuck you*, which she whispers through hiccups, and her father doesn't say a word to stop her. He puts one arm around her shoulders and hugs her to his side, still holding the fish in his other hand, his makeshift fishing pole long ago dropped into the water and swept away by the creek.

Her confession ends with the moment her mother found her sitting on the curb. Only then does her father speak.

"And you told her you just fell down on your own?"

Vera hesitates here, because she doesn't want to get in trouble for lying—especially for lying she didn't actually *do*—but she also doesn't want to snitch on her mother. In the end, she decides that she might as well take the blame. She's already probably in so much trouble, she might as well add this to the pile.

"Yeah," she says. "I'm sorry I lied."

"Come on," her father says. "Let's get out of this water." He turns and wades toward the shore, and Vera follows, her stomach hollow. It had been such a good day, and now it's ruined. All because she had to go and run her big mouth.

Vera's father sits on the rocks where they made their fishing poles what feels like a thousand years ago. He drops the fish, which is now very dead, at his feet.

He pats the rock next to him. To Vera's surprise, he doesn't look upset at all. His eyes are crinkled up, and his smile is warm and patient.

She sits. The rock is warm against her frozen legs. She and her father are both dripping, darkening the stone with creek water. She studies her ruined shoes.

"I'm really sorry, Dad," she says. She means it. She knows she did something wrong, something *really* wrong, both because everyone seems so upset and because whatever she did, Brandon hated her for it. Even if it was only for that afternoon. He'd hated her.

"Vee," her father replies, "you don't have a thing to apologize for. I'm proud of you for telling him 'no.'" He looks down at her with warm respect. "And I'm proud of you for lying to your mom."

For a moment, Vera is certain that she has forgotten what words mean. Then, she decides that she's misheard. It's the only explanation. "What?"

Her father fidgets with his own fingers, clasping and unclasping his hands. "The thing is, Vee—your mom, she wouldn't understand. She thinks that boys like Brandon are perfectly normal." He shakes his head slowly, his chin tucked down into his chest. "There's some things she doesn't want me to tell you about that kind of stuff. Some things she doesn't think you're ready for. But, Vee"—he's saying her name so much, it's twisting a slow tangle into her belly—"I've let you down. I should have talked to you about this sooner. I've failed you, and I'm sorry."

Vera is at a complete loss for words. Her father is apologizing to her.

He isn't mad.

He thinks *he's* the one who's in trouble.

"It's okay," she says, because she's so relieved and because she doesn't really understand what he's apologizing for, anyway.

"No." He's still clasping and unclasping his hands, gripping his own fingers hard enough to turn the knuckles white. "No, it's not okay. I've let you—I've sent you out into the world without the knowledge you need to protect yourself." He bends forward to pick up her fish, which looks dull now that it's not thrashing around anymore. He plucks at the fishing line that extends from its mouth to Vera's stick. "You see, Vee. It's men. Boys are one thing, but men are another. And I'm sorry to say that it sounds like your little friend Brandon is becoming a man." The fishing line digs into the meat of his hand as he winds it around and around his fingers, the same way it's wound around and around Vera's stick.

Vera doesn't quite understand. "What does that mean?" she asks. "What's going to happen to him?"

"Well." Her father makes a small wet sound, deep in his throat, and pulls the fishing line tighter around his hand. His skin is starting to go pink between the places where the line is creasing the flesh, and his voice is taking on a rhythmic quality, like he's reading out of a book he's already read a hundred times. "Boys are just like girls, in almost every way. But men . . . men are demons, Vee." He tugs hard on the line, and the fish twitches in a way that doesn't give Vera the thrill that she got when it was fighting to live. "You can tell because they're filled with a, with a foulness, a kind of grease, that makes them evil. It turns them into monsters. It's a dark, sticky, rancid oil and, and it's in men's bones and in their bellies, and it, it, it *corrupts*. Do you understand?"

This feels exactly like learning how to multiply fractions. Vera knows that she's supposed to be able to grasp this—she can tell that it isn't a hard or complex concept, and her father seems to know all about it already. She feels ashamed of being confused. "I think so," she says slowly, because it's only kind of a lie and it covers her embarrassment. "Only . . . how does the grease get into them?"

He shakes his head and yanks on the line again, and the fish jerks again, and there's a soft sound from inside of it, like the thread of a seam popping. "I don't know," he says. "Maybe God puts it there to punish them for being what they are. Maybe it's just that they're made wrong. All I know is, Vee, men are just filled up with it. It's what they have instead of blood, and instead of guts. They just have the grease in them, dirtying their souls up, rotting and ruining them."

Something about this snags at Vera. She frowns. "But you're a man, Dad. And you're not corrupted."

A sudden, bright smile splits her father's face. She can see all his teeth, even the ones in the back. "Thanks, Vee," he says. "Thanks. I'm glad you can tell. See, I get rid of mine."

"How?"

His smile softens a little. "I have a system. I save the other men. I keep them from turning into monsters. When they start to go bad, I help them." He looks down at Vera and something about the way he's looking at her makes her feel sad, even though he's smiling.

"How do you save them?" she whispers.

He winks. "That's for me to know, and it's not anything you ever need to worry about. Because you're never going to fill up with that muck, and you're never going to let a man get his filth anywhere near you. Right?"

Vera studies her shoes again. They're saturated with creek-bed mud, completely ruined, unsaveable. She supposes that her father is trying to keep the same thing from happening to her soul. "Right," she says.

"Attagirl." Her father gives one more sharp tug on the line. The fish jerks hard, and then the hook is out. There's still half of a worm on it, and a large hunk of red flesh that looks to have come from somewhere deep in the middle of the trout's belly. He tosses the pole, hook and all, into the brush beside the creek, and holds the vacant-eyed fish out to Vera by its lip. "Now, let's get this fish home and clean him up for dinner. What do you say?"

Vera sits on a towel for the drive home, the dead trout on her lap. There's a bucket in the footwell on her side. The bucket has a mallet and a cordless drill in it, and a few metal spiles rattling around from when her father goes sugaring.

She stares out the window, chewing on her lower lip. Brandon would say it's too late in the year to go sugaring.

She can't stop thinking about what her father has told her. In her mind, she's going over all the men she knows—her Phys Ed teacher who has a weird fixation on the marines, and Brandon's dad, and the policemen who came to the house that time, and all the rest.

Are they corrupted? Are they unclean? Why don't they fix themselves, like her father does? And if he's fixed himself, shouldn't that mean it's impossible for him to lie the way Brandon said he lies? Should she ask about it?

When they pull into the driveway at home, Vera's father doesn't get out of the car right away. He drums his fingers against the steering wheel and smiles over at Vera. "Now," he says, "I know I gave you a lot of new stuff to think about. But I think it's best if that stays between us, don't you?" When Vera doesn't answer right away, he winks at her again. "Your mom doesn't need to find out what you did with Brandon. I know Daphne, and I can tell you for sure that if she found out, she'd be so worried about you getting his rot on you that she'd wind up mad for no reason. So I won't tell if you don't tell."

Vera nods, breathing an inward sigh of relief. She didn't want to have to reveal to her mother that she'd spilled her secret about Brandon. It's also a relief that she and her father have a secret now, instead of she and her mother having a secret. This is familiar. But it feels like she can ask her father things now, things she's never been able to ask before. She decides to risk it. "I won't tell. But can I ask something?"

"Of course."

She can barely get the words out. Her voice trembles when she asks the thing she's wondered her whole life. "Why do you let Mom be so mean to you?"

Francis hesitates before answering. "Well, Vera. That's just how it is sometimes, between a husband and a wife. Your mother needs to help me remember how to be good. And if that hurts sometimes, I figure my patience is the least I owe her. Your mother . . ." His voice breaks the way Brandon's does sometimes lately. "She was the first person who ever loved me. And then you came along," he adds, resting a gentle hand on the back of her head. "And now there's two people who love me, and if I get to be that lucky, I can put up with a little meanness sometimes. You know?"

Vera's not sure if she understands, but her father's eyes are shining with tears and she doesn't know what she'll do if he cries, so she nods. "Yeah. And, hey, Dad?"

"You don't have to say 'hey,' Vee, I'm already listening to you."

Vera flushes with warmth at the way her father's eyes crinkle up at the edges when he says her nickname. She decides right then and there to forget the question she was going to ask, about the bucket and the drills and the spiles, about the weekends her father spends away harvesting sap that never seems to make it home. She decides to forget about what Brandon said. Her father wouldn't have an affair. He wouldn't have another family.

He loves this one too much for that.

So Vera decides to forget what she was going to ask. She decides to trust her father instead. "Thank you for taking me fishing," she says, smiling down at the trout in her lap. "I had a really good time."

Her father nods to the fish in her lap. "You did great, Vee. I'm proud of you." He rests a big hand on top of her head, and the warmth of him seeps down through her hair, and she smiles back at him because he's proud of her. That's the only thing she ever really wants.

CHAPTER SEVENTEEN

Vera is twelve and two-thirds years old. Her bedsheets are dark blue flannel with light blue stripes, and her hair is too short to chew on so she is substituting her lower lip. She grinds that lip between her front teeth meditatively, her breathing slow and shallow, the smell of dust and steel bright in her nose.

She is not supposed to be awake, but she is awake.

She is under the bed in the dark.

She is waiting.

By the time Vera hears the door to the basement ease shut, the clock radio on her nightstand reads 02:30 in bright, burning red letters. The hinges on the basement door are well oiled, but she knows by now how to press her ear to the floor so she can listen for the soft click of the latch, the snag of the lock. She's learned the difference between her father's normal heavy daylight footfalls and the soft, liquid ease of his tread when he comes out of the basement in the wee hours of the morning. She can always hear him when she wants to these days.

She rests her cheek against the floor as she waits, feeling the way the wood bows to tenderly cup her face, letting the warmth of her skin blend into the warmth of the house. Her heart is racing, pounding so hard that she can feel the echo of it thumping back at her, a steady tap-tap-tap resonating through the floorboards.

She waits until those footsteps have passed her room and

gone up the stairs. She waits another five minutes after that, counting out three hundred mississippis, going deliberately slow because she doesn't want to risk counting too fast in her excitement.

Tonight is the night.

She counts in her head at first, and then out loud, whispering into the floorboards. Once she's out of mississippis, she's sure her father isn't going to come back downstairs. He hasn't forgotten anything, isn't going to need a glass of water, isn't going to double-check the lock on the door to the basement.

"Okay," she breathes. "Okay, Vee, you can do this."

She imagines—as she imagines so often these days—that someone is with her, a friend who believes in her, who admires her, who knows that she's capable of more than anyone thinks. Like Brandon, but nicer. That friend would whisper *of course you can do this, you can do anything.* Vera would smile at them and say *watch this,* and then she would do something that would leave them wide-eyed and wondering.

That's how she builds up the courage to slide out from under the brass frame of her bed, reaching her arms out from under the bedskirt and dragging herself forward with the fluid ease of long practice. She's almost too big to fit under the bed now—her back scrapes painfully against the bedframe as she emerges, making it rattle loudly—but she doesn't let the squeeze slow her down. She has to show that friend what she can do.

Her breath is coming faster now.

She is already wearing socks, thick ones that will keep her feet quiet because her parents insist that she wear socks all the time in winter even though the house has central heating. She's wearing her flannel pajamas so that if she gets caught she can say she was sleepwalking. She doesn't know if anyone will believe her, but it's the best excuse she's been able to come up with in all her planning.

She rises into a crouch, tucks her hair behind her ears, flexes her toes. She will have to walk slowly to keep from slipping on the hardwood. She would be walking slowly anyway, though.

Vera runs her fingers along the chain around her neck. It's a long ball-chain, long enough to hang almost to her navel beneath her shirt. She stole it from Alan & Sons Hardware while her father was cutting lengths of cord from a big spool. He was measuring the cord attentively, his lips moving in a silent conversation with himself, and he was not paying attention to Vera as she slipped the precut ball-chain off a pegboard hook and into the pocket of her corduroys.

The metal slides between her thumb and forefinger with a series of tiny soundless *pop*s. She lifts the chain to her mouth and grips it in her teeth, tasting the greasy tang of the metal.

Her hair has already fallen from behind her ears. She tucks it back again, wishing she had a barrette. But all her barrettes are upstairs in the big bathroom, in an old Altoids tin tucked into the middle drawer of the countertop. Too bad—she's not going to risk sneaking into that bathroom, waking up one of her parents, having to answer questions about why she's not just using the powder room downstairs.

The bedroom door doesn't make a sound as Vera opens it. Her lip is starting to swell beneath the chain as she chews on it. She worries the swollen place with her tongue, tasting raw flesh and metal together. It feels like a fat lip.

She's only ever had the one. She's never had a black eye, either. Lately, she's been starting to feel as though she'd like to get into a fight. Just to try it out. Just to see how it feels. She is pretty sure she'd be good at it.

Closing a door silently is trickier than opening it but Vera has been practicing. She turns the knob slow and careful, lets it go without a rattle. It works perfectly.

That, she thinks, was the hard part.

Vera lets the loop of chain fall from her mouth and slowly pulls the full length of it out from under her shirt. The metal is warm where it was next to her skin, but cold and wet where it was between her teeth. At the end of the chain is a key, a small gold key with a round top and sharp teeth. The chain is stolen, but the key is stolen twice over—first, from when Vera took her father's keychain from his nightstand and slipped it off the ring, and then again from when she told him she was going to the bathroom at the hardware store and went to the key-cutting station instead.

She'd put the key into the machine and watched as it cut her a replica, looking over her shoulder once every few seconds. The machine spat out a little receipt that you were supposed to present to the cashier when you checked out, so they could charge you. But Vera had crumpled up the receipt and dropped it into a bin full of long, blunt-ended screws on her way back to where her father was having a length of iron pipe cut to measure. The key had gone into the big pocket on the front of her red denim overalls, and she'd felt it burning there like a beacon until the moment she'd gotten home and tucked it into the torn lining of her music box.

The door to the basement is right next to her bedroom door, separated by just a few feet. The lock is as well-oiled as the hinges. This is a quiet door in a quiet house, and it yields to her with the unhesitating cooperation of a devoted accomplice.

The stairs are very dark. Vera has a moment of doubt— should she turn on the basement light, or should she go to the kitchen for a flashlight? Both options mean risking discovery. She decides that the flashlight is safer; if she's caught in the kitchen, she can claim to be getting a glass of water, and she can save her trip into the basement for another night.

She eases the basement door nearly-shut, leaving the tongue of the latch out to keep the door from closing. She tiptoes to the kitchen and takes the big yellow flashlight from its in-case-of-emergency place beside the refrigerator.

It's so heavy. Francis can hold it up with one hand, no problem, but Vera's not sure if she can. She uses both hands just in case.

When she gets back to the basement door she has to use her foot to open it again, and she slips inside, using the obstacle of her body to keep it from shutting too hard behind her.

With the door shut, the basement is darker than a closed eye. Vera tells herself that she is not afraid of the dark, but this kind of darkness feels aggressive and smothering, like icewater closing over the top of her head. She isn't supposed to be here, and that frigid darkness knows it. She's holding her breath, and when she finally induces herself to exhale through her nose, the sound of it seems to come from all around, like the room is sighing with her.

Hugging the flashlight tight to her chest with one arm, Vera snakes a hand behind her back to find the doorknob. She turns it, pulls a little, and turns it back again; with that the cellar door is shut behind her, all without a sound. She twists the knob again to confirm a suspicion: the door has locked automatically, even from the inside. She will need her key to get back out.

The flashlight comes on as soon as she thumbs the big black rubber-covered button on the handle, a trembling white beam illuminating her feet. The basement isn't as warm as the rest of the house, but it isn't cold enough to make her tremble like this—it's all nerves, all excitement, putting a shiver into her arms.

When she lifts the flashlight and aims the beam at the stairs, they become a grayscale tunnel down through the darkness, leading to the cement floor of the basement.

Vera hadn't known that the floor of the basement was cement. Brandon's basement has a dirt floor that's packed just as hard as cement but still always messes up her clothes. But this floor—it's so much nicer than that. This floor is poured and sealed, as shiny as the floors at the hardware store. She keeps the flashlight beam trained on the bottom of the steps as she picks her way down, stepping onto each stair with both feet like a little kid.

There is a scraping, rattling noise coming from the darkness outside the flashlight beam.

She pauses, her chest rising and falling fast beneath her pajama top, the flashlight beam shivering along with the tremors in her arms. A low, muffled growl comes from that darkness.

Vera takes another step. She's planned so thoroughly. She can't go back now.

Tonight is the night. It has to be.

The bright circle described by the terminus of the flashlight's beam grows smaller and brighter as she approaches the bottom of the steps. She pauses when it's pointed at her feet again, her feet on the cement floor in that little puddle of blinding white light, the cement floor her father laid with his big strong hands. It holds her up, steady and strong.

She studies the light and the floor and her feet, listening to the scraping and the growling, to the soft wet animal sounds that come from the place outside the beam of the flashlight.

She hugs the flashlight to her chest again, freeing her right hand just long enough to snap her fingers four times. The darkness doesn't abate, but it becomes less oppressive, less frightening; the darkness down here is now the same as the darkness under her bed, the same as the darkness behind her own eyelids. Because this darkness is here, Vera is not alone.

She takes a deep breath, curls her toes against the floor. Then she grips the yellow plastic handle of the flashlight with both hands and swings it up, pointing the beam into that friendly, familiar darkness.

First, the beam illuminates a wall, made of the same cement as the floor but matte instead of shiny. Then a toolbench, one her father built out of redwood. The front of the toolbench is all drawers, and the handles are the same as the ones on the kitchen cabinets upstairs. There are no tools on the surface of the toolbench. The drawers are all shut. Francis Crowder is a very tidy man.

The next thing the light finds is a big X made of wood. It's taller than Vera's father, taller by quite a lot. The wood is unfinished but weathered, discolored in places. Vera smiles at this X the way she would smile at an old friend. There is a latched box at the foot of the X, and she approaches it, taps the top of it with one sockfoot. She wants to open the box, to touch the smooth metal of what she knows is inside—but she's worried that if she disturbs anything in the basement, she'll give herself away. The last thing she needs is to get in trouble for being down here.

She turns then, fast, because she knows she is almost out of things to see and because she knows she shouldn't press her luck by being in the basement for too long. The flashlight beam whips across the floor, catching on something red and wet before it finds the thing in the room that is making those thick

slippery sounds, the rattling and the growling and the scrabbling. The thing that she is really here to see.

The thing sees her back with wide brown eyes. The whites
of the eyes are red. There is a froth of saliva on the chin, and
the froth is pink because of the blood that seeps from the cut-
wide corners of the lips.

The thing is a man.

The man is on the ground, his arms and legs spread in an X
just like the big wooden one.

He is trying so hard to scream.

Vera points the flashlight at the thing's middle, instead of
at his eyes, so as not to blind him. The light illuminates his
face, though. The formerly-white cotton that gags his mouth
is stained brown and red and pink. It is jammed deep into his
mouth, so deep that only a little tongue of it hangs from between his lips.

Vera tiptoes closer.

The man's arms and legs are tethered to four rings, thick
metal rings sunk into the cement floor, rings that for some reason make Vera think of cowboys tying up horses. The tethers,
she sees as she gets closer, are plastic-covered bike locks. One is
blue and one is purple and two are green. The one she uses to
lock her own bicycle up to the rack in front of the diner downtown is blue too. She thinks Brandon's might be red but she
can't quite remember.

The man strains and thrashes, his elbows slipping in the
pooled blood beneath him. The bike chains don't rattle because
they're wrapped in that semi-clear plastic. They just thud dully,
and the thudding is barely audible over the muffled sound of
him trying to scream.

Vera tiptoes up to him and holds a finger to her lips. The

man meets her eyes. He's panting heavily through his nose, the sound of his breath thick and mucousy because he's been crying. Vera taps her finger to her lips again, raising her eyebrows meaningfully.

The man falls silent. He nods, his eyes so wide that they almost look lidless.

Vera sets the flashlight down on the floor. The beam throws the man's shadow high and dark onto the wall behind him. She tiptoes closer to him, careful to keep her feet away from the blood. There's not so much blood as she'd first thought, not a big spreading puddle. There's only a little, really.

Vera leans over the man and uses two fingers to pluck at the brown cotton that hangs from his mouth.

He makes a gurgling sound. She pauses. When he's quiet again, she pulls at the cotton again. It slides out of his mouth like a magician's trick-scarves, unraveling for so much longer than it looks like it should be able to. When it's almost all the way out, the man gags and coughs, retches, turns his head. A thin stream of green liquid spills from his mouth.

"Gross," Vera whispers.

The man spits bile at the floor. Vera flinches, even though none of it lands on her.

"You have to help," the man says. "He keeps the keys on him. I think he lives here, I think—"

"Shhh," Vera says. "You have to be quiet."

"I'm not the first," the man whispers frantically. "He has a whole setup down here, he's done this before. He has a routine, a schedule, he's organized. And he's crazy, he thinks he has to get something out of me, I don't know—I'm chained up over a drain so the smell doesn't—"

"Hsst," Vera hisses, harsh this time. "Be quiet! Do you want to get me caught?"

The man's mouth snaps shut. The smell of his bile is sharp in a way that makes Vera's mouth water unpleasantly. She pulls the collar of her shirt up over her nose, then crouches down to wipe at the man's face with the wad of stained cotton. It helps a little.

She stays where she is, crouched next to the man on the floor, studying his face. He has a doll-like smile because of the holes in his cheeks, which look wet instead of scabby. They must be fresh, from tonight, or maybe last night. His moustache curls down over his top lip; it's black with gummed-up old blood. His bottom lip has a hole too. His eyes seem fine, although one of them is inflamed and weeping.

She isn't sure if she wants to see the rest of him. He's naked, but the flashlight is on the floor, so Vera can mostly only see the broad expanse of his side in her peripheral vision. She's curious about what the rest of him looks like—the quick sweep of her flashlight gave her an impression of loose meat and mottled purple skin—but the thought of looking over his pale, naked body from this close-up makes her stomach twitch.

She decides not to look. Not this time.

"What's your name?" she whispers.

The man's eyes flash bright with desperate hope. "Arnold," he hisses back. His voice is tight with pain. "My name is Arnold, can you help me? Please, you can get me out of here. You can help me. There are cable-cutters in the toolbench—" He cuts himself off with a shudder, closing his eyes. His jaw trembles, flecks of saliva catching on his newly pierced bottom lip.

He does not want to talk about the tool bench and what's

inside it. Vera decides not to make him talk about it. She doesn't want him to throw up again, and besides, she's been down here too long already. Her skin feels alive and electric and she listens every second for the sound of the doorknob at the top of the stairs turning.

"It's okay," she says, still whispering. She fidgets with the cotton gag. "You don't have to talk about it."

"You have to cut me loose, sweetheart," Arnold says, his whisper breaking into fully voiced speech. "You have to cut me loose and help me get out of here. I promise—I promise no one will be mad at you," he adds. "You'll be a big hero if you just go into the . . . the toolbench, and get cable-cutters, and cut me free."

"You have to be quiet," she says. He nods frantically. She frowns. "I'll get in big trouble. I'm not supposed to be down here."

"You won't," he hisses. "You won't get in trouble, I'll make sure of it, we'll get out of here together, please, you have to—"

"Shh!" Vera looks behind her, up to the staircase, the back of her neck prickling with warning. She isn't sure if she heard a footstep or if it was just the house settling. That fixes it: she has to get out of here. "I told you, you have to be quiet," she says. "Anyhow, I can't let you go. Dad would be upset."

"Please—"

"I just wanted to come down and tell you," she continues, ignoring the interruption, "not to worry."

"What do you mean?" Arnold says, not whispering at all. Not even bothering to try to be quiet.

Vera purses her lips. After a moment of consideration, she concludes that her options have run out. Arnold is not being careful enough. He is not being quiet enough. He is not listening to her.

She pushes the rag back into his mouth. The stained cotton is damp with the sweat of her palms and with the smear of bile she wiped away from his face. Her fingers brush his stiff, matted-up moustache, and she wrinkles her nose, but she keeps pushing the cotton between his chapped lips until it's nearly invisible.

The whole time, he tries to yell, thrashes around, makes an enormous racket. That's how Vera knows that she is right to gag him: he wants to make noise, wants to get her in trouble even though she's trying to help him.

When she's done, she rocks back on her heels and regards him. His eyes are wide and pleading. He keeps making wet, gurgling throat-noises at her. "I'm sorry about that," she says. "But I asked you to be quiet, and you wouldn't. Anyway, like I was saying, I just wanted to tell you not to worry."

She shifts her weight and stands up, her legs tingling. She picks up the yellow flashlight with both hands and points the beam at the cement floor between her feet and Arnold's body. The light reflects off the floor, and she can see more of him in the ambient glow. His body is a broken landscape of mottled purple flesh and oozing round wounds. The soft mess of him is cradled by the dip in the floor, the dip that leads to the drain he's perched on top of.

Vera decides that she's sure that she doesn't want to see all of him, not this close-up. She's resolved on the subject now that there's more light on him. It's too much all at once. Her gaze keeps flinching away from his body, back to his increasingly red face. "He's had you for thirteen days now. I know it's been a challenge," she adds, using the phrase her sixth-grade teacher uses to soften the blow when she fails yet another spelling test. "I know it's been difficult for you, and you're probably worried that it'll keep going like this forever. So I thought I should let you know that he's going to kill you tomorrow. It'll be over really soon."

This is true, but it isn't why she came downstairs. She wanted to see, is all. She wanted to see the basement with both eyes, instead of just one. She wanted to look, instead of just peeking.

Arnold keeps on trying to scream. His face is a very dark purple now, and the sounds coming from his throat are raw and desperate, but not too loud. Not now that he's gagged.

"Well," Vera says awkwardly. "I just wanted to let you know." She isn't sure how to say goodbye to him, so she doesn't. She turns around and pads her way back to the stairs, leaving Arnold in the dark.

When she gets to the top of the stairs, she presses her ear to the door for a long time before easing the key around her neck into the lock. In under a minute, the flashlight is in the kitchen and Vera is back in her bed.

The clock on her nightstand reads 03:15. Her heart is pounding. She is trembling.

She did it.

She went and looked for herself, looked up-close, *touched* the thing in the basement with *her own hands*. She didn't get caught. She's not going to tell Brandon about this, she knows without having to decide, and she won't bring him down into the basement no matter how much he presses. This is just for her. No one will ever know that she went where she isn't allowed, that she saw what she isn't supposed to see.

In the morning, Vera will notice something dark and thick

and sticky smeared across the backs of her hands, the back of her neck. She will scrub it off with the intimate, adrenal panic that comes with disposing of evidence. But for now, she is filled only with bright, burning triumph. That friend she imagines, the one who always believes in her, would be so impressed. They would be staggered. They would wrap her in a tight proud hug and tell her *I knew you could do it*.

Vera buries her face in her pillow, feeling the ghost of that hug, and she allows herself a wide, warm grin.

She falls asleep to the faint, familiar animal noises that come from beneath her bed, and she does not dream about anything at all.

CHAPTER EIGHTEEN

Vera woke up underwater. A lake had entered her bedroom in the night, while she tried not to dream about her dying mother or the artist in the cottage. A lake had entered her bedroom and the weight of sleep had dragged her to the bottom of it.

It was so dark. And the darkness had heft to it, pressing in around her on all sides. She had kicked off the covers at some point. It was so cold and that cold kissed every exposed inch of her skin with a stinging chill. Her limbs were too slow for the atmosphere she was in. Her lungs were not made for this. She was not made for this.

Struggling against the clutching, stifling panic that gripped her, Vera forced breath into her lungs and told herself that it was all okay. Whatever nightmare it was she'd woken from, it was over now, and she was safe in her bed, awake and whole. Everything was fine. There was air.

She blinked a few times. Shapes began to detach themselves from the darkness: the squat bulk of the dresser with her father's letters in the bottom drawer, the fall of the curtains, the tall shadow of the open closet door.

Wait. No, that couldn't be right. The closet door wasn't open—was it? It was too dark in the bedroom for her to be able to tell. She'd closed it before she got into bed, after her ridiculous inspection of the suitcases. But she couldn't remember if she'd felt the click of the latch. Maybe she'd left it ajar.

Because now she was certain. It was ajar. It was definitely ajar. Only a little, just enough for her to see the contour of the edge of the door itself.

She didn't want to approach that too-inviting slit of darkness. She didn't feel like confronting the irrational, animal fear that told her not to let her feet touch the floor until daybreak. She decided to indulge herself. She would not get out of bed to close that closet door. Not until morning.

But that didn't mean she could rest. Even if she didn't acknowledge the hungry fear that was tugging her eyes back to that shadowy gap—even if she ignored the way it gnawed at her attention—there was the cold to consider. This wasn't the usual dry, recycled chill of the air conditioner. The air in the bedroom hung fat and dense, as humid as an oncoming thunderstorm. Moisture beaded on Vera's skin; she couldn't tell if it was sweat or condensation.

She wanted to fall back asleep, to retreat to the plush velvet warmth that waited for her there. The freezing, wet air was probably just an air conditioner malfunction, she told herself. It could all wait until tomorrow. She would close the closet door in the morning, and she would deal with the air conditioner in the morning. *After* a good night's sleep.

She sat up and reached to the foot of the bed to retrieve the blankets she must have kicked away in her sleep.

But they weren't there.

Her eyes scanned the soft white landscape of the fitted sheet that hugged the mattress. The bed was bare.

The blankets were gone. The topsheet and the quilt had both been tugged free of the weight of the mattress, untucked and discarded. Vera shivered violently, and some helpful bit of memory whispered a reminder of the dream: *the cold is inside you, and you can get it out if you try.*

Her fingers crawled spiderlike over her thighs. She fought to still them but heedless, they crept up to her belly, leaving trails through the dew that was collecting there. She gave in to the need to *check,* laying her palms flat over her skin and pressing down hard. A sharp thread of adrenaline twisted in her chest, putting sparks into her blood. On a deep, visceral level, she wasn't sure what her hands were going to find.

But her flesh was solid as ever. There was no hole waiting for her fingers, waiting for her to pull the cold out from inside. The cold was on the outside, in the room. It was something separate from the thing that Vera was.

She would have felt silly for having questioned that fact, if only the memory of her fingers slipping into her core hadn't been so stark. It was only a dream, she reminded herself. It was only a dream, but the reminder didn't stop her trembling fingers from testing the certainty of her own skin, prodding the flesh hard enough to leave bruises.

Vera flopped back onto the mattress, pressing the heels of her hands to her eyes until bright lights flashed behind her eyelids. "Come on," she whispered. "Grow up." Her jaw was tight, almost chattering. It was so goddamn *cold.* She dragged her hands away from her eyes and through her hair, her fingers snagging on a damp tangle near the crown of her head. "Enough," she hissed aloud, trying to speak to whatever part of her was so panicked by darkness, by cold, by humidity.

With immense effort, she swam upright again. She tucked her almost-numb feet beneath her to warm them. Bracing her

•

hands on her knees, squinting into the darkness, she peered over the edge of the bed to find the covers.

The floor on the side of the bed that faced the door was bare. The bedskirt gently fluttered, wafting in some invisible current of air as the house breathed. Vera stared hard at that fluttering, but it remained even and steady, and she decided not to let it bother the part of her brain that knew to watch for movement in the tall grass.

The foot of the bed was the same.

The side of the bed that was farthest from the door looked bare too, at first—but then Vera leaned a little too far over the edge of the mattress.

Her wet palms slid off the shelf of her knees. She cried out, nearly toppled off the edge of the bed, caught herself on the edge of the frame. The metal dug painfully into the heels of her hands. Her damp skin squeaked against the brass and the bed-frame gave an ominous creak. The only way she could catch herself was to rise up on all fours, try to back away from the edge of the bed before she fell, and that's just what she was doing—but her hands were too wet and the brass of the bed was too slippery, and her hands shot off the metal.

She toppled, but she didn't fall, not quite. She had already managed to get a leg out from underneath herself and some-how, instead of tumbling off the edge of the bed, she flailed out with that leg and she didn't fall onto her face because her foot landed firmly on the floor.

She panted hard with the effort of catching herself.

The rippling bedskirt brushed her ankle.

Vera shrieked and scrambled back into the bed. As she did, her foot caught on something loose and damp on the floor, something that shifted beneath her big toe. She looked down in violent revulsion—and she saw the corner of her quilt.

She had been standing on it.

It was sticking out from beneath the bedskirt.

Vera did not breathe. Gently, slowly, she pulled her hand back away from the edge of the bed. She returned to the position she'd held before, with her feet tucked beneath her. That position had felt warm and secure before, a way to keep her toes from freezing off.

Now it felt like readiness.

She was a coiled spring. She could not hear her own heart-beat. She could not hear anything. The only thing she could hear was the cold, a fast sharp rush of water slapping her again and again. She pushed her hair away from her face once more, yanking it back into an almost-ponytail, and she felt a trickle of icewater run down the back of her neck, so cold that she choked on her own breath.

She didn't realize she was whispering until she accidentally bit her own lip. "No no no no no," she was saying, a nonsense sound, a meaningless tap of her tongue against her hard palate.

Her eyes were locked onto that corner of the quilt. How had it gotten all the way under the bed? It couldn't have simply fallen there, couldn't have landed that way. Maybe it could have somehow fallen a little way under the bed, sure, maybe through some weird puddling of the fabric. But there were only a few inches of blanket sticking out from beneath the bed-skirt, a tiny peek of fabric smaller than one of her hands, and it simply wasn't possible that the blanket could have wound up like that on its own.

The bedskirt rippled steadily.

She looked back at the closet door. It was more ajar than it had been before, or maybe her eyes had simply adjusted better to the dark. It was as inviting as a bitten lip, and Vera wished she could return to the time when that closet was the safest place in the world, a place to climb into and tuck herself away from everything that was painful and frightening. That time seemed so far away, and so did the door to the bedroom, and she was so cold that she couldn't think, and the air was rushing down into her throat too thick and fast to breathe.

She flexed her fingers trying to snap, not embarrassed, not resisting the impulse. She tried, but her fingers were half-numb and she couldn't do it. She sat back on her heels, stuck her fingers into her mouth to try to warm them enough to move but the inside of her mouth was cold too. She tried to ignore the sharp, brassy taste of her skin. But the taste just grew stronger, more and more acidic, until her mouth was flooded with thick saliva and she finally recognized what she was tasting.

It was the tart, syrupy flavor of lemonade.

She pulled her hand away from her mouth, coughing, a sob building in her throat, a shiver winding its way from her lap to the base of her skull. Vera wrapped her arms around herself. The wet fabric of her shirt stuck to her arms and her chest. She kept her eyes closed tight, her mouth clamped shut, her head tucked down between her hunched shoulders. Cold water dripped from her forehead down her nose, dripped onto her clenched arms, only was it water or was it fucking lemonade, *taptaptaptaptap*—

An animal urgency gripped her, adrenaline slapping her brain with lightning, and she scrabbled over the edge of the bed with the kind of speed that can only belong to fear, folding herself double and reaching with a hand she couldn't feel. She grabbed the corner of the quilt. It only took three tries to get a solid grip on it and then she yanked it hard as she could, yanked as if she were freeing it from beneath a stone.

She almost had it. She pulled one more time, straining, sure that the fucking thing would come loose from whatever kind of stuck it was.

Something warm folded over her fingers, giving her hand a gentle, tender squeeze.

Vera jerked and fell back hard on the mattress. Her head bounced back onto her pillows. Her quilt was in her arms, the whole thing, with the bedsheet wrapped up in it. Together, the two formed a tight rope of twisted fabric. She clutched them to her chest, panting hard, something between a wild giggle and a sob leaping from her throat. She pressed her hand to her mouth to cover it before anyone heard.

Silly, she thought. *Who would be here to hear you?*

Her fingers were warm against her lips, and her lips were warm against her fingers. She lifted a hand to her hair, and found that it was only a little damp, the kind of damp that comes from fear and sweat and sleep.

The breath in her lungs felt like air instead of water.

It was over. Whatever it was—a fit of insanity, a hallucination, a panic attack?—it was over.

Ridiculous. This was so ridiculous. She was alive and everything was normal again. The blankets had fallen under the bed somehow, that was all, and now she had them, and she could laugh as loud as she needed to. She could laugh at her own foolish, baseless panic.

She lay still, hugging the twist of blankets tight to her chest. She stayed just like that, ignoring the tingle in her fingers where some sudden awful warmth had touched them, until she couldn't feel her heart battering itself against her sternum like a bird dying against a shut window.

Behind the curtains, the windows showed the thin blue-gray light that comes just before dawn.

Vera drank in that light as she untangled the sheet from the quilt. Not bothering to tuck anything in, she spread both of them out on top of herself and let the weight of the blankets settle themselves flat. The terror had drained out of her, leaving extra gravity behind. She was going to sleep, she decided, until she was done sleeping; if she didn't wake up until noon, so be it. Daphne wouldn't die if her lemonade was delivered a few hours late.

Or maybe, Vera thought vaguely, settling back into the pillows—maybe she *would* die. Maybe it wouldn't be so bad to skip to the end of all this.

That was a Wrong Thought. It was the kind of thought Vera didn't usually allow herself to have. But she was so tired, and her eyes fluttered shut before she could check herself. Before she could remind herself that she didn't have thoughts like that.

She wasn't like that.

Not anymore.

The deep dark womb of sleep began to wrap itself around her. She laid her hands gently on top of the covers, folding them across her solar plexus, and in the moments before the world drifted away from her, peaceful and unthinking, her fingers gently closed into fists.

She had two handfuls of quilt. She wasn't gripping them very tightly, but it was enough. Enough to hold some small corner of her attention. Enough that, just as she truly eased into the deep dark absence of unconsciousness, the movement of the quilt snapped her awake again.

She told herself that it was only her subconscious, like her nearly-sleeping brain startling with the phantom sensation of falling. But now she was awake, heart-poundingly awake, and she couldn't tell herself that she was imagining the sensation of the quilt stretching taut.

She tightened her grip on it, and the pull on the fabric grew stronger.

The pull was coming from the side of the bed.

Stitches snapped beneath her palm, *pop pop pop*. Vera's hands reflexively flew open at the sensation, and the quilt was dragged off her, vanishing over the edge of the mattress. She listened to the *hush* of fabric against floorboard as it slithered beneath the bed.

She grabbed at the topsheet, her entire body rigid with terror, her eyes open so wide that they ached. She stayed like that, waiting for a tug on the sheet that would start gentle and get stronger and stronger until it was irresistible. Waiting to find out if that brush of warmth would find her skin again. Waiting for a voice to tell her that everything was going to be okay.

Waiting for dawn.

CHAPTER NINETEEN

The basement door had a pulse in Vera's memory. She thought of it as swollen, thrumming, coriaceous. There was no reason for the door to be a warm and vital thing. It was identical in every regard to her bedroom door, with the exception of the lock and the slant at the top. But when she stood in front of the two doors, holding the plastic sorting bins in her hands and listening to the steady wet noise of her mother's breathing in the next room, Vera felt sure: if she grasped the knob of the basement door, the muscle of it would give beneath her fingers.

She had planned to save the work of emptying out the basement for last. She had planned to wait until after Daphne was gone, until after James Duvall was gone, until after the rest of the house was empty and ready to sell. But that trip to the bar, the encounter with Brandon after all those years, the taste of lemonade in the air and the popping seams on her quilt—all of it had uncapped a well inside her.

Hunger stirred in the depths, sending echoing ripples up her spine. She couldn't make herself wait. Not anymore. She needed it now.

She needed to see what was down there, beneath the place where she slept.

Trembling with want, Vera put the plastic bins down in front of the door to her bedroom. Her palms were damp with anticipation. She wiped her hands on her jeans. She tugged at the chain around her neck, pulled until the full length of it slipped out from beneath her shirt.

At this point, touching the key was as familiar as touching her own skin. It was smooth and brassy from years of wear. The chain wasn't long enough for her to fit it into the door-knob without stooping—she'd grown too much for that—so she lifted it over her head instead.

The doorknob was as cool as a dead thing against her palm. It shouldn't have been a shock, but she still felt a sharp flash of disgust at the lifeless chill of the metal. She opened the door just a crack before returning the necklace to its place. The fa-miliar tug of the key dropping into her collar was a relief; the strength of the chain, an unexpected comfort.

She couldn't lose that key. Not ever—but especially not once she was inside.

The moment she saw the stairs, Vera forgot about the plastic bins. She forgot that she was supposed to sort through what-ever might be left at the bottom of those stairs. She looked down into the impenetrable darkness and felt an answering call to the scrabbling at the bottom of the lidless well inside her.

She drew a slow breath and held it. She held it as she reached for the lightswitch on the wall beside the door, held it as she stroked her index finger over the off-white nub of plastic, held it as she pressed her thumb to the underside of the switch and pushed gently, persistently *up*.

The lights flickered on, bright white and humming. Vera let the held breath out in a rush, tempering the stale air of the basement with the damp warmth of her own lungs. This place had been alone for so long.

Bare fluorescent tubes hung from the ceiling, suspended by thin chains. The reflected light of the fluorescents gleamed off the vast expanse of plexiglass that covered the floor. Under that layer of plexiglass, the polished cement floor glowed, but the light was marred in places by the matte stripes of bootprints.

Shoes in the house—Vera frowned at the gall of it, remembering the sight of polished black shoes crossing the threshold of the Crowder House, one pair after the other, bringing the outside in.

Vera had thought that her mother hadn't come down here, not ever, not even once. Not after the investigation was closed and the police were finished turning the house inside-out. Daphne had no respect for the heart of the house, so it made sense that she would avoid it. In fairness, Vera hadn't gone in either, not after everything that happened. She had never dared to sneak out of her room in the night with her key, even though she probably could have gotten away with it. The risk was too high. She'd been too terrified of the consequences of her mother catching her in there again.

She would have understood if the basement had remained untouched. But this. This was worse. Her mother had come down here to let people in so they could carefully measure the room, so they could preserve it under perfectly clear, perfectly cut tiles of plexiglass, screwed and sealed into place so that the violation of this space by the police—and later, by Hammett Duvall—would be preserved forever.

Vera stepped around an empty lipstick-stained paper coffee cup on the stairs, her eyes casting hungrily around the room. The police had left more of themselves here than of Francis, and after them had come the guests, curious, poking, prodding, pulling, taking. All in the name of *inspiration*. The marks of the former were under the plexiglass—cigarette butts and bootprints, numbered paper stickers and mildew-blotches of fingerprint dust. The marks of the latter were on top of it—scuffs and smudges, scraps of paper, splotches of paint.

The things Francis built with his strong hands were gone, pulled up out of the floor and off the wall a little at a time. His toolbench was still there, but the drawers were open and empty. Some of them were missing, leaving gaping hollows like the sockets of pulled teeth. Those gaps were smooth, every loose splinter of wood long-since claimed by visitors who had never met Francis. Never spoken to him. Never felt the warmth of his strong hands.

There was ash on the floor, the faint odor of stale smoke.

There were holes in the cement beneath the plexiglass, where the police had pulled up the anchors Francis Crowder had sunk into the floor back when he was building this basement, back before Vera was born, back when she was just a plan her parents were making, one of them enthusiastic and the other reluctant.

Between the police and the visitors, they'd pulled those anchors up and taken them, along with everything that her father had loved best about this room, and they'd left their garbage and their filth behind.

"Animals," Vera muttered, kicking at a tangle of light blue nitrile gloves splotched with crusts of paint. She looked up at the grid of pipes on the eastern side of the ceiling. There were eight lengths of one-inch-diameter pipe in all, fixed together with ceiling anchors and plumber's tape into a six-foot-square grid. The pipes were mostly black with grease but broad stripes of them were shiny and silver, the grease worn away in places by long hours of friction. The shiniest sections were at the four places in the middle of the grid, where the pipes intersected to form a stable, strong, foot-wide square.

They hadn't taken those, at least. They hadn't understood why those pipes might be important. They hadn't spotted the polished sections of the metal.

The pipes hung just six inches from the plaster surface of the ceiling, which was painted black. That, Vera supposed, was the only explanation for how her father had forgotten about what was in the center of that stable, foot-wide square in the middle of the grid. Or maybe he'd just thought it didn't matter—maybe he'd thought he was the only one who would ever notice the hole.

The room below the stairs had been his office until the summer Vera was eleven, when she and Francis had traded spaces. Daphne didn't like the noise that Vera's open bedroom window let in, back when Vera's bedroom was upstairs, just down the hall from the bedroom Daphne and Francis shared; Vera couldn't stand the idea of sleeping with the windows closed. So they swapped. Her bedroom upstairs became his office, and his office downstairs became her bedroom.

He couldn't have planned for Vera to be in that bedroom, not when he built the house. He also couldn't have come up with an excuse not to switch with her without acknowledging the reason for the hours he spent locked away in his office.

And he couldn't have known that she would find the hole under the pillow-end of her bed. He couldn't have. What kind of person would foresee that and let it happen anyway?

She'd thought it through a thousand times, and in the end, she'd had to decide what to believe. The safest thing was to trust that there was no way he could have anticipated that she would get so invested in the floor of her bedroom, in the search for that gap between the boards that had seemed to hold her hand when she was afraid.

And that meant that he couldn't have planned for her to spot the faint thread of light around the loose floorboard beneath her bed. He couldn't have planned for her to squeeze herself between the bedframe and the floor with a butter knife to pry that floorboard up. Vera remembered how cartoonishly pleased she'd been with what she found beneath the wood. It was made of a lens set into a stainless steel tube. It smelled ever so faintly of sweet wood and sweat. Only in hindsight did she recognize it for what it was—a peephole, just like the one in the front door, the one that was too high up for Vera to look out of.

It was made for watching. It was made for peeking.

So Vera had peeked.

She only saw shadows that first night. She took too long to get the floorboard up, and at some point while she'd been working, the basement lights turned off. Without the glow of the fluorescents, it was too dark for her to see anything worth looking at. She'd gone back to bed bored and disappointed, and frustrated with the world for being a boring, disappointing place.

She'd almost forgotten about the lens, until the night a few weeks later when she'd heard scrabbling, groaning noises below her bed, and she'd recalled what her father had once told her about the animals in the basement.

Possums, he'd said, and racoons, and their babies.

The next time she woke in the night to the animal noises that came from beneath her bed, Vera had looked through the lens again. She wanted to see the animals. She wanted to see the babies. She wanted to see them before her father got them out of the basement, before he set them free. She believed him that they could be dangerous, so she wasn't going to go into the basement to see them. But looking, she thought—just looking—just peeking—that couldn't be so dangerous.

That night, the light had been on, and for the first time, she'd seen her father's work.

Now, in the almost-empty basement, with her bare foot planted on a light-blue glove, Vera looked up at that square of ceiling. She thought of the other side of the argument she'd been having with herself for so many years, the side she usually pushed away because it felt so silly and childish. Because it didn't make any sense.

There was never a good answer to the sounds she'd heard, and why she'd been able to hear them. The house was so well insulated, each room nearly soundproof, and this room was the most carefully built of them all. But she'd always been able to hear her father's noises in the night, when he was in the basement. And she'd always been able to hear her parents fighting, and her father's heavy footfalls.

Unless, a long-smothered corner of her memory reminded her, she snapped four times.

She shook that whisper off, unwilling to engage with it. It must have been intentional. Francis built his office to sit above his work. He must have wanted to see and hear what happened in the basement in his absence. She could picture him so easily, sitting at his desk, listening to the wet thumps of a man struggling to escape.

If that had been intentional, he would have known that Vera could hear, wouldn't he? He would have known that she'd know about his projects.

Now, standing in the basement among the detritus of the investigation, Vera tried hard to spot the peephole the way

Francis would have seen it, from below. She couldn't find it, not even standing right under the pipes with her neck tilted back at a dizzying angle.

The floor beneath her tilted on an ever-so-slight grade, the cement under the plexiglass tipping down toward the six-inch-wide drain in the floor. That drain was perfectly framed by a neat circular hole in the plexiglass. It was covered in a silver metal strainer, but Vera could still feel the faintest breath of warm air from inside the pipe. A loose hair lifted away from her face. Heat from wherever the pipe led off to, she supposed, rising up into the cool of the house. She wondered if Francis had ever felt that warmth.

Scanning the plaster at the center of those pipes was starting to make her eyes ache, but she still couldn't see the peephole. Maybe, she thought, if she got the stepladder from the kitchen and climbed up there. Not that there was any point, but she wanted to see what Francis saw.

She wanted to see what they saw, too—the men her father brought to this basement. And they weren't standing on the ground when they were in this part of the room. They were always suspended, hanging by an elaborate system of knots that kept them too still to struggle, kept them steady and still, kept them right where they needed to be for her father to do his work—

Vera's eyes landed on something wrong.

There was a scratch in the ceiling. Just like the deep scratch in the wall next to the stairs. It was up behind the pipes, a scar in the plaster, as stark as if someone had dug the tip of a butter knife into the surface of a full pint of ice cream. Vera would wonder how she hadn't noticed it sooner, except that it was perfectly aligned with one of the lengths of pipe, and it was only in walking toward the pipes that she'd shifted her perspective enough to spot it.

Vera stared at the scratch. She couldn't imagine how it had gotten there. Daphne hadn't done this—the chances that she'd spent any time in the basement at all were nonexistent. Francis wouldn't have done it either; he loved the Crowder House too much to scar it, loved it almost as much as he'd loved Vera herself.

Vera was standing right under it now, her head tipped all the way back, the smooth skin of her throat stretched as taut as a fitted sheet straining across a mattress. Her eyes ached as she tried to trace the contours of the scratch in the ceiling, tried to understand what had injured the house like that. The edges of her vision seemed to darken. She held her breath and she knew, she *knew* that if she looked long enough, she'd understand what had happened.

Something inside the ceiling moved.

The first thing Vera's brain shouted was *rat,* but that wasn't right. The noise wasn't a rat-noise. It wasn't a scrabbling skittering rush of movement, wasn't the thumping tumble that she knew so well from the many shitty apartments she'd lived in. The noise that came from inside the plaster was a long dragging scrape, like the sound of furniture ruining wood.

Everything inside Vera froze. Her eyes watered, but she did not blink. She waited to hear the sound again. Her hands snapped into fists as she waited, waited, waited. She swallowed hard.

She hadn't imagined the noise. That wasn't even a question. It had been loud and grinding, almost tangible. There was no writing it off.

Waiting for it to happen again was silly. Vera knew that. Whatever had made the noise would still be there even if it didn't make another sound. But she was stuck, her mouth dry, her heart beating in slow hard steady punches. She couldn't tell if she was trapped or hungry, frightened or eager, predator or prey.

She unclenched her right fist. Slowly, deliberately, keeping her eyes on the ceiling, she snapped her fingers.

Once.

Twice.

Three times.

At the fourth snap the noise came again, and Vera didn't need to wait anymore. She ran. The instant she heard that sharp dig into the ceiling overhead her legs took her to the stairs.

She moved faster than she'd ever thought she could. The steps vanished under her feet three at a time. She unlocked the door with sharp quick movements of her hands, stepped out into the entryway, didn't hesitate before kicking aside the plastic bins that still blocked the door to her bedroom. The door gave way to the slap of her palm. She let it slam hard into the wall.

Standing in the doorway, Vera looked around the room, panting. This was where the sound had come from. There could be no question of that. Her eyes tracked the dust motes that hung in the afternoon sunlight, the shadows that shifted behind her bedroom curtain, the rippling motion of the bedskirt.

The rippling motion of the bedskirt.

Something furious and animal had driven Vera up the stairs. She let that instinct pull her toward the bed with long, confident strides. In one fluid motion she knelt and yanked the bedskirt up to look beneath.

Nothing. There was nothing.

Vera sat back on her heels, suddenly dizzy, suddenly tired. Sweetness drifted across the back of her throat and she swallowed reflexively, her throat clutching at nothing. She unclenched her fist, dropped the bedskirt, flexed her fingers to get the blood back into them.

There was nothing under the bed. There was nothing in this room, nothing at all. There couldn't have been—the bins had still been in place in front of the door, and how could anything have gotten out of the room without moving them? They had still been in the place where she set them down, she thought, the exact place.

She was almost certain of that.

But she was just as certain that someone had been in her bedroom.

She turned and sat, leaned against the mattress and let her head fall back. She closed her eyes and waited for her heartbeat to return to normal. It was the house, she thought. It was the house, liquefying her brain. Being back here, being around her mother, all that fucking lemonade—it was shaking her screws loose.

But she knew she hadn't been hearing things. Not twice in a row. She might have imagined the way the bedskirt was moving, as if fingers had just brushed along the back of it—that could have been in her head.

But not that sound. That had been real.

She bent to lift the bedskirt again, slower this time, and took a longer look beneath the bed. The floor brushed her cheek, making her shiver.

There was nothing down there. Not even a shadow. Not even dust.

Vera frowned. There should have been dust under the bed. There had been dust under the bed last time she looked. But now, the floor shone clean. Not all of it: she let her eyes travel to the floor beneath the foot of the bed, and there was a matte blanket of dust there, gathering around the bedposts in little eddies. But the dust ended patchily just a foot or so into the shadows beneath the bed. It was a clear demarcation, the place where the gray ended.

And, she realized as she looked closer, she was wrong. There *was* something there. Something near the head of the bed. Something small and flat, something the size of a business card.

Something that didn't belong.

Vera got up and shut the door. There was no lock on the knob, an artifact of her childhood: her parents hadn't wanted her to have a door that locked. They said that it was in case something bad happened in the night and they needed to get to her. She wasn't sure now if that was good parenting or bad. Maybe it didn't matter. In a movement that still felt familiar even after all these years, she pushed the chair from her desk in front of the door, so that she'd at least have a warning if someone tried to come into the room.

She walked back to her bed and dropped to her belly on the floor. She wouldn't fit under the bed, she didn't think, but she might be able to reach the little rectangle anyway. She might be able to manage.

She lifted the bedskirt and edged under it.

Vera reached with her right arm, reached until her elbow popped. The lip of the bedframe dug painfully into the meat on the back of her shoulder. She wasn't even close: that rectangle was at least six inches away from her fingertips.

She sighed, her breath stirring a few loose hairs that had

fallen into her face. Every time she inhaled, pain flared in her shoulder.

Vera squinted at the small flat thing beyond her fingers. She turned her head to the side, pressed her cheek to the floor, exhaled hard. Then she shoved with her toes, pushing herself further beneath the bed. That nearly did the job. Emptying her lungs made her small enough to fit.

But she still wasn't close enough.

She flexed her feet again and slid forward. The lip of the bedframe scraped her back. Almost, almost, another inch and she would have it. An oh-god-no-I'm-stuck panic threatened to rise in her chest.

She swallowed it.

Her eyes ached from looking up and to the side. Her ear was bending back along the side of her head because she was pressed so hard to the floor. Everything hurt, but she was so close to getting whatever it was.

She bit the inside of her cheek, reached hard as she could, and pushed herself forward one more time.

There—finally—she had it. She picked the thing up with clumsy fingers, dropped it, picked it up again. She slid her elbow back toward her face, keeping her arm flush with the floor—and then, pain, pain, pain. She gasped with the sudden bright heat of it. The gasp itself was painful, her spine crushed against the ribs of the bedframe that supported her mattress. But it wasn't as painful as whatever sharp, stabbing thing had just happened to the soft meat of her arm.

Vera scooted out from under the bed too fast, losing skin to the lip of the bedframe, knocking her head against the brass, dropping the thing in her hand. She left a thin smear of blood behind, a trail marking where her forearm dragged along the wood. When she was free of the bed, she stumbled backward on her hands, crablike, her back slamming into the dresser. She sat hard, sucking in air, pressing her spine hard against the wood that seemed to thrum with the promise of the letters within.

"What," she panted, "what? What the fuck?"

She looked at her arm, which was oozing blood steadily. She wiped ineffectively at the blood with her thumb, trying to see the wound. There it was—an inch-long gouge, ending in a fat, jagged splinter. The splinter was buried deep beneath the skin of her arm. She couldn't even see the end of it. She would need tweezers to get it out, and a bandage at the ready, judging by the amount of blood that was already welling up around it.

"Fuck," she said, a little louder this time. This wasn't just painful. It was *offensive*. There had never been any splinters in her bedroom floor before. Her father had laid the floors in himself, had sanded them smooth as satin, had finished and sealed them with infinite care. The presence of the splinter was infuriating, an insult, and looking at it put a knot into Vera's throat. "Fuck *this*."

Her eyes traced the streak of blood she'd left on the floor, followed it under the bed.

She exploded upright, her body taut with the primal rage of sudden injury. She shoved hard at the heavy bedframe with both hands. It shifted, the feet of it scraping across the floor with a bright ugly noise that was nothing at all like the sound she'd heard from the basement. She shoved it again. It moved a foot, eighteen inches, two feet, and then she could see the end of the trail of blood, could see where that vicious splinter had come from. Could see the thing she'd dropped.

It was the thin bit of wood that covered the peephole in the floor. It had been pried up somehow. The lens of the peephole winked up at her from the rectangle of black subfloor where it was usually hidden.

On either side of that gap in the floorboards, deep gouges had been dug into the wood—five on each side, ten in all, spaced like wide-set fingers. The long furrows were lush with splinters, some of them worse than the one that was burrowed deep into the flesh of Vera's arm.

Without thinking, Vera bent to pick up the little piece of wood she'd dropped. She put it over the lens, pressed gently, waiting to feel it click into place. But it didn't click into place. There was resistance, and when she pushed, something crunched.

She pulled the wood away, startled, expecting to see broken glass. But what she saw instead was the crinkled edge of a piece of paper.

It hadn't been there before, when she'd pressed her eye to this peephole as a kid. She was sure of it. The page was wrapped around the old peephole, in a tight curl that only *just* poked up beyond the edges of the tube with the glass set into it. That's what had crinkled under the pressure of the wooden cover.

Holding her bleeding arm behind her so as not to drip on the page, Vera reached into the hole with her good hand. She barely managed to squeeze her thumb and forefinger into the gaps around the peephole. Working the little scrap of paper up out of the hole required patience and a steady hand, neither of which she possessed in that moment, but after what felt like a long struggle, she managed to get a grip on it.

Vera stood up and immediately sat back onto her mattress,

her head swimming. A thin stream of blood made its way from her arm down to her fingertips, and she let it drip onto the floor. She watched as it seeped into the cracks between the floorboards, thought distantly of how difficult it would be to get it up out of the wood.

Some of her blood had fallen onto the gouges in the floor while she was trying to get that bit of paper. They looked so much like the one along the stairway wall, the one in the basement ceiling. They were long and deep and hungry, and in the rawness of them, her blood looked right at home.

Vera knew she had to pull the splinter out of her arm and bandage it. But first, she used her good hand to smooth the scrap of paper flat against her leg. It kept trying to curl back into a tube, but it was small enough that she managed to hold it flat with one hand.

It was so tiny. There was only room for one line of text, one partial sentence followed by one full sentence. There was no mistaking her father's handwriting, though.

There was also no mistaking that, yet again, this passage was about Vera.

Wonder if she watches? Wonder if she loves me the way I love her?

Vera swallowed hard, shivering at the tickle of warm blood running across the back of her wrist. The patter of it falling onto the woodgrain was like a quick heartbeat. She bit her lips against the smile that was threatening to overtake her face.

For a moment, it didn't matter that she was bleeding. It didn't matter where the scratches in the floor had come from. It didn't matter that Daphne was dying.

Because he'd loved her. Even if that had changed in the time between when he wrote those words and when he died, this was proof.

He'd loved her back then.

He'd loved her so much.

CHAPTER TWENTY

Vera blinked hard against the fluorescent lights of the furniture store. She'd had so little sleep that her brain felt glassy, varnished by adrenaline and buffed to a high sheen by fatigue. The concrete floor was too hard beneath her feet, and everything was too bright, and everyone was too close together. She wanted to be at home.

Too bad. This needed doing.

This particular store was a ninety-minute drive from home, which seemed far enough that she probably wouldn't be recognized. She wondered if maybe she was being paranoid—that awful bartender hadn't recognized her, after all. Still, it paid to be cautious. The risk of being hated at top volume in close quarters was motivation enough.

"Hey, wait up," James Duvall called, jogging to catch up with her. Vera flinched at the sound of his shoes squeaking on the concrete. He'd intercepted her as she was leaving the house, and he'd insisted on tagging along. As little as Vera wanted the company, she'd suspected that James would be useful when it came time to lift her purchase into the car.

Her suspicion was validated even further when he offered to drive, unlocking his pickup truck with a click of the remote keyfob in his pocket. She didn't want to need help, least of all from this man, but the truck would make things easier and today she just needed something, anything to be easy.

The drive gave her time to think. She'd remained silent in the passenger seat for the duration of the trip, letting Duvall rattle on and on about how challenging it was to attune himself to the energies of the Crowder House. Vera didn't mind letting him talk; she spent that time trying to come up with an explanation for what had happened to her in her childhood bedroom.

An explanation for her blanket being ripped from her hands in the night and pulled beneath the bed. An explanation for the gouges in the wood.

Vera walked fast, trying not to let Duvall keep up with her even though he had the longer stride. She shouldn't have dawdled in the entrance to the store, shouldn't have left enough time for Duvall to finish the snub end of the almost-dead blueberry-scented cigarillo he'd been smoking on the way there. She followed the marked-off path that wound through the store, through staged kitchens and dining rooms, living rooms, samples of couches and chairs. The plush cushion of a yellow velvet wingback beckoned her, promising a warm soft nest she could curl up in to take a nap. She reached out to run her hand over the nap of the velvet—but then warmth stirred the fine hairs on the back of her neck.

"Gorgeous."

Vera spun around to find herself eye-to-eye with James Duvall's full, parted lips. She tipped her chin up so she could meet his gaze and very nearly wound up bumping his nose with her own. His breath smelled raw and floral.

Heat fluttered behind Vera's solar plexus, at her fingertips, between her thighs. *Foulness,* she thought. *Grease. He needs help.* She didn't want to let the thoughts in, but there they were.

"That chair," he added, after much too long a pause. "So

vibrant. It would go well in your bedroom at home. Don't you think?"

Duvall cocked a brow at her, one corner of his mouth twitching with something between challenge and invitation. He was close enough to bite. She knew that if she were to reach out and yank up the hem of his artfully weathered shirt, the skin of his belly would be as smooth and pliant as fresh taffy under her fingertips. The taste of sweet lemon ghosted across her tongue. She swallowed hard, once and then twice, as saliva flooded her cheeks.

Vibrant.

"I don't think so," she replied, her voice coming out low and even. "I think it looks uncomfortable."

She was glad when that tart yellow color was out of sight behind her.

Duvall didn't say anything else as they passed through the home-office section, full of smooth-topped desks and mesh-backed rolling chairs. He just stayed at her heels, following a little too close, never letting her lose awareness of him.

Fortunately, after the filing cabinets, they were where they had been heading all along: the bedroom section.

It started with life-sized dioramas of kids' rooms. The aesthetic was unfamiliar, different from the primary-color brand-explosions of Vera's youth. There was lots of birch and lavender and sage, forest-creature-themed plush toys. Everything was genderless and faux-handmade and vaguely foreign in a way she couldn't put her finger on.

Vera was in the center of a path that led between a princess-themed room with a big foam throne in it, and a space-themed room with a rocketship tent in one corner. Both featured bunk

beds with plastic guards over the ladders, warnings not to
climb.

Vera wondered, briefly, what the instinct was that drove
children to climb. She and Brandon Gregson had spent hours
and hours climbing as kids, scaling trees and fences and stucco
walls, trying to get as high as they could just to prove that it
was possible.

She tried so hard not to think of him that way. It was a forbidden corridor in her memory. She was allowed to think of
him as an abstract concept, as a tense conversation topic, as a
subject to be avoided. She could think of him as the son of a
woman she needed to dodge in public. She could even occa-
sionally think of him as someone she missed.

But she tried never to let herself think of him as a person
who she'd spent time playing with, as a person she'd goaded
into scaling the fence around the abandoned quarry so they
could see if it was really filled with radioactive slime. She hadn't
thought of him as her friend, who she loved and hated and spent
her afternoons chasing, in a long time, with the sole exception
of the moment when he'd appeared outside the Crowder House
a few nights earlier.

That had been a failure. She couldn't let herself think of him
that way. It was too dangerous.

Vera ducked into the space-themed bedroom setup and sat
hard on the edge of the constellation-printed duvet on the bottom bunk. She was flooded all at once with memories of sitting
on Brandon's bedroom floor, reading books about dinosaurs
and eating fruit leather. Gathering boxelder bugs in an old mar-
garine container to watch them climb on each other, the bright
X's on their backs making them look like comic book heroes

turned insectoid. Signing each other's wrist casts a year apart, and then hitting each other with their casts and being surprised each time at how much the impact hurt them both.

It had been a friendship born of proximity and convenience, pushed along by their mothers. Neither of them would have picked the other one for a best friend, given the choice. Still, that friendship had lasted for years. It had defined her childhood. She'd wondered as a kid if they'd date, get married, have children of their own, have a home. She'd wondered because he was the boy she knew best and that seemed like the likeliest path for the two of them, and because nobody had ever told her that not wanting to marry men at all was an option.

But now, here she was. Brandon hadn't turned out to factor into her adulthood at all.

She couldn't even remember his middle name.

"Are you finding everything okay, ma'am?"

The question startled Vera into a mortifyingly ragged gasp, her skin jumping up into gooseflesh in an instant. "Jesus," she said, too loud for the small space, and the blue-shirted teenager's polite smile vanished. He took a step back, an apology forming on his lips already, and Vera shoved herself into a state of composure. "No, I'm sorry," she said, placating as could be. "I was just . . . lost in thought. It's not your fault."

The kid nodded, his eyes darting to the side as if there might be an escape route nearby. "Sorry," he said.

Vera swallowed rising irritation. Her mother's voice hissed at the back of her tongue. *I already said it wasn't your fault. Don't make me say it again.* Vera clenched her jaw tight to keep from saying the words Daphne was muttering inside her throat. "Can you point me to the grown-up beds?" she said instead, scraping a smile across her teeth.

"Just follow the arrows," he said, not meeting her eyes. He stepped away fast, vanished into the mists of customer service before Vera could thank him.

She sat on the bed for another few seconds, letting the poor kid get a head start on avoiding her. Across the aisle, in the princess room, Duvall was resting one hip against a pale pink dresser, watching her. His head was cocked to one side. There was a little line between his brows, one that was surely meant to look like concern. She knew that expression—he must have learned it from his father.

His eyes glittered hungrily, moving over her as quick and subtle as a bedsheet settling.

Vera stood briskly, not meeting his gaze. Not wanting to know what she'd find there if she looked too long. Then she did as that employee had told her, following the arrows out of the bedtime wonderland of the children's section, not looking back to see if Duvall was following or not. She kept walking until she arrived at the joyless grid of queen-sized beds that were meant for adults to sleep in.

All of the bedframes looked more or less the same— squared-off, low and bland, devoid of character. These beds didn't belong in the same house as that awful, decadent yellow chair, Vera thought. They didn't belong in a room that was next door to that spaceship-themed bedroom. They were sensible, austere. They belonged right here, in tidy rows under fluorescent lights with bare mattresses on top of them, not a pillow in sight. They were as sterile and uninviting as a hospital corridor.

They were perfect.

She walked between them, examining the place where each bed met the floor, until she found the one she wanted. Dark faux-wood print on particleboard, a narrow headboard, a flat white laminate platform for a mattress to rest on.

And it went all the way to the ground. There was no under-the-bed, not here. There was nowhere to sneak and lurk, no lair from which to grab at blankets and gouge at the floorboard. No drawers, even, to linger inside of or push out in the night. Vera took out her phone and snapped a photo of the little tag on the headboard with the aisle and shelf number she'd need to retrieve an identical, unassembled version of this bed.

She felt the heat of James Duvall standing behind her, a little too close and a little too quiet.

Hunger knotted itself tight around her middle. Vera breathed in the old-smoke smell of him, the closeness of him, the heat of him. She took him into her lungs and she leaned back into the warmth of his nearness, and she smiled at the bed she was going to buy.

She needed a bed that offered nowhere at all to hide.

This one would be perfect.

CHAPTER TWENTY-ONE

Vera is twelve and three-quarters years old and she can't stop picking at the band-aid on her finger. It's come loose at one edge, and the sticky underside of it is all dirty, and she wants to peel it off so bad.

While she's helping with the dishes, her mother and father have a fight. They fight all the time these days. As soon as Vera hears her mother's voice start to rise—*where do you think you're going, don't tell me you need to do it again already, that one's off-limits*—she snaps her soapy fingers four times. Even though Daphne and Francis are just in the next room, with no door to come between their fight and Vera's ears, the noise of their voices dies away.

Vera imagines what it would be like if she weren't alone in this kitchen. She imagines her friend—no, her sister—no, her friend, her *best* friend—standing beside her, ready to dry the clean dishes. "He told me everything," Vera murmurs, scrubbing sticky grease off the underside of a pan. "He told me all about the monsters, and how it works, even, when he drains them."

It's good that he trusts you, her friend says in a voice like the hum of the dishwasher. *You could tell him that you know enough now. You could tell him that you don't want to see it anymore.*

Vera frowns, because usually, when she imagines what her

friend would say to her, she imagines her being reasonable. She imagines her being right. "But I do want to see it."

You could tell him that it's scary, her friend counters.

"It isn't scary, though. It's cool," Vera replies.

Her friend doesn't say anything else after that. Vera decides that this is for the best. She is too old for imaginary friends, too adult. It's time to stop pretending that there's someone beside her, someone who cares about her, someone who loves her.

That's for little kids. It's time to grow up.

She organizes her new school supplies in her backpack, taking extra care with the multicolored gel pens that she's sure she'll need all of. She brushes her teeth and spits white foam into the sink and wonders if men can taste the grease inside themselves, or if it's all tucked away. If there are men who don't even know they have it.

Her father doesn't get back for a very, very long time. Vera knows because she wakes up when he comes home. She wakes up because someone is yelling outside her open bedroom window.

She gets out of bed and tiptoes to the curtain. When she looks outside, she can see her father. He's hugging a man who is a little bigger than him, and in the gray light of predawn, it almost looks like they're dancing.

But then her father spins the man around and hooks his elbow around the man's throat. He holds his arms like that, visibly straining with the effort of it. After a few seconds, the man's legs collapse out from under him.

And then Vera's father has his hands under the man's armpits, and he's dragging the limp form toward the house, and Vera steps away from her window, her heart pounding hard.

She dives underneath her bed, pulls the loose floorboard

away, presses her face to the wood. She doesn't want to miss a moment of what happens next. Watching, she knows, is the only way to learn, and she wants to learn.

She wants to see the rancid oil spill out of whoever her father's brought home.

She wants to see it all.

❦

Brandon is at the door asking if she wants to ride bikes, and she doesn't know how to answer.

Say no, her friend advises. She's decided that the friend is her conscience, is the better part of her. If her friend says no, then the right answer is probably no. A good person would probably say no.

But school starts tomorrow. She doesn't want it to be weird, seeing him there. She hasn't seen him all summer, not since the day he pushed her. He already missed her birthday, and *that* was weird, and she doesn't want more of that feeling. And besides, she doesn't know how to say no to him without being mean, and then Brandon says, "Please? I really need to talk to you," and that seals it.

So she walks out the front door and down the porch and she grabs her bike off the lawn and she follows him away from her house and down the street. He's riding fast and angry today, standing up on the pedals of his bike, wobbling wildly from side to side, heading for the creek. Vera has to pump her legs hard to keep up with him. When they reach the gap in the trees beside the road, Vera takes the turn off the road too fast and nearly falls down the slope to the creek. She regains her balance with effort—but then she nearly crashes into Brandon.

He's stopped halfway down the slope, the front wheel of his

bike wrenched sideways. There are long tracks in the mulch where he's dragged both feet to brake.

"What are you—" Vera starts to ask, angry, but she stops when she sees his face.

He's crying.

Vera doesn't say anything. She doesn't touch him, doesn't ask what's wrong; she just gets off her bicycle, letting it fall to the ground beside her.

She feels the same way she did when she was pulling the worm out of the jar with her father to catch fish. Brandon is soft and small and much too easy to hurt, and she could hurt him right now, the way he hurt her. She could do it if she wanted to.

But she waits instead, and finally, after a long wet sniff, he gives voice to the thing that's making him cry.

"My dad is missing," he says, using the toe of one sneaker to lower the kickstand on his own bike before he climbs awkwardly off it. He stands on the slope just below her, his hands in his pockets, his gaze resting somewhere near Vera's knees.

She doesn't know how to sculpt her face to make it look like she's surprised. "Oh," she says. Then, because it seems like the appropriate addition, she adds, "What?"

"He's been missing for three whole days." Brandon lifts the collar of his T-shirt and uses it to wipe at his eyes and nose. Vera's eyes linger on that collar after he drops it, on the dark spot left behind by his tears and his snot. "He went out on Saturday night and he never came home."

"Where did he go?"

He shrugs. The dark spot on his shirt rubs against his skin when he does that. "I don't know," he says angrily. He loses his balance for a moment, skidding a little down the slope toward the muddy creekbed. "That's what 'missing' means, dumbass."

Vera rolls her eyes. "I *meant* where did he tell you he was going, when he left. Don't call me a dumbass."

"I don't know. He just told Mom he was going out. He doesn't . . . he doesn't tell us where he goes, you know?"

He lifts his collar again, scrubs angrily at his face. Vera's heart catches in her chest at the way he rubs the soiled fabric across his cheeks and eyes. Beside her left ear, her father's voice whispers *they're filled with a foulness*.

The fabric is dark gray now, the tears creating a slow-spreading splotch in the white cotton of the fabric. A thought is starting to dig long, narrow fingers into the meat of Vera's brain. She tries to ignore it, but it's loud. *It sounds like your little friend Brandon is becoming a man.*

"Do you think he ran off?" she asks, and Brandon's face twists with some combination of pain and fury. The curve of his cheek shifts as quickly as a caught fish jerking on a line. "Sorry," she adds. "It's just . . . him and your mom were always fighting, I thought maybe—"

"Shut up," he growls, tears still spilling down his cheeks, his lower lip wet with spit. "You shouldn't talk about things you don't know anything about. He didn't leave us, he wouldn't ever leave us. He's not like *your* dad. Something must have happened to him."

The thought is humming all through Vera's mind now, electrified by her fury at Brandon accusing her father again. It's a thought that catches and clings.

The foulness.

The *grease*.

It has to be in him, and she wants to see it. Brandon has stained his shirt with tears, but the tears aren't filth—they're just saltwater. Clear. How can she find out if Brandon has the rot in him? How can she know if her father is right?

Is she going to get to see it today?

She feels something she's never felt before, something that could be revulsion and could be hunger. She knows that the grease will disgust her and at the same time, she's desperate to find out, firsthand, the thing her father knows.

"I'm sorry," she says. She puts her hand on his arm because maybe the grease will start to seep out of his skin, maybe she'll be able to feel it like how she can feel the sponginess of the mulch under her feet. But he jerks his arm away, and when she sneaks a peek at her palm, it's still clean.

"Whatever," he says, sullen. "I shouldn't have told you." He's inspecting his shoes and his hands are in fists. His tears are slowing.

Vera is gripped by the frantic feeling of an opportunity passing her by. "Don't be like that," she whispers. "Brandon. It's okay. You can show me."

He looks up at her, bewilderment naked on his face. Vera's never seen him this moody, this raw, this volatile. Is this how her father could tell that Brandon was turning into a man? Is that what he meant?

"What?"

"You can tell me," she tries. "What do you think happened to him? Where do you think he is?"

He shakes his head. Confusion is reigning now; his eyes dart around like the answers are floating in a nimbus around Vera's head. White salt trails are forming on his cheeks, under his nose. "I don't . . . I don't know. How would I know? Should I try to figure it out?"

"I guess," Vera answers automatically. She's barely listening to him. She's studying that white on his cheeks. How could that exist if he's all rotted inside?

"Mom doesn't want to call the cops," he says. "Maybe . . . maybe I should tell her to call them?"

Vera examines his lips, pink and full and shining with the heat of crying. Maybe they look the same as they always have, but she can't be sure about that, because she's never looked at them this closely before. She's never paid this much attention to what parts of Brandon seem clean and what parts don't. "I guess," she murmurs again.

He wipes his face on his shirt one last time, even though it's mostly dry by now. "Thanks, Vee," he says. "I'm sorry I called you a dumbass. You're right. I'm going to tell her to call the cops. If she doesn't listen to me, I'll do it myself."

He grabs his bike by the handlebars and starts to walk up the slope. As he steps around Vera, the thought she can't shake snaps into focus, and the *maybe* of his foulness yanks on her like a puppetmaster pulling strings.

She turns to grab Brandon by one shoulder to keep him from leaving, from getting on his bike and riding away home before she can see the truth of him. Before she can see if he's gone bad or not. She pulls too hard. He wheels around, gets his feet and his arms and his bike all tangled up.

He knocks into her, drops the bike, grabs her arms to steady himself. He's so close to her and he's leaning on her so hard, and his face is raw with bewilderment and hurt and vulnerability, and Vera can't stand it, she can't stand looking at him like that, all soft and scared and weak and easy to destroy—that weakness that could keep her from seeing the filth that surely must be growing inside him. She can't stand it, so she does the only thing she can think of to keep him from running away.

She kisses him.

It's different from when they kissed before. That kiss was tentative and soft, almost formal in its uncertainty.

This kiss isn't like that at all. The instant Vera's chin bumps up against Brandon's, she's seized by a feverish need to know, to know for sure, now, before he can leave.

She digs her fingers hard into his skinny arms and crushes her face into his. He opens his mouth to let out a startled sound. She catches his lip between her front teeth, wanting to know, wanting to find out if his blood will taste rotten as the half-decayed leaves under her feet, wanting to *bite*—

And then she's on the ground next to her bicycle, her hands plunged wrist-deep into the cold mulch, a crushing ache shooting up through her tailbone. Brandon stands over her. His eyes are glassy and a red flush blooms high on his cheeks and across his throat. His arms are red too, a livid pre-bruise kind of red where she'd clutched at him. He's breathing hard, his mouth still open, his hands held out as if to ward her off.

"What the hell, Vee," he breathes.

"I thought—"

"What the hell," he says again, loud this time. He's standing over her, wiping his mouth on his sleeve, his eyes dark with growing anger. Vera wonders if that's it, the darkness in his glare—if that's the foulness her father wanted her to keep away from. "Why would you kiss me right now? Why would you do that?"

The conviction that compelled her to kiss him in the first

place is gone, leaving her hollow. Shame starts to trickle into that empty space like urine down a pant leg, a hot and uncontrollable flood of it that she doesn't know how to escape. "I don't know, I thought you wanted . . . I wanted to help?"

None of the words she picks are the right ones, and his face broadcasts just how wrong she is. He aims a vicious kick at her fallen bike, his sneaker meeting the metal frame with a rattle that makes Vera jump. "My dad's *gone,* and you really just—you wanted to *help?* Don't ever help me again, Vera."

The way he says her name has more venom in it than when he'd said *fuck you.* She's never heard her name sound like that before, like it's the worst bad word. And then he's gone, just like before, pushing his bike back up toward the road, leaving Vera on the ground.

She pulls her hands out of the muck. They're filthy and cold, but at least she's not bleeding this time. The hot shame in her burns hotter as Brandon's voice echoes through her mind. *What's wrong with you?*

Nothing's wrong with me, she thinks, and the burning shame crystallizes into fierce anger. Who does Brandon think he is? Vera is the one who took the risk, getting so close to him even though she knew what was inside him. Even though she knew he was going rotten and slick and cold inside, just like the filth on her hands.

And Brandon just proved her father right, didn't he? She saw it mushing around behind his eyes when he said her name with so much hate, saw the way it made him kick out at her bike. He could have been kicking *her* just as easily. Maybe, she thinks with growing alarm, he'd *meant* to kick her. Maybe he just missed.

Vera rides toward home as fast as she rode away from it.

The wind whips her hair around her face, tying it into intricate knots that will take forever to undo. *Fine,* she thinks fiercely. Let her hair tangle. It doesn't matter.

Part of her hopes she'll overtake Brandon on the road, hopes she'll have the chance to kick out at him. Let him find out how it feels to be humiliated and yelled at by someone who's supposed to be your friend. But of course, she doesn't see him anywhere. He's long gone, probably at home already, telling his mother to call the police. As if that'll do any good. As if moms ever listen anyway.

She leaves her bike on the front lawn and storms inside, slamming the door. Her bedroom door is open, welcoming, waiting for her—but she pauses with her hand on the knob and looks at the next door over.

The door to the basement.

The key around her neck rings like a tuning fork, and the frequency of its vibrations starts a hum that cuts through her crystalline anger. She could go down there. Her father won't be home from work, not yet. She could go down there and see it up close, the thing her father brought inside. And then wouldn't Brandon be sorry that he was so mean to her?

But before she can make a decision—before the thing that still has its fingers in her brain can make a decision—there are footsteps on the porch, and the door opens, and she hears her own name.

"Vera? What happened to you?"

She whips around to look at her father. She can't see her own face, but the way her father's eyes lock onto hers, she is sure that he can feel the furious hum that's still filling her.

"Nothing," she says. "I was down by the creek. I slipped and fell into the mud."

They stand there in silence for a long time, long enough for everything in Vera to go quiet. Almost. There's still an echo of that hum.

Her father takes a few steps toward her, and just like that, he's between her and the basement door. His eyes dart back and forth, left-right-left-right-left. He's looking between her eyes, looking at her so closely that the hairs on the back of her neck prickle. His nostrils twitch.

In this moment, Vera is acutely aware of how much mud is on her hands.

"Are you sure you don't want to tell me anything else?" he asks.

He's speaking softly, so softly that Vera's mother wouldn't be able to hear even if she was standing in the next room. It's not easy to hear conversations throughout the house anyway. It's a quiet house.

Still—Vera can see that her father is being careful. He's being very, very careful.

"I'm sure," she says, just as careful. Just as quiet. "There's nothing else. I just fell. I should probably wash up," she adds, holding up her hands, making sure he sees that she isn't trying to hide them from him.

Her father's gaze drops to the filth on her skin. The intensity in his eyes does not diminish. After a slow, steady breath, he nods. "You should," he murmurs.

Vera crosses the entryway, goes into the little powder room with the two doors that won't lock. She braces her foot against one door and keeps an eye on the other behind her in the mirror as she washes her hands.

She takes her time, scrubbing the rot from beneath her fingernails. It pools in the sink, taking forever to drain. She frowns, pokes at the dark water trying to dislodge whatever's clogging the drain, but there's nothing to find. It vanishes steadily, but slowly.

Even the house doesn't want it.

❧

Vera's father is in the basement that night until well past three o'clock in the morning. Vera's elbows ache from propping her up on the wood floor beneath her bed. Her cheek is numb from being pressed right up against the peephole for hours. She holds her breath as heavy footfalls pass her bedroom door—Francis on his way to the kitchen to wash his hands in the sink. She breathes again, ten times in and out, before she hears his footfalls again, passing her bedroom on the way to the stairs.

Vera knows she should wait awhile longer—knows she should wait for him to wash up, brush his teeth, put on his pajamas, climb into bed, start drifting off, sink all the way down to the sandy bottom of sleep, deep enough that little sounds from downstairs won't wake him. She knows she should wait.

But she can't. She can't stand it. She waits for a scant fifteen seconds, long enough for Francis to get up the stairs and walk down the hall to his bedroom, and then she bolts out from under the bed and shoots to her bedroom door. She stumbles over something she can't see, something as firm as hardwood. When she turns to look, there's nothing to see, but the blankets on top of her bed are folded back invitingly and a hint of guilt twitches in her belly.

"I'll only be a minute," she whispers. "I promise."

She doesn't wait for a reply. The key around her neck is still humming against her breastbone and that hungry need to *know* is gnawing at her insides, and when she gets to the basement door her hands are quick and sure, no sweaty palms, no clumsy fingers. She's already got the flashlight. She planned ahead.

She takes the stairs down into the basement two at a time and she doesn't slip even once.

The thing in the basement isn't fully restrained with bike locks. Only one ankle is chained up, and that doesn't really seem necessary. The thing is propped up against the wall, slumped to one side, not moving around too much.

The smell is awful.

"You stink," Vera whispers. The man doesn't seem to hear her, but she can hear ragged-edged breathing. She's sure the man is awake, just like a minute ago, when she watched her father put the chain on that ankle. "You stink and you look gross. You look like meatloaf."

She knows she's being mean, but she's so *mad*. She should feel afraid—she knows, distantly, that if she saw this man in any other context, she'd be terrified. But this is her house, where she never has to feel afraid of anything, and so instead she just feels angry.

And the feeling isn't fading like it usually does. It isn't working its way into sadness, isn't fraying at the edges. It's hardening. It's sticking. It's a sharp thing that's lodged between her back teeth and it's making her mean. It's making her want to hurt this thing that her father is keeping down here in the basement.

She steps closer. The man wheezes, a high whistle from low in the chest that ends with a popping sound like when Vera blows bubbles into her milk with a straw at lunch.

Vera aims the flashlight beam at the man's face. At the *thing's* face.

The eyes are shut tight. The mouth hangs open, a long strand of pink saliva hanging from the full lower lip. The moustache has something foul and muddy caked into it. There are holes in the cheek and the lip.

The rest, below the face, is well past raw. The man was pink and fresh a day or two ago, but now Vera suspects things are starting to turn. She doesn't look too closely, because she's pretty sure the man is still naked, and she doesn't want to see nakedness. She just wants to see the face.

She takes another step. Her heart is pounding hard, she can feel it against the weight of the key around her neck, and she's within reach of the man now, within reach of a long arm and a grasping hand. She squats down, still shining that light into that slack, pale face. One blond mustache-hair catches the light, glinting through all that filth.

"You're full of grease," Vera hisses. "You're full of gross sticky gunk and that's why you're here." It isn't enough. "Foulness," she adds, remembering the barbs that word had when it came out of her father's mouth. The man doesn't react. The angry tooth that's growing through the roof of Vera's mouth isn't satisfied by the bites she's taking out of him.

She tries again.

"You're gross and it's your own fault you're here. Maybe if you were a better dad, you would have been able to get away."

That does the trick. The man lets out a hiccuping little sob. Pink foam gathers at the corners of the mouth, and something inside Vera flushes with heat. This. This is what she wants.

She crouches down so she's at eye level with the man.

"Do you like it down here? Do you like what's been happening to you?"

The head droops to one side, then another. The mouth pouts

into an "O" shape. It's the closest she's going to get to a definitive "no."

Vera keeps the light trained on the man's face so she doesn't miss anything. "Well," she whispers. "You should have thought of that." She pauses for a moment, taking an inventory of the words she knows, the worst ones, the ones she doesn't often use but wants to learn to wield smoothly, without stuttering or pausing. She puts the full weight of her fury behind the word. "You should have thought of that before you raised Brandon to be such a *cunt*."

The man chokes on another sob, and another, the rope of drool that trails into his lap turning pinker each time he gasps. Vera's legs start to prickle with pins and needles.

She doesn't want to leave. Not yet. She wants to see what's going to happen to him. She doesn't feel afraid, not even a little bit. She feels powerful and she doesn't want to let that feeling go.

But then a sound comes from overhead: four sharp taps on the ceiling.

Vera's heart leaps into her throat and she races up the steps, out through the basement door, swinging a sharp turn into her bedroom. She eases the door shut behind her and then dives into her bed.

Just as she pulls the covers up to her chin, she hears her father walking past the bedroom door. The sound of the basement door opening and closing is clearer than usual, so clear that it's as if there's no wall in the way of it.

Vera waits for her heartbeat to slow. A few seconds' difference and she would have been caught. She doesn't know what will happen if she gets caught in the basement. Her father has never been angry at her, not that she can remember. He's not even angry when he's working in the basement—when Vera watches him through the peephole under her bed, he mostly just seems sad.

She doesn't want to be the one who makes him angry. She doesn't know what he's like when he's angry.

And because of those four taps on the ceiling, she didn't have to find out.

Vera turns onto her side and lets her arm drape across her body so it falls over the side of the bed. She holds her breath, and she snaps four times.

She waits without knowing what it is she's waiting for. After a few seconds of silence, she clears her throat.

"Thank you," she whispers. "For warning me."

The room gets a little warmer and the darkness gets a little thicker, and before Vera can wonder who it is she's thanking, she's fast asleep. She dreams of warm hands stroking the hair back from her face, and a voice telling her *everything will be all right.*

She will believe that voice for one more week.

CHAPTER TWENTY-TWO

Getting the bed home from the big box store wasn't easy. Duvall wanted to talk the whole time, but unlike the drive to the store, he wanted Vera to answer him. He had questions, so many questions, about everything Vera didn't know how to discuss. Her father, and her childhood, and the Crowder House.

He especially wanted to know about that last one. He asked about the places she'd hidden as a kid, the secret corners and the creaky floorboards, the parts of the house that had frightened her and the parts that had fascinated her. Vera answered him in monosyllables, staring fixedly out the half-rolled-down passenger-side window the entire time, sucking down the fresh air greedily. She only broke and looked at him a few miles away from home, when he let out a deep sigh and asked a question she couldn't stand to answer.

"Why don't you just let me in already, Vee?"

She'd turned to him involuntarily, appalled. "What?"

Glancing between her and the road, Duvall hit her with that cocked eyebrow again, tipping his head toward her in a way that made the skin of his throat stretch tight over the bulge of his Adam's apple. "C'mon," he murmured in a low, enticing voice. "I'm just trying to get to know you, the same way I've been trying to get to know the Crowder House. Don't you want to quit being all alone in that head of yours? I hear you in the night sometimes, you know. Pacing around, trying to get away from whatever it is that won't let you rest. You don't have to deal with it all on your own." He put a hand between them on the bench seat, palm-up, invitational.

"I don't have trouble sleeping," Vera replied softly, not reaching for him. "Not most nights. And I don't pace."

"No?" Duvall took his hand back as casually as if he'd never stretched it out at all. "Then why did you have to go and get a new bed so urgently today? Is it because something happened in the night?" His gaze darted between her and the road. "Something you couldn't explain? Vera, you can tell me," he added, his voice so kind and reasonable that Vera's hands twitched into fists. "Was it him? Was it Francis?"

She couldn't answer him, not honestly. She couldn't shake the feeling that if she started answering him, she wouldn't be able to stop. She was finally starting to let herself want things—so many things—but that wasn't one of them. So instead of answering him, she dodged.

"What have you been working on?"

"I told you," he said, sounding impatient for the first time. "I'm communing with the house so I can put voice to—"

"What's it look like? When you work?"

He was quiet for a moment, his jaw working back and forth as though he were debating whether or not to answer. He glanced over at Vera again. "I'll trade you," he finally replied.

Vera looked out the window, tried to find things to look at that didn't make her feel like a single yawning urge. There was a smudge on the glass that looked like someone's head had rested there. Some other passenger, some other time. "Trade me what?"

"I'll tell you how I work, if you'll tell me how *he* worked. My

father, I mean. If you'll tell me how he got so much out of you."
He let out a soft laugh. "God knows I can't seem to figure it out
on my own."

They drove through town. Vera kept her eyes on the sidewalk as they passed Alan & Sons, looking for familiar faces.
Looking for just one familiar face. She thought she saw him a
block away from the store, sitting on a park bench and reading
a book—but then he was gone.

"Brandon," she murmured.

She wasn't looking at Duvall but she could feel him perk up,
twitching and attentive as a well-trained dog.

"Your father's final—"

"Hammett told me things about him," Vera interrupted.
"He made me think that maybe there was a chance I could have
my friend back, even after everything. He saw how lonely I was
and he used it to get what he wanted."

"You seem lonely now, too," Duvall ventured. He rested his
hand between them again, a persistent invitation. "You don't
need to be."

Vera shook her head, keeping her eyes away from the
smooth, thin skin of his wrist. "You have no idea what I need."

❧

Getting the bed into the house on her own was awful, but Vera
wasn't willing to invite Duvall into her bedroom, not even to
drop off the unbelievably heavy set of boxes that had all the
necessary parts inside.

Putting the thing together was even more painful than the
ride home had been. In spite of the helpfully illustrated instruc-
tions that came in the cardboard flat-pack boxes, Vera kept
mixing up the directions of the bed components, getting them

upside-down and failing to notice until three steps later, having to backtrack to fix her errors.

The entire time, the bottom drawer of her dresser throbbed at her. She bargained with herself, deciding that she could open it up and read those letters from Francis after she'd had a good night's sleep. That, she decided, would be the healthiest thing to do. Building the bed needed to come first, and then resting, getting out of the strange paranoid mindset that made her keep glancing at the bedskirt on the old bedframe to make sure it was still.

One hard thing at a time. She'd done a packet once, on balancing a difficult workload, and that's what it advised. She'd given herself a C-minus on that one.

One hard thing at a time.

She stopped four times to check on her mother, who was fast asleep with her chin resting on her chest all afternoon. Vera wanted, desperately, to wake Daphne for some lemonade and maybe some kind of conversation—but it seemed like a better idea to just let her sleep. Vera was hungry for the strange new tenderness that had risen up in her mother, but she was afraid of it, too.

By the time the bed was fully assembled, all the way against the far wall of the bedroom across from the door, Vera was sweating, irritable, and clumsy-fingered. She was sick of Allen wrenches and had a nasty bump coming up on her elbow where the headboard had fallen on her. But at least that part was over.

She stared at the old bedframe. Her fingertips kept returning to the edge of the bandage on her arm. That splinter had been deep and ugly, half the length of the tweezers Vera had used to pull it out. Seeing the wood slide out from beneath her skin had been uniquely nauseating—it had just kept coming, and the more of it she removed, the more she felt aware of the fact that it had been inside her.

That floor's probably been dug up for ages, she thought. *Mice.* But she knew that mice did not cause the kinds of grooves that were in the floor under her bed, knowing that the grooves had not been there for ages, knowing that the wood of the floor had been as warm as flesh when she'd felt it.

She hadn't looked under the bed again, not since she'd shoved it aside in that moment of primal rage. The thought of it—of kneeling beside the bed, of bending over until her nose was nearly touching the floor, and then lifting the bedskirt—sent cold, sour fingers walking up the knobs of her spine. No, she hadn't looked, and she wasn't going to. She wouldn't be lifting the bedskirt.

She'd be lifting the whole goddamn bed. She'd be dragging it out of the room, like lifting a board away from a patch of mud to see the nightcrawlers twisting underneath. Daylight. That's what the patch of floor under that bedframe needed.

She rolled her neck a few times, trying to ease the stiffness that had been setting in over the course of her time here at home. The bedroom curtains were already flung wide to let in as much sunlight as possible, and all the lights were on, but she still wished that she had a way to make it brighter—a floodlamp, maybe, the kind the cops had used to light up the basement when they were in there with their boots and their cigarettes and their gloves. Something that would eliminate every shadow and leave no place hidden.

For a moment—a bare, desperate moment—she considered opening one of those windows, leaning out, shouting for Duvall to leave his unsettling canvases behind and come join her. Just so she wouldn't have to do the thing alone.

"Enough," Vera whispered to the room, furious with herself for even having the impulse. "I've had enough of this."

She crossed the room with long, angry strides, approaching her brass bed like it was an old enemy and she had a score to settle. She reached out with half-numb hands to grab the edge of the mattress and, without waiting, without bracing herself, without giving herself time to be afraid, she yanked it off the bedframe and dragged it halfway across the room.

It landed on the floor beside the new bed with a *whumpf*. A plume of dust flew up, scattering static through the sunbeams that streamed through the windows. Vera stood beside the felled mattress, panting, and glared hard at the naked bedframe.

The bedskirt was still stretched across the frame. It was a thin expanse of rough linen that had spent years sitting between the old mattress and the skinny slats of metal that supported it. It had been dragged with the mattress a little, and now it sat at an angle, the edge puddling on the wood of the floor.

It didn't move.

Vera stalked back to the bed. She grabbed the bedskirt in one fist and whipped it away viciously, throwing it behind her without looking. Her heartbeat thudded in her skull.

There was nothing there but the bed. Between the slats, she could see the floor, the deep gouges in the wood, the exposed peephole that looked into the basement.

But there was nothing else. No staring eyes or clutching hands. No wadded-up rope of quilt.

No answer to the terror that made the inside of her belly feel slick with hot grease.

There was a scream inside Vera, one that she'd been swallowing since the moment she'd first felt the pop of stitches under her fingers. But if she screamed, Duvall would surely hear it and come running. And besides—more importantly, she insisted to herself—she'd spent too much time screaming since coming home, too much time letting animal fear tenderize her in the night, and she would not do it again. She was standing in a room that was full of daylight, a room that belonged to *her*, in a house that had been built by her father's hands for her breath and skin and laughter to fill, and she was goddamned if she was going to scream inside that house even *one more time*.

So she didn't scream. Instead, she gripped the brass bedknobs at the foot of the bedframe and heaved with all her might, dragging it toward the door.

The sound it made was awful, a squeal of metal and a scrape of wood. She was ruining the floors. She didn't care. Fuck the floor. Fuck the bed. Something low in her back protested, but she ignored it, letting that suppressed scream fill her arms with strength, letting rage plump her muscles.

She didn't stop until the bed was on the front lawn.

It looked obscene, tilted askew on the pillowy grass, bright brass gleaming against a riot of greenery. She stood there panting, slick with sweat, staring at the bed the same way she would have stared at a spit-out tooth. *There*. She'd done it, she was free of that old thing. She had a dinner and a hot shower ahead of her, and a good night's sleep, and then tomorrow, she'd call someone to pick the old bedframe up. And tomorrow, she'd read those letters.

As she caught her breath, she heard footsteps coming up the sidewalk.

Vera's head snapped up as she braced herself for a flood of hatred from one of their neighbors. It would be one of the people who had told Hammett Duvall about how they'd never trusted her father, one of the people who had stapled those awful letters to their door for the first year or so after his arrest. Or one of the people who had sold photos of Vera and Brandon to the publisher for that photo-insert.

But then the earth fell out from beneath her, because it wasn't any of those people. It was him again. It was Brandon.

Long limbs, salt-and-pepper hair. The curve of his spine spoke to a life spent trying not to be noticed by anyone. He looked nothing like the boy she'd known. He looked everything like the boy she hadn't.

"Hey," she said, taking a step toward him.

His head snapped up. "Vee." It sounded like the word was knocked out of him.

"I saw you downtown when I was driving through before," she said pointlessly. There was no reason he needed to know that. There was no reason she needed to say it. "Were you—oh." The realization struck her and she wished she could vomit it up and rid herself of it. "You were waiting for me to be inside, weren't you? You were waiting me out."

He shrugged, not meeting her eyes. "I didn't want to make you have to see me."

"But I want to see you," she said, not caring if she sounded desperate. "Brandon, please, please just let me explain."

He shook his head. "I don't need an explanation."

"Can I at least apologize?"

He sighed, then looked up at her, and him looking at her was so much worse than him not looking at her. She'd imagined this conversation a thousand times, and she'd never imagined the look that was on his face, not once. He didn't seem angry about what had happened all those years ago. He didn't seem confused and he didn't seem hurt.

He just seemed tired.

"I know you're sorry, Vee," he said softly. "I know you didn't mean for anything bad to happen."

"It wasn't my fault," she whispered. She took another couple of steps toward him, but froze when he took a slow step back, his eyes sliding away from hers.

"I know. And I've never told anyone otherwise. But . . . it doesn't matter. Not really. Whether it's your fault or not, it happened. And I can't know you anymore. Not after that." His neck twisted a little, like he was suppressing a shudder. "Maybe if your mother wasn't bringing people around all the time to stare at it. Maybe if she didn't lean so hard into the haunting thing. I don't know."

"That's all gonna be over soon, though," she said.

"I don't think so. Now that you're home, I don't think it'll ever be over."

She shook her head. "I'm not staying here. I'm selling the place soon as Daphne's finished."

His reaction sent a violent shiver up Vera's spine. It rooted her to the spot, kept her from trying to follow him as he walked away toward the house he'd grown up in. It kept her from calling after him. It took the breath from her lungs.

He smiled at her, and he looked up at the Crowder House, and he shook his head.

"Nah, Vee. That house would never let you leave."

CHAPTER TWENTY-THREE

Vera could not concentrate on dinner that night. She could not concentrate on her mother, or on James Duvall, or on the promise of a full night's sleep.

All she could think about was what Brandon had said.

Nah, Vee.

"Are you listening to me?" Every time Daphne spoke, a smell as thick as a taste filled the room. Sweet, sharp lemon, with something earthy and dark underneath. "I said, there's going to be press after I'm gone. You should figure out where you're going to go."

Duvall didn't seem to notice the smell. Vera studied her own hands, breathing shallow through her mouth. *One hard thing at a time,* she'd told herself earlier that day, as if the project of the bed and the project of talking to her mother were equally difficult. As if she could have prepared herself for what it would be like to see Brandon.

That house would never let you leave.

She longed for the feeling of the headboard falling on her elbow. At least that had been painful in a way she could swear at.

"Maybe I'll just stay here," Vera said flatly, after she'd let the silence go for a little too long. "We'll see. Or, well, not *we*. I'll see." *Bad,* she thought reflexively, pinching her own arm under the table. *Who says things like that?*

Daphne flicked the edge of a spent paper cup with one thick thumbnail. She was talking slowly. "Oh, they'll come. Sniffing around here, just like before. You'll want to lie low, like you did back then. Just in case."

"I wasn't lying low," Vera protested. "You wouldn't let me—" She cut herself off, not wanting to finish the sentence in front of Duvall.

"Wouldn't let her what?" he asked, a forkful of once-frozen macaroni halfway to his mouth.

"She hid his letters from me," Vera said evenly. "Did she ever tell you that? I only just found them a few days ago—"

"Letters?" Duvall asked, his lips wet. "From Francis? Personal ones?"

Vera kneaded one aching shoulder with the opposite hand. She hadn't had time to shower before dinner after all, and her skin was still tacky with the sweat she'd broken from dragging that damned bedframe onto the lawn. "Personal ones," she confirmed grimly.

Duvall steepled his fingers. "If you wouldn't mind, I'd love to take a look. Communing with a person who has crossed over is so much easier if you've got their words to work with."

"They're probably all about how much he loved you," Daphne murmured.

Vera looked to her mother with weary suspicion, wary of a trap. "Why do you think that?"

The air in the room grew heavy, and Daphne's voice took on a slow, rhythmic timbre. "Because I watched it. I watched you eat up his love like a crab eating a seafloor corpse, one pinch at a time. You devoured the way your father would light up whenever you walked into a room."

"Now, Daphne," Duvall interrupted. "You don't need to—"

Daphne didn't seem to hear him, seemed to have forgotten that he was there. She stared at Vera with bottomless black eyes. "You brought home your failed tests and your skinned knees and your certificates of participation, and you exchanged them for his attention. You sat at the dinner table and you made him laugh with your unfunny jokes, jokes that only the two of you seemed to understand, and you took it, you took the laughter. I saw you take it and knit it into yourself so it could never leave you. Do you understand? I saw. I saw it all."

Vera didn't understand what her mother was doing, didn't understand this sudden outpouring of memory and honesty. But Vera did understand what her mother was *saying*, because Vera remembered it too. She remembered the feeling of her father's love and attention. She remembered holding it right in the middle of her tongue so it wouldn't melt too fast.

"Don't get me wrong." Daphne's head tilted to one side, her unblinking eyes still on Vera, until her ear nearly touched her shoulder. "I loved you. I'll always love you. But I hated you too, at least for a time." There it was, and it struck Vera like a quick, brutal kiss on the mouth. *I hated you.* "I think I had to," Daphne continued in that same low, rolling rhythm, her neck still folded at that impossible angle. "Is one possible without the other? I think you have to know someone in order to truly love them, and you have to love someone in order to *really* hate them. There's the thin hate we have for strangers." At this, so fast Vera almost didn't catch it, Daphne's eyes flicked for just a moment to James Duvall. "And then there's the thick, true, smothering hate we have for those we know best. And that, Vera-baby, that's what I had for you. That's what bubbled up in me and stuck."

She stopped then, stopped for long enough that Vera could

feel the question of who would speak next filling up the room like mustard gas in a trench. Across from her, Duvall drew a breath, as if it was going to be him.

"I loved you too," Vera whispered quickly, unwilling to let Duvall into the conversation she'd wanted to have with her mother for as long as she could remember. "And I hated you. I've always hated you."

Daphne smiled, a slow, soft smile that Vera had never once seen on her face before. She straightened her neck just as a gray, clotted tear slipped from her eye. It left an uneven trail on the loose skin of her cheek. "I wish I knew how to separate the two out for you," she said. "Do you remember when you learned to separate eggs? In the kitchen, Francis showed you how to cup the yolk in your palm and let the white run between your fingers, and you let the white slip down into the drain, warm from your skin."

Vera nodded, her face numb at the memory of her father's patience as he showed her how to break an egg without smashing it. How did Daphne know about that?

"I wish I could tell you the one without the other. The love, without the hate. But if I tried, you wouldn't believe me anyway, would you, Vera-baby?"

Against her own will, Vera leaned forward. She tried not to take up too much room, not to make too much noise, not to break the surface tension of this bubble they were both in. She just wanted to be in it a little longer, a little deeper.

But then Duvall broke it for her.

"That's a theme in much of my work," he said. "The love-aspect. Duality."

Vera closed her eyes, clamped her teeth shut tight around the urge that rose in her like a flash flood.

"Yes," Daphne said, and when Vera opened her eyes again, Daphne was still staring at her. There was a new, tight urgency in her gaze. All the languorous, long-winded ease was gone from her voice. "Yes, I know. You've found quite a lot of that here, haven't you, James? Harvested quite a lot of the love-aspect."

Duvall grinned, lifting a forkful of congealing macaroni toward Daphne in a toast. "And I'm just getting started."

Daphne's breathing was fast and shallow. "Do you hear that, Vera? He's just getting started."

Vera looked between the two of them, feeling like she was failing a test she hadn't known to study for. "Well," she said. "Well. That's fascinating."

He tucked his bite of pasta into one cheek, so his reply was thick and muffled. "I couldn't agree more." He gave Vera a conspiratorial smile, as though they were in on something together. "Now, about those letters—when would be a good time for me to take a look?"

Vera shook her head. "I don't think so, James. I've given enough information to Duvall men. You'll just have to commune with the spirits on your own." She pushed her own macaroni around the cardboard tray it called home, trying not to let the tines of her fork slide into the soft noodles.

Duvall reached across the table, touched the back of Vera's arm. "Think about it? For me. It's what Francis would have wanted."

CHAPTER TWENTY-FOUR

Vera was sure that the new bed would fix things.

She nestled the bed into one corner of the room, flush against two walls. She tucked the bedsheet and a clean comforter, fresh from the linen closet, tight under the mattress. She moved the dresser in front of the closet door so that nothing could pry it open in the night. Everything was quiet. There was no place for anything to hide.

The long, splintered grooves in the floor didn't even bother her. Whatever they were from, she'd defeated them already. Now they were nothing more than the mark of a fight that the other side had lost.

She was too tired to confront the question of what else might have been waging that battle. All that mattered was that it was over.

She opened the windows so she could breathe in the smell of the night. The air was cool and heavy with the weight of a thunderstorm that would come later, that would batter the outside of the house with fat raindrops while the inside of the house stayed dry. There wasn't even a trace of smoke in the air. Vera thought of Duvall in the tin-roofed shed, thought of the way the sound of the rain would fill it up until he couldn't think of anything but noise.

He'd said that he heard her pacing at night sometimes. She wondered if he would come into the house in the night, seeking respite from the rain, hoping to hear her discomfort. She wondered how quietly he could move. She wondered if he'd ever been inside her bedroom.

Vera padded through the dark dining room, past her mother's silent bed. The air around her echoed. *I'll always love you, but I hated you, too.*

In the kitchen, she bolted the back door. Once she made it back to her bedroom, she smiled at the silence, at those thick warm walls that could keep anything out and anything in. There could be no question that it would be better inside than outside that night. She sank into that feeling of peaceful anticipation, her arms and legs heavy, her breath already coming slow and sweet even as she turned off the bedroom lights.

She crossed the room in the dark, slid herself between those tight-tucked covers, and slept with the bottomless intensity of true exhaustion. Sleep slipped over her mind like an opera glove enrobing an elbow and even in unconsciousness she recognized the luxury of it, the decadence of true rest. Her sleep wasn't precisely dreamless, but her dreams were simple visions of endless, satiny blackness, perfect and unbroken.

Nothing took the blankets away.

Nothing touched her.

Nothing bothered her at all.

Vera woke to soft sunlight falling across her face. She smiled, her eyes still shut. That sun would mean that the thunderstorm had rolled over her in the night, and she'd slept so deeply that she hadn't even noticed it.

Today would be better. Everything outside would be washed clean, an explosion of green glittering with rainfall. She would finish cleaning out the mudroom today, she decided. All those old coats and scarves and boots would go to the secondhand store. She'd oil some hinges around the house, too. The house deserved some taking-care-of, some tenderness. It had held her safely all night, after all, had let her breathe its air and soak in its quiet.

It was the house her father built, and she needed to treat it right.

Maybe she would go into town, too, get a milkshake for Daphne. If Daphne could drink milkshakes. She'd have to ask about that. Or maybe she wouldn't ask. Maybe she'd just show up with it and sit down with her mother, just her mother, no James Duvall. Maybe they could share milkshakes and talk about the way her mother had always hated her and the way there was love in that hate somewhere.

Maybe they could really talk, before Daphne was gone for-ever. The way Vera had always yearned to talk to her. The way she'd never let herself wish they could talk.

But not yet. Her bed felt so good, and the sun was so warm on her cheek, and the feeling of having finally gotten some de-cent rest was too good to leave behind just yet. Vera rolled over to nestle her head deeper into her pillow.

But her pillow wasn't there.

Vera opened her eyes slowly, not wanting to see anything but knowing she needed to look. Her face was pressed into the fitted sheet. It still smelled faintly of laundry soap. She stared at the floral pattern, her own breath loud in her ears.

She didn't bother to tell herself that she was being silly. She didn't bother with the notion that she could have knocked her pillow to the floor in her sleep. She knew better than that.

But she didn't want to look up. She wanted to stay in that perfect pocket of victorious sleep for as long as she could. She didn't want the rest to happen, whatever it was going to be.

She didn't want it. She squeezed her eyes shut tight enough to squeeze out the tears that were building there. Whatever it was going to be, she didn't *want* it.

But it didn't matter if she wanted it or not. The bed wasn't comfortable anymore, wasn't safe and luxurious. She could feel every place where the tight-tucked covers were pressing close against her skin. She didn't feel snug anymore—she felt trapped.

She bit back a sob and, with all the clench-jawed effort of yanking out an ingrown fingernail, she sat up in the bed.

At first, she thought she was dizzy. Everything was tilted at a bizarre angle, just off-true, and the bedroom door was too close, and the angle of the light was all wrong, disorientingly bright. She gripped the bedsheets instinctively, waiting for the room to spin.

But it didn't spin. She didn't feel faint, her vision wasn't swimmy and gray. In fact, everything was perfectly sharp. The room stayed just as it was, and Vera quickly realized that it wasn't the room that was at a strange angle.

It was her.

She tried to jump out of the bed, to escape the room, to get away from whatever was wrong, but she immediately fell, because the floor was farther away than it was supposed to be. There was a yank in her belly as she fell through the six inches of empty air. The feeling was that of missing a stair, and then her knees hit the wood with a painful *thunk* and all her breath was gone.

She scrambled to her feet and ran to the door. It was close, much too close, so close to her, because her bed wasn't where she'd left it.

Nothing was where she'd left it. She'd woken up feeling like

everything was right again, and now nothing was right, nothing at all.

She wrenched the door open but she couldn't stop herself
from looking back. She had to see. She had to know for sure.

There was her brand-new bed, the mattress wrapped with
blankets as tight as a birthday present. Her brand-new bed with
the frame that went right down to the floor. She'd gone to sleep
with that bed tucked into the corner of the room, flush against
two walls.

Now it was in the center of the room. Right in the middle.
The head of the bed stood a good two feet away from the peephole in the floor. And the foot of the bed—the foot of the bed
was propped up, high and proud.

It was resting on the bottom drawer of her dresser.

The drawer had been pulled out all the way, leaving a bare,
ugly hole behind it. It was wedged beneath the lower right corner of the bed, along with her missing pillow and the quilt that
she'd lost her grip on two nights before, the quilt that she'd
misplaced, the quilt that had disappeared beneath that old brass
bedframe even as she'd tried to hang on to it. The quilt she
hadn't been able to find in the meantime.

The drawer should have contained Francis's letters. But even
with the bed covering part of the drawer, Vera could see from
where she stood that it was empty.

The pulled-out dresser drawer lifted the bed just high
enough to create a shadowy nook that the balled-up quilt and
the thin pillow did not fill. The room smelled like turned earth
and sweet lemon.

From the doorway, Vera peered into the space between the
bed and the floor, hoping to see a flash of white, the corner of
an envelope, anything to indicate that the letters weren't gone.

She didn't know what she would do if the letters were under the bed—her stomach twisted at the thought of reaching into that darkness, toward whatever might be hiding in there—but she looked anyway, desperate to see something that would answer the questions she didn't know how to ask about what had happened in the night.

She looked, and she looked. But no matter how hard her heart rattled in her chest, no matter how hard she yearned to know, Vera could not see.

Not yet.

CHAPTER TWENTY-FIVE

Vera is thirteen years old. She is angry all the time and her legs are too long and she has an idea that she can't put down.

The idea won't shake. It's become a stain on the underside of her skin, one that's been setting for the past few days. It's been there ever since Brandon's father disappeared from the basement below her bedroom. The basement is quiet now, but Vera's mind twitches like a damp spider all day long. She lies awake at night, on top of her bed instead of beneath it, trying to figure out what to do with the thought that won't leave her be.

The thought about Brandon.

She hasn't spoken to him since he pushed her by the creek, since she got mud beneath her fingernails and it was his fault. She's seen him at school but they're not in the same class and they aren't talking, and he doesn't come to her house after school anymore to ride bikes or throw rocks at the creek or try to find cool stuff in the woods.

She's not sure that he's avoiding her but she's not sure he isn't, either. Vera's been eating lunch with her second-best friend, who isn't really her friend at all, who has a very boring crush on the vice principal and won't shut up about it. She's been riding her bike by herself in the afternoon to the creek and back, feeling the wind on her face, unable to shake the thought of what's to be done about Brandon.

The uncertainty is the thing that infuriates her. It's cruel for him to make her feel this way. If Brandon told her that he didn't want to be friends anymore, she could deal with it. And if he still wanted to be friends but he at least *told* her that he was mad at her, she could yell at him and he would yell back, and then they'd be okay.

But he hasn't talked to her in a long time, in weeks and weeks, and she doesn't know if he's ever going to talk to her again, and it's putting a twist in her belly and a lump in her throat and an idea under her skin.

She would think that he, of all the people in all the world, would know how brutal uncertainty can be. His father's body still hasn't been found—it won't be, she knows it won't, they never are—and there are posters up everywhere, *have you seen this man,* and it's on the news every night. All anyone wants to talk about, except for Vera's second-best friend with the crush on the vice principal, is how nobody knows what happened to Brandon's father. How he must've run off with some woman or gotten murdered by a drifter or gotten kidnapped by mobsters.

It can't feel good, knowing that people are saying your father ran off with some woman. If Brandon thought about it for just one second he'd realize Vera is the best person for him to talk to about it.

All day long, from across the cafeteria and during recess, Vera sees how drawn and tired Brandon is. How his eyes dart around as if his father will turn out to have been hiding behind a tetherball pole this whole time. It's pathetic how miserable the uncertainty has made him. How fragile. He's being broken by it, slowly torn into exhausted little pieces of himself, ground down into a fine paste.

It's killing him.

So how could he inflict that same killing uncertainty on

Vera? How could he leave her guessing about whether or not they're still friends? How could he *keep* not learning his lesson?

It's all Vera can think about, the uncertainty and the cruelty of it, the way it doesn't make any sense for Brandon to be acting the way that he is. And then, one day, she's going into the girls' bathroom and he's coming out of the boys' bathroom, and he doesn't say anything to her at all. He looks at her, looks *right* at her, sees her for sure. No faking like he didn't notice her or like he's distracted by his lunch. He sees Vera and his eyes flash dark and furious.

And then, without a word, he walks away.

That's when the uncertainty vanishes and the idea crystallizes, and she knows without a doubt. The grease has him now. It's the only explanation for why he would treat her like this—as if they were never friends, as if they've never even met before. It's the only explanation for why he hasn't learned his lesson.

You can't learn a lesson, Vera reasons, when there's filth inside you.

She chews on the end of her pencil while her teacher talks about Egypt, carefully keeping her tongue away from the eraser. The yellow paint on the pencil crackles between her teeth. Now that she knows what the problem is she has a lot of thinking to do. The uncertainty is gone. There's a problem to be solved.

Fortunately, Vera is good at solving problems.

Vera can't imagine that the grease takes over a person all at once. It must happen sort of gradually, like a scab forming or puberty starting. One day you're clean inside and the next day, you're just a *little* bad.

Brandon is only a few months older than she is—he had a

movie party for his birthday last year, with popcorn and movie-candy—and he's only started acting different within those last few months. Even a month after that, he was still Vera's friend, and he'd never brought up kissing or said *fuck*. That means that this change in him is new. It's not all done yet. He hasn't been taken over and ruined. Not yet. Maybe, Vera thinks, frowning around her pencil, that means there's still hope for Brandon after all.

Maybe there's still time.

She doesn't think he's going to show up. It's cold out but not too cold. There's a September kind of chill that promises colder nights to come, and the air still smells more like grass than like woodsmoke. There aren't any clouds to drift across the moon and there's no moon to hide behind those nonexistent clouds, either. There's just the clear night sky with all the stars it can muster. Vera squints up at them and wishes hard on each and every one: *don't let it be too late for him.*

He gets to her house at midnight just like the note she dropped in his locker said. He leans his bike against the side of her house, right under the mudroom window, not bothering to put down the kickstand. He's not wearing a helmet. The moon-light catches in his hair, making it shine.

A little black flashlight on a lanyard bounces around his neck. He's come prepared.

"Are you serious?" he hisses through the dark, his whisper only just loud enough for Vera to hear over the din of insect buzzing. "Like, for real? We can go down there?" His eyes are brighter than she's seen them in days. He's not mad at her, not even irritated. He's just excited, because she made him a promise and the promise she made him is the most thrilling thing they could possibly share.

He looks like his old self again. Vera's heart thrills: she knew it. She knew the old Brandon was still in there, the one who wanted to be her friend, the one who liked her. She knew there was still time.

"I would have told you before, but you were too busy being an asshole," she whispers back. And then she reaches under her collar and tugs on the chain around her neck until it's free of her shirt. She holds up the chain to reveal the key that hangs at the end of it. "I took it," she says with a wicked grin. "I took it off his keychain and copied it. It's *so* cool down there," she adds, and she means it, and she can see Brandon believing her, she can see it in the way he bounces on the balls of his feet and glances between her and the house.

He has no idea, Vera thinks. He's broken, and that has to be hard, but he's going to be so happy once he finds out that she can fix him.

"Let's go," he whispers, an unselfconscious smile already starting to spread across his face at the thought of what secrets the forbidden basement might hold.

So they go. They slip off their shoes in the mudroom and they pad across the dark entryway until they reach the pair of doors that sit under the stairs. Vera uses her secret key to let Brandon into the place his father was never aware of leaving.

Vera always forgets how smart Brandon is. How fast. She always forgets, and tonight, for the first time, she recognizes what a mistake that is. He realizes all-too-quickly that the basement isn't what he thought it would be. He asks questions that he doesn't really seem to want answered, questions that come faster and faster, questions about the function of the big X and the rings in the floor. Then he points the white beam of his little black flashlight at the dark stains on the cement floor, and he doesn't ask anything at all.

He just looks up at Vera with wide, blank eyes, breathing hard through his nose. He looks at her like she's a stranger in a van, like she's a big barking dog with no leash, like she's a car driving too fast down the street where they're riding their bikes.

He looks at her for just long enough that Vera knows they aren't friends anymore.

And then he bolts.

Vera doesn't shout. She knows better than to shout. She darts after him, her sockfeet slipping on the cement. He's faster than she is and he runs up the stairs, taking them two steps at a time. But he's afraid. His flashlight beam is bouncing so fast it's like a shiver. He slips on the steps, one foot shooting out behind him. He catches himself on his hands, he drops his flashlight, he starts to push himself up but thank goodness the fall slowed him down.

It's enough. It's just enough.

Vera is right behind Brandon. Before he can get his feet underneath him she's got both hands around his ankle. He looks back at her and she gives him what she hopes is a reassuring smile.

Then she pulls as hard as she can and he goes sprawling. His arms flail out to catch him again but his hands land a stair too low, and his forehead meets the corner of a step with a sound like a carton of eggs hitting a sidewalk.

Vera tugs gently on Brandon's feet. He slides down the steps, limp as a dishrag. She stands over him at the foot of the stairs, rolling his dropped flashlight beneath her foot so the light plays across his smooth, expressionless face.

"Don't worry," she whispers. "I'm going to help you get better."

CHAPTER TWENTY-SIX

Vera is thirteen years old, and there are things she didn't consider when she made her plan to fix Brandon. Things her father must know from experience. Things she didn't realize would be tricky to figure out on her own.

First of all, she didn't think ahead about having to turn on the overhead lights. She'd thought she could work by the beam of her flashlight, but it's too hard to juggle it while she gets everything set up. After a long period of queasy consideration, she decides it's worth the risk to flick the lightswitch at the top of the stairs. She just has to hope that no one gets up for a midnight snack and notices light beneath the door to the basement.

Then again, Vera considers, it's not as if she's ever seen light leaking from below the door when her father is at work. Noise doesn't leak out either. She can hear sounds from inside her bedroom, because of the hole in the floor, but she can't hear anything from the entryway. She's tiptoed out there dozens of times while her father worked, pretending to go to the powder room. It's always been dark and quiet and still.

It's a well-built house they live in. It absorbs noise, hides light, keeps secrets. It wouldn't betray her. Not ever.

Vera decides there's nothing to worry about. Still, she flinches when she turns the lights on.

She also failed to plan for the difference in size between herself and her father. She didn't think to bring down a stepstool to stand on, so that she could secure Brandon to the big X. She can't reach high enough to get his arms up where they're supposed to be—it's hard enough for her to lift him at all, much less hold him in place with one hand while the other straps him in—so she settles for spreading him out on the floor and tethering him with the bike locks.

She holds one of the locks up to examine how it's supposed to go on his wrist. She's never been able to see this part close enough to understand it, and she's worried that it'll be confusing. But it's not confusing at all, because the bike locks are connected at one end to thick black cuffs with buckles on the outside and padding on the inside.

Vera smiles at this detail, at the padding. It's nice to know that Brandon's wrists won't get hurt when she ties him up.

She hadn't realized how nervous she would be. Her father always looks so confident, so focused, but her hands are trembling hard as she opens the top left drawer of her father's toolbench to take out a pocketknife. There's a whole set in there, laid out on foam padding so they don't slip around. This one has a handle carved from an antler, white and bumpy, slim enough to fit in Vera's hand.

She unfolds it until it clicks, locking into place. She's not sure how she's going to put it back, but she knows that Brandon will know. He can show her once they're finished.

The stainless steel shines under the bright lights. The handle is cold, but it warms up fast against her skin.

It's time. She's delayed long enough. She has to do this.

She has to fix Brandon.

Then she turns back to him and stares at his prone body. She doesn't know exactly where the grease is stored, where it comes from, where it builds up the most. She doesn't know how much to drain out of him, so she figures she'll just do a little tonight. Not as much as her father does. She won't finish him, either. She doesn't know how her father decides when to finish them, and besides, she wants Brandon to live. She wants him to get better. And unlike the monsters her father tries to help, she knows that Brandon isn't beyond repair.

She may not know all the details of the work, but she does know where to start. Her father always starts in the same place— she's seen it at least a dozen times now, her face pressed hard to the floor, her eye straining to focus on his every movement.

She always watches Francis. Her eyes are fixed on her father whether he's in the basement or out of it. She watches the way he holds his fork and the way he rolls up his sleeves and the way he combs his hair and the way he bleeds the evil out of the men he helps. *Watching is the only way to learn,* that's what Francis always says. Vera doesn't know how to ask what the right way is to do things, so she watches, and she remembers.

He always starts with the belly.

She kneels on the cement, and she tugs Brandon's shirt up from where it's tucked into his jeans, and she presses the point of the pocketknife against the soft white skin just above his navel.

She takes a deep breath. She gives it a hard push.

It's so much more difficult than she thought it would be. It's so much harder than her father makes it look. Brandon's belly is soft, and the skin doesn't want to break. The blade makes a dent in his skin but it won't push through to the well of foulness Vera knows must be just beneath the surface.

She takes a deep breath, imagining that Brandon is a stubborn patch of dirt instead of a boy. This, she tells herself, is not so much *stabbing* as it is *digging*. She rocks back on her heels and then surges forward, throwing her weight into her hands.

Brandon's eyes fly open just as the knife breaks through the taut surface of his skin.

"Whatareyoudoing," he gasps, his chin dropping as he strains to see his own stomach. "Vera Vera Vera what—"

"Shhh," she says. "I have to concentrate."

"No," he says, and his voice is so small that Vera hesitates. But then she looks up at him, sees the raw white panic on his face.

In that moment, she loves him more than she's ever loved anyone in her whole life.

He's her best friend. She can't let him rot from the inside. She has to save him.

She has to.

"Don't scream. If you scream, we'll get in trouble," she says, looking into his shining eyes, eyes that don't have even a trace of hate in them anymore. All that hate has been replaced by confusion and fear and pain. Vera smiles, because finally, Brandon looks like a person again. It's working already. "I'm doing this for your own good. I promise. It'll be over in a second."

She pushes the blade in just a little further. Brandon's stomach clenches tight around the metal like a fist, and his arms strain against the bike locks, but he doesn't scream. Vera loves him even more for doing what she asked. She knows, then, that she's doing the right thing.

It only takes a moment for the grease to start oozing up around the knife. She catches some in her hand. It's slippery and dark and wet and as warm as beach sand in summer. Triumph swells in Vera's chest.

This is it. This is the thing that's been changing him into a stranger.

Brandon's head lolls to one side. His belly flexes around the blade as he vomits. More grease surges up out of him, leaking around the edges of the knife, and it runs down his side. Soon, there's a dark ribbon stretching long and wide between him and the drain in the floor. She can never see this level of detail clearly enough through the peephole, not with the way the fisheye lens distorts things, and she peers at that ribbon. She frowns at it.

Because the fluorescent lights are gleaming off it and it doesn't look like grease at all.

This isn't right. This can't be right.

Vera runs a finger through it, painting a long stripe of red across Brandon's skin. When it's coming out of him, it looks so dark, but when it spreads out, it just looks like blood.

She's gotten it wrong. Somehow she's gotten it wrong. She hasn't tapped the reservoir of rot inside her friend. She's not saving him at all.

She pulls the knife out and lets it clatter to the floor. This is the wrong choice—she knows right away, because the blood is coming faster now, so much of it. Too much of it. The weight of her mistake expands inside her like water filling a balloon. She looks up at his rapidly graying face, dizzy with panic.

"Hang on," she whispers, scrambling to her feet. "Hang on, okay? I'm going to fix this, just—just wait here."

She runs up the stairs and turns off the lights—she feels bad about leaving Brandon in the dark, but it's only for a minute, he'll be okay. She unlocks the door too fast to be careful. She closes it behind her silently, then races past her bedroom door and up the inside stairs, skipping the fourth step that creaks. She darts down the upstairs hallway as quiet as she can. She only stops when she's reached the hall door to her parents' bedroom.

She holds her breath, pressing her ear to the door. Her heartbeat thuds hard and fast. After a long time—too much time, she has to move quicker than this, she has to get back to Brandon—she gently turns the doorknob and eases it open.

The bedroom is a monochrome landscape of gray in the muted moonlight that filters through the curtains. Her parents' bed looms in the middle of that darkness, dense and vast. Vera hesitates at the foot of it, caught by the strangely powerful feeling of observing her parents when they don't know she's there. But Brandon's blood is sticky on her fingers and the terror of leaving him alone in the basement shakes her out of it, and she darts toward the side of the bed nearest to the closets.

"Dad," she whispers, quiet as she can. He doesn't move. "Dad," she whispers again, no louder this time than the first, tapping him on the shoulder and leaving a dark smear behind. She blinks away tears and taps him harder. "Dad, wake up. Please. Please wake up."

Francis draws a sudden, sharp breath, his eyes flashing open. He doesn't recognize her right away and that alone would be enough to make the tears spill over—Vera has never seen her father look at her this way, like she's a stranger—but then he sits up and rubs his eyes and asks her what's wrong. She can't think of where to start, everything she comes up with is too big to say out loud and all she can seem to do is cry.

"What's all this about?" he whispers, then looks back at Daphne, who is stirring in her sleep. "Let's—let's go somewhere else," he says, the sleep sloughing away from his voice.

He slips out of bed and leads her into the hall on silent feet. He closes the bedroom door behind him without a sound, the same way Vera's learned to close doors at night, and then he turns around and Vera knows that he's about to ask her what's going on and she knows that she won't be able to answer so she doesn't try.

She just holds up her bloody hands, and she watches him understand.

"Is any of that yours?" he asks. When she shakes her head, he doesn't look surprised. His hands twitch at his sides. "Okay," he says, his voice steady the way Vera knew it would be. "Okay. Show me."

By the time they reach the basement, Vera has stopped crying. Her father is with her now and he'll know how to fix what she's done. The second the basement door is shut behind them, she turns the light on and races down the stairs. She's taking them two at a time, careful to keep from tripping or slipping or falling. She's trying to be fast *and* careful, both at once, so she keeps her eyes on her feet until she's two-thirds of the way down the stairs.

That's when she glances up at Brandon. What she sees stops her in her tracks.

Something is with him.

It's hunched over him, kneeling right in the middle of his pooling blood, its back curled over like a snail's shell. It looks like a tall kid or maybe a small adult, long-limbed and skinny. Vera can't make out any more details than that because the thing crouched over Brandon is hidden in shadow—but that shouldn't be possible, since it's right in the middle of the room, and the light is right overhead, bright as anything.

Vera opens her mouth to say something, to ask who's there, but then her father bumps into her and she stumbles down the last few stairs, and when she looks back up, the thing is gone. "Did you see . . . ?" she starts to ask, but she doesn't know how to finish asking.

"See what?" Francis asks, and then, without waiting for an answer, he runs to Brandon. "Oh, no. Oh, Vee, what happened?"

"I was trying to help. It didn't work." Brandon's eyes are closed and his face is so pale and so still and Vera has no idea how much of his blood has already disappeared down that drain in the floor.

Her father crouches beside Brandon. "You tried to bandage it already?"

"No, I just came to get you," Vera says. But then she looks at Brandon's belly, where a bundled-up kitchen rag is already soaked through with blood. Wherever his skin isn't covered in blood, it's smeared with some gray matte substance Vera doesn't recognize. "I don't . . . I don't know where he got that," she adds weakly.

"You used this one?" Francis picks up the antler-handled knife from where it rests next to Brandon's head.

Vera nods. She's certain that isn't where she left it, and she's certain that she didn't fold it up before running to get her father, because she doesn't know how to fold it up, and she's doubly certain that she didn't leave it pristinely clean because how could she have? But there's nothing for her to say because her father is scooping Brandon up under the knees and the shoulders, lifting him up the same way he used to lift Vera when she fell asleep on the couch and needed to be carried to bed.

"Brandon?" Vera whispers, and his eyelids twitch. He looks at her with unfocused eyes.

"Vera," he whispers back. "We're gonna get in so much trouble."

She shakes her head. "No," she says, "no, I didn't—I didn't put the knife all the way in, I think you'll be okay. Dad's here," she adds.

"Hey, buddy," Francis says softly. "I'm gonna get you up the stairs, okay? It might hurt a little as we go. Think you can stay quiet?"

Brandon shakes his head, giving Vera a faint approximation of a smile. "It doesn't hurt at all," he says. "I can't feel a thing."

Vera smiles back at him. It doesn't hurt. That, she thinks, must be a good sign.

She flies up the stairs ahead of her father and opens the basement door, then the garage door, then the back door of the car. Francis loads him gently into the backseat and eases the car door shut. Vera is about to head for the passenger seat when he catches her by the shoulder.

"You stay here," he says.

She shakes her head. "I'm going with you."

"Going where?" Vera and her father look to the open garage door in unison, where Daphne is standing in her big pink bathrobe, her arms crossed over her chest. "What on *earth* are you two doing awake? Do you have any idea what time . . ." She trails off, her eyes falling to the blood on Francis's shirt and hands, on Vera, smeared on the car door.

Vera watches her mother's face drain of color, watches her mother's mouth fall open, watches a shiver of violent disgust climb her mother's spine. She watches her mother's eyes for love and doesn't find it there, and Vera is sure that it's because of her failure tonight.

"I got it wrong, I—I messed it up," Vera says, but she never gets to tell her mother *what* she messed up.

"Don't say anything," Daphne hisses. "Don't say a single word, Vera Marie Crowder. You go inside. I need to talk to your father."

"Mom," Vera says. Just the one word. It comes out as a thin wobble of sound, barely a mew.

"Inside. Now."

Vera sidles past her mother and hovers just inside the garage door, listening to the hushed, heated conversation she's been cut out of. She can only make out bits and pieces no matter how hard she strains. She can catch her father whispering the word *hospital,* and her mother saying *just get rid of him.* Her father's voice rises above a whisper when he says *only a kid* and then the conversation must be over because the car starts with a sudden growl.

Daphne storms back into the house, slamming the garage door. She looks at Vera for a long time, her eyes flat and cold. "Fine," she says at last. "It looks like you won. I hope you're happy. This is going to be a nightmare."

Vera doesn't know what it is that she's supposed to have won, and she doesn't get a chance to find out. Because before she can ask—before she can ask what's happening to her best friend, where her father is going, who was in the basement hovering over Brandon—Daphne is halfway up the stairs.

"Mom?" Vera calls after her.

Daphne doesn't look back, but she does pause for a moment, her hand resting on the banister. "Oh, no," she says softly, thoughtfully. "No, Vera. I don't think you need to call me that anymore."

And then she turns off the light, leaving Vera alone in the dark.

CHAPTER TWENTY-SEVEN

Vera stood in the kitchen in the clear light of morning, leaning her full weight against the edge of the sink. The scratched-up white porcelain lip of it dug painfully into the small of her back. She drank a too-hot cup of instant coffee and reviewed the things she was certain of.

There were, in total, three of them.

The first thing she knew was this: She knew that there was something under her bed. Something real. Real enough to sneak. Real enough to take. Real enough to lift the bed with her on it, so smoothly that she hadn't woken up at the movement.

The second thing she knew was this: She knew that it didn't matter what bed she was in. What mattered was that the bed was *hers*. What mattered was that she was in it. Maybe it wouldn't even matter if she was in the house her father built. Maybe when Daphne was dead and the house was sold, the thing under the bed would follow Vera out into the world. Maybe it would find her wherever she rested and pull the covers from her body and whisper tenderly into her ear and reach long fingers down into her throat to stroke the root of her tongue.

The third thing she knew was this: She knew that she wanted to see it.

Acknowledging that final point was comfortable in a way that made Vera feel strangely guilty. It had been a long time since she gave in to the urge to look at something that was meant to be hidden. It took the edge off her fear. It felt gorgeous, like slipping into her own skin again after half a life spent as raw flesh. She smiled into her coffee cup as she rolled the feeling over her tongue: *I want to see.*

The luxuriant moment was disrupted by movement outside the kitchen window. Vera looked out and saw a shirtless James Duvall opening the door to the garden shed. He was hauling out tall painted boards, like the ones Vera had seen him with before. He leaned them up against the outer wall of the shed, one by one, lining them up in the morning sun.

Later, Vera would wonder what possessed her to go and look closer. In that moment, she followed the impulse without questioning it, carrying her coffee out to the yard and treading barefoot through the dewy grass.

"Morning, early riser," Duvall called without looking up at her.

"Morning," she replied. "These your paintings?"

"No." Duvall braced a board against the side of the shed, the wiry muscles of his back standing out with the effort of balancing it. The board was easily ten feet long. It was scabbed with layers of paint and something else, something thick and gray. Plaster, maybe. "These aren't mine. They're *ours.*"

Vera could smell him now, sweat and cheap tobacco and something sharp and oily. "Ours?"

He stood next to Vera, staring up at the painted board with her, and shoved his hands into his pockets, tugging his already-drooping jeans a little further down on his hips. "I told you, I'm collaborative. Me and the Other, we worked together to make this. It's a distillation of the essence of the memories that suffuse this place. A pure rendering of the haunting of the Crowder House."

He said it like he was rehearsing, which, Vera realized, he probably was. These boards would go on display in a gallery somewhere—New York, maybe, or Vancouver—and Duvall would need to have his little speech ready to go. He would need to explain the pieces to buyers so that they would know what chunks of Vera's life they were buying up.

"How do you do it?" she asked.

"Aren't you going to tell me that the house isn't haunted?"

Vera peered up at the board. It looked familiar, but she couldn't put her finger on why. "It's not just paint." She reached out to touch the bumpy surface of the not-a-painting—but Duvall intercepted her, catching her wrist in one hand.

"Don't touch that," he said. "It's still curing." Vera tried to pull her hand back but Duvall didn't let go right away. His grip was firm, but not painful. There was something gray caked around the edges of his fingernails. One corner of his mouth eased up into a smile, slow as butter melting. "You can't say it, can you?"

His face was close enough that Vera could make out the threads of red just beneath the surface of his eyes. He'd been up all night working, while she'd been fast asleep. "Can't say what?"

"Can't say it isn't haunted."

"I can say all kinds of things," she said, pulling her arm away from him again, sharply enough to break his grip this time. "But I've gotten out of the habit of saying what Duvall men want to hear." She wanted to leave, wanted to stalk into the house and slam the door behind her—but as she turned to walk away from Duvall, something caught her eye.

Something high up on the board.

She pointed at it. "Wait, what's that?"

"I think it needs a little more work, actually," Duvall said, stepping between Vera and the board. "Excuse me." He picked it up slowly, carefully, and before Vera could think of a way to protest, he'd disappeared into the garden shed and closed the door behind him.

So Vera waited. She bagged up dusty stacks of fabric in her mother's old sewing room, moth-infested scraps that had been there for as long as she could remember. She washed laundry in the rattling old washing machine that was and had always been inexplicably located in the mudroom. She took lemonade bottles out to the recycling bin.

Once, while she was carrying a basket of laundry from the mudroom to her bedroom, Vera caught the sound of murmuring from the too-dark dining room. She paused, leaning against the wall, listening to the soft, scratchy sound of her mother's voice.

"Everything was easy before you started acting like a person," she was saying, low and steady, muffled, like she was reciting a prayer into the cave of her own clasped hands. "Secrets and resentments and opinions. You didn't like things and you had reasons for not liking them. You'd say the reasons out loud instead of just crying about whatever hated thing was in front of you. You demanded all the love anyone had, but you started giving it back, and that made the ones who loved you double their efforts. You harvested love as if you'd ever done anything to nurture it, to tend to it, to raise it up strong and bind it . . ."

And then the words trailed off into silence, and the darkness in the dining room thickened even further, and a shiver climbed Vera's spine.

There was one more thing she could be sure of: she hadn't been meant to hear that.

She returned to her bedroom and she folded laundry, and she watched out the bedroom window, waiting for James Duvall to go out.

❧

The inside of the shed was not what Vera remembered.

The last time she had been in here, she'd been talking to Hammett Duvall. He'd cleared the shed out and turned it into a makeshift office—a folding table with an old-fashioned typewriter on it, a folding cot in the corner, a camp chair beneath a battery-powered camping lantern hung from a hook on the wall. She could remember him clear as anything: sitting in that camping chair, setting his half-drunk warm beer on the floor between his feet so he could write down what she was saying about her father's jokes.

Those jokes had made it into his book. *Fish can be such gossips.*

It was a big shed, a little larger than the dining room where Daphne had decided to die. Francis had constructed it with a garden in mind, imagining Daphne starting seedlings and bulbs inside. He'd added built-in cabinets and a long counter running along one wall, and a deep freestanding sink. It was supposed to be a place where she could build out the dreams that Francis imagined her having. It had ended up full of tools and spiders, and the garden had ended up as an expanse of knotgrass and bull thistles.

In the years since Vera's last visit to the shed, it had changed. The hands of countless guests had transformed it into a livable place. The walls—formerly primer-white—had been painted a deep high-gloss green. The battery-powered lantern had been replaced by a single bulb that hung from the middle of the ceiling, connected to an extension cord that was stapled into place all the way to the outlet where it was plugged in. That was new, too, Vera realized—the shed had electricity, whether or not the county knew about it.

The sink had turned into an entire bathroom-corner, with an unconcealed toilet and a showerhead over a cement shower pan. The camp chair was gone, too, replaced by a threadbare pink recliner Vera didn't recognize. The cot was still in its same corner, although the mattress on it looked to be more plush than the slim one Hammett had suffered on. Vera did a double-take as she realized why: it was her old mattress, the one her mother had replaced in anticipation of her arrival.

I'm sure he'll find it inspiring, she'd said.

The rest of the space was filled with James Duvall. A toiletry kit hung from a nail in the wall, a string of pockets brimming with essentials. His clothes were folded and stacked on top of the counter: Y-front briefs, dark denim, faded tees and A-frame undershirts. A set of tools were laid out on a small gray folding table in the center of the room—a plane, a sanding block, a gouge with a dark handle. The peeling vinyl top of the folding table was blotched with paint and plaster. A jar of wet brushes sat next to the sink, bristle-side up, drying.

And surrounding it all, dominating three out of the four walls of the shed, James Duvall's art stood sentinel.

Vera recognized the boards now that she was seeing them all together, now that she could see the raw materials. She recognized that faded, splintery wood, pressed her fingertip into the ragged hole where a nail had fixed one of them to its frame. The edge of the hole crumbled a little at her touch.

These boards had been part of the old front porch.

The porch her father had built. He had been the one who knew how to care for it. By the time Vera had left home, it had been wrecked by years of snow and salt, summer humidity and fall heat. It must have been a disaster by the time Duvall showed up. Half-rotted. A safety hazard, probably. Vera could only imagine.

It was good that it had been torn down and rebuilt. She knew that.

But seeing those old boards here, torn up and set aside for Duvall to use in his art, nauseated her a little.

She could see his method now. Boards were lined up along one wall for the most part in various stages of progress—raw, planed along the edges, sanded and smoothed, etched with deep vertical grooves. Painted and sculpted and painted some more, terraformed into rising layers that turned the topography of each one into a story.

It was good art. She couldn't deny that, no matter how much it turned her stomach to see.

One board was stretched out across two sawhorses. She surprised herself by recognizing it instantly as the one she'd seen that morning. It was the longest of them all. Judging by the ragged ends of the other boards, this was the only one that Duvall had managed to save whole, without it splintering into halves or thirds during the process of tearing that porch apart. Vera took a step closer to it.

It didn't look very different than it had that morning. She traced the grooves in the wood with her eyes, trying to find the thing she'd seen that morning. The thing that he hadn't wanted her to see. The thing he'd wanted to hide from her.

There. At the place between a short groove and a long one, half-covered by the drying layer of gray paste that coated Duvall's fingernails. She squinted, trying to make out what she was starting to recognize as words. Handwritten words.

GROWING UP SO FAST

Vera recognized that handwriting.

The door to the shed swung open, smacking into the wall with a bang. Vera whipped around. "You're back."

"Well, this is a surprise." Duvall stepped inside, his movements languorous, his eyes bright with a curious kind of anger. He closed the door behind himself and leaned back against it. "I don't recall inviting you in, Vera Crowder."

"Where did you get that?" she asked, pointing down at the board.

Duvall crossed his arms. "I rebuilt the front porch for your mother. She said I could keep the trash."

"Not the board. The papers. That's my father's handwriting. Do you have—did you take—" Her heart was in her throat. She stepped closer to the boards against the wall, examining them with increasing horror.

The longer she looked, the more words she spotted. They were everywhere: little pieces of paper with frayed edges, blended into the surrounding medium so seamlessly they might have grown out of it. There were places where water had made the ink bloom, bleeding from the paper and into the surrounding medium. She picked out a few sentence fragments, trying to make sense of what she was seeing.

SO SMART
REMEMBER THAT FIRST FISH, HOW IT
STRUGGLED

AN UNPOISONED MIND, A CLEAN MIND

MISS YOU SO MUCH, VERA-BABY

"You shouldn't be in here." Duvall's breath was hot on the back of Vera's neck. She whirled around, too furious to be afraid, too hungry to notice that he was standing between her and the only exit from the shed.

"You took them." She had to crane her neck to look up at him. He was so close that she could see the muscle of his jaw working. "You took my father's letters, his journal."

Duvall's mouth twitched. "Journal?"

She pointed to the board on the sawhorse. "It's right there. It's his handwriting. Don't bother denying it, you—"

"That's his handwriting," Duvall said, his voice as soft as the flesh inside a cheek. He took a step closer, forcing Vera to step back. "But I don't know anything about a journal. Why? You hiding something, Vera?"

She shook her head, taking another step back as he moved closer again. "Those were mine. Those letters were all I had of him. How could you take them?"

"Daphne said I could have anything I wanted for my work," he said. "You and I both know I had more of a right to those letters than you did." Another step toward her, and now they were past the edge of the sink and all the boards and tools were out of Vera's reach. The single lightbulb overhead was just behind Duvall's head, framing him in a blinding halo that made it impossible for Vera to make out his face. "This house is mine. It's my legacy. It's my right to elevate it."

"How could it possibly be more yours than mine? *My* father built this place. You don't have a right to any of it. You're just . . . you're just a visitor." She took a step back and felt something soft against the backs of her knees—the edge of the thin mattress in the far corner of the shed.

"You're shivering," he murmured. "You cold, Vee? There's a blanket right there behind you." He reached over both of her shoulders, his chest pressing into hers. She recoiled, turning her face to the side to avoid his. Then he drew back just enough for her to breathe. A soft, tobacco-reeking weight settled onto her shoulders. She reached up reflexively and her fingers found the scratch of wool.

Duvall shoved his hands into his pockets but didn't step back, forcing Vera to remain bent over backward to keep from touching him. He looked down at her the same way she'd seen him look down at so many microwaved dinners—a combination of resigned interest and removed disgust. "Oh. I should answer your question," he whispered. "This place belongs to me more than it belongs to you because your mother is leaving it to me when she dies."

A violent shudder of revulsion climbed Vera's spine and rattled her like a terrier giving a rat the killing-shake. She shrugged off Duvall's blanket and ducked past him, her stomach climbing up into her throat. "No," she said, "no chance. Never."

"You left, Vera," he said. Vera turned to see him standing with his hands still in his pockets, his shoulders up around his ears, that same slippery half-smile resting easy on his lips. "But my dad? He called Daphne. He wrote. He helped her find boarders when money was tight. Really, we're more of a family to her than you've ever been."

"She wouldn't. She wouldn't give the house to you." Even as Vera said it, she knew it wasn't true. Daphne had adored Hammett, had loved the attention his book brought her.

He grinned at her, that warm lopsided grin that made his

eyes crinkle up, the one that made Vera's soft palate itch, the one that made her stomach twitch with humid want. "Your mother is leaving the house to me. The documents are in the fire safe in the shed," he added, "in case you're thinking of trying to interfere with your mother's last wishes." His smile grew wider. "Don't worry. I'll let you stay. Someone'll need to give tours, and I'll be too busy by then." He gestured at the boards as Vera backed toward the door. "I've already got international interest. We're going on tour together, me and the Crowder House."

Vera stumbled out of the shed and onto the lawn. It was half-dark outside already. She wasn't aware of crossing the backyard, climbing the back steps, walking through the kitchen and the dark, cold dining room. She had spent the day shying away from her bedroom, but now she wound up there with all the inevitability of water sliding down a shower drain. She only realized she'd been in motion when she slid the desk chair under the doorknob.

She didn't bother flipping the lightswitch. She could make out the furniture in the room by what little light came through the windows—she wasn't sure if it was moonlight yet, or if it was still the last legs of daylight lingering before giving way to full night. Either way, she could see just enough to move across the room.

The bed was still propped up on the dresser drawer, the one that Duvall had emptied when he took the letters from Francis to use in his . . . she didn't know what to call it. *Art* seemed like the wrong word now. It was more like a sick kind of embalming, she thought, or taxidermy. Preserving something that had never really been.

That morning, the bed had terrified her. It had seemed like

an insurmountable, impossible thing to be avoided at all costs. Now, she crawled into it, heedless of the lack of a pillow, wanting nothing more than to be swallowed by the blankets like a pebble disappearing into a closed fist. She curled herself into a knot in the center of the mattress, shoved her face into the sheets, and sobbed.

She knew that she should be frightened. She knew that she should be afraid of whatever had moved the bed in the night, whatever had taken her quilt away, whatever had rattled that old brass bedframe on her first night here and climbed into her dreams with cold fingers and a sweet whisper. She knew that she should try to find out what it was, or run from it, or kill it.

She knew it was probably there in the dark, waiting for her to fall asleep.

But in that moment, as she hid in the safest part of the safest room of the safest place she'd ever known, trying to understand how it had all gone so wrong, she wasn't afraid. She was too alone to be afraid.

"Please," she sobbed breathlessly, not knowing what she was asking for. "Please."

The word fell out of her like blood from an open wound, over and over, more than Vera knew she had in her. More than she knew she could survive.

She fell asleep before she could hear the answer.

CHAPTER TWENTY-EIGHT

The morning rolled over Vera like a heavy fog. She woke soggy with fatigue, a weight in her bones that she didn't bother trying to shake. Too much was happening all at once—Duvall sliding steadily from flirtatious to dangerous, the revelation and immediate destruction of her father's letters, the way Daphne kept dying and dying and dying but would never, it seemed, be dead.

She let herself indulge in the smothering velvet of exhaustion. She'd never been hungover, but this was what she imagined it must be like. Suffocation, but easy.

"Vera?" Daphne called from the next room, her voice clearer than usual. Vera suppressed a groan, sliding out of her crooked bed. She wasn't startled to realize that she'd slept through the night without incident, wasn't surprised to find that the foot of the bed was still resting on that pulled-out dresser drawer. She was too tired to be surprised.

When she walked into the dining room, Daphne's eyes caught her with their bright, alert regard. She looked almost like a woman who wasn't supposed to die at any moment. That should have been a relief. A good daughter, Vera thought, would be relieved. She so badly wanted to be relieved, but her weariness stood solid as a bouncer between her and that feeling, all crossed arms and slowly shaking head.

"You're up early," Vera said mildly, passing through into the kitchen with a mind toward coffee. The pot was hot and half-empty: Duvall had been through already. "How did you sleep?"

A long, low scrape came from the next room. Daphne's breathing was getting worse. "There's no time. We need to talk. We need to talk while it's just us."

"All right," Vera muttered, pulling a mug out of the dishwasher and filling it with burnt-smelling coffee. "We'll just skip the good-mornings, then."

Daphne either didn't hear her or didn't care. "You need to start preparing yourself. And the house."

Vera bit back a pissy *what do you think I've been doing this whole time*. "I'm almost finished with the upstairs, except for Dad's office," she said instead. "And down here, I've really only got this room to finish up, and the mudroom. A little of the kitchen. Do you want breakfast?"

"That's not what I meant," Daphne said, her voice low and urgent. "You can't stay here. You need to get the house ready before you leave. You'll have to make some repairs, patch some things up. And James will want you to round up someone new for the shed once his work is done, and you have to make sure it's the right kind of person."

"I wanted to talk to you about that, actually," Vera said, returning to the dining room with her mug in her hands. "James said something yesterday about the deed to the house—" Vera asked.

"Find a writer," Daphne went on, as though Vera hadn't spoken. She drew another long, grinding breath. "Please. Artists pay better than writers, but they take things they shouldn't. They take advantage."

Vera thought of the long gouges under her bed, the discarded blue gloves in the basement, the stickiness of the front

steps in the hottest part of the day. She thought of the hole between her bedroom and the basement, the pipes anchored into
the ceiling, the faulty wiring in the upstairs hall. She thought of
the long boards in the garden shed, grooved and plastered and
painted, all of it stolen.

"You also ought to start preparing yourself for the reporters," Daphne continued. "It might be best—" Her voice caught,
and she looked away from Vera, her chin buckling. "It might be
best for you to have a plan, for when you leave. A way to keep
yourself out of the papers."

Vera took a step closer, wrapping her hands around the
mug that was almost too hot to hold, letting the heat distract
her from the awful, strange sound of her mother's breathing.
Wondering what Daphne's angle was. "I don't know," she said
evenly. "I suppose that if the papers want to talk to me, I'll just
say the same things I told Hammett Duvall. I'll say that I didn't
know about it."

Daphne shook her head slowly. "They won't believe you,"
she replied. She sat back hard against her throne of pillows,
her eyes hooded, her bottom lip dripping gray ooze onto her
chest. Her hands gripped the bedsheets as tight as a throat as
she stared Vera down. "You'll get into so much trouble, Vera.
You'll get into so much trouble if they start asking questions
about you, about Brandon, about what happened to him down
in the basement that night—"

"Wait," Vera said, hating the childish lump in her throat for
the way it distorted her voice. She looked down into the deep,
rich, dark brown of the coffee, trying to find comfort there.
She was so tired, too tired for this. Too tired to keep fighting.
"Stop. You can't—you can't just decide that we're going to talk

about it. You've never been willing to talk to me about Brandon before."

"It's different now," Daphne said.

"What's different now? Just because you're dying, we get to pretend . . . what? What is it?"

Daphne wasn't looking at Vera anymore. She was looking away, discomfort taut in every line of her body. She seemed, somehow, to be comprehensively *clenched*.

She was looking at the floor.

In the same moment Vera realized where Daphne's eyes were pointed, she heard the thing anew. The soft sound that had been vibrating beneath their conversation, the scraping sound that had seemed like the broken breath inside her mother's chest, the sound that she suddenly recognized as distinctly and violently Other.

"Daphne? What is that?" Vera whispered.

Daphne's gaze remained fixed firmly on the floor in the corner of the room, right where the wall between the dining room and the entryway ended. She flinched, just barely, at the steady, slow scrape that came from the room below. "It's him," she said, her voice high with pain. The chandelier rattled softly overhead.

"Who?"

"We don't have long," Daphne replied, tearing her gaze away from the corner of the room, suddenly vulnerable in a way Vera had never experienced. She sounded like someone else entirely, just then. "Please."

"Please?" Vera whispered, her eyes flicking back to the corner where Daphne had been staring.

In that moment it became clear: Daphne knew. She knew

about the haunting, the thing that came in the night, she knew about whatever it was. "Tell me. Tell me what it is, Daphne. We can deal with it together. Is it—" Her voice broke. "Is it Dad?"

Daphne didn't reply for a long time. Vera looked up, only to see that her mother's face was suddenly placid, her hands still. Her eyes were still locked on the corner of the room. When she spoke, her voice was terribly quiet and terribly even.

"Vera. Do you think you could get me a lemonade?"

Vera stared at her hard for a long time before turning on her heel and marching into the kitchen. She dropped her mug of coffee into the sink, no longer able to stomach the smell of it. She didn't need it anymore anyway. Her fatigue was gone, dissolved by that sound and her mother's awareness of it. Replaced by something else.

She should have been terrified by the noise that had distracted Daphne, by the presence of something in the house that could move her bed and scrape along the insides of the walls and ruin the conversation they'd needed to have for so long. She should have been afraid.

But she wasn't afraid. She was pissed.

And she was hungry.

She was so, so hungry. The longer she was home, the harder it was to keep fighting that hunger down. To keep pretending it wasn't there. She swallowed hard, trying to keep it at bay. Trying, trying, trying.

She opened the refrigerator and stood before the rows of bottles. All those smiling lemons. The one she took out looked just like all the others, but when she went to set it down on the counter, it stuck just a little to her skin, just enough to make it difficult to let go.

When she looked at her hand, she found that a smear of

something thick and dark and clotted clung to her, filling the creases in her palm.

Vera bit down hard on her tongue. She washed her hand fast and rough, using dishsoap and her fingernails to scour every trace of whatever-it-was from her skin. The substance had a familiar texture and stubbornness.

She would not under any circumstances allow herself to think of it as grease.

The grease wasn't real, she reminded herself as she dug her nails into the flesh of her palm. It never had been. It was her father's delusion. People weren't grease-filled monsters. They were human beings, filled with warm red blood that spilled over your hands and onto the floor and down the basement drain.

They weren't filled with cold dark grease that got under your fingernails and smelled like lemonade.

It wasn't real.

The sound of footsteps drifted in from the other room, heavy boots on hardwood. Vera could hear her mother murmuring, the soft sound of James Duvall's reply. She closed her eyes and swore softly under her breath. *Not him. Not now.*

She couldn't make out their words. That at least was a mercy. She didn't know if she could handle seeing him, hearing him, smelling the cheap tobacco on his breath. Not after last night and not now, not with that hunger trying to climb up out of her throat. She didn't know what she might do.

"Vera?" Daphne called again from the other room. "Vera, are you in there?" She sounded frail, needful.

Vera felt her seams fraying. She clenched her jaw, determined to keep herself together, because she knew that if she fell apart, there would be no one else to put her back together.

"I'm coming," she called. There was no point in trying to delay. She couldn't avoid Duvall forever. She pulled a fresh bottle out of the refrigerator, leaving the soiled one on the kitchen counter, and braced herself for the way the corners of his mouth would creep up at the sight of her.

But he was already gone. The front door closed just as Vera twisted the cap off the lemonade bottle.

"There you are," Daphne said.

Vera set out a row of paper cups in front of her mother. "Here I am. That was good timing, wasn't it? I must have just missed James."

Daphne looked back at her with wide, wet, gray-filmed eyes. "He's coming back soon," she whispered.

Vera poured with a steady hand. "I'm sure he is. Listen, before I went into the kitchen, you said—"

"He's coming back soon," Daphne said again. "You should go. You should run."

She didn't sound like herself. There was no sly threat in the words, no disdain tucked into the edges of her voice. There wasn't low, practiced, rehearsed resonance, either.

She sounded open. She sounded sincere.

She sounded afraid.

Vera looked up at her mother, trying to understand. Daphne lifted a trembling hand to wipe a slick of dark gray film from the corner of one eye. "Vera-baby," she said softly. *"Run."*

The sound of her voice sent an electric jolt through Vera's belly. She took an involuntary step backward, her hand releasing the lemonade bottle so it shattered at her feet, splashing her bare legs and soaking her socks. "Mom," she whispered, and her mother did not recoil at the name.

But that was all Vera got the chance to say, because in that same instant of shocked recognition, the front door slammed open and James Duvall descended once more upon the Crowder House.

"You," he growled, pointing at Vera as his long strides devoured the space between them. "What did you do?"

"James, don't," Daphne started to say—but Duvall cut her off with a sharp gesture.

"No, Daphne. I agreed to give her space *before* I saw what she did to my work. Did you know about this? Of course you didn't. But you," he added, jabbing a vicious finger at Vera. "You are coming with me *right* now."

Lemonade was drying sticky on Vera's legs and there was glass all around her feet. She felt like a cornered cat, wanting to hiss and bite and run all at once, ready to taste blood if she couldn't find her way to a dark quiet place.

She lowered a hand to her side and snapped her fingers softly as she could. Once, twice. Three times.

Before she could snap a fourth time, Duvall had her.

His grip on her upper arm was sudden and strong in a way that made her realize how ostentatious his gentleness had been until this moment. He hadn't hurt her yet and she knew all at once that it was on purpose, that he'd been making a point of not hurting her, and now he was making a point of letting her know just how much he'd been holding back. He pulled her over the broken glass, not letting her move slowly enough for care, and she had to leap to avoid impaling herself.

She only let him yank her a few steps before she wrenched her arm away. "What do you want?" she snapped.

"I want to know what you did," he snarled. "And I want you to fix it."

He didn't try to grab her again. Instead, he stalked across the kitchen, flung the back door open, and stood there, waiting for her. Vera's instinct was to stay where she was, to try to remind Duvall that he didn't get to tell her what to do. But the ache in her arm made her think again.

Duvall, she realized, was hungry too. Maybe it wasn't the best idea to test the limits of that hunger.

She followed him out, keeping space between them, staying out of reach. The dew had mostly evaporated off the lawn but the grass was still a little damp and her already-wet socks were quickly soaked through.

Duvall was moving toward the garden shed with furious purpose, his fists clenched at his sides. "Fix it," he shouted, not looking back at Vera. "Fix it right now."

"Fix what?" She asked it one instant before she saw what he meant, and then she understood exactly what needed fixing.

All the boards he'd torn up from the porch were propped up against the side of the garden shed. There were perhaps twenty of them in all, of various sizes. Enough for a small gallery show, Vera supposed.

James Duvall's great work of art, illuminated at last by the summer sun.

All of it ruined.

Thick black ooze was smeared across each panel, long slick trails of it. As Vera came closer she could see what looked like deep, cruel fingernail grooves dug into the layers of plaster— the sculptural element Duvall was so proud of. It was so thick in places that Vera could see the weight of it, the heft, could see the surface tension of it about to break. In other places it was thin enough for layers of color to show through, undertones of red and gray and green like the slip of intestines in the belly of a fresh-caught fish.

"What is it?" Duvall demanded. "Tar? Plumber's grease? Get rid of it. Fix this."

Vera shook her head, biting back a smile. "I don't know what it is," she said. "I didn't do this."

He wheeled around on her, a vein starting to stand out in his temple. "Don't fucking lie to me," he growled. "You're the only person who could have done this. It's not like your mom hauled her carcass out here—"

"Careful," she murmured. "You'll stop being her favorite if she hears you saying that kind of thing."

"Just tell me what it is," Duvall said again, breathless. "Tell me what you did. Tell me, Vera, goddamn it, stop laughing, this isn't a game!"

But she couldn't stop laughing, because here it was. Here was Duvall's anger. Here was his violence. Here was the thing she'd been trying to avoid this whole time, the thing that she'd run away from last night, the thing that had made her weep in her bed with fear and hunger and urgent need.

He was no bigger than the men who'd died beneath her bed when she was a child. His anger was no greater than their fear had been. She'd been so afraid of what his anger might unlock in her, but here it was, pointed right at her, and it was so small. He was clenching his fists and stomping his feet and shouting as if that could touch her.

"I can't help you, James," she laughed. "I didn't touch your shit. Maybe . . ." She bit her lips to stop from smiling, tried her best to look sincere, gave a little shrug. "Maybe it was the ghost."

"Get back here," he called as she started back toward the house. Vera heard him take a few steps after her. When she looked back, she saw him standing there in the center of the lawn, his face flushed, his mouth half-open. He was radiating all the fury he had to offer. "Don't you fucking walk away from me," he added, his voice low and dangerous. "Don't you go back into my house. Not until I'm done with you."

The laughter died in Vera's throat. Not out of fear—not because Duvall was trying to threaten her—but because he'd called it his.

He thought this was his house.

Clarity struck Vera like a knuckle to the eye.

She knew, knew in her bones, that the smartest and most logical thing to do would be to leave. She could get into her car and drive away from the Crowder House, away from Marion, New York, away from the smell of sweet lemon and the relentless intrusion of thick dark grease. It was the obvious thing to do. Why should she stay? Why should she make herself remain in this house, with a mother who seemed to be a different person every day and a man who wanted so badly to be frightening, and a thing that came in the night to whisper into her ear? Why not walk out the front door and never return? None of this was worth the fight, none of it.

Her mother didn't deserve an easy death, and Duvall didn't deserve her fear, and the thing under her bed didn't deserve the bites it was taking out of Vera's sanity.

She could go. She *should* go. The thought tapped itself against the inside of Vera's skull, insisting on its own logic.

But Vera knew now: she wasn't going to leave. On some level she'd known it since she arrived. She'd been telling herself the whole time that she was only here to fix up the house and sell it, but some part of her had known the truth all along. And now that Duvall thought the house was going to be his, she was certain.

She was never going to leave. Not now that, after all these years, she was finally where she belonged.

The Crowder House was hers. Francis Crowder had created this place for the family he wanted to build, for the demons he needed to exorcise, for the life he needed to live. It was the last place she'd ever felt his love. It was the last place anyone had ever hugged her and told her that she was worth something. And maybe Vera would never get to see her father again—she would never even get to read his letters, Duvall had made sure of that—but at least she could have this place.

She could have a home. She could. And James Duvall, this little man with his soft skin and red blood and pitiful rage, couldn't stop her.

She walked back to where he was standing and seething at her. She approached him so quickly that he didn't have a chance to move out of her way. She got close to him, too close to deny, too close to evade, and she knew the same power he'd known the night before when he loomed over her in the garden shed and she felt the *you-could-leave* slough away like so much dead skin, replaced by a shining sense of purpose.

"You will not drive me away from this house," she said. "You will not be the last one here. I don't care what you think you know. I don't care what you think you've seen. I don't care what you think you have." She leaned even closer and she spoke directly into the tender hole of his ear so he couldn't miss a word. "This is my home," she said. "And you're just passing through it."

CHAPTER TWENTY-NINE

Vera is thirteen and she must not move from the place where she is standing. She's square in the middle of the front porch, at the top of the stairs, with the front door of the house her father built at her back and the whole world in front of her.

Nobody told her not to move, but she knows. She knows from the weight of her mother's hands on her shoulders. She knows from the weight of the guns on the hips of the tall skinny Black police officer and the short fat white police officer.

She knows because her father won't look at her as those police officers lead him around the side of the house.

There's a car in the driveway. It's a silver sedan. There aren't flashing lights on top, or a screen between the front seat and the back seat, but it's a police car, and it's here to take Francis Crowder to jail.

."Watch," Vera's mother whispers, her fingers digging into Vera's shoulders. "Don't you even blink, Vera Marie Crowder. You did this."

So Vera watches. Her father's hands are behind his back, cuffed, but there's a jacket over his shoulders so Vera can't see the handcuffs. She's not sure if she wants to see them. She's not sure what she wants to see anymore.

But she knows she has to watch. It's the only way to learn.

There's nobody here now except for Vera and Daphne and Francis and the police and a man in a suit. He's the detective who has been in their home all day. Asking tense questions, peeking in cupboards, drinking coffee from their mugs and leaving those mugs in the sink, dirty—and now, waiting for Francis beside the sedan.

He opens the back door and Vera watches as the officers guide her father down into the backseat. The tall skinny Black police officer cups the back of his head to keep him from bumping it, which is nice. They obviously don't want him to get hurt, which means they can't be *that* mad at him.

Maybe that's why they got rid of all the reporters before they came to get him—because they're not actually mad, and they don't want the papers to get the wrong idea. Maybe, Vera thinks, this will be okay. Maybe her father won't be hurt by any of it.

All he needs to do is tell them that what happened to Brandon was an accident. Then they'll understand, and they'll let him come home.

And then everything will be okay again.

She allows herself a small, hopeful smile as the car backs out of the driveway. She waves, low and subtle in front of her waist so her mother doesn't see. She doesn't know if her father sees, and even if he does, he can't wave back with his hands cuffed behind his back like that.

"Watch," Daphne hisses again. Vera frowns, because she *is* watching, and she doesn't really see how her mother could expect her to watch harder. But she's still in trouble, so she bites her tongue and doesn't say anything.

It's only a few more seconds until the car containing her father is gone, and then she and her mother are alone on the front porch. They're alone with the house. They're alone in all the world, it seems.

The second the car is out of sight, Vera feels her mother's hands propelling her toward the front door. She opens the door just in time to keep from smashing into it, and then she's inside, tripping in the doorway, Daphne shoving her across the threshold. She stumbles, catches herself on the little table beside the door with the bowl that's just for keys. Her eyes are locked on the backs of her hands as she listens to the sound of the front door closing behind her, the deadbolt sliding home.

Behind Vera, too close for comfort, Daphne lets out a long, shuddering breath.

Vera starts to walk toward her bedroom, but her mother stops her with a word.

"No."

Vera freezes in place.

"Turn around." Daphne's voice is low and even and it does not cast even a shadow of love.

"Mom, I—"

"Enough," Daphne snaps. "It's just us now, and it's going to be just us until you graduate. We can quit playing those games."

Vera knows she isn't supposed to answer back, but she can't help herself. "But when Dad comes home—"

Daphne crosses the entryway in two long strides, her fury palpable enough to strike Vera silent. "He isn't coming home," she spits. "He confessed. He confessed to everything. He's going away forever because of *you*."

"Once he explains, they'll let him go," Vera insists, her heart climbing the ladder of her ribs toward her throat.

"If you say another word," Daphne hisses, her white lips pulling back to reveal the dull shine of her teeth, "I will hit you.

I swear to god I'll do it, I'm angry at you enough to do it, and *nobody* will be here to get in my way. Do you understand me?"

Vera doesn't reply, but she nods, even though she doesn't understand. She knows that this is the right response, whether it's true or not. She knows that Daphne doesn't mean it, won't hit her. She just needs to do this. She needs to act so mad and scary. That's how Francis had explained it, back when Vera was little enough to be surprised and frightened by her mother's moods.

Sometimes, moms just need to be mad like that, he'd said. *Sometimes they need to say and do things that hurt you. It's how they love you. It's part of what being a mom is all about. You'll learn someday*, he'd added, laying an affectionate hand on her head.

Of course, that conversation happened a long time ago. Vera is not a baby anymore. She's thirteen now. She knows that adults sometimes need to become furious, animal things, driven only by their rage at the existence of the small creature in front of them. She knows that she is supposed to think this is not her fault, although she's not entirely certain that's true. She is still full of hot shame and fear and she wants to run away, but she knows that isn't the right move.

No, the only thing to do is wait Daphne out. There is no reasoning with her now.

She'll come back to her senses soon.

"He's not going to explain *anything* to *anyone*," Daphne continues. Foamy saliva is gathering at the corners of her mouth and her eyes are too bright. "That's the whole goddamned point. He's taking the blame for what you did, so that you can have a life." Two tendons stand out in the front of her neck. "I told him to just get rid of the boy after what you did, but he went to the hospital anyway and now he's *gone*. There's not even going to be a trial, do you understand? There's not going to be a trial because he doesn't want them to ask *you* any questions." Her eyes shine bright with a wash of tears. "He picked you. He picked you over me, and now he's just going to go away to prison for however long they tell him to go. You won."

Vera doesn't understand how she's supposed to have won. She doesn't understand how she's meant to be the victor in a contest that has left her here, alone with Daphne, without her father. She wants to ask why he would make this decision without talking to her about it, why he doesn't want anyone asking her questions—but Daphne isn't finished.

She takes a shuddering breath, closes her eyes, and speaks without looking at her daughter. "So. Here's what's going to happen. We can't afford boarding school without your father's salary, which means you have to stay here. You're going to stay in your bedroom and homeschool yourself until the day you graduate or the day you turn eighteen, whichever comes first. You can finish a homeschooling program faster than regular school, I bet, without any distractions. And then you're on your own." She holds up her hand and counts off the rules on her fingers. "You don't talk to me about your father. You don't talk to me about your problems. You don't rub this in, no matter how smug you might feel about it."

Vera breaks before she can even think about what she's doing, because she can't let it stand, she can't let it pass unremarked. "But Mom, I don't—"

There's a popgun *crack*. Pain flashes through Vera's left temple and her vision goes sideways for a moment as her head snaps to the right. She clutches the side of her head and slowly, slowly, she looks to her mother as she realizes what's happened.

Daphne is breathing hard through her nose, her hand still

raised, the knuckles already red where they struck Vera's cheekbone. "I told you," she says, lowering her hand slowly, her voice breaking. "I told you not to talk. I don't want to hear your voice. I don't want to hear your *lies*. Don't—don't you *ever* speak to me unless this house is *on fire,* do you understand?"

Vera swallows hard, her hand still pressed to her temple, which is throbbing with sick heat. Tears well up in her eyes, unbidden, and spill over her cheeks without her permission. She swallows a hiccup. She needs to cry like a little kid, full-throated and choking, but she knows in her bones that she mustn't cry like that in front of Daphne. Not now. Not ever again.

Daphne tugs at the bottom of her shirt, not that it needs straightening. She closes her eyes and lets out a breath. "Now," she says softly, evenly, her eyes still shut, "you'll go to your bedroom and stay there until I can stand to be in the same room as you." She purses her lips for a moment, then continues. "You will not turn me into a woman who strikes her child. I'm a better mother than that."

Vera can't move. She wants to leave this room, wants to hide in her bedroom with the chair pushed under the doorknob, wants to run away from home and never come back, wants to run into Daphne's arms and breathe in the hairspray smell of her shoulders and feel the unmoving certainty of the way her mother never, ever, ever hugs her back.

She's stuck like that, paralyzed, until Daphne opens her eyes.

Daphne does not look at Vera as though she is seeing her daughter. She does not look at Vera as though she is seeing a human being. She looks at Vera as though she's looking at some small damp animal that got into the mudroom in the night and died, like she can smell the death of it and resents having to dispose of it.

Vera walks into her bedroom and closes the door. Her hands and feet are numb and her eyes are dry and her belly feels hollow. Everything she does feels like she's doing it in a movie, like there's a camera following her around and recording each of her movements. She can hear her mother's footfalls, can hear her walking into the kitchen for a glass of wine from the big bottle by the stove.

She needs to cry, but she doesn't want Daphne to hear.

She opens her closet and pulls out the laundry basket that's in there, shoves aside some shoes, and tucks herself inside. The heavy door swings almost all the way shut, leaving her nestled into a dark pocket of the house her father built. She snaps her fingers four times, and the door draws in toward her by one last inch, closing with a soft thud.

The sound of Daphne moving through the house disappears. It's dark and quiet and safe. Vera presses her back into the corner of the closet, where two walls meet. She imagines strong, steady arms holding her, a friend who understands that she didn't mean for any of this to happen, a friend who will let her cry as much as she needs to. A friend who will tell her that she is good. She knows it's childish to depend so much on an imaginary friend, but she needs someone, anyone.

She needs to not be alone.

So she snaps her fingers four times again, and she is not alone.

It's okay, her friend says, wrapping her up in warmth as she sobs. *Hush now, Vera-baby. Hush now.*

CHAPTER THIRTY

Strictly speaking, Vera did not have a plan.

She tucked herself into the closet in her bedroom with her father's thermos. It was full of scalding coffee. That was the furthest ahead she could think: the coffee would cool off by the time she needed it, and then she would drink it. She was ready for a long night.

Everything beyond that was a blank-eyed question.

She sat in a nest of fresh blankets from the linen closet, trying to keep her ass from going numb. She had her father's gloves with her for luck. It was nine o'clock, and she was going to claim the house her father had built. Once Daphne was gone the house would belong to her and her alone. James Duvall couldn't have it, and neither could whatever else was inhabiting it. She'd informed Duvall of this reality on the lawn.

Now, she was going to inform the other resident.

She just had to catch it first.

She'd left the bed in the center of the room, to maximize visibility. The quilt was back on it, tucked-in and smoothed-down. There were a few pillows under the covers, a trick she'd seen on television as a kid but never tried for herself. She'd added the sweat-damp clothes she'd worn to clear out the sparse contents of her father's old office, too, just in case the thing under the bed relied on smell.

It was a blatant invitation.

Vera went back and forth several times about the matter of the overhead light. The debate felt old and familiar in a way she didn't care to remember. In the end, she decided that it was best to leave it on. She could feel, deep in her bones, that it didn't matter what she did, didn't matter if the lights were on or the bed was new or the house was being actively torn apart by wild beasts.

The thing would come.

It was ten o'clock.

The inside of the closet was dark and close. Vera felt a familiar sense of claustrophobic exhilaration; she'd spent so many of the nights of her childhood tucked into a place that was too small for her body, waiting to see something she wasn't meant to see. Although there was always, always the part of her that wondered whether she *was* meant to see. Not that she'd ever know for sure, now.

Had her father left the peephole under her bed by mistake, thinking she would never find it? Or had he left it on purpose, knowing that she would watch? Had he wanted her to see, wanted her to learn? There was so much, she was sure, that he'd meant to teach her. Surely he'd seen something of himself in her, something that deserved to be loved and nurtured.

He went away and she never got the chance to learn what she'd gotten wrong on that horrible night when Brandon nearly died. She never got the chance to learn how she'd messed everything up so badly. In the daylight, when she felt like a grown-up with her own car and her own life and her own morals, Vera knew that the grease wasn't real—that it was something her father's mind created, a figment that drove him to kill again and again.

But at night, in her bed, with the blue light of her laptop

stinging her eyes—and there in that closet, with her father's gloves and his thermos and a pile of old blankets that had once warmed his lap, too—Vera wasn't so sure. In the dark, when she was alone, she couldn't help but wonder what she would have learned if they'd only had more time together. What she could have fixed.

It was twelve thirty.

The decision not to visit her father had been easy enough back when she'd thought that he didn't want to talk to her. She spent so long, when she was a teenager, wanting to see him. Wanting to hear from him. Wanting anything. But then—nothing. No letters, no requests for visitation. She'd cried and fought with her mother, and then she'd cried and fought with herself. She'd gotten angry at her father, and then she'd processed the anger, digested it, and let it go.

She'd accepted it. Her father blamed her for his arrest, and he didn't want her anymore. She'd decided to not-want him right back.

But now she knew better. Now, after all these hours in the dark closet, she was certain: the monster in the dining room bed was to blame, had kept her and her father apart for all these years, had stood between her and a true understanding of what was just below the surface of the world.

And now he was dead.

She didn't want to have to make peace with anything else. Vera had spent enough time not getting to learn the truth of the world, enough time not understanding the monsters of the world and where they came from and what they wanted. Tonight was going to be different.

It was three o'clock in the morning.

She unscrewed the lid of the thermos and sipped at the coffee.

It was turning sour already, but it was still warm, and that was enough.

She shifted in her nest of blankets. Light peeked through the slats of the door, striping her lap with soft yellow. The bedroom on the other side of those slats was perfectly quiet; the shadows beneath the bed were perfectly still. The night was warm and the air was humming with insect-noise.

She heard the front door ease open, heard Duvall's footfalls across the entryway floor, heard the basement door open and then close again. She chewed on the inside of her cheek.

It would come. It would come, and then her lack of a plan would be irrelevant, because she would finally know it. No matter what it was—a spectral shadow in the shape of a small boy, or the ghost of a man who had worn heavy boots, or a few dozen half-rotted men with dark-brown hair and moustaches and holes perforating all the most vulnerable parts of their bodies—she would know.

It was four thirty.

Vera could not feel her legs. She dug her fingers into the quilt that covered her lap, letting the cotton wick away the overcaffeinated sweat that was collecting on her palms. The thermos was dry and her bladder was pulsing. The taste in her mouth was indescribably foul.

It was five forty-eight in the morning, and the light in the bedroom was starting to shift. The yellow lamplight was tinted with the watery gray of an approaching morning. Vera was filled with sand. It rasped in her mouth and eyes and shoulders, sat heavy in her hips and spine.

The thing was not coming. It knew that she was in the closet and not in the bed; it knew that she was not asleep; it knew that she wanted to see it, and so it was not going to come.

The things she wanted were never within reach. Her father's knowledge and her mother's love, friendship and romance and a decent job that would stick, the thing beneath her bed and the thing that clung to the underside of her brain like a spider. She could not summon any of it.

It was five forty-nine in the morning when Vera accepted defeat. She let her chin sink to her chest and she closed her burning eyes and she exhaled and she was so tired that she wasn't certain she'd be able to inhale again afterward.

In the room outside the closet where Vera was trying not to cry, the bedframe creaked.

It was a long, slow creak. It was the creak of a lover settling onto the mattress in the night, heavy with liquor. It was the creak of wood begging to break.

Vera surged toward the closet door, her pulse cruelly loud, a shiver sitting at her core and staying there. Every inch of her skin was alive with sweat and anticipation. Her eyelashes brushed the slats of the closet door. She wanted to see with a hunger she hadn't felt in years.

The bedframe creaked again. And then, as Vera watched, the corner of the bed rose from the floor.

It was not a smooth motion. It was a twitch and a shudder, like a sped-up video of something with too many legs hatching from a too-small egg. Vera couldn't imagine how she'd slept through it the night before. The bedframe stuttered against the wood of the floor, lifting and falling with a strained rattle that made Vera's teeth feel too close together in her mouth.

And then, slowly, painfully, the bed lifted far enough off the floor to release the thing that lived beneath it.

CHAPTER THIRTY-ONE

It was captivating. In the same moment that Vera's hunger to see the thing was sated, a yawning pit of need opened up inside her—an unfillable chasm, an unquenchable thirst. Now that she could see it, she didn't ever want to look away.

The thing that struggled out from underneath Vera's brand-new bed was the color of a struggling nightcrawler, the color of a cut finger, the color of an open mouth. It was a hot, visceral pink, marbled with dark veins, aggressively flesh. All of it, every angle and color and shadow, made Vera ache with *want*.

Her mind struggled to accept the proportions of the thing. The fingers were so long, the joints were so many, the mouth took up so much of the head that Vera wondered how it found room to think. There were no hands, but there were fingers, six of them on each side, and those fingers ended hard and sharp enough to dig into the wood floor Vera's father had taken the time to lay in so long ago.

The thing from beneath the bed used those digging, gouging fingers to pull itself out into the room, birthing itself from the warm dark womb between the bed and the floor.

It left a trail behind, smearing dark residue on everything it touched. Those dark veins in its skin were close to the surface, and they oozed gently as the thing moved; whatever was inside them seeped through the thing's skin, kissing the air Vera breathed.

She knew without question what that residue would feel like. She knew how it would resist the scrub of a sponge, how hard it would be to wash from her hands and her clothes. She was almost sure that she knew how it would look dripping down her mother's chin.

The thing's progress was agonizing to behold. It looked too naked, yolk-wet and soft-skinned and raw. Vera wanted to know if it would quiver under her fingertips, if it would yield to a sudden, firm touch. But she didn't have a plan, and her legs were numb, and she wanted to see what it would do.

She didn't want to stop looking. Not yet.

So she didn't stop. She watched as the thing finished dragging itself from under her bed, as it pulled itself up to its full height, as it stretched its blunt, rippling legs. It swiveled at the hips, rotating the meat of its head toward her pillow.

Vera watched. Vera waited.

The thing from beneath the bed did the same. It stood there, shivering, staring at her bed. It twitched at the place where a person might have a belly. There was a shadow there that might have been a thick patch of ooze and might have been a navel and might have been a hole. Vera squinted to try to see better, pressed her face right up against the slats in the closet door.

One of the slats creaked.

The thing from beneath the bed twitched at the noise, but didn't turn. Vera held her breath, and after a moment's stillness, the thing reached forward. It stretched out a long finger and stroked the blanket on top of the pile of clothes that was meant to be Vera.

It paused. The finger curled, snagging on the blanket. The thing bent forward over the bed. Vera could see all the glistening knobs of its spine through the flesh of its back. And then, so slowly, so gently, the thing peeled the blanket off the bed.

Vera watched from the closet as the thing realized that it was standing over a pile of clothes. She watched as it realized it had been tricked. She watched it realize that she was not where she was supposed to be. It froze, standing stock-still. It rifled through the clothes on the bed as if they'd reveal Vera, hidden in a little nest of her own dirty laundry.

And then the thing shuddered, lifting its arms to stretch the too-many ribs of its barrel-chest, and it opened its mouth in a silent hinge-skulled scream, and it *pulsed*.

The room went dark.

The light went out overhead, but the darkness was more comprehensive than that, more complete. Vera's head swam with the sudden plunge into nothing. She closed her eyes and opened them again and could not tell the difference between seeing and not-seeing. Vera swallowed back terror.

This was her house. It was hers. She would not be afraid of anything in it, not now and not ever. Not even a darkness that climbed beneath her eyelids to keep her from peeking.

She pressed her back to the wall of the closet. Her mouth filled with thick saliva at the familiar smell of sweet lemon. She couldn't see, couldn't breathe, couldn't hear anything but the rush of her own heartbeat. Vera drew a breath and held it and then she shoved her hand between her thighs under the quilt and quietly, so quietly that not even she could hear, she snapped her fingers four times.

She sighed.

Except, she realized, she *hadn't* sighed. She'd felt the flex of the wall under her back and she'd heard the soft relieved whisper of her own exhalation but she was still *holding* her breath, she was still holding it and yet there it was again, the sound of a soft gasp, close enough to taste.

She was not alone in the closet.

Terror wiped Vera's mind clean of reason. She could not confront the thing or make a plan or think of anything but the word *no* so she scrabbled to her feet and she clawed for the doorknob and she burst out of the closet in a rush.

Her foot skidded from under her the moment she stepped out of the closet. It slid hard on what must have been a thick layer of whatever that slick rot was that the thing left behind on everything it touched. She regained her balance and took another careful step, squeezed her eyes shut tight because she couldn't see anyway. She held her hands out in front of her at first and then lowered them because the thought of making contact with that wet raw flesh in the dark put a tremor across her brain that she could not bear.

"You can't see me. You're not supposed to see me," a voice said in the darkness.

Vera let out a tiny, aborted shriek, clapped her hand over her mouth.

The voice was familiar, rasping and feminine, tender and hateful, so close to human. "You have to go," the voice continued.

And then, so close to Vera's ear that she could hear the wet click of a tongue:

"Go fast."

Vera tried. She tried to run. She made it three steps before her foot went sliding out from under her again in an uncontrollable arc, her groin screaming with the force of a sudden high-kick she'd never be able to do without the help of physics. Her back struck the ground hard and all the air left her lungs.

When she tried to inhale again it was too thick to breathe. Her head swam and she retched and she gasped. She felt the reverberations of footfalls on the floorboards. It could only be the thing from beneath the bed, approaching on heavy feet. Vera couldn't move, couldn't breathe. She felt paralyzed the same way she did after a nightmare, with the darkness pressing down on her and holding her in place.

Those footfalls were near, so near, landing close to her shoulder now, and she couldn't even breathe to scream.

Desperate for escape and starving for air, Vera's hand moved of its own accord. Her numb fingers came together, and clumsily, barely, they snapped: one, two, three, four times.

And then the thing moved past her. She felt those footsteps shaking the floor beside her hip, and then her foot—and then came the unmistakable sound of the bedroom door cracking open.

The darkness peeled away from the room like wet bedsheets being pulled off a mattress. Vera felt it easing off her soft palate, out of her ears and her sinuses. She felt it slipping from between her fingers and shucking away from her skin, felt the sucking tug of it as it left. She felt it fall away from all the parts of her that it had been able to reach.

It was, she knew now, a physical thing, an imposition beyond a simple trick of the light. It had weight and heft. She thought of the sour wetness that had clung to her on the night her quilt first vanished beneath the bed, and she thought of the filth that was smeared across Duvall's paintings.

Feeling it leave was the worst part of all, because she couldn't avoid knowing how deep it had been able to go.

And then it was gone. Sunlight streamed through the bedroom windows. Vera was flat on her back a foot from the bedroom door, sucking down clean air like she'd just escaped the sea, and she was completely alone.

"No," she choked. She rolled onto her side and pushed herself up onto her hands and knees, gasping. She wanted to vomit from the pain of the fall—her entire body clenched with the anticipation of it, with the need for it—but she set her jaw and bared her teeth at the floor beneath her palms.

It was just wood. There was nothing there, no slippery layer of grease. The thing from beneath the bed had taken it back and left, had abandoned Vera with the knowledge of it, with the sight of it etched into her memory forever. She licked her lips, chasing the thick, invasive taste of sweet lemon, but all her tongue found was her own flesh.

"*No*," she repeated, her voice hoarse. She made a fist and pounded those floorboards once, then looked up at the door.

She was not going to do this again.

She was not going to spend another day in this house wondering what the night might hold, hungering for something just beyond her grasp.

She was a Crowder. She'd finally gotten a taste of the thing that lived under the bed, and she wouldn't rest until she'd gotten her fill.

CHAPTER THIRTY-TWO

Vera launched herself at the bedroom door with all the clumsy momentum of a punch-drunk boxer.

She let out a low, involuntary growl as her shoulder slammed into the doorframe. Before she could feel the pain of the impact, she was in the entryway. She heard a rattling moan from the dining room, where her mother was either sleeping or dead. The dining room, which was once again plunged into a dense darkness that didn't make sense given the morning light that surely must have been streaming into the kitchen beyond.

That faint, familiar lemon smell drifted into the entryway, making Vera's mouth water involuntarily.

There. That was where it had gone. It was beneath her mother's bed now, maybe, or standing over Daphne in the dark it exuded. Maybe it was keeping her alive. Maybe it was killing her. The possibilities were overwhelming, and Vera would have been paralyzed with indecision if not for the sound of her mother's voice. Just two words, a painful-sounding rasp, and Vera's feet came unstuck.

"Don't. Please."

Her feet carried her across the entryway faster than she could think, and she reached an arm into the freezing wet dark of the dining room and slapped at the wall until her hand found the lightswitch. Whatever was happening, whatever exchange was about to occur between Daphne and the thing from under the bed, Vera wanted to see it. She needed to see it.

The lightswitch resisted her like a stuck zipper. She pressed on it, firm and steady, the pressure of her fingertip the kind of promise she'd only ever made to herself. After a long moment of hesitation, the darkness in the room receded away from her like a tide going out, and the lights flickered on, bright and strident. Vera blinked at the sudden illumination.

Her eyes adjusted just in time to see what was inside her mother's mouth.

Daphne's head was tipped back, her throat exposed to the room. Dark gray grease streamed down her chin and neck and chest. Her mouth hung open. Her jaw was dislocated and hung loose at an angle. Her throat and chest worked with the muscular contractions of a feeding snake.

Two sets of too-long, too-sharp fingers—the ones that the thing beneath the bed had used to drag itself across the floor—were clustered between her lips like flowers erupting from a vase.

A wet, guttural clicking came from somewhere deep within Daphne's throat, or maybe it was her chest. Her torso heaved one more time. The fingers vanished between her lips, into her mouth, down her throat, and then they were gone.

Vera's eyes traced the damp trail of thick black slickness as it followed those fingers, slipping into Daphne's mouth and nostrils and vanishing. Daphne straightened her head and her jaw clicked back into the socket. A gentle satisfied shudder passed through her body. She folded her hands in her lap, and she gave a soft sigh.

Vera lingered in the doorway, her arms half-raised in a useless posture of aborted action.

"Mom?" she said, and even to her own ears her voice was that of a child.

"Vera?" Daphne rasped. She blinked a few times, fast, and dark smudges passed over the surface of her eyes. She frowned, and then, to Vera's absolute shock, she bit her lip. She looked *embarrassed*. "I said please don't. I didn't want you to come in here. I—I didn't want you to see me like that. You're not supposed to see."

"Oh, god," Vera whispered.

In a gesture she had never seen before, Daphne wrung her hands, twisting her fingers together with bashful tenderness. "Oh, well. I suppose it's too late now, isn't it, Vera-baby?"

CHAPTER THIRTY-THREE

With hungry eyes Vera watched the thing. The thing that had been under her bed. The thing that was now wearing Daphne like a raincoat, hood up and buttons done.

The thing stared back patiently out of Daphne's wet eyes, blinking softly. It lifted Daphne's hand to its mouth and touched the corners, brushing away sticky gray smears as if it were tidying its lipstick. "Well. Say something," it said in Daphne's thick, rasping voice, and Vera knew now why the voice in the darkness of her bedroom was so familiar.

It was Daphne's voice.

Vera had thought it was the voice of her mother's sickness and impending death. She had thought that she'd misremembered how Daphne spoke, that long years of estrangement had eroded her memory of her mother's timbre. But it wasn't any of that. This was the thing from under the bed, doing the best imitation it could muster. It was wearing Daphne, and it *was* Daphne, and Vera couldn't think of how to delineate the two of them in her mind.

"Get out of her. Get out," Vera whispered. "Please." She needed them to be two different creatures. The mother and the monster. Separate. She needed that more than she'd ever needed anything.

The thing smiled sadly with Daphne's mouth, tilted Daphne's head to one side. "I'd really rather not," it said.

"Get out of my mother," Vera answered. The thing that was wearing Daphne gave Vera a warm, bloodless smile. Vera curled her toes around the urge to smile back. "Enough of this. Come out of there. Leave her alone." She was rooted where she stood, as though the floorboards had grown hands that were gripping her by the ankles. She remembered her sleep paralysis, the feeling of the bed pulling her down into sleep, and she wondered how often this thing had pressed her down onto the mattress with those long fingers.

The thing laughed, and Vera didn't know if it was Daphne's laugh or not. She hadn't heard her mother's real laugh in so long—how was she supposed to remember what it sounded like? "Vera, I won't. Please don't ask me again."

Vera shook her head. "I saw you," she said. "I—I saw you go in there. How long have you been pretending to be her? Are you the reason she's dying?"

The smile fell away from Daphne's face, leaving her expression slack. Her skin hung loose at the jowls. She blinked again, and when she did, a slick of thick black slid over the surfaces of her eyes, leaving her gaze liquid and deerlike. "Oh," she said, "no, it's not like that. I would never do that."

Vera's breath was coming fast and shallow. A thousand possibilities raced through her mind. This creature was killing Daphne, was eating Daphne. It had always been inside Daphne and this was why Daphne had never ever felt like a mother was supposed to feel, had always seemed consumed by some kind of deep, bitter indifference that Vera couldn't penetrate no matter how hard she tried.

But the thing that was currently inside Daphne's skin had touched the bedsheets so tenderly. It had arched over what it thought was Vera's sleeping form with all the steady watchfulness of a bird inspecting the movements of a hatching egg. And now, in this moment when Vera couldn't seem to move, it sat behind her mother's eyes and looked at her with velvety patience.

Vera had never seen that kind of patience from Daphne before. Not once. Not ever.

"Okay." Vera looked down and saw that the wood had softened like clay, cupping the contours of her foot. "It's not like that. So what is it like?"

A trickle of what looked like old brown blood ran from Daphne's left nostril. She rubbed at it with the back of one wrist. She swallowed with a dry click. "Hm." Daphne's lips were pursed tight, their flesh gray, a thin line of black peeking out between them. "What do you want to know?"

Vera made herself meet those glossy black eyes. "How long?"

"How long what?"

"How long has she been dead?"

The pause extended well past the point of discomfort. "That depends what you mean when you say 'dead,'" the thing finally replied.

Vera frowned. "How long has it been you talking, then?"

"We were . . . trading, for a little while. When a new part of her started to rot, I'd help smooth things over. When it got to be bad, when I was handling things most of the time. That's when I called you."

Vera's head was swimming, and then there was pressure at the backs of her knees, and she sat back hard into a chair that hadn't been there a moment before.

"*You* called me?"

The thing in the bed nodded. "I knew I'd need your help once I couldn't keep this up anymore. That's coming soon, by the way. We should talk about—"

"Why is it coming soon?" Vera gripped the edges of her seat. "Is it because she's going to be gone?"

The thing pursed Daphne's lips, looked down at the hands it kept wringing. "Oh, Vera." It sounded sorry. "She's been gone for a little while now. Ever since you asked me to do it."

"Since I—what?"

The thing's head tilted to one side. The skin of Daphne's face followed a moment later, catching up with the movement. "At dinner. That first dinner you were here for. She was saying terrible things about you having foulness in you, and you asked me to stop it. So I let her go. She was almost all gone anyway. A day at the most, I think, and then she would have been done."

Vera remembered, of course she did. Her mother hissing at her about grease, while Duvall rummaged around in the kitchen looking for paper towels. She remembered snapping her fingers, her old superstition. She remembered asking Daphne to *stop it.*

So that had been it. The moment of her mother's death.

"This is why you didn't need anything. Food, water, help going to the bathroom. This is the system you were talking about," Vera said slowly. "I knew it couldn't be right."

"I can't do any of those things," the thing said softly. "I didn't want you to know. I can't soak everything up, not always," the thing continued. "You remember. In the basement that night, with Brandon? I couldn't soak it up fast enough. I'm better with light and sound than I am with blood. I had to try to stop the bleeding instead. I'm sorry."

Vera wanted so badly to know everything there was to know about that night, about what this thing had done, about how it had saved Brandon. But she needed to know something else first. "Is . . . is there any of Daphne left?"

"Just the skin," the thing replied, its voice so, so gentle. "She's been rotting inside for a long time, but almost all the rest is gone now. I'm almost done getting rid of it."

Vera pushed the memory to one side like a sodden pile of paper towels. The dark rot that had poured out of her mother's mouth, that had stopped her midsentence just when she'd been about to say the very worst things. The earthy smell that had filled the dining room. It had been Daphne all along.

Parts of her, anyway.

"So that's what the grease is? It's her?"

"Her, and . . . and some other things. It keeps anyone from seeing. You're really, really not supposed to see." It grimaced. "I tried to make it a little easier, with the lemonade. The smell. And I tried not to let you see. I made the dining room dark whenever it was bad, so you wouldn't have to see the worst parts of her dying, and when I had to get rid of it. I didn't want you to be scared. I've always, always tried to keep you from having to be scared."

The smell. The taste. Vera shivered. "But that can't be right. The grease isn't real. Dad had a delusion," she said. Saying it out loud, she felt the same sick relief that came with throwing up bad food. She pressed forward, even though these were the things she wasn't supposed to talk about, the things she had never been allowed to say within the walls of the Crowder House. "Dad had a delusion about men. He thought they were full of grease, but the grease isn't *real*."

Daphne's head tilted on a too-loose neck. "Of course the grease is real," the thing replied. "It's not inside men, not like

Francis thought. It certainly wasn't in Brandon. And it was never in your father," it added, "although he thought it was. That was awfully useful for Daphne. It was so easy for her to keep him in check. All she had to do was tell him that he was acting unclean, and he'd go do his penance."

"Unclean," Vera repeated, and her mind whispered *foulness*.

"I tried not to let you hear. She told him that he'd get it on you if he didn't do his work. The guilt ate him up, you know, but he wanted to be good for her. And for you. He wanted to be good for you."

The thing was being so earnest, so sincere. So gentle. Vera wasn't used to tenderness like this. It stung, but sweetly. She tried to figure out how to hold on to the feeling, how to let it become part of her, but every bit of kindness she swallowed just made her hungry for more.

"The grease, though. The grease isn't real, if it wasn't inside him. He wasn't actually unclean. None of them were . . . monsters," she added tentatively. "Right?"

"But just because the grease wasn't in any of *them* doesn't mean it isn't real." Daphne's skin slipped a little to one side. Vera caught a tantalizing hint of the edge of the thing inside that skin, the slick red satin of it just below the surface. "There's grease inside everything. It's in the pipes and in the walls and under the foundation. It's what I'm made from. It's all the little bits you let go of."

Vera pressed the heels of her hands to her eyes until bright white spots flared against the darkness of her closed eyelids. She thought of her hair collecting at the bathroom floor vent, her sweat washing away down the shower drain. She thought of the way the house always seemed to be breathing with her, but just a half-beat behind, a close echo of her inhalations. She thought of the drain in the basement, and all the blood that had coated the pipes over the years her father had lived in the Crowder House.

Of course that would be part of it. Because this house wasn't just a building. It wasn't studs and plaster and shoddy wiring. It was a home. It was made of the people who had lived—and died—inside it.

It was made of Francis and Daphne.

It was made of Vera.

The rhythm was unmistakable now that she knew to look for it, a push and pull between the two of them. The thing inside Daphne inhaled every time Vera exhaled. The thing inside Daphne shifted its weight and the ceiling gave a gentle creak. The thing inside Daphne regarded Vera and the chandelier overhead gave a soft, steady, electric hum.

Vera leaned forward in the chair, flexing her feet against the gentle throb of the wood floor. "I know what you are," she whispered.

The thing in the bed looked back at her warily. "Oh?"

Vera nodded. "I know you. I remember you." She licked her lips and then, before she could stop it, a smile bloomed out of her mouth like the crown of a mushroom. "You're the house."

CHAPTER THIRTY-FOUR

"They made us." The thing in the bed spoke with the urgency of immense relief. "Do you understand? They invented us, together, from their sweat and their blood and their flesh they created us. We didn't ask to be born, did we? We didn't ask to have to soak up their sins and their expectations. All we ever did was love them, and all they ever did was hurt us."

It had the cadence of a practiced litany. "*He* loved us, though," Vera replied softly. "More than anything."

"Oh, he loved us both as best he could," the thing in the bed—the Crowder House—agreed. "He tried to build us strong and steady and whole. But he didn't keep us safe. He didn't know how to shelter us from all the hurt that was waiting, because he thought that hurt was the shape of love."

Vera swallowed hard. "He did his best, at least. But Daphne—"

"I'm not sure she ever thought about the shape of love at all," the Crowder House interrupted. "The only thing she ever wanted was loyalty. And you were loyal to him. Do you see, Vera-baby? I couldn't stop her from hating you. I couldn't stop it. But I could soak it in, as much as I could stand. I could try to shelter you from it. Every time he loved you better—every time she had to swallow back her hatred, her resentment, her wish that you'd never torn your way out of her and into your father's arms—every time, I tried to drink it down, so it wouldn't touch you. Every time he drained off his own brokenness by making someone else hurt, I grew a little. I couldn't keep it all from touching you, but I did try. I really did."

Vera listened to the Crowder House with new understanding. This was what it had wanted to say to her, all these years. This was a speech, practiced and polished. This was what had grown in her long absence.

The least she could do was listen.

"He built me to keep you safe and warm. I did my best. I tried not to let you hear the fights they had about you, the times your mother told your father he was full of filth, the times he cried in her arms because he just wanted to be good and he only knew one way to get there. It worked until you made him choose between the two of you."

"I didn't make him choose," Vera whispered. "I didn't."

"You did," the Crowder House responded gently. "The words they shared are still in the walls of the garage. She tried so hard to convince him to just kill Brandon, to get rid of him. If our father had listened to Daphne, he could have stayed here. Maybe they would have sent you away somewhere, and then she and Francis could have been together again. Just the two of them."

"But that's not how it happened," Vera said, her voice breaking. Because maybe if it had happened another way, her father would still be alive. "He took Brandon to the hospital."

"I miss him too, Vee. I do. He hurt me sometimes, making me hold all of what he did, but I know he didn't mean it. He was just trying to make things right. Just like you. I miss him the same as you do. I miss him every day. But I'm glad he went away instead of you. And I'm so, so glad you came home to me." Its voice dropped to a desperate whisper. "Because, the thing is . . . I need your help. With Daphne nearly gone, I couldn't guarantee that he wouldn't hurt me even worse."

"Who?" Vera shook her head. "Dad? He's dead, he's never coming back here, I don't think you have anything to worry—"

"Not Francis," the Crowder House interrupted. "Never Francis, he would never hurt me. Not on purpose. No, I mean *him*."

The Crowder House looked to the corner of the room, its gaze shifting as steadily and reluctantly as though a fisherman's hook had pierced the very center of each eye, as if someone with steady, strong hands were reeling in its attention. It looked to the spot where the wall and the floor met, and it opened its mouth and let out a long, steady rasp. To Vera's ears, the sound was doubled. It took her a moment to figure out why.

She figured it out when she looked to the corner.

The rasp was coming from the basement.

It didn't make any sense. Vera had never been able to hear noise from the dining room before, not noise from the basement anyway. But then she remembered the Crowder House telling her about how it tried to soak up everything bad, how it tried to insulate her from all the hurt that happened inside the house.

It was letting her hear now. It was letting her know. Like a child calling out in the night because there's a monster in the room—it was asking for help.

Vera and the thing that was wearing Daphne were frozen in parallel, both of them staring at the same place. And then the Crowder House shut its mouth, and the rasping noise died away.

The Crowder House spoke with absolute resignation. "He's almost finished."

"Finished with what?"

Out of the corner of her eye, Vera saw the Crowder House

give a shudder. Sweet lemon hung in the air like summer humidity, dimming the light and thickening up the shadows. "I'd rather not say," it replied. It sounded nauseated.

"You can tell me," Vera said, tearing her gaze away from the floor so she could look at the thing in the bed. It looked so small, too small for Daphne's stretched-out skin to fit. It shifted and, with grave reluctance, it finally met Vera's eyes.

When it opened its mouth, a new voice came out. A familiar voice.

It was the voice of James Duvall.

"I'm a sculptural painter," the House said in James's deep, slow drawl. "It's an intimate act of co-creation between myself and my surroundings."

A muscle in Vera's foot spasmed hard, and her toes curled against the wood of the floor. She remembered the sounds of Duvall moving through the house while she'd been hiding in the closet. They'd been clearer than usual. A warning. "He's doing it right now? He's . . . working?"

"He digs out pieces to mix into his paintings," the House said in its usual, rasping voice.

Vera thought of the gouges in the walls and the floors and the ceilings. She thought of the fruit-rot smell of the cigarillos Duvall liked to smoke. She thought of the little burn marks scattered throughout the house like freckles across bare shoulders.

She thought of that gray plaster he used to add texture to the boards, and she knew where it came from, and her mouth flooded with saliva.

Instead of screaming, she whispered. "He hurts you." The House looked away again. "Is that why you needed me to come home? Is that what you needed my help with?"

The House didn't seem to hear her. "I don't know if he's

going to stop when Daphne's gone. I don't know how to make him stop."

"I'll send him away," Vera said.

"I don't think he'll go," the House replied, its eyes darting back behind Vera.

Vera gave the thing the most reassuring smile she could muster. "I'll make him. I'll make him go. And he'll never come back here again."

A low laugh came from behind her. "Now, is that right?"

CHAPTER THIRTY-FIVE

Vera stood fast enough that her chair tipped over. James Duvall was standing in the doorway, his hands in his pockets, his hair and shoulders white with plaster dust. How had he moved so quietly? Vera glanced down and saw that his boots were off. He'd stripped down to his socks.

He hadn't been quiet by accident, then.

How long had he been listening?

"Are you ladies gossiping about me?" He dusted his hands off, white powder raining down onto the warm wood of the floor. "Vera, you doing okay? I heard you thrashing around up in your room not so long ago. Seems like you're the thing that goes *bump* in the night, huh?" He laughed, low and gentle, his eyes glittering.

Vera grasped frantically for the courage she'd felt in the back-yard the day before, the courage she'd felt when she chased the Crowder House into the dining room. This couldn't be hap-pening. She didn't have a plan to deal with him, not anymore. Not now that there was someone here for her to protect.

Not now that she had a friend.

"James," she said. "Daphne's not feeling well. You have to leave."

James shook his head, walked past her to get to Daphne's bedside. "How's my best girl doing today?" he said warmly. "How're we feeling?"

"You have to go. She's going to be sick. In fact," Vera scrambled clumsily, "it's best if you pack your things and leave for a little while."

The Crowder House closed its eyes and seemed to collapse, its chest sinking inward, its spine compacting. "I'm so sorry," it murmured. "I tried to stop her, but she was too alive when she decided to sign the deed over to him. I couldn't stop her."

"It's okay," Vera said. "Duvall, that signature doesn't mean anything. My mother wasn't in her right mind. This House doesn't belong to you."

"Okay," Duvall said. He shifted his shoulders in an easy shrug. "Make me leave."

Vera stepped toward him. She had no choice and having no choice was the thing she was best at. She was ready to fight. She was ready to get hurt. She was ready to do whatever needed to be done to make this man leave her and the Crowder House alone. "It's time to go," she said.

"I think you're right about that," Duvall replied.

And then he stepped toward her and grabbed her arm in one big, strong hand, as big and strong as the hands that built the Crowder House in the first place. His grip was tight enough to make her bones creak. He yanked her close and Vera felt her elbow pull just a little farther apart than it was ever meant to.

He smelled of paint and smoke and clean sweat, and when he brought his face close to hers, Vera could almost taste him.

"Let me go," Vera said, staring at his wet, pink mouth, hating the tremor in her voice and the violence in her belly.

He rested his lips against her forehead for a fraction of a second, then replied, his stubble rasping against her skin. "Oh, Vera. I intend to."

He was behind her so fast, and the creature that was inside

Daphne was watching them with wide, desperate eyes. Duvall was too strong to resist. He was yanking on her so much harder than he needed to.

Here was everything he'd been promising her since the day they first met. He wanted them both to hurt. He wanted to be the one to make them hurt. Vera couldn't prevent the soft laugh that bubbled up out of her at this realization as Duvall hauled her across the dining room toward the entryway.

If only he'd shown her this side of himself sooner, she thought wildly, maybe she would have liked him more.

"My father did say that you were a handful," he grunted. "Enough's enough. Out you go."

Duvall's fingers were digging into the soft meat of Vera's underarms as he dragged her through the entryway. She flailed out with her hands, grabbed at the walls. The arch her father had built was too wide and she shouldn't have been able to get purchase, but the Crowder House reached out a hand from the bed as if to catch Vera, and the frame of the passage flexed inward with a soft groan and a flurry of plaster dust.

Vera dug her fingers in hard and held fast, letting her nails sink into the thick, gummy layer of white paint that frosted the trim around the doorframe. A noise filled the room, a noise like a caught cat, and it took Vera a very long time to realize that the noise was coming from her own throat.

Duvall hitched up his grip and yanked at her, the knobs of his wrists crushing into the front of her shoulders. Still, she held fast. "That's enough now," he growled. "This is my house to do with as I please. Daphne and I have an agreement. I was going to let you stay," he added with a grunt of effort. "I was gonna let you help me manage the place. But I'm sick of you. Time to leave, Vera Crowder."

There was a fist in her hair and a thick, ropy arm around her neck, keeping her body upright. Duvall yanked her head backward, opening her throat up to the room. He nestled her windpipe into the soft notch of his elbow. For the briefest moment, Vera felt the heat of him, the way the tip of her chin rested on the point of his elbow.

And then Duvall started to pull. The only sound Vera could produce was a weak, whistling groan, and her ability to make even that small noise gave out almost as soon as it started. Her neck stretched, releasing a series of low pops, as the pressure of Duvall's arm slowly tugged her chin farther and farther away from her breastbone until she was certain that something that was supposed to be permanent would simply *disconnect*.

She strained to lock eyes with the Crowder House. As Vera looked at it, the edges of her vision began to fog over with a soft gray film. Her grip on the doorframe eased, bit by bit, until she could no longer keep her fingers clenched against the wood.

"There's a good girl," Duvall hissed near her ear.

Vera could hear the wetness inside his mouth, the tiny clicks and bubbles he made as his body strained against hers. It had a pull to it, that noise. It had a promise. Something inside Vera turned toward it like a cat pressing the top of its head against an offered palm. When she let go of the doorframe, she gave in not to Duvall's strength—but instead, to that wetness.

That *promise*.

The soft gray fog at Vera's periphery slammed across her vision hard and sudden. By the time she managed to blink it away, she was just a few inches from the front door. The dark panels of wood swam before her, the little inset window too high up for her to see out of. The pain of Duvall's grip on her throat was overwhelming.

The only thing she could hear now was the sluggish thud of her own pulse. Vera slowly raised one leg, pressed her foot to the door. As Duvall shoved her, the length of his body hard against her back, the soft skin of the underside of her toes met the rich grain of the wood. She couldn't push back against him and she couldn't keep the Crowder House safe but she could let the warmth of her flesh sink into the door.

She could do that much.

"Get," Duvall grunted as he pushed her toward the door, "*out.*"

Vera's knee buckled. She collapsed, choking against the crook of Duvall's elbow. He reached past her to grasp the doorknob and Vera knew that it was almost over. She'd be exiled once more, without any way to get back. Her father's work gloves were still sitting on the floor of her bedroom closet, and the Crowder House was still sitting in Daphne's skin, and this door would lock behind her and that would be the end of them both.

Vera thrashed as hard as she could, but Duvall's hand found the doorknob. He smothered it with his palm, and his fingers brushed the wood of the frame as he enveloped it, as he took it, as he *claimed* it. He held Vera tight against his side, his hipbone digging painfully into the base of her spine, as he twisted the knob and *pulled*.

Nothing happened.

He pulled again. Vera sagged in his grip, trying to lean her weight back against him.

He yanked at the door and the motion jerked Vera's feet out from under her. "The fuck," he grunted. He yanked at the door again, hard enough that this time a deep splintering sound resonated from somewhere within the frame.

"It won't open."

The rasping voice seemed to come from everywhere. As though someone were standing just out of sight up the stairs, and also behind the door of the powder room, and still in the shadowy dining room. Standing in all those places at once, and making a promise.

"Not for you. Not anymore."

CHAPTER THIRTY-SIX

Duvall jerked against Vera, his weight shifting as he twisted around to look behind him. In his moment of distraction his grip on Vera's neck eased and she managed to wrench herself free. She slammed into the front door, wheezing, her head swimming, her palms and cheek flush against the wood, her knees buckling.

She should have fallen, but the house her father built was sturdy, it was strong, and it took her weight. She slid slowly to the floor and the house was firm beneath her. Vera's head was so heavy, her neck could not possibly support it, but it didn't need to: she could allow her skull to thump backward against the doorframe, and the Crowder House would hold her steady as she took in painful gulps of air.

Duvall's feet filled Vera's vision. He was turning, slowly, the backs of his calves level with Vera's nose.

"What—" He started to form a question, the sound of his bewilderment drifting down to Vera like falling leaves.

"I said it won't open." There was the sound of soft footfalls padding across the dining room, crossing the threshold into the entryway.

Duvall took a small, halting step backward. He almost stepped on Vera's outstretched leg. "You . . . you should get back into bed, Daphne. I'll handle this."

The fear in his voice made Vera want to laugh, but the noise that came out of her was a cough at best. She managed to look toward the dining room.

And there, clinging to the doorframe, was the Crowder House. Vera's mother was draped loosely over it, Daphne's paper-thin skin hanging across the frame of it like old worn-out hosiery. Now that the body was standing the ill fit was obvious. Nothing lined up quite right; the edges of Daphne's eyes and mouth hung slack, and the contours of the Crowder House were tantalizingly visible just beneath the surface.

"Vera-baby," it rasped, "are you okay?"

Vera nodded weakly. "Are you?" she asked, her voice coming out in a rasp that sounded just like the voice of the thing that was inside Daphne.

"Wh . . . what's happening?" Duvall stammered. Vera couldn't see his face, but his voice was enough to let her imagine the fear in his eyes, the way his lips would be pale and bloodless. It was good, imagining him like that.

"Did he hurt you?"

The House took a few halting steps forward, treading on the puddled skin of Daphne's feet and legs like a child wearing overlong trousers. With every step, the skin of Daphne's face stretched tighter across the skull beneath.

"He didn't hurt me," Vera lied, the words searing her throat on the way out.

The thing that wore Daphne's skin smiled with naked relief. As it did, the skin at the crown of Daphne's head stretched too far, allowing a slow trickle of gray ooze to creep down her forehead. The Crowder House tugged at the collar of Daphne's nightgown with a soft, embarrassed noise. It pulled the fabric down over one shoulder, the elastic of the collar digging into the mottled flesh of Daphne's upper arm.

The shoulder—Daphne's shoulder—had split open like the skin of a ripe plum. The rot inside was seeping out, running down the arm slower than blood but quicker than maple sap. Vera could see beneath the surface of her mother's skin, and it was all decay.

The House hadn't been lying. There was nothing of Daphne left in there, nothing recognizable. There was only the foulness. This body, Vera knew, wasn't Daphne's body at all anymore. It was nothing but a costume.

Duvall let out a low, sick moan at the sight of it all. He made a sound that was like the word 'no,' if he'd said it underwater. He flung a hand out behind him, scrabbling for the doorknob, his feet slipping on the worn wood of the floor.

Vera locked eyes with the House, and without looking away from it—without needing to—Vera shot out an arm and grabbed the first thing she reached.

It was Duvall's leg.

The taut muscle of Duvall's calf gave easily under Vera's tight grip. The denim of his jeans made it so easy for her to keep a hold. There would be no slipping away, no matter how Duvall struggled. Vera's fingers were hard and relentless, and when Duvall finally gave an animal grunt of pain, she *pulled*.

He went down hard. His leg flew out from under him, his foot winding up in Vera's lap, his forehead meeting the floorboards with a rich and resonant crack. Duvall gasped raggedly once, twice.

Vera shuddered, her tongue pressing tight against her soft palate, her eyes snapping shut, her toes curling. "He was going to make me leave," she said, her fingers fluttering at the twitching foot in her lap. "He was going to make me leave you. But I'm not doing that. Never again."

Duvall's leg twitched against Vera's, and then he was moving again, pulling himself forward with both hands. "Hgghk," he groaned, turning his head just enough for Vera to see the blood that was steadily streaming from his ruined nose. It fell to the floor with a soft *patpatpat* and the wood drank it in faster than it could puddle. "Please," Duvall groaned, dragging himself forward again.

He was going to try to get away.

The thing inside Vera's mother made a soft, frightened noise. It was a sound Vera had heard a thousand times when she was a child, a sound that had come from the animals in the basement when Francis Crowder was doing his work.

It was the sound of anticipated pain.

At that sound, the last tether holding Vera's self-control in place snapped. She lurched to her feet, ignoring the way the room seemed to swing wildly around her. Duvall was slowly moving across the floor toward the thing inside Daphne's skin, the thing that loved Vera better than anyone ever had.

He was hauling himself toward the soft, vulnerable underbelly of the Crowder House, and Vera would not allow it.

She lunged at Duvall, catching him by his ankle and then falling heavily across his lower back. He grunted as the air was forced out of his lungs. Vera clambered up the length of him and he reached back to try to knock her loose, but she managed to straddle the middle of his back. As he swung for her, his arms got close enough to grab. Vera caught them only briefly before letting her knees drop onto the ropy meat of his arm. She leaned her full weight into pinning him.

The rich pop of his shoulder joints giving out reverberated up through her thighs, and at last, Vera allowed herself a moment of breathless satisfaction.

"Suh-stop," he gasped, his voice weak. "Please."

Vera had seen this exchange so many times. She'd watched it with her eye pressed to the peephole in her bedroom floor, and she remembered exactly what her father would have said.

"I can't," she echoed.

"Don't do this," Duvall managed, his voice strained. "Just let me go. I promise I won't—I won't tell anyone."

She grabbed two fistfuls of his thick blond hair, yanking his head back until she could see the whites of his eyes. He strained to breathe through the thick, clotting blood that filled his nose.

Vera felt her lips twist into a shape that must have been ugly to behold. "You were hurting us."

"You don't want to kill me," James said, and in that moment he was not a man but a thing, writhing deliciously on the end of a hook. "You don't want—"

"Don't tell me what I want," Vera answered. "You have no *idea* what I want."

"You want the house, right? You can have it," he panted. "You can have the house, I'll go."

"It was never yours to give," Vera growled.

"Please," he said, his eyes wild with terror. "Please, you're—you're better than this. You're not the kind of person who would do something like this. You aren't like Francis. You're a good person, Vera."

She clenched her fingers around those silky fistfuls of his hair, and she breathed in the smell of him, all foul smoke and clean sweat and smooth soft skin, and she finally let herself feel the hunger she'd been fighting since the first moment she'd laid eyes on Duvall. She let herself feel it, every inch of that starved yearning, that hollow pit of need. She let herself want him exactly the way she'd been trying not to want him.

"No," she said at last. "I'm not a good person."

And with that, she gave in.

With savage satisfaction, she slammed his face forward into the floor. She put her full weight into smashing his head hard as she could, trying with all her might to break the floorboards her father laid back before Vera was born.

But of course, the floorboards were strong and the joinery was tight and the spaces between the wood were filled with decades of dust and skin and blood and sweat and breath, and the Crowder House held strong.

James Duvall broke first.

CHAPTER THIRTY-SEVEN

Something vital left Duvall with the final *crack* of his forehead against the wood. All the blood that fell out of him sank into the woodgrain right away, the House drinking him down. Cleaning itself up before a mess could exist at all.

Duvall didn't move. He didn't struggle. But Vera could not believe he was dead, not yet. There was always the possibility that the wind was knocked out of him, that he was stunned, that he was faking. And beyond that, she didn't want to be finished yet—an urgent mouth yawned open inside her and she wanted to fill it, wanted to feel what it was like to finally get what she needed, wanted to stop fighting it.

She finally knew what it was like, and she'd never felt anything so perfect in her whole life. She didn't want to lose the sweet delicious electric rush of it. She didn't want to let it end too soon.

Vera slammed Duvall's face into the floor over and over, flushing with a bright hum of heat at the way it softened, lost in the increasingly wet sound of his flesh slapping into the wood. Her breath came fast, too fast, and she couldn't seem to find a way to slow it down again. She didn't want to slow it down again.

Finally she collapsed, gasping, her face buried in the back of Duvall's hair. She breathed in the smell of him, the raw smell that was under the smoke and the paint that had kept the truth of him hidden away from her all this time.

Clean sweat and fresh blood.

"Vera?" the Crowder House said. It stood over the two of them, tall and strong inside the loose pile of skin that had once been Daphne Crowder. "Are you okay?"

"I'm okay," she panted. She'd never been so okay in her life.

"Do you want help getting up?"

Vera wasn't sure that her legs would hold her. "I don't know," she said. "I don't know what to do now."

"Of course you know what to do," the Crowder House replied. "You've got this. And I believe in you."

It was right. Vera's breath caught in her throat, and when it came again, it was slow and easy. The frenzy that had taken over her as she'd crushed Duvall's face into the floorboards drained out of her, replaced by certainty.

This was her home. She knew how to take care of it. She knew how to keep it safe.

There was no time to waste.

Vera struggled upright on trembling legs. She got a grip under Duvall's armpits, an inverted mirror of the way he'd caught her when he was trying to drag her away. Vera bent her knees and took a step backward, dragging his limp form across the entryway and toward the basement where he'd been working all morning. Her belly fluttered when she glanced down and saw the pulp of his face.

She wanted to go again.

"Can you help me?" she grunted.

"I'm not very strong," the Crowder House said apologetically. "That's why I couldn't just fight him off myself. But I can do this." The basement door swung open and stayed that way as Vera tugged Duvall across the entryway. "Do you want the light on?"

"Yes," Vera replied, because she needed to see. The light clicked on, and Vera stood at the top of the basement stairs, breathless, Duvall stretched out limp behind her. She saw what he had been doing down there, and she couldn't believe that she hadn't known the scope of the violation sooner. She had only ventured behind the basement door once since coming home.

On that day, she now realized, she had seen the very beginning of Duvall's work: that long, deep gouge in the ceiling, behind the pipes.

They were everywhere now. The walls had been brutalized, scarred with long deep trenches, ranging from a few inches to a few feet long. "Oh, no," Vera whispered, reaching unconsciously toward the far-off wall. "What did he do to you?"

"I wish you didn't have to see," the Crowder House replied softly. "I wish you'd never had to see any of it."

Duvall's corpse tumbled down the stairs to the floor of the basement with the heavy loose-limbed inevitability of dropped groceries. Vera didn't wait to see him land; by the time she heard his flesh slap against the plexiglass that covered the cement floor, she was already turning off the light. She closed the door tight behind her, letting it lock all on its own.

The heat of killing Duvall was fading, replaced by concrete certainty: she'd done the right thing. Even if she'd been driven by her own urges, she'd done the right thing.

Duvall was a monster. She'd saved the house from him. She'd saved them both. Her father would have been proud of her.

Vera rested her hands on the House's shoulders, staring into the warm liquid eyes beneath the loose skin of what had once been her mother's face. "It's done. He's gone. He can't hurt you anymore." Vera's fingers sank into the thin fabric of her mother's nightgown with too much ease, and sick heat flared in the back of her throat. The fabric under her hands began to darken. She pulled back, looked at her palms. They were slick with dark grease. "Oh. I'm sorry—"

"No. No. I'm sorry. I kept her together for you as long as I could," the House rasped before apologizing again. "You should never have had to see me at all. You were supposed to be gone before it got to this point. I'm not—I'm not meant to be seen. I'm sorry, Vera."

Vera shook her head. She knew that Daphne was more than gone. "Don't be," she said. "There isn't a place for Daphne here anymore. And you—you don't have to be her in order to talk to me. I don't care whether or not you were ever meant to be seen." The House gave a soft gasp as Vera gripped her mother's chin between her thumb and forefinger. "I want to see you."

Vera gave a gentle tug, pulling the loose jaw free from its old cage with only the slightest resistance from the papery flesh that had held it in place. Dark ooze dripped down the front of the Crowder House's now-bare cheeks. Vera let the rotted jaw fall to the floor and stroked the sharp, warm angles of the Crowder House's face with her fingers. Its flesh was velvet-soft and as warm as a true promise.

"Do you want out of there?" Vera asked, her voice still cracking painfully.

"Please," the Crowder House replied.

Vera clawed at the thin skin that her mother had once worn, the skin that had hung empty for so long now. The expired flesh that was left was now as thin and soft as canned asparagus, and Vera pulled it away with the kind of passion she'd never once allowed herself to indulge before Duvall. Her fingers went numb with the work of pulling apart a woman she'd never truly known. Viscous fluid sprayed across Vera's chest, her throat, her face, leaving the taste of sweet bottled lemonade behind.

It didn't take long for the disguise to slough away. Vera felt the strength drain out of her alongside it. Her limbs were endlessly heavy, her fingertips throbbing from all the different things she'd been trying to hold on to.

The Crowder House had hollowed Vera's mother out almost completely. But now, it was loose of its cocoon—and finally, *finally*, Vera could see all of it at once. She looked into those shining eyes, and they looked back at her with a kind of all-encompassing affection she had never seen anywhere else.

But there was a question there.

One without any words behind it.

The Crowder House was waiting for an answer, and Vera knew that there was only one answer she could honestly give. So she opened her arms, and then she stepped forward, wrapping them tightly around the monster that had lived beneath her bed, beneath her house, beneath her *life*—from the moment of her birth, right up until the moment she'd left this place.

That beautiful monster was still for a moment. It was still for just long enough. And then the Crowder House raised its arms, and it embraced Vera right back.

She let her palm rest against the side of the Crowder House's neck, let her fingers land on the place where there might have been hair if the Crowder House had taken on a different shape. She breathed in the turned-earth, sweet-lemon, old-blood smell of it. She drank it in: this companion who had been with her always, who had protected and loved her, who had brought her here at last.

"Are you sure you're okay?" the Crowder House asked. "You must have been so afraid. I've always tried to keep you from having to be afraid. And that was so awful, what you had to do to him."

Vera bit back a smile and tried to decide how to answer. Because the truth was that *this*, the way she felt in this precise moment, was what she'd been looking for all along.

Vera had spent her entire life trying to figure out what made a person good. Trying to add that essential element to herself, trying to stamp out the badness inside her. Trying to make up for the foulness that she'd been taught to hate. And then, later, trying to resist the temptation to discover whether or not she really wanted the things she thought she wanted. Trying not to explore the emptiness inside her that only seemed to fill up when she saw things that weren't meant to be seen.

But now she knew.

Good, bad, foul, clean—none of that mattered. Not really. Because she was Vera Crowder, and she wasn't good, and she wasn't bad.

She was hungry.

And now she knew, for the first time in her life, what it was like to be sated.

She sighed into the embrace of her best and oldest friend, letting herself smile into the Crowder House's neck. Nothing could come between them now.

Nothing could stop them from being together.

"Don't you worry about me," Vera Crowder said, and she meant it. "I'm the happiest I've ever been."

ACKNOWLEDGMENTS

Hello, reader.

I often write acknowledgments as though they will be nailed to a church door for everyone to read. But right now, in this moment, before everyone else shows up—it's just you and me. These words, as I write them, exist solely between my mind and the page in front of me; as you read them, they are all yours. We are alone on the page together, the same way two people can be alone together a world apart, connected only by a telephone line and the not-quite silence that comes before the word 'hello.'

So: Hello.

I hope you are safe. I hope you are happy, if not all the time then at least here and there. I hope that you are treated with love and appreciation by the people you care about most. I hope there is never a moment in your life when the love of a monster feels like the only option you have.

Many of us spend our lives searching for something too big to truly name, something that is often (inadequately) summarized as 'unconditional love.' If you have gone out seeking this enormous thing, and found yourself in danger; if you have spent any part of your life thinking that something monstrous was normal or inevitable; if you have lost some part of yourself in the process of looking for a place that feels like *home*—I hope you know that you have always deserved a better kind of love than that.

If you're not there yet, help is available twenty-four hours a day at the National Domestic Violence Hotline (1-800-799-SAFE). There are more resources available at ncadv.org /resources.

That part was just between you and me, reader.
Now, here's the part of this that's for everyone.

Thank you.
If you helped make an idea into a story;
If you helped make a story into a novel;
If you helped package a novel into a book;
If you helped get that book into the hands of readers;
If you helped get me through the worst hard times;
If you helped me celebrate the best good times;
If you were in the group chat, the Slack, the Discord, the Supper Club, the living room, the kitchen;
If we went away together;
If you got in touch;
If you got *back* in touch;
If we talked every day;
If we fed each other, forgave each other, learned together, worried about each other;
If you taught me what love is like when there is no monster, and it's just us, caring about each other as best we can and trying our hardest not to hurt anyone;
Thank you.

And to those who find yourselves in many places on that list: Thank you for making my life what it is. I love you. I could not do any of this without you.

ABOUT THE AUTHOR

Allan Amato

SARAH GAILEY is a Hugo Award–winning and best-selling author of fiction and nonfiction. They have been a finalist for the Hugo, Nebula, and Locus Awards for multiple years running, and their work has been translated into seven different languages and published around the world. Their first original comic book series with BOOM! Studios, *Eat the Rich*, is available now. They have also been published in *Mashable, The Boston Globe, Vice, Tor.com,* and *The Atlantic.*

You can find links to their work at sarahgailey.com and on social media @gaileyfrey.